# BY
# HONOR
# BOUND

# ALAN MORRIS

GUARDIANS OF THE NORTH

# BY HONOR BOUND

## BETHANY HOUSE PUBLISHERS
### MINNEAPOLIS, MINNESOTA 55438

*By Honor Bound*
Copyright © 1996
Alan Morris

Cover illustration by Joe Nordstrom

Published by Bethany House Publishers
A Ministry of Bethany Fellowship, Inc.
11300 Hampshire Avenue South
Minneapolis, Minnesota 55438

Printed in the United States of America.

---

**Library of Congress Cataloging-in-Publication Data**

Morris, Alan B., 1959–
    By honor bound / Alan Morris.
        p.   cm. — (Guardians of the north ; 1)

    1. Title.  II. Series: Morris, Alan B., 1959–     Guardians of the
north ; 1.
PS3563.087395B9      1995
813'.54—dc20                                                    96-4442
ISBN 1-55661-692-9                                              CIP

# DEDICATION

To my father
Though the very soul of generosity
'tis prize enough to be his son

ALAN MORRIS is a full-time writer who has also coauthored a series of books with his father, best-selling author Gilbert Morris. Learning the craft of writing from his father, this is Alan's first solo novel. He and his wife have three children and make their home on the Gulf coast of Alabama.

# ACKNOWLEDGMENTS

After plotting this novel, I confidently walked into my local library with a book bag, ready to relieve the place of a dozen or so books on Canadian history. The supplies would be endless; after all, our "Neighbors to the North" share our continent, and throughout our short history they have been our loyal allies and best friends in the world. I thought arrogantly and magnanimously, "They can even call themselves the 'Northern United States' if they want to, which they surely do. We speak the same thoughts and share the same culture anyway. Right?"

For someone who considers himself a history buff, this was shameful naiveté, and for that I apologize to the proud people of Canada. Yours is a history rich with chronicles of sacrifice and bravery, and I am proud to live in a country that is *your* ally.

Imagine my surprise when I found *no* books available. Not one. I tried three more libraries and was disappointed three more times. I did find many photographs of the country available, but this was due to the simple reason that Canada is one of the most scenically beautiful nations on the planet.

I did find help, however, in the form of four people.

Loren MccRory and her mother, Lola M. Beck, were extremely patient with my greedy borrowing.

Dan Torgunrud of the Cypress Hills Provincial Park graciously took the time to send rare information to a complete stranger and harried author.

And to Sergeant A. (Tony) Brezinski, Rtd. R.C.M.P., who gave me invaluable materials that proved instrumental in the writing of not only this book, but also future ones, I extend my most heartfelt gratitude.

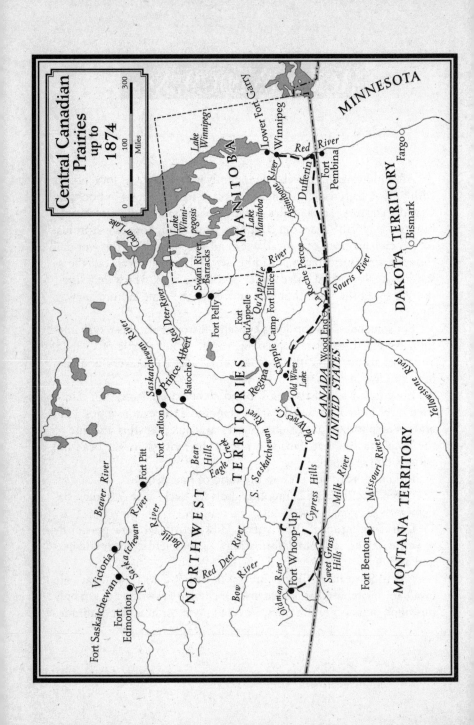

Central Canadian Prairies up to 1874

0    100    300
Miles

MINNESOTA

DAKOTA TERRITORY

Fargo

Bismark

MANITOBA

Lake Winnipeg

Lake Winnipegosis

Cedar Lake

Lower Fort Garry

Winnipeg

Red River

Fort Pembina

Dufferin

Assiniboine River

Swan River Barracks

La Roche Percée

Souris River

Fort Pelly

Fort Ellice

Fort Qu'Appelle

Qu'Appelle River

Cripple Camp

Old Wives Lake

Old Wives C.

Wood End

Regina

N.W.M.P.

CANADA

UNITED STATES

Prince Albert

Batoche

Red Deer River

Saskatchewan River

Fort Carlton

NORTHWEST TERRITORIES

Bear Hills

Eagle Creek

S. Saskatchewan River

Cypress Hills

Milk River

Missouri River

Yellowstone River

MONTANA TERRITORY

Fort Pitt

Battle River

N. Saskatchewan River

Victoria

Fort Saskatchewan

Fort Edmonton

Beaver River

Red Deer River

Bow River

Oldman River

Fort Whoop-Up

Sweet Grass Hills

Fort Benton

1874

# CONTENTS

# PROLOGUE

To: HONOR COURT
NORTH-WEST MOUNTED POLICE


From: JAYE ELIOT VICKERSHAM
SUB-INSPECTOR
"C" Division
NORTH-WEST MOUNTED POLICE

September 10, 1874

Sirs:

I wear the scarlet.

At this moment, so does my friend and fellow officer Hunter Stone. You are here to judge whether or not he shall continue to wear it. I am here to tell you why he should. Indeed, if this distinguished and honorable police force finds that he is unworthy to lead its men in the stamping out of injustice, corruption, and deviousness, then I, too, am unworthy.

I am from England, from which sprung the lore and glory of knights. Courageous men who would offer the ultimate sacrifice for the sake of God, king, and, most of all, truth and justice. I was breast-fed the tales of honor, nobility, and morality. I dreamed of these men—always they were faceless strength wrapped in armor, astride a milky white charger running at full stride to right a wrong. These extraordinary men were dead long before I was born. But I am here today, before this court, to proclaim that I have found a knight in our present day. He is in your great country, Canada. He is, gentlemen, sitting directly in front of you, awaiting your judgment. His name is Sir Hunter Stone.

You have heard through the testimony of witnesses the

events of September 7, 1874. By the grace of Commissioner French and Assistant Commissioner Macleod, I have been granted the opportunity to humbly inform this court that a fair and impartial judgment cannot be ascertained without knowledge of prior issues. These issues directly affected Sub-Inspector Stone's actions on that day, and I fully believe that this honor court could not be satisfied with its findings without all of the evidence presented. . . .

# THE GAUNTLET

*God answers sharp and
sudden on some prayers,
And thrusts the thing we
have prayed for in our face,
A gauntlet with a gift in't.*

Elizabeth Barrett Browning
*Aurora Leigh*

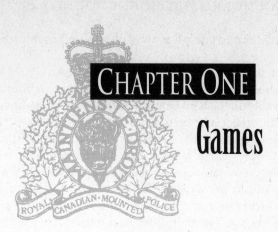

# CHAPTER ONE

## Games

The crack of wood on wood split the air, followed by a girlish squeal that rolled over the expanse of freshly cut grass.

"I did it! I did it! I made it through the little hoop!" Sally Ames cried. She bobbed up and down excitedly, her curly, honey-blond hair shimmering in the sun. "How many feet was that, Reena?"

"Oh, I'd say about four," Reena O'Donnell answered with exaggerated disinterest. "And it's called a wicket."

"Four? It *had* to be farther than that!" Sally's whole body sagged, and the head of the croquet mallet she was holding touched the ground.

Reena rolled her bright blue eyes but smiled with affection. Sally was twenty-one years old, but her sense of measurement was as poor as a child's. To Reena's never-ending amusement, Sally played the lawn game with the same innocent enthusiasm as a child, too.

Despite the crystal clear April day in Chicago, Reena shivered. She wore a lace-trimmed white dress with straight sleeves that ended in turned-back cuffs. A light jacketed bodice made of silk with a long *basque* formed an overskirt. From inside her bedroom the weather had looked warm and inviting, but the constant wind blowing in from Lake Michigan magnified every particle of cool air, raising goose bumps on her arms. She waved at Hiram, the stable boy, as he headed toward the corral. *Even Hiram had the sense to wear a jacket today*, she thought. The stable was only about sixty feet from the start of the croquet lawn, but thankfully upwind.

"What does . . . enn . . . enn . . . 'ennuyees' mean?" asked Charlotte Thibodeaux, her violet eyes momentarily baffled. She and Reena's sister, Megan, were sitting a few feet away on an iron bench with ivy embroidery.

"It means you should stop trying to read Walt Whitman," said Megan O'Donnell, bored out of her mind. She shifted her well-formed figure uncomfortably on the hard bench they occupied, mentally cursing the huge bustle on her blue dress. Two years separated Megan and Reena, Megan being the oldest at twenty-two, but there was little evidence that they were sisters. Megan had light brown hair, while Reena's was so black it sometimes appeared blue. Reena's slender, well-toned body held an easy grace that belied her claims of awkwardness. Megan was four inches shorter than Reena's height of five feet eight inches, and truly clumsy. The trait differences were many, with both girls wishing for qualities the other possessed.

Offended by Megan's remark, Charlotte retorted icily, "We don't all attend Mrs. Bright's College of Genteel Young Ladies and know everything like *you* do, Megan. *You* probably don't even know what it means."

"Only Mr. Whitman knows for sure, because it's not a word. But I think it's a play on the word 'ennui,' which means listless or dull." Megan again tried to adjust her bustle to a more comfortable position. By the time she was through, she was practically sitting on it. She didn't see Charlotte make a face at her, but she heard Sally and Reena giggle. Mistaking their amusement for her struggle with her dress, she said, "I hate these things. Why do we have to wear them?"

"Would you rather wear a hoop skirt as big as a barn and knock everything over that you pass by?" Reena asked.

"I wouldn't be caught dead in a hoop skirt!" Sally announced. "*Nobody* wears those anymore."

"They do in Louisiana," retorted Charlotte, getting back to her reading. Her Southern accent rang clear as she rolled the state's name off of her tongue in lazy, syrupy syllables.

Reena saw that Megan nearly shivered from the sound of it. Charlotte was visiting Sally for the month, and this was the first time Megan and Reena had been around a deep South cadence. Reena thought it quaint and fascinating; Megan tried to keep from cringing every time Charlotte opened her mouth.

"I hear some of you people still have slaves," Megan commented innocently.

"Megan!" Reena blurted, horrified.

"It's all right, Reena," Charlotte said and turned to Megan with a tight mouth. "Slavery is against the law, or didn't you learn that in your school? Unfortunately, ignorance isn't, and there are still a few people around who think like that." She turned back to her book, facing away from Megan.

*Hurrah, Charlotte!* Reena mentally applauded. Few girls could trade barbs with Megan and come out on top. Instead of lashing out as Reena thought she would, Megan withdrew her claws and gave Reena a look that conceded a draw—for now.

Sally, ever the peace-keeper, changed the subject. "Are you staying long enough for the ball next week, Charlotte? By the way, it's your turn."

With obvious reluctance, Charlotte put down *Leaves of Grass* and took her turn. "I can't *wait* for the ball. You say you have one every spring, Reena?" After missing the wicket, she immediately sat down and picked up the well-worn book.

"Yes, my father says it's an old tradition in our family, starting way back in Ireland. A celebration of planting."

"What a grand idea! I need to tell my father about it. But your family is in banking, isn't it?"

"Yes, but everyone before us were farmers. Our great-grandfather came to America and settled in what was then outer Chicago. When the city boomed, he sold his land for about a thousand times what he paid for it."

"That's how *we* got rich, too!" piped Sally. "It's your turn, Reena." Since Sally had finally knocked a ball through a wicket, she could hardly wait for her next turn.

"Sally, you really ought to stop bragging about being rich," Megan said. "That's the first thing a rich person should learn."

Sally appeared genuinely confused. "But . . . we're all rich here. I don't brag around the poor."

"It doesn't matter. The rich don't even brag around the rich." Megan lazily plucked at lint on her dress.

Reena felt a twinge of jealousy that her sister had had the sense to wear a woolen walking-out day dress with jacket bodice that looked toasty warm to Reena's chilled skin.

"What's Louis doing today, Reena?" Sally asked, pronouncing his name in a musical taunt. Her rebuke from Megan was already forgotten.

"He's at the bank with Da."

"And you still haven't set the wedding date?"

Reena didn't meet Sally's or Megan's eyes. Charlotte was again absorbed in her book. "Not yet."

"Well, what are you two waiting for?" Sally asked abruptly but playfully. Fluffing her hair and batting her eyes, she added, "If you don't hurry up, I just might have to steal him from you."

Charlotte suddenly gasped and put a dainty hand over her mouth. "Listen to this! 'The married couple sleep calmly in their bed, he with his palm on the hip of the wife, and she with her palm on the hip of the husband.' Isn't that just—" She paused, searching for the right word, found it, and gushed, "—as naughty as you can get?" The sense of immorality was so strong, Charlotte's cheeks turned pink, and she took a quick look around for any lurking boys or men.

"Does it really say that?" Sally asked, wide-eyed, as she and Reena went to look over her shoulder.

Charlotte pointed triumphantly. "Right there!"

Megan snorted derisively, and all eyes turned to her.

"What's the matter with you?" Reena asked.

"Nothing," she answered immediately, nursing a secret smile.

Reena had seen Megan's ploy before—she loved to have facts begged out of her—but Reena didn't feel like playing Megan's game today. She looked at her sister's profile, again struck by the eerie feeling she was seeing a double of herself. From the side, the sisters had the same cheek structure, fine, straight noses, full lips, and elegant chins. However, at full face they were as different as complete strangers.

Sally was having none of Megan's holding out and took the bait with the enthusiasm of a sparrow on a bug. "What is it, Megan? Pleeeaaase tell us!"

Megan made them wait for a few moments, as was her way. Then, as if having the thoughts wrested from her under torture, she said casually, "You girls are too much. Don't you know there's more to life than sneaking around and reading Walt Whitman?"

"Like what?" Sally asked, breathless.

"Like learning about boys all on your own—not from some ancient, egotistical, fifty-year-old man."

"Ego—what?"

"Never mind, Sally. The point is, Mr. Whitman's poems and prose are admired for the way he seems to take life by the throat and *live* it. Take a chance on your dreams and desires. *Feel* life! And you don't have to do it by reading him—make your own experiences."

"As I'm sure *you* do, Megan?" Charlotte said sarcastically.

Megan shrugged. "Believe what you want. And don't you roll your eyes at me, Charlotte. I hate it when my sister does it, and I hate it when anyone else does it."

Reena watched her sister for a moment, gauging her seriousness.

Megan had hinted at having many beaux come knocking on her door at school in St. Louis. Reena had ignored her, thinking it was only big sister bragging. But after hearing her words just now and seeing the look on Megan's face, Reena wasn't so sure. *She looks so grown-up and sure of herself—and she sounds different.* All at once, Reena didn't want to know what had happened to make her sister come back changed. Tapping Megan on the shoulder, she rolled her eyes with gusto. "It's your turn to croquet, sister."

Irritated, Megan shrugged off Reena's touch and stood. Surveying the lawn, she saw something that made her smile with genuine pleasure. Taking her mallet in hand, she strolled to her black painted ball, gently tapped it, and watched as it traveled a few feet to Sally's red ball and nudged it with a soft *clack.*

"No, Megan!" Sally wailed. "I just made it through that hoop!"

Still smiling, Megan positioned her ball next to Sally's and placed her booted foot on her own ball. Like a lumberjack preparing to start hacking on a two-foot-thick tree, she cast her lively brown eyes on Sally, pretended to spit on each hand, and with a mighty stroke sent Sally's red ball flying through the air like a rocket. All four heads turned to follow as the red blur flew sixty feet, struck the side of the stable diagonally, and ricocheted into the horse corral. For a moment, the three spectators stared at Megan dumbfounded: first for the sheer cruelty of the act, second for the surprising strength that had been displayed.

"Oooohhh!" Charlotted exclaimed with curled lips. "Did you see what that landed in, Sally?"

"I'm afraid so."

"I've changed my mind," Megan said sweetly. "I *like* this game!"

Reena put her hands on her hips. "Megan, you go get that ball right now!"

"Why? I'd say Sally's out of the game, wouldn't you?"

"Then so am I! Why do you have to be so mean, Megan?"

"Mean!" she said, genuinely surprised. "I'm just playing the game."

"You didn't have to hit it so far." Reena glanced at Sally, who was now staring blankly at the corral. "Sally, go get the green ball if you want to keep playing." Sally didn't move, except for her lower lip trembling.

"I'm tired of playing," Charlotte pouted.

"You haven't even *been* playing, Charlotte!" Megan pointed out. "All you want to do is read that book you stole from your father's library."

"I *borrowed* it."

"That's enough!" Reena pronounced. As had been the case all of their lives, Reena found herself having to keep her older sister in line, instead of the other way around.

"You ladies seem to be getting along in the usual way," a man's voice called. Liam O'Donnell strolled casually toward the group, smiling, conscious of the four pairs of eyes locked onto him in surprise. His hands were stuffed carelessly into the pockets of his black knee-length coat, as were his trouser legs into riding boots that gleamed with new polish. His white shirt was unbuttoned to a gray vest with button-down lapels.

"Liam!" Reena exclaimed, dropping her mallet and hugging him fiercely. He stood one inch over Reena's five-foot eight-inch height, and she felt the scrape of young whiskers when their cheeks touched. "When did you get back?"

"Just now. I heard the merry chatter of female voices, and you know how that draws me." He felt Reena's thin dress while holding her arms. "You must be freezing! Here, take my coat." She felt a rush of affection and watched his face as he removed his coat. As if to round out his sisters' physical features, he was a cross between Megan and Reena. He had Reena's fabulous blue eyes, but Megan's light brown hair. His frame was solid, neither fat nor slim, but well proportioned and reliable. High, prominent cheekbones and full lips tilted his overall appearance to Reena's side.

"I'm freezing too, Liam," Sally pouted playfully.

"Sally, the warmth of your smile should keep the rest of you heated."

Sally sighed and pretended to swoon, then giggled. "You're such a flirt, Liam! Have you no shame?"

Megan went to him and pulled him down to her, planting a rough kiss on his stubbled cheek. "No, he's just like me—not a shamed bone in his seventeen-year-old body."

"How are you, Megan?"

"Bored."

"Then I see nothing *has* changed around here, and I can go get some sleep knowing that the world still turns and God is in His heaven."

"Sleep?" Reena asked. "It's eleven o'clock in the morning."

"George and I rode all night."

"So how was West Point? Are you going to go there?"

Liam smiled his crooked smile tiredly, and his eyes came to rest on Charlotte. "I'll tell all after someone introduces me to this lovely lady."

Before Sally could introduce her friend, Megan drawled, "This here's Miss Charlotte Thibodeaux, all the way from Lou-eeee-siana."

Liam's grin faltered at the mischief in Megan's voice, but he recovered quickly. "Miss Thibodeaux, it's nice to meet you. Please don't mind my sister—we only let her off of her chain on Tuesdays and Thursdays."

"The pleasure is mine, suh." White, even teeth gleamed for a moment, until the light went behind the clouds of Charlotte's violet eyes when they fell on Megan.

Liam turned back to Reena. "West Point was fine, Reena."

She waited for more, and when he didn't go on, she leaned forward and made a wheeling motion with her hand. "Yes? Go on, Liam. You've been gone for a week."

Uncertainty overcame his easy confidence, and he glanced around at all four faces before answering. "I don't know what to do, Reena. I hate the banking business, but I don't really want to be a soldier either. To tell the truth, I'm not interested in anything." He tried to smile, but Reena saw the frustration in his features.

"We should go, Sally," Charlotte said, sensing the private family discussion. "We have to meet your mother for lunch, remember?"

"Yes, I suppose so." Sally looked longingly at her croquet mallet and the course. "Well, it's been fun! At least until my ball was shot off the course." She playfully pinched Megan's arm.

"I was just having fun, Sally," Megan said.

"I know," Sally smiled. She could no more hold a grudge than an infant.

Reena wondered what it was like wandering around from day to day, experiencing life with nothing but anticipation for the next interesting event to be thrown your way.

"Master O'Donnell, it was very nice to meet you," Charlotte said, with only a minimum batting of her eyelashes.

"Call me Liam, please, and the pleasure was all mine. May I get your carriage?"

"Thank you, suh," Charlotte responded with a deep curtsy.

After he'd left, Charlotte said to no one in particular, "He's only seventeen? He seems much older."

Reena and Megan exchanged amused glances, and Reena said, "I hope you brought your ladder from Louisiana, because you'll have to climb over every girl in Chicago to get to him."

An hour later, Reena and Megan were having tea in the parlor of their father's huge house. Liam had gone straight to bed without another word, clearly exhausted. Megan was flipping through a copy of

*Godey's Lady Book*, a quarterly publication that Reena referred to as "Megan's Bible." It contained the latest official information on how to put on airs and be socially conformed. It covered everything from the proper way of sitting at the dinner table to the correct manner of admonishing a servant in front of guests. The editor, Sarah Josepha Hale, held the distinction of being the first female editor of a magazine in U. S. history and was credited with the establishment of Thanksgiving as a national holiday as a result of her prodigious efforts. The proclamation had come from Abraham Lincoln in 1863.

"Well, would you look at this," Megan said thoughtfully. "Walt Whitman has another book coming out this year—*Passage to India*. Another opportunity for Charlotte to commit theft." Hearing no comment, she peered over the top of the well-worn magazine to find Reena staring with sightless eyes at the arrangement of waxed fruit on the black walnut table in the middle of the spacious room. Megan turned back to her magazine with mischief playing at the corners of her small mouth. "Oh, and here. Mrs. Hale has outlawed raven-haired beauties with fabulous blue eyes from high society. You know how her word is law, Reena—out you go!"

"Hmmm?" Only the sound of her name brought her back. "What did you say, Megan?"

Megan lowered the magazine but didn't let go of it. "Where are you? I've been talking for the last five minutes, and you haven't heard a word of it."

"I'm sorry . . . I'm just . . . I don't know."

"Thinking about Louis?"

Nodding, Reena confessed dreamily, "He's a wonderful man."

"I still haven't figured out how you got him first, Reena. The man was destined to be mine and buy me everything I want for the rest of my life."

"You didn't even meet him until we'd started courting."

Megan set down her magazine on the table and leaned forward, her dark brown eyes fastened on Reena's. "I'm talking about destiny, dear sister. Don't quibble with the details."

Reena reached beside her to the whatnot built into the corner of the room and picked up a marble carving of a boy in a straw hat sitting on a log, fishing. Made of polished black wood, the shelves of the whatnot held curios and ornaments of an unusual nature, their mother's passion. "Have you ever been in love, Megan?" She kept her eyes on the blue figurine, thinking that if she didn't make eye contact with her sister, the answer would be from the heart instead of one of her joking evasions.

"Hundreds of times."

Reena looked at her without smiling.

"Mercy, we are serious today, aren't we?" Megan said, leaning back into the thickly padded wingback chair. With fearful nonchalance, she casually draped one of her black-stockinged legs over the arm of the chair and laid her head back to stare at the ceiling. "In love, in love. . . ."

"It's a simple question, Megan."

" 'What is love?' " Megan cried, theatrically throwing her hands in the air, frustrated and beseeching.

"Oh no—" Reena groaned.

" 'It is that powerful attraction towards all that we conceive, or fear, or hope beyond ourselves.' " After making the statement, all signs of banter had disappeared from Megan's face, and she stared at Reena with a calm, questioning look.

Reena had been prepared for a bawdy, contemptuous reply, but as Megan spoke, the words registered in her mind as an incredibly swift dawn. One moment her sister was speaking, then in the silence that followed, each syllable was mentally caressed and stroked and coddled. Megan loved to draw a reaction from people, and Reena was more stunned than when Megan had sent Sally's croquet ball flying into the stable. Just when Reena would think that her sister was beyond hope, she would show an intimate and deeply pensive part of herself that defied explanation.

"Your mouth is open, Reena. It's not very becoming."

Realizing she was right, Reena swallowed and whispered, "That's beautiful, Megan. Who said it?"

"Percy Shelley."

Nodding slowly, not wishing for her to return to the arrogant, spoiled rich girl just yet, Reena asked, "And have you ever felt that way?"

Megan continued staring at her for a long moment, the only sound in the room being the clock on the fireplace mantel ticking softly. "A girl's got to have her secrets, dear sister. Doesn't she?"

# CHAPTER TWO

# A Powerful Message

Reena started down the curving staircase on Sunday morning, and before she was even halfway her nose was treated with a pleasant, buttery smell that quickened her step to the kitchen. Elmira Cotter was at the stove, her broad back to Reena and her body shimmying as she whipped batter in a bowl. Without turning around she observed, "You's late, chile."

"Ellie, how do you always know it's me?"

"Reconnize you step upstairs." Ellie gave her an amused look, which changed at once to surprise. "My lands, Miss Reena, that dress do bring out your purty eyes!"

"Do you like it?" Reena asked, whirling around once for the cook. She'd bought the dress that week at the insistence of her mother. Reena's closet was full to overflowing with elegant dresses, and she always felt a twinge of guilt when she added another fine garment to her wardrobe while there were so many needy families in Chicago, especially after the horrible fire of 1871.

"Whatchoo call that fashion?" Ellie asked, still wide-eyed.

"Princess style."

"Well, you sho look like a princess *in* it!"

"Thank you, Ellie." The dress had a close-fitting bodice with a square-cut neckline. Long sleeves with turned-back cuffs were decorated with pearl buttons and a small frill. But the appeal was the color— the royal blue accented Reena's sky-toned eyes and naturally tawny skin. Reena knew the effect was stunning, but was nevertheless uncomfortable with the attention she was sure to get. The only reason she'd agreed to buy the dress was that her mother had picked it out specially.

"Flapjacks comin' up," Ellie announced, turning back to the stove. Sunday morning breakfast was always Reena's favorite because she and her mother were the only ones to go to church. Her father slept in, while Megan and Liam had no interest.

"Mr. Louis still goin' wit you this mornin'?"

"Yes, I made him keep his promise. I don't really know what a good Catholic boy is going to think of Reverend Moody, but we'll soon find out."

Cackling, Ellie set a plate piled with sausage on the table. Reena's father had hired her during the War. She'd appeared out of nowhere on the day after the battle of Gettysburg and had claimed she'd heard through some mysterious grapevine that Jack O'Donnell was in need of a cook. Her connections were well informed, because the prior cook had died only the day before. Jack O'Donnell had suspected she was an escaped slave, but when he'd questioned her about how she'd known about the death, Ellie had stared off into space as if she hadn't heard him. She was loving, kindhearted, a good cook, and had fit well into the family, but her past was never discussed or questioned.

"Sho' wish I could hear that Reverend Moody," Ellie said, shaking her head. "He sound like he the very thunder himself, mm—mm."

"I think you should go with me sometime."

"Whoo, chile, don' be talkin' that way!"

"I don't care, Ellie. You should be able to attend whatever church you want, just like everybody else."

"No, I's satisfied with my Negro church. Reverend Anderson mightn't win all the souls that Mr. Moody do, but he a good preacher." Ellie placed the heaping mound of pancakes in front of Reena and stood wiping her hands on her apron, waiting for her usual protest.

"Ellie, this is too much! I only eat one or two, and this could feed the neighborhood. We go through this every Sunday." Reena contemplated the six flapjacks with wide eyes. As she watched, a lump of butter slid down its slick path from the top of the pancakes to the plate.

"Hush and eat, chile. Maybe someday you—"

"Good morning, all," Virginia O'Donnell called as she entered the kitchen.

"Morning, Mama," Reena said, then noticed her mother was still in her nightgown. "Why aren't you dressed for church?"

Sighing and easing down into a chair, Virginia said, "I just don't feel well today. Couldn't sleep, either."

Reena observed the bloodshot eyes and the dark rings beneath them. Her mother was having more stomach trouble than she wanted to admit. She had definitely lost some weight, mostly evident in the face; the normal, full roundness had been chipped away until her mother held a slightly gaunt look. "Mama, you have to let Da take you to the doctor."

"That's right, Miz O'Donnell," Ellie agreed as she poured coffee. "You listen to Miz Reena. You sho won't listen to me! You want breakfast?"

Virginia glanced down at the plate of sausage with a look of brief disgust. "No, I believe I'll just have some milk, Ellie." She turned and passed her eyes over Reena. "You look lovely, dear. I feel sorry for the men in the congregation this morning. They'll be so busy looking at you, they'll miss the sermon."

Reena blushed. "Now, Mama—"

"Ain't that the truth!" Ellie exclaimed, setting a glass of milk down in front of Virginia. "Eat, chile, it's gettin' cold!" she barked at Reena.

"Mama, you're avoiding what I said," Reena said, putting a hand on her mother's. "Will you go to the doctor?"

"Yes, yes, I'll go, but everyone's getting stirred up for nothing! I'm just having a little stomach problem that won't go away, that's all."

"Good," Reena nodded. "I'll hold you to it, you know that."

"Me, too," Ellie chimed in. "By the way, Miz O'Donnell, if you need to lay yourself down today, do it in Miz Reena's room so's I can wash your sheets."

"Thank you, Ellie. It looks like rain today, though."

"I don' care. You fooled around and wouldn't let me git to 'em yesterday. Today's the day. Ain't nobody likes to be sleepin' on dirty sheets."

"I didn't feel well yesterday, and—"

"Shoulda let Mr. O'Donnell take you to the park like he asked. Prob'ly woulda done you good."

"I'll decide what does me good, Elmira," Virginia said sharply.

A stunned silence followed. Reena couldn't remember the last time her mother had spoken harshly to Ellie, much less call her by her proper name.

Ellie stared at Virginia for a moment, her liquid brown eyes saddened. Softly she said, "I's sorry, Miz O'Donnell."

"No, no, I'm the one that's sorry." Virginia took a deep breath and put a hand to her forehead. "I didn't mean to snap. . . ."

Reena looked down at her untouched pancakes, suddenly without an appetite. She squeezed her mother's hand and said, "I'll try to get Reverend Moody to pray for you today, Mama."

"Thank you, dear." Virginia smiled at Reena, then turned to Ellie.

"Don't you say nothin', Miz O'Donnell," Ellie said, wiping her eyes with her apron. "You got ever right to get after me and my big black mouth." A knock sounded at the kitchen's outside door, and she rose, mumbling, "Oughta take a horse whip to me. . . ."

"Now, Ellie, I don't want to hear that kind of talk."

Ellie opened the door to find Hiram, the stable boy, with his hat in his hands. "Mornin', Ellie—mornin', Miz O'Donnell, Miz O'Donnell—"

"Hiram, you bring the horse whip?" Ellie asked.

"Huh?" Hiram blinked.

"Ellie, that's enough," Virginia said. "What is it, Hiram?"

"It's Mr. Louis, ma'am. He be comin' up the road."

"Thank you, Hiram," Reena said.

Hiram bowed slightly, started to turn, then faced back around. "Miz O'Donnell, it good to see you . . . you lookin' mighty fresh today, fresh as a daisy."

Virginia smiled. "You always were a bad liar, Hiram, but thank you just the same."

"I's not lyin', Miz O'Donnell. I's tellin' the truth!"

"Get on back to the stable, nigger, and see to Mr. Louis!" Ellie barked. "You's just standin' there lettin' all the warm air out!" Hiram bowed at Virginia and Reena, stepped out of sight, and then Ellie was shouting, "Don' be blowin' no kisses at me, fool! Git on outa here!"

---

The Great Chicago Fire of October 8, 1871, had destroyed more than three square miles of the city—over 17,000 buildings. Some 250 people were killed by the raging fire, and the damage was estimated at $200,000,000. Neither the West Side, where the fire originated, nor the North and South Sides escaped damage. On the North Side, the fire ran unbroken to Fullerton Avenue, but did not reach Reena's home on Lake Michigan.

However, Illinois Street Church, where Reverend Dwight Lyman Moody preached, had been consumed by the flames. Reverend Moody had considerable talent in raising money, as he'd demonstrated in being instrumental in building the first YMCA in 1867, along with scores of churches and missions across the land. As was his way, he disclaimed all honor for his share of the work and politely declined attempts to use his name. After only two months, on a lot close to the previously flattened church, Moody dedicated a new building. On Christmas Eve, 1871, the North Side Tabernacle opened its doors for its first service, and a new church was born.

All of this was explained by Reena to Louis Goldsen as they rode their way through the fire-ravaged ruins of the district. "And you say this man is an easterner?" Louis asked. He'd listened intently, soaking up all the details without interrupting. That was one of the things Reena loved about him—his quiet manner that carefully processed all the information available around him before questioning.

"From the *North*east—Northfield, Massachusetts." Reena pulled her cloak around herself tightly. The absence of sunlight on the overcast day was making it difficult to deal with the never-ceasing wind.

"Why did he come to Chicago?"

"A restless spirit, he claims. Boston was too confining, and he wanted to see the West. He started out as a shoe salesman, you know."

Louis glanced at her, dark eyes stretched in surprise. "A *shoe* salesman! Imagine that," he finished thoughtfully. The strong wind blew his dark brown hair directly back from his face, accenting his features sharply. An oversized nose held gold-rimmed spectacles, and his generous mouth seemed constantly turned up in amusement at everything he experienced. Broad, dark eyebrows over widely spaced, intelligent eyes rounded out a not unhandsome face.

They rode in silence for a while. The desolation that the Great Fire had caused was clearly visible, even seven months afterward. Here and there, charred chimneys rose from the black ground—silent, accusing, and mocking to the aspirations of man. A light fog had partially lifted from the district, creating a fitting gray shroud to brood over the somber earth. The only building to be seen in the ash-bitter landscape was the North Side Tabernacle in the distance—a refuge in a vision of hell.

"Church is *needed* after driving through these dismal streets," Louis commented, reflecting Reena's thoughts exactly.

"Let's talk about something that has nothing to do with it," Reena suggested. "Something happy. Da says you have the golden touch in banking."

"Your father exaggerates. I still feel like I'm a lamb among wolves in the investment community. Whenever I squeeze out a chancy deal, I swear I hear jaws snapping shut right behind me."

Reena reached up and picked a piece of lint off his black suit. "But the point is, the deal is made before the trap closes. That's what counts."

"I suppose so." He rubbed his nose and shifted on the bench seat. "Um, Reena. Have you thought any more about setting a date for the wedding yet?"

Keeping her eyes carefully trained on the nearing church, Reena said, "Yes, I've thought about it."

When she didn't go on, Louis laughed softly. "And?"

"I don't know, darling. Something just . . . keeps telling me to wait and not rush in."

"Rush? We've been engaged for a year."

Reena placed her hand on his arm, her eyes pleading. "I know, and thank you for being so patient with me. I can't explain it . . . it's just . . . a feeling."

Louis sighed deeply but said nothing.

They had arrived a bit early for the service, but many carriages were already parked around the building. When they walked inside, the wooden pews were nearly full, but Louis found them a spot midway to the platform on the left. Before entering the pew, Louis had to catch himself before automatically genuflecting. Reena noticed his nervousness and put her arm through his with her other hand resting there also. He smiled at her uncertainly but attempted to fit in. They nodded to a few acquaintances, with Louis receiving a few open-mouthed looks from people who were aware of his religion.

"So far, so good," he whispered when they were seated.

"Just relax, Louis. No one's going to bite you!"

The church was plainly furnished, seventy-five by one hundred feet, and it was no secret that it was only a temporary structure until money could be raised for a permanent, sturdier building. A large carved cross hung over a twenty-by-twenty platform at the front of the auditorium. The platform held a few chairs behind a pulpit that was off to the right of the dais. From the pulpit stretched a railing to the other side, where a small piano rested. Reverend Moody's favorite spot to preach was from the rail; he rarely stayed behind the pulpit.

Two men extricated themselves from a crowd that had formed in the front and made their way to the platform. Reverend Moody followed Ira Sankey, the song leader and instrumentalist, up the short stairs, and Reena again noticed the contrasting physical features of the men. Sankey stood a full head and shoulders above the preacher, and with Moody behind Sankey on the stairs, it reminded Reena of a father leading his son. Sankey's balding head made him appear much older than Moody, but Reena had heard they weren't far apart in age.

"Good morning!" Sankey called out in a rich baritone. The crowd answered as he took his seat behind a small piano. "It's wonderful to be in the house of the Lord this morning, isn't it?"

"Yes!" came the answer.

"Stand and turn in your hymnals with me to page sixty-eight, and let's worship Him in song."

Louis held the hymnal and struggled through four songs, ending with "Holy, Holy Is What the Angels Sing." Reena carefully avoided making a move or looking at him when he missed a key or word. She only felt overwhelming joy that he had come to church with her at all and was about to hear the most exciting preacher in the country.

Reverend Moody thanked Sankey, who took a seat at the rear of the dais. Moody went directly to the railing and said in a booming voice, "Are you as excited about singing with the angels to our Savior as I am?"

"Yes! Amen!"

" 'I will sing about my Savior, who upon dark Calvary—freely pardoned my transgressions, died to set a sinner free!' Glory be to the Lamb of Lambs, for He died for YOU, sir." Moody pointed directly at a man in the front row, who visibly started. "And YOU, sir, and YOU, ma'am!" Reena's heart jumped to the back of her throat, for he seemed to point right at her nose. "Let us pray."

Moody prayed gracefully and easily for the Spirit of God to move among the congregation and the unredeemed of the city. The nasal utterance of the northeast rang clear in his voice.

"I didn't mean to scare you folks with the finger pointing. I just love sharing about the love of our Lord Jesus." As he began walking along the rail he added, "I also want you to be awake for what I have to say." Good-natured laughter filled the hall. "My enthusiasm outweighs my good sense sometimes, I must say. The other day I was walking along the riverfront and heard a dock worker cursing another man in the bluest language you've ever heard—pardon me ladies for bringing up such a vile subject—but I ran to the man and asked, 'Sir do you know Jesus as your Savior?' " Moody paused and shook his head. "Well, the man didn't pitch me over the rail into the Chicago River, but he became quite agitated with me." More laughter and guffaws.

A serious look came over the reverend's face, and he turned his short, squat body to face the crowd, which was hanging on every word. A full mustache and beard covered most of the man's mouth and concealed what little neck he possessed. The eyes were dark and wide-spaced with heavy bags beneath. Quietly, but loud enough for every ear to hear, he said, "That man had the Spirit of Almighty *God* move over him, and he accepted Jesus right in front of the very man he was abusing!"

"Amen! Hallelujah!" cried the congregation.

Reena glanced at Louis and smiled, receiving a halfhearted effort in return. He'd been listening intently to Moody, mesmerized by the man's speech and commanding presence. Though no one who heard him preach could identify the appeal of the plain former shoe salesman, everyone agreed on one thing: Moody seemed to speak to every person individually, as if only he and the listener were present.

Moody continued: "Do you realize what a privilege and an honor it is to tell people about Jesus? Mr. Griffin, there in the third row—if that man next to you saved you and your family from the disastrous fire of last year—if you were disabled, and he came into your house and carried you out one by one through blazing walls of flame, would you feel something for that man?"

"Yes, Reverend."

"Would you be proud to call him your friend?"

"Yes, I would."

"Would you do anything for him, give him anything he asked?"

"Yes."

"Why?"

Mr. Griffin appeared flustered for a moment and tugged at his tie. "Well, Reverend Moody, because he would have risked his own life to save mine and my family's."

"That's right! Now, what would you do if a man you didn't even know saved you and your family from eternal—I said *eternal*—pain and suffering by dying a painful and grotesque death, and then asked of you only three little things. Would you do them?"

"Of course!"

Moody grinned and winked at the congregation. "I do believe I've got him now, don't I?" The audience responded with more laughter. Moody turned back to Griffin and counted the points one by one with his fingers. "Mr. Griffin, that man only wants you to love Him and His Father in heaven, to try to be like Him, and to tell other people about Him. Pretty simple, isn't it?"

"Yes it is, Reverend."

"Would you say that's too much to ask?"

"No."

"I don't either, and, friends, that's what we should strive to do every day. Let me tell you about a man named Paul who tried to do it every day, too, but every day of his life he was in mortal danger for

ALAN MORRIS / BY HONOR BOUND

*doing* it." He went on to tell of Paul's first and second missionary jour-
neys from Antioch, and the wondrous works God allowed him to do
in His name.

Reena listened intently, but at one point, Moody's voice seemed to
become louder and clearer than usual to her. All peripheral vision, even
Louis, vanished until her unobstructed sight was trained on the powerful preacher. "Are there those out there who seem to be treading the
water of life? Who seem to be waiting for the Lord to reveal His plan
for them? Who somehow feel that they need a direction in life?" To
Reena's astoundment, Moody again seemed to be staring directly at
her. "Paul and Silas were chosen of God, but at one point in their second mission, they were uncertain of which way to go. The Holy Spirit
didn't reveal the path they were to follow, only blocked the way to
where He *didn't* want them to go. The Holy Spirit said no to the Turk-
ish provinces of Asia Minor. He said no to the province of Bithynia.
And then something strange and wonderful happened—Paul had a vision.

"He dreamed of a man over in Macedonia, Greece, pleading and
begging and waving to him to 'Come over into Macedonia and help
us! Help us!' " Moody shook his head solemnly. "Brothers and sisters,
few of us are chosen to serve the Lord by leaving our homes and going
to another country to minister to other people's needs for salvation.
Could *you* be one of those?"

Reena felt a shiver despite the warmth emanating from the stoves
along the walls. ". . . one of those, one of those, one of those," the
words echoed through her mind.

Moody continued to speak of Paul and Silas' imprisonment, and
the subsequent conversion of the Philippian jailer. But Reena's world
and vision had returned to normal, and she was now only listening with
half an ear. *What does this mean, Lord?* she prayed. *Why was that revealed to me so forcefully?* Louis seemed to sense her anxiety and took
one of her hands with a questioning look. She tried to give him an
encouraging smile, but wasn't sure if she succeeded after seeing his
face.

Silence from the podium caught Reena's attention. Moody was absolutely still as he gazed at two doors on the right side of the hall.
"Before the Great Fire, I would tell people to consider all that they'd
heard, and think about a decision for Christ for a week, until the next
Sunday. One time when I did that, there was no next Sunday for some
folks, and the burden was almost too much for me to bear." His voice
caught with emotion, and he looked over the congregation with tears

in his eyes. "Indeed, I couldn't have borne it without the grace and forgiveness of our Lord. So today, as every Sunday now, I want each of you who need to make a decision for salvation to go to our inquiry rooms over there." He pointed toward two doors on the right. "*Next* Sunday is not the time for a decision—the Lord Jesus calls for you *to-day*!"

Twenty or thirty souls rose from their seats and made their way to the rooms during the invitation. Reena's heart rejoiced, for Moody always received a response from his sermons. The Lord's moving in him was strong.

After the service, Reena told Louis that she wanted to meet Moody. Louis asked if she wanted him to go with her, but she could tell he was uncomfortable with the idea and told him to meet her outside.

Making her way to the front of the hall, she saw a crowd of people around Moody and thought she would be kept waiting for a long time. But as she approached, a few parishioners left, leaving a natural path directly to the man. Their eyes locked, and held by his intense yet warm gaze, Reena felt herself to be alone with him instead of with the ten other people around him. Apparently, when his attention was fixed on an individual, there was no one else around.

"Good morning," he said cheerily.

Reena found herself standing a full head taller than him. "Good morning, Reverend. I don't want to take too much of your time. I know you're busy—"

"Nonsense, my dear! I always have time for our church members. I've seen you in the congregation, but I've never had the pleasure. You are usually with an older woman—is that your mother?"

"Yes, sir. My name's Reena O'Donnell, and . . . and . . . I—"

Moody waited patiently, his hands clasped in front of himself. "Please, Miss O'Donnell, tell me what's bothering you."

*How does he know something's bothering me?* "It's my mother, Reverend. She's really ill, and I was wondering if you could pray for her this week."

His eyebrows raised into arches. "This week? My dear girl, we'll pray for her right now!" Before Reena could wipe the surprise from her face, Moody grasped her hands in his, bowed his head, and began to pray. His words, words so right that Reena could only stand and admire, pleaded for a complete recovery for her mother if it was God's will. He also prayed for Reena, for the Lord to ease her burden for her mother. By the time he was through, Reena had helpless tears streaming down her cheeks.

"Thank you, Reverend Moody."

"No, no, it's my pleasure."

Reena glanced around at the other people waiting to talk to him, but when her gaze came back to his kindly face, he showed no hurry to send her on her way. "Your message was wonderful, sir—"

"The Lord's message, my dear. The Lord's message. I'm only the mouth that speaks His thoughts."

"Yes, the Lord's message. One part, about treading the water of life and waiting for something . . ." Reena was suddenly at a loss for words.

"Did that touch you, Miss O'Donnell?"

"Yes . . . yes it certainly did. I felt as though you were speaking directly to me."

"Maybe it wasn't *me* speaking directly to you, remember?"

Reena stared at him open-mouthed for a moment as his words hit home.

"Have you ever had thoughts of the mission field, dear?"

"No, I—no, never."

Moody smiled beneath his thick beard. The edges of his wide eyes crinkled with tiny lines. "Then, maybe you should." He patted her hand gently. "Maybe you should."

Reena practically stumbled outside into the gray day, the preacher's words swirling through her head. *A missionary? Me? I couldn't possibly. . . .*

"Did you see him, Reena?" Louis asked. She'd made her way to the buggy without remembering a step of the way. Louis helped her in, then went around to his side.

"Yes, I met him," she said through numbed lips.

"What's he like?"

Reena met his eyes, searching for words. "He's everything I'd imagined him to be—and more."

# CHAPTER THREE

## Spring Ball

"...so—when Mrs. Turginson talked for what seemed *hours* about the wonderful properties of eggs, I had an idea." Megan ran on and on as she applied dark shadow to her eyes with careful strokes. A dancing gleam came into her face.

"No, Megan, don't tell me," Reena said, momentarily forgetting about applying her own makeup. The girls were in Megan's bedroom getting ready for the ball that evening. Megan was in one of her talkative moods, but instead of being irritated, Reena welcomed the distraction from her own mind. The Sunday message was still foremost in her thoughts five days later, with no relief in sight. She had told no one, but the urge to confide in *somebody* had grown stronger every day.

"Well, it's so *boring* in that science class, and the other girls need a refreshing outlook."

"What did you do?" Reena sighed.

"The next morning she brought her old, stiff self into the class, went to her desk, and sat down in her chair—right on an egg!" Megan erupted in laughter. "Right before she sat down it was the quietest it had ever been in that room. Everyone was waiting for the crack and the squash!"

Reena shook her head. "I don't suppose I have to ask who put the egg there?"

"It wasn't me, Reena, I promise! It was Susie McAlister."

"And who put her up to it?"

Megan smiled and shrugged, continuing with her application.

"So, what happened?"

"Old Mrs. Turginson got mad and turned so red in the face I

thought she'd explode, but she couldn't really expel the whole class, could she? So we just ended up writing 'I will not assault Mrs. Turginson again' until our arms almost fell off. Can you believe that? Assault?"

"Sounds like you got off easy. Why do you even bother going to school if you hate it so much?" Megan gave her a you-should-know-that look, and Reena held up a hand. "Never mind—bored, right?"

"Some of us aren't set up for marriage with a promising, rich man. Have you set the date yet?"

Reena threw down the pad she'd been using to put on her rouge. "Why does everybody keep asking me that?"

Megan whistled. "Sor—ree! I didn't know it was such a touchy subject."

"What's a touchy subject?" Virginia O'Donnell asked as she entered the room.

"Mother!" Reena breathed. "You look beautiful!"

"Thank you, dear." Her hands unconsciously went to the gold overskirt of her ball gown. The underskirt was long and trained, and, like the overskirt, heavily flounced. The bodice was off-the-shoulder, with short, puffed, lace-filled sleeves. Reena thought that the deep gold color was just what her mother's pale, slightly drawn face needed.

"Da better not let you out of his sight tonight!" Megan admired.

"So—who's touchy?" Virginia repeated as she went to sit on Megan's four poster bed.

"Reena is." Megan caught Reena's warning look reflecting in her mirror but innocently ignored it. "Whatever you do, don't ask about her wedding plans."

"Why not, Reena? Did something happen?"

*Only that I think God is telling me to leave everything and everyone I know to go to some strange country*, Reena thought with a trace of bitterness. Sitting back down beside Megan, she gave her sister a biting look and picked up her rouge pad. "Not really," she said quietly.

Virginia stared at her daughter for a moment before saying, "Megan, would you excuse us, please?"

"Mama, this is my room! We only have an hour to get ready!"

"Go to Reena's room to finish. You both have the same things anyway."

"But, Mama—"

"*Go*, Megan."

"Yes, ma'am," Megan conceded, casting a withering glance at Reena, who smiled prettily. Dressed only in her undergarments, Megan threw on her robe and flounced out.

"What is it, dear?" Virginia asked after the door closed. "What's bothering you?"

Reena turned her chair to face her mother. The late afternoon sunlight came through the window beside the vanity, and she felt the left side of her face grow warm in the glow. Picking up a brush, she needlessly skimmed it through her hair while trying to hide her nervousness. She and her mother had always been close, but it had been a long time since Reena had come to her with a serious, life-changing problem, and Reena didn't quite know how to start.

"Do you love Louis?" Virginia asked.

"Yes—it's not that. It's something else."

Virginia waited patiently, a pleasant, trusting smile on her lips.

Taking a deep breath, Reena stopped brushing and met her mother's eyes. "You know, Mama, I had something happen in the service Sunday that was . . . strange. Strange, but good in a way. And scary." Reena shook her head in exasperation. "Let me start from the beginning." She told of her excitement when Louis had asked her to marry him, then of the months that followed when a nagging doubt plagued her mind. The prospects of being a wife and mother were intriguing, but only that. She felt something else was in store for her, something big and good and satisfying that would make her proud of herself. She'd waited for an answer and prayed about it, but nothing came to mind, and nothing was revealed by God.

"So Sunday," she continued, "Reverend Moody said something that aimed at me like a cannon and hit me with just about as much force." Reena paused, still afraid to reveal something that even *she* wasn't sure about.

"Go ahead, Reena. You can tell me." Virginia was leaning forward on the bed, listening intently.

"He talked about people merely going through the motions of life, as if waiting for something. Then he said that maybe the mission field was the calling for those people." Reena stopped and watched her mother's reaction. What she saw totally surprised her.

Virginia kept her dark, marble blue eyes on Reena and nodded slightly. Then she leaned back until her back was straight, took a deep breath, and said thoughtfully, "So that's it. That's what God had in store for you."

Expecting anything but the reaction she'd received, Reena asked, "*Had* in store for me? What do you mean?"

Virginia rose and came over and sat beside her daughter at the vanity. "Do you remember when Megan stopped going to church with us? You were—I don't know, about ten?"

"Yes."

"It really hurt you, and made you—well—angry at your sister. I thought it was cute at the time, you telling Megan what was right and wrong when she was two years older than you. But after thinking about it, that's the way it's always been with you two. I believe that Megan tries to show a wild side around you so that you can tell her what's right and what's wrong. It's just something she needs. You're her rock, her cornerstone."

Reena stared at her skeptically.

Patting her hand, Virginia went on: "Anyway, that's not what I was going to tell you. At that time, when Megan stopped attending church, I was praying for her, when suddenly the Lord revealed to me something about *you*. He gave me a verse in Proverbs: 'Train up a child in the way he should go: and when he is old, he will not depart from it.' You see, Reena, God gave me a gentle peace about you even back then. In a way, He told me that you were His—that He had special plans for you. Do you understand?"

Reena thought a moment, then asked, "Why haven't you told me this before?"

"Because I didn't want to put pressure on you. I wanted you to find your own way in the world, and let God lead you. That's why I'm not really surprised with what you've just told me."

"So—you think I should do this? Just leave everything and go?" Reena's heart was pounding in her chest as she asked the questions. Her whole future could depend on her mother's answer.

Virginia sensed the weight that accompanied the questions and saw Reena's breathless anxiety. "I think it's between you and God. I'm not going to tell you His will—only He can do that."

Shoulders sagging with a mixture of relief and disappointment, Reena stared at her hands in her lap. She'd hoped her mother would solve her dilemma with either a word of encouragement or discouragement. But now she was right back where she had been before—unsure of what to do.

"Just wait on the Lord, dear," Virginia smiled. "He'll let you know what to do."

Reena nodded without meeting her eyes.

"Guess who arrived in town today?" Virginia asked, changing the subject.

"Who?"

"Your Uncle Faron."

"You're joking!" Reena said, surprised and pleased. "What's he *doing* here? We haven't heard from him in months!"

"Who knows what your father's brother has in mind?"

"Where is he? Will he be at the ball tonight?"

"He'll be there. Right now he's at the bank with your father."

"Uncle Faron," Reena breathed, staring out the window. Her eyes came back into focus on her mother. "He hasn't gotten into some kind of trouble, has he?"

"Faron?" Virginia laughed. "Probably."

"Well—what's he doing? For a living, I mean."

Virginia stood, still smiling. "I'll let him tell you tonight. *I'm* not really sure."

————

"Trapping! Beaver, mink, sparrows—anything!" Faron O'Donnell boomed as he held Reena at arm's length and looked her up and down appreciatively. "I swear, Reena, you're the very sight of heaven, you are!"

His speech was still thick with an Irish brogue. The tuxedo he'd borrowed from Reena's father was too small and fit poorly, but Reena hardly noticed. Her eyes were locked on her uncle's heavily bearded face and smiling eyes, remarkably similar in color to Reena's.

They stood outside Sally Ames' house with Louis and Jack, Reena's father. The spring ball had once been held in a meeting hall that had fallen in the Great Fire, but Charles Ames had taken it upon himself to offer his own huge ballroom in his house. Like so many of the people that had had fortune come their way suddenly in Chicago, Ames had spared no expense in the building of his home and would have no trouble accommodating fifty or so guests.

"Beautiful like me, eh, Faron?" Jack asked.

"Ah, Jack, me brudder, I see you're still suffering from those blinding delusions. Haven't gotten any better, hey?" Faron slapped his brother on the back with a resounding *whack!* that sent Jack forward a half step. The brothers were the same height and stocky build, but Faron exuded a liveliness that made him seen taller and bigger. He turned to Louis, who was standing beside Reena quietly. "And you, me boy—I hear ye'll be marryin' me favorite niece."

"I hope so, sir."

"Don't ye be sirrin' me! That's fer old folk like Jack here!"

"You're older than I am, Faron," Jack pointed out. "By four years."

"But you *look* older! Anyway—what was the name—Louis?"

"Yes—Louis Goldsen."

"What kind o' parent names their son 'Louis'?" Faron muttered into his red and gray beard. "Frenchys?"

"I beg your pardon?" Louis asked, round-eyed.

"Frenchys! French people!"

"Um . . . no, s—I mean, no, we're from English ancest—"

"Never ye mind!" Faron turned to his brother and said, "Boy seems to ramble, don't he?" He turned the full force of his presence to Louis again. "I hear that in some parts of these United States, it's considered customary to use force to keep the wifey in line, if ye know what I mean. I'm here to tell you that, by Gabriel's trumpet, if I hear of any of that I'll—"

"Uncle Faron!" Reena said, horrified.

"—fix yer head in a beaver trap and nail ye to the nearest tree for archery practice!"

"Uncle Faron, please! Louis isn't like that!" Reena protested.

"I assure you, sir . . . I mean Uncle . . . er—" Louis stammered.

Faron glanced at Jack knowingly. "There he goes again! Get yer thoughts together in yer head, boy, before ye open your maw!"

A small orchestra began playing inside, and the lilting music flowed from the front door as two couples entered. Faron's face lit up like a lantern, and he extended his elbow to Reena. "Sweet music, lass! What are we standin' out here for?"

Reena cast a helpless, laughing look over her shoulder at the bewildered Louis and allowed Faron to lead her inside.

Jack noticed Louis' slightly dazed air and said, "Don't be alarmed, son. Everyone is a little shell-shocked after meeting my brother."

"Is he . . . always like that?"

"I've only seen my brother different on one occasion. That was after his wife, Margaret, died back in '67. He came over here from Ireland after that a hard, bitter, angry man. Didn't stay around too long, and ended up drifting to Canada." Jack shook his head thoughtfully and took Louis' arm, steering him toward the door. "He seems to have made peace with his demons, though, hasn't he?"

The Ames' ballroom was decorated with bright green streamers hanging from the twenty-foot ceiling and vases of flowers scattered all about the huge room. A large banner over the double doors to the hallway proclaimed, "Spring Ball, 1872," and various menservants dressed in tuxedos carried trays of sweets and drinks around to the people hovering at the edge of the dance floor. The room was arranged in royal blue, from the velvet curtains hanging in front of the tall windows to the fabric on the furniture. The walls were painted a bright golden color nearly identical to the flooring, making the dance floor seem even larger than it was.

Faron whirled Reena around in a breathless waltz, unmindful of the other dancers. He received more than a few glares from the gentlemen, and Reena noticed Mrs. Ames and her friends on the side staring in disapproval, but Reena didn't care. Uncle Faron was simply too much fun to be with to worry about what other people thought. His eyes shone with mischief and his graying, chest-length beard swayed back and forth with his agile movements.

Reena greeted her friends as she zipped by them and noticed Charlotte Thibodeaux dancing with Liam, her dark eyes shining. Sally was watching them with ill-concealed envy for Charlotte, and she attempted a smile at Reena when she saw her. Megan was nowhere to be seen. She'd come to the ball early, since Reena and her mother had talked until Megan couldn't wait any longer.

While everyone was clapping politely for the orchestra after the dance, Faron suggested, "Care to have another go?"

Reena put a hand to her heaving chest. "No, you've worn me out with one dance, Uncle. Let's have some lemonade and talk."

"Lemonade! Don't they have anything stronger?"

"I don't know, but I won't let you have anything *but* lemonade."

"Yes, your ladyship," Faron said, disappointed.

Reena found a vacant sofa, and after they were seated, she carefully arranged her red satin skirt. The dress was short-sleeved and had a neckline trimmed with white lace. Embroidered roses delicately intertwined through it, and her hair was tied back with matching red lace. Reena asked, "So what brings you back down to civilization?"

"That man right over there," Faron pointed.

Reena followed his finger and saw a tall man in some sort of uniform with heavy sideburns and a full mustache. "Who's he?"

"That is Captain James F. Macleod o' the Canadian Militia." Faron caught Macleod's eye and waved for him to come over. Macleod's posture and bearing as he crossed the room was undoubtedly the strictest Reena had ever seen. He stopped in front of them, clicked his heels together, and bowed to Reena.

"Captain Macleod, my niece Reena."

"And the loveliest girl in the ballroom, I must say," Macleod said in a quiet voice. His speech held a trace of a British accent.

"Thank you, Captain. My uncle tells me that you're the reason we're able to see him again. For that I thank you, even though I don't know what it means."

Macleod continued standing painfully erect, his light blue uniform shining like a lighthouse in the sea of black tuxedos. The gold buttons on the front were arranged in double-breasted order, and the four huge chandeliers in the room made them shine brightly. "I've come from Ottawa to study some techniques of the Chicago Police Department. My country will be organizing a troop for security in the North-West Territories within the next year or so."

"You hope," Faron added with a hint of a smile.

"Yes, we definitely hope for that."

Macleod obviously didn't catch Faron's sarcasm, and Reena imagined that a sense of humor was not one of James Macleod's strong suits. "Is there trouble in the Canadian West?" Reena asked.

"Not as bad as in your American West, but we don't want to take any chances and be caught unawares."

"The Indians are peaceful, for the most part," Faron added. "But settlers are starting to head that way in Canada, and then there's the whiskey traders."

"Blackguards and villains, all of them!" Macleod erupted, then immediately looked at Reena. "My apologies, Miss O'Donnell, I forget myself when the subject is broached. They force their rotgut whiskey on the peaceful Indians, and then they aren't so peaceful anymore. Not to mention the traders themselves acting as if they own the area—but why wouldn't they, when there's no police of any sort?"

"None at all?" Reena asked.

"There are a few odd justices of the peace here and there, but no organized force. If Sir Macdonald, our prime minister, and I have anything to say on the matter, we'll have a troop established there in no time."

"If the prime minister is for it, then why can't it be made into law right now?"

"Parliament." Macleod practically spit the word out. "They don't see the use in spending all that money when there aren't many white people there anyway. But there will be, mark my words." His eyes found Charles Ames, and he said, "Would you excuse me, please? I need to thank our host."

Reena watched him go and commented, "I sure wouldn't want to be on his bad side."

"No, you don't. He's probably the best soldier in Canada."

"What do you think about all that, Uncle?"

Faron drained his small glass of lemonade in a single swallow, pursed his lips, and glared at the empty glass. "Needs sugar. What do *I* think? I'm all for it. I did most o' my tradin' with some Assiniboine Indians in the Cypress Hills for a while. Nicest race o' people ye'd ever meet, but when they get ahold o' that whiskey they change completely!"

"Sounds just like white men," Reena said with a slightly accusing glance at her uncle.

"Aye, ye got me there, darlin'! Just the same as white men. But the Indians seem different somehow. When the supply runs out, I think they'd nearly kill their own brother if he was hidin' some and didn't let on. And those poor Assiniboine! Their chief, Lone Elk, is as fine a man as ye'd ever meet—'cept when he gets on the whiskey. And he's been on it more than off it lately." Faron shook his head and snatched another glass from a passing attendant's tray. "I'll tell ye what those fine people need, little Reena—it's some o' your Bible learnin'!"

Reena stopped her glass midway to her mouth and stared at him. "What?"

Thinking she didn't hear him, Faron raised his voice until he was almost shouting. "I said, those Assiniboine Indians need some o' your Bible learnin' and God talk. What's the matter, lass? Ye look like ye've just seen a banshee!"

Reena leaned back on the sofa and let the thick, blue cushions surround her shoulders. Only an instant before, she'd let her eyes wander to take in what was going on around the large ballroom, to see who was dancing with whom, unconsciously searching for a new subject to discuss. Faron's word had intruded like a thunderclap.

"Are ye all right, girl?" Faron asked, leaning forward and grasping her arm.

"Yes . . . I . . . just felt faint for a moment there."

"Do ye want to lie down?"

"No, Uncle, I'm better now. Just a passing spell, I suppose." Reena sat back up straight and set her glass on a nearby oak table. *Was that a coincidence? If it was, they sure are piling up lately!* She turned to Faron and asked, "So you think the Indians need a missionary?"

Faron looked surprised to hear the word and said thoughtfully, "A missionary—now that ye mention it, yes they do. They've got their old ways, o' course, and their own sort of religion—" He caught the faraway, contemplative frown on Reena's face and looked at her askance.

"What's on your mind, darlin'? I've seen that look before on me beloved wife Margaret's face, God rest her soul, and it's questionable whether anything good come of it."

Taking a deep breath, Reena said, "I've already told this story once today, but here goes. . . ." She told him everything, stopping every once in a while to greet a newcomer that stopped by. Once when Louis hesitantly walked up to them, Reena stopped abruptly. Faron noticed but said nothing. Reena told Louis she wanted to visit a bit more. As soon as he walked away, she finished her story. "So when you said that about the Assiniboine needing God, it was just like when Reverend Moody was speaking and everything around me just sort of—vanished. I could only hear your words over and over."

Faron continued to stare at her when she'd finished, his face neutral. He'd nodded from time to time, but had let her get it all out with no comment.

"What do you think, Uncle Faron?" Reena asked, growing nervous under his direct, stony stare. The very fact that he was so quiet was starting to frighten her. *He looks like he's about to call the police to take me away.*

Suddenly snapping out of his scrutiny, Faron rubbed his nose and cleared his throat. "Weel, that's a very interesting story, me girl. The first query that comes to me mind is, what does our Louis think of it?"

"He . . . um . . . doesn't know about this yet."

Faron was nodding even before she'd finished. "Aye, aye," he mumbled. He fixed her with a serious gaze. "I'm not one to be givin' advice, Reena. You know that, especially when it comes to matters of the Man upstairs. We aren't on the best of terms, which is *my* fault. But I've always followed me heart, and it's taken me to some pretty strange places. I think that's what you should do, no matter what anybody says."

Reena nodded, and when her eyes broke away from him, they landed directly on Louis dancing with Megan. They were moving very slowly to the music, not laughing and talking, but studying each other's faces as if for the first time. Jealousy rose in Reena, unbidden and sudden and sharp. Louis and Megan were in sharp contrast to the other dancers, who were laughing and talking. She found their silence more disturbing than the close way Louis held Megan.

Aware that her uncle was still watching her intently, Reena gave him a crooked smile and uselessly adjusted her red skirt. "Thank you for listening, Uncle Faron. I'm just trying to figure out where my heart is right now."

"Good girl," he said, patting her hand. "Now, I've got to go find me brudder. We've got a lot of catching up to do."

Faron had no sooner left than Sally appeared and plopped down beside Reena, oblivious to wrinkling her blue dress. The color matched the royal blue of the room perfectly, and Reena wondered if Sally's mother had dressed her that way intentionally. It was difficult for Reena not to think of Sally as a China doll, with her porcelain, rosy-cheeked features and childish personality. Apparently her mother felt the same way.

"Do you *see* that, Reena?" Sally asked with round blue eyes.

"See what?"

"Those two making a spectacle of themselves!" she said, nodding toward Louis and Megan.

"They're just dancing, Sally." Reena sounded more confident than she felt, but when she looked at the dancers, Louis and Megan were as close as ever.

"You're so innocent, Reena!" Sally announced with a sniff. "She's *catapulting* herself at him!"

Despite her mounting anxiety, Reena had to laugh at the idea of Sally accusing someone else of being innocent, but her laugh ended with a hollow note. *There's too much happening too fast! I've suddenly lost control of my life, and I don't understand it!*

At that moment the dance ended, and Reena saw Megan glance at her, then quickly look away. She waved at someone across the room and went toward them. Louis was making his way to Reena, and in the absence of music playing, she could hear his heels clicking on the hardwood dance floor. Reena turned to say something to Sally and found she'd disappeared.

"So you're finally free," Louis observed with a faint smile as he sat down. "I was beginning to wonder if you'd find any time for *me* to-night."

"I was beginning to wonder some things, too," Reena blurted, all at once not able to control her feelings of jealousy and betrayal. "Why didn't you and Megan just go outside on the balcony and dance where no one would see you?"

"What are you talking about?" Louis' face was totally guiltless, but for a moment, in the blink of an eye, Reena had seen guilt pass over his features.

"You *know*, Louis," Reena said harshly, "everyone in the room saw how closely you two were dancing."

"It was a slow waltz, Reena. And you know how clumsy your sister is on the dance floor. I was just trying to keep her from—"

"Megan isn't *nearly* as clumsy as she seems." A helpless anger kept rising in Reena, and she couldn't stop it—didn't *want* to stop it.

"Reena, darling, you're upset, and—"

"Yes I *am* upset!" she stated as she rose. The volume of her voice had people around them turning to stare, but she didn't care.

Louis lowered his voice and stepped toward her. "People are watching, darling."

"I don't care!"

Louis glanced quickly at the curious faces around them. "Darling, let's calm down—"

"Leave me alone, Louis!" Reena spun and made her way past the small crowd that had gathered and stopped at an adjoining room. She paused at the door and saw Megan watching from across the room. She seemed neither surprised nor alarmed; her face only held a blank, observing look, as if she were watching a play in which she had lost interest. Reena shot an icy glare her way but didn't wait for her reaction.

————

Louis stared unbelievingly at Reena's receding back. He'd never felt so humiliated in front of so many of his peers before, and inside he burned like a blacksmith's forge. *No one has* ever *done that to me!* he thought darkly as his eyes came to rest on a violin player in the orchestra. He was watching Louis with the faintest glimmer of a smile on his lips, as if he were aware of everything that had happened and was enjoying it immensely. Louis immediately headed straight for the man to give him a good dressing down. The musician's face turned pale and wary as he saw the aggression in Louis' movements, but he sat frozen in his chair.

At the last moment, Louis considered the damage that had already been done and the attention the incident had brought to him. Deciding he wanted no more confrontations, Louis veered away from the man and went directly to the balcony doors and stepped outside, shutting the tall doors behind him.

*And that uncle of hers!* he continued as he stomped to the rail overlooking the expansive lawn and Lake Michigan beyond. *What a cad! What skeleton closet did they drag him out of?* He shook his head and gripped the rail tightly as he watched a freighter steam its way south, white smoke billowing from the smokestack.

"Louis?"

He turned to find Megan standing in the doorway with a concerned look on her face. He hadn't heard the door open, and his immediate reaction was anger at her for getting all this started.

"What do you want?" he asked rudely.

Megan ignored his gruff tone and came outside. "I just wanted to see if you were all right—if there was anything I could do."

"No, thank you, you've done enough."

"What does that mean?"

"It means if we hadn't danced, Reena wouldn't have gotten angry."

"That's not true!" Megan pouted as she came up beside him. "She's been acting strange lately anyway, always brooding and staring off into the distance."

Louis said nothing and kept his eyes on the lake. Megan had always been pleasant to him, sometimes to the point of flirting, but he'd considered her actions innocent—until they'd danced tonight. The way she'd looked at him and held him—along with the seriousness of her face—had confused him. He'd kept dancing with her, waiting for her to say something, but she hadn't spoken a word. For Megan to be silent *and* demure was a phenomenon that had made him take pause, and he'd found himself waiting for what would happen next.

Shaking his head, he thought out loud, "I don't know what's wrong with Reena. She still doesn't want to set a wedding date. What am I supposed to do, wait around forever?"

Megan didn't answer him, but she put her hand on his and squeezed lightly.

Louis looked down at her hand briefly, then considered her face. She watched him a moment, seemed ready to say something, then abruptly turned and walked along the balcony to stand beside a tall potted fern. "What is it, Megan?"

Fingering a broad leaf, she mumbled something that he couldn't hear.

"I didn't hear you," he said, going toward her.

Megan turned and locked her eyes with his. "I said *I* wouldn't make you wait."

Her calm statement stopped him, and he could think of nothing to say.

"I really believe that you and I are better suited for each other," Megan said in the same matter-of-fact voice. "I know I shouldn't be talking about my sister behind her back, but she's *not* the sort who would guide you to the heights of high society. She just wouldn't take the time, because it doesn't mean as much to her as it does to you." Megan walked slowly toward him. "That *is* important to you, isn't it, Louis?"

His mouth worked, but no words came as she stopped directly in front of him, their faces inches apart. He caught the scent of a lilac perfume, different from Reena's, and briefly wondered what it was.

"Megan, I . . . I . . . don't know what to say. I had no idea—"

"You don't have to say anything, Louis. Just remember that with my help, there would be no limit for us in this town." Louis felt her fingers intertwine with his. "No limit," she repeated softly.

Neither one of them noticed Reena through the tall glass balcony doors, standing at the back of the ballroom and staring at them in confusion and pain.

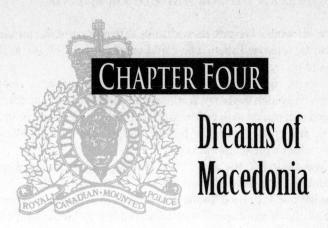

# CHAPTER FOUR

# Dreams of Macedonia

In her dream, Reena was walking steadily toward the West Coast. She could tell she was trudging along a huge map of the United States. The endless terrain meant nothing to her; she glided over the rivers, trails, and hills with an easy stride and felt nothing beneath her feet. Sensing she'd passed into Iowa, she turned and looked in the direction of Chicago and saw her family and friends, tiny but discernible, watching her go. Their faces were blank and staring, the masks of the dream-drunk.

When she turned to the front she found a snow-covered, flat prairie that she instinctively knew was Dakota Territory. The vision was of a cold day, with a freezing wind blowing the sparse grass that the snow didn't cover, but she felt no chill. She was walking northwest now, and saw massive herds of buffalo grazing, and even witnessed a band of fur-clad Indians as their ponies dashed among the beasts of one herd, shooting arrows at close range. The speed with which she moved was incredibly swift, but her senses took in every detail.

Suddenly her movement stopped, and she found herself standing on the summit of a mountain with a breathtaking view. A river wound its serpentine path to the north, disappearing into a gray wall of mist. Somehow she knew the fog was the border to Canada, and even as her eyes tried to penetrate the barrier, the ashen-colored mist began to dissipate and swirl. Reena knew that something was on the other side, and she felt a knot grow in her stomach, unsure whether she wanted to see what lay behind the swirling tendrils of fog. She attempted to tear her eyes away, but she had no peripheral vision—only the same tunnel-like view she'd had when Reverend Moody had been preaching.

The fog lifted completely, and Reena saw a figure standing on a rise of low, rolling hills. Despite their altitude difference and the hundreds of miles that separated them, she could see the man as clearly as if he were standing right in front of her.

He was an Indian, and by the look and bearing of him, a chief. A headdress of golden eagle tail feathers adorned his head. The feathers were dyed red, tipped with yellow-tinted horsehair. His face was strong and stoic and creased with the burden of ages. He held no weapon, and his clothes were plain buckskin.

He was Lone Elk, the Assiniboine chief that Faron had spoken of. Reena didn't know how she knew, but she did.

Slowly Lone Elk raised his hand, palm inward, and gestured toward his side of the dreamscape. Twice he waved her to him, and then he cocked his head to the side in a questioning manner. "Come to us," she heard, but his lips hadn't moved. "Please!"

Fear invaded Reena, and as the emotion grew, the figure of Lone Elk began to recede until he *did* seem hundreds of miles away. "Please come!" she heard, as if from the bottom of a well.

Reena woke with a start and found her sweating hands gripping the bedsheets painfully tight and a light sheen of perspiration covering her face. Realizing she was in her bedroom, she sat up and found she'd fallen asleep in her ball gown. The windows were dark, and even though she had no idea what time it was, she could tell that the house was empty from the heavy silence. Apparently her family had not returned from the ball yet.

Reena had an expansive bedroom, but sudden claustrophobia enveloped her. The shift from the wide-open expanses in the dream to the relative closeness of her bedroom put her in a momentary panic.

"Oh, God, help me!" she cried, burying her face in her hands. "I don't want to go, I don't want to go!" Scrambling from her bed and kneeling beside it, she clasped her hands together tightly. "Father, please don't ask this of me, I *beg* you! I don't understand this—I don't understand *any* of this! Why me?" She took a deep breath and with difficulty forced herself to calm down. The magnitude of what was being asked of her was a great weight, as real as an iron yoke. She began to pray with a fervency and impassionedness that she'd never before experienced.

In a sudden blast of ironic insight, she remembered how many times in her life she'd casually prayed for God to reveal His will to her, and she'd never been sure of His answer. Every matter that had caused her to go to Him for guidance now seemed as trivial as a drop in the ocean. Now, kneeling on shaking knees with her thumbs pressed against her eyes tightly, she was certain of one thing: this *was* God's will. A few minutes into her fearful pleading for deliverance from this revelation, she heard herself saying, almost in a chant, "Let this cup pass from me, let this cup pass from me. . . ." The words came naturally to her mind, since the passage in the Bible of Christ's lonely agony had always affected her so deeply.

Opening her eyes, she stared at the green and gold leaves printed on her bedspread for a long time.

Jesus' cup had not passed from Him. He'd embraced it as His Father's will and met His sacrifice with dignity, ready acceptance, and honor. And what a sacrifice!

When she rose from her knees half an hour later, her tears were gone. Fear and dread had been replaced with acceptance and self-confidence. Even her memory of the pain she'd felt at the ball when she'd seen Louis and Megan on the balcony had faded. She went to a window and looked out on the night. Her eyes turned to the northwest, and she smiled as she searched the star-laden horizon for the great Indian chief in her dream. He was real, and one day soon Reena would find him.

————

"You want me to what?" Louis asked, disbelief filling his eyes.

Reena smiled. She knew perfectly well that he had heard her. "I said I'm going to Canada to be a missionary, and I want you to come with me."

Chuckling, Louis lined up a shot on the billiard table. Just before he hit the cue ball, he looked up at Reena and saw that he'd been wrong—she wasn't joking. "You're not serious?"

"I'm as serious as I've ever been in my life."

"But . . . that's preposterous! You don't know anything about Canada! And don't they have their own churches up there?"

"Not the Indians."

"Indians!" Louis erupted. "What are you talking about? You can't go live with Indians!"

"Why not?"

Louis sputtered, searching for words. "Would you like a list of reasons?"

"Yes, Louis, why don't you give me a list," Reena said testily. She knew this was probably the worst timing imaginable. They'd only resolved their spat that morning, three days after the ball. She still didn't understand what his dance with Megan had implied, and Louis had maintained his innocence, but Reena didn't want to fight with him. Maybe she *had* been overly jealous.

She'd sent Hiram to Louis' house with a message that she wanted to meet with him, only to find that soon after he'd left, a messenger from Louis arrived with the same idea in mind. She had yet to find out what he'd wanted to see her about.

Louis laid the billiard stick on the table, all interest in his favorite game forgotten. He didn't even know where to *start* in trying to talk her out of her strange idea. Besides, he was still nervous about telling his news to her. Taking her arm, he attempted to calm himself down as he said, "Let's sit down." The huge game room had a small oak table in one corner with a green marble chess set on top. He didn't let go of her hand when they were seated and absently kneaded her fingers as he thought.

"Louis, I know this is shocking—"

"No . . . no, it's not. Not after thinking about it."

"It's not?"

"Your delay in setting our wedding date had me baffled, but I should have realized it would have something to do with your religion. This is really too much, Reena," he smiled as he waved his hand around at the impressive game room. "You belong in these surroundings, not in a tepee."

Reena kissed him softly. "I love you, but you don't understand. This is God's will; I couldn't be more sure of it." She briefly recounted all the signs that had led to her decision, watching his face closely. He listened to her without interruption, which surprised her. She'd expected an argument from him on the key points, but his face showed only interest instead of the outrage she'd been frightened of seeing.

When she'd finished, his eyes slid away and came to rest on the chessboard. After a pause, he asked quietly, "What does your family think about all this?"

"I've only told my parents and Uncle Faron. My mother, as you know from what I just told you, supports me, as does Uncle Faron. But, he would support me if I told him I was running for president."

"And your father?"

Reena sighed deeply. "He thinks it's just a passing phase."

"But that's not what it is—you're really going to do it?"

"Yes, I am . . . and I want you to come with me."

Louis shook his head, stood, and paced up and down beside the billiard table. "Do you have any idea how preposterous this all sounds, Reena? I'm a banker, not a preacher!"

"But we could be happy, Louis! Think of the new things to see, the new experiences. And the rewards for doing that sort of work would be more fulfilling than anything in the world!"

"For you, Reena, but not for me!" Louis argued. "I hate to throw mud on your party, but have you forgotten that I'm a Catholic? How would you get around that? You seem to have everything else figured out!" he finished bitterly, then, realizing he'd spoken more harshly than he'd intended, he apologized. "I'm sorry, I don't mean to hurt you." He squatted down in front of her with his elbows on his knees. "I'm a banker, Reena. It's where I get *my* fulfillment. I'm not going to live with a lot of stinking Indians." He picked up a pawn from the chessboard and held it up to her. "This is not me. You can't keep moving me around where you want me."

"I don't *try* to—"

"It's the way *I* feel, Reena." He moved to sit beside her again. "My place is in the bank, living by the lake in that house near my father's, with a nice society wife by my side to give me children. I thought that would be you."

Reena couldn't meet his eyes. "I have to do this," she whispered. "It's God's will. How can I say no?"

"Easily. It could all be a coincidence, just something you've dreamed up."

"How can you say that? Haven't you heard a word I've said? You know me better than that, Louis!"

"And I thought you knew *me* better, too! I'm not going to throw away a promising career, preaching something I don't believe or know anything about to Indians!" He sighed and ran a hand through his thick brown hair, still gripping the pawn tightly in his other hand. "I had a good life planned for us, Reena, a perfect life. Anything you'd asked for, I'd have given you. But not this!"

Reena considered what he said and felt the need to ask him a question—but she wasn't sure she wanted to know the answer. "Why are you talking about us in the past tense, Louis?"

He took a deep breath, nervously fingered the chess piece, and said, "We're not very compatible, you and me. I would want us to stay friends, of course, but—" He shifted his feet and sat up straight in the chair. "I've asked Megan to marry me, and she's accepted."

"What?" Reena breathed, feeling her pulse quicken and her heart drop to the pit of her stomach. She suddenly felt sick.

"That's what I was going to tell you today." Louis attempted to smile but failed. "Seems we both had big news, didn't we?"

"I don't believe this!" Reena voiced in wonder. "How could you? How could she—?"

"Well, after hearing what you've planned, it sounds like it's the best for all around, don't you think?"

"Louis, don't you love me?" Reena asked, still in shock as she gazed at him open-mouthed.

"I had everything planned out—"

"That's not an answer!"

"I think you're a wonderful woman, Reena—"

"You don't love me!" Reena whispered, her eyes falling to the hard wooden floor. "How could I have been so stupid!?"

"I *do* love you in a way, darling—"

"Don't you dare 'darling' me, Louis!" Reena exploded, rising to her feet. She snatched the pawn piece from his hand and held it an inch from his face. "And you accuse *me* of manipulating *you*! How could you be so cruel?"

"Stop and think for a moment, will you? You've just told me you're going to another country, and I *must* have a wife by my side!"

"No . . . no . . . don't you try to use *my* decision to justify your actions! You asked Megan *before* I told you anything—you didn't even have the decency to break our engagement before you proposed! You're a *snake*, Louis!" she cried, throwing the pawn onto the chessboard. As she walked out it occurred to her that the pawn had, fittingly, scored a direct hit on the king, sprawling the larger piece into the queen.

At the door, she turned and said with tears in her eyes, "You and Megan *deserve* each other!"

Louis stared at the chessboard, hearing the thunder of the heavy oak door slamming.

———

Reena spent all afternoon in her bedroom. She'd considered marching straight down to the parlor where she knew her mother and Megan were sewing but decided against it. In her state of mind and feeling deeply betrayed, she just might try to strangle Megan. Thinking of her sitting there with Mother, chatting on and on about inconsequential things while hiding the truth, made Reena want to throw something. She couldn't avoid crying and hated herself even more for doing it. *He's not worth crying over!* she kept telling herself, but an alarming amount of tears still came. Eventually she fell into a restless sleep. Some time later she was awakened by a knock at her door.

"Reena, darling? It's time for dinner."

"I'm not hungry, Mother."

"May I come in?"

"I'd rather you didn't right now."

A long pause. "Well, come down when you're ready, dear."

*I'll never be ready to face anyone in this house again!* Reena thought bitterly. She suddenly wondered if Megan had told their parents. *Or had Louis come to them, hat in hand, and asked for their other daughter's hand? "So sorry, Mr. and Mrs. O'Donnell. Wrong daughter the first time around. You know how it is!"* She shook her head, still seething inside, and suddenly realized something else: *Hiding in my room is exactly what Megan wants!*

Running to her makeup table, she began arranging her dark, tangled hair and stopped short when she saw her eyes, red and swollen from crying. Then she waved a hand at her reflection and did the best she could, saying a quick prayer for patience and for her anger to subside.

Just before entering the dining room, she heard Uncle Faron grumbling, ". . . backhanded business, Megan, you've less tact than a warthog!"

"Uncle Faron!" Reena heard Megan protest, and Liam laughed.

"Good evening, all," Reena greeted, trying to sound cheerful as she went to her chair between Virginia and Liam.

A brief, stunned silence was broken by Faron, who recovered first. " 'ello, luv! Glad ye could make it." He glanced quickly at Megan, who continued to stare at Reena in shock for a moment, then speared a cut of roast on her plate.

Virginia patted Reena's arm and Liam smiled at her sympathetically. Jack O'Donnell chewed his food thoughtfully. Reena wasn't hungry, but she began to spoon yellow corn onto her plate and secretly enjoyed the stunned silence. Unable to resist, she asked, "So, how was everyone else's day today? Mine was pretty eventful."

If there were any doubts that Megan hadn't told them about her engagement yet, they were gone when Reena saw Megan almost choke on her roast and Faron cover his laugh with a white cloth napkin, blue eyes dancing.

"Reena, darling, I'm sorry," Virginia murmured.

"Thank you, Mother, but I don't think you're the one who needs to apologize."

"Why should *I* apologize?" Megan demanded. "Louis asked *me*. What was I supposed to do, say no?" The sisters glared at each other for a moment, then Megan dropped her eyes. "You're right, Reena. I apologize—I'm *really* sorry. I just—I couldn't say no to him! I hate that you and he had problems, but—"

"That's funny—I didn't know we *had* problems until today. How did *you* know?"

"All right, girls, that's enough," Jack admonished, laying down his knife and fork. "This situation is very uncomfortable for everyone involved—"

"Amen to that!" Faron muttered.

Jack gave his brother a burning glare but said nothing to him. Slowly and deliberately, he placed his knife and fork on each side of his plate. "Reena, Megan wanted to ask you something."

"You want me to ask her *now*?" Megan wanted to know, her eyes wide.

"Yes, I do."

Gently patting her mouth with her napkin, Megan looked at Reena and said meekly, "I would really like it if you'd be my maid of honor."

Reena had thought she was through with being shocked that day, but Megan's request was another twist that took her breath away. She looked at her mother, who kept her eyes on her plate, and her father, who nodded. Turning to Megan she declared, "That's the most insulting—no, let me rephrase that—that's the *second* most insulting thing you've ever pulled, Megan!"

"On the contrary, Reena," her father said. "I believe it would show marvelous family unity to the public."

Staring disbelievingly at him, Reena asked, "Do you suppose I really care what the public thinks?"

"I *do* want you to be my maid, Reena," Megan said. "For no other reason except that you're my closest friend."

"If that's true, I'd sure hate to see how you treat your enemies," Reena stated coldly.

Liam spoke up, trying to change the subject. "Da told us about your decision, Reena. It's very admirable."

Reena continued glaring at Megan for a long moment, then reluctantly turned her attention to her brother. "Thank you, Liam."

"When are you leaving?"

Reena glanced at her uncle, who was concentrating on stuffing as many boiled potatoes in his mouth as possible. "I was hoping Uncle Faron would be kind enough to take me when he goes back to Canada."

Faron looked up quickly, his cheeks round with food like a chipmunk gathering acorns for the winter. "Mmpff?" He began chewing as fast as he could so he could give an answer.

"Surely you're staying for the wedding?" Jack inquired.

Nearly laughing out loud, Reena said, "No, I'm not, Da."

Jack's beefy face reddened noticeably, as he wasn't accustomed to people going against his will. "It's very important to me that you attend, Reena."

"I'll be leavin' in a few days, girl," Faron announced. "Ye don't want to go that soon do ye? Not that you're unwelcome, mind ye."

"Stay out of this, Faron," Jack commanded.

"She's twenty years of age, brudder! Ye can't *force* her to stay!"

"Don't be too sure." He cast a stern eye at his daughter, who stared straight back.

"I'm leaving with Uncle Faron, Da," Reena contended in as strong a voice as she could muster. "And that's that." Their eyes remained locked for a few moments that seemed agonizingly long to Reena. She'd never stood up to her father before, and she saw anger and surprise in his face.

Jack looked away first, then rose abruptly, his scraping chair sounding impossibly loud in the still room. To his wife he said, "Excuse me, my dear. I seem to have lost my appetite." His heavy boots pounded on the oak flooring as he left.

"Mother, I'm sorry," Reena whispered.

Taking a deep breath, Virginia said, "Well, if you're leaving so soon we've got a lot to do." She gave Reena a weak smile.

Later that night, when her mother had left her room after helping her make plans, Reena walked confidently down the hall to Megan's room and knocked on the door.

"Come in." Megan was lying across her bed, face up and staring at the canopy overhead. When she saw Reena, she sat up and said, "You're the last person I thought would be knocking."

Reena closed the door and crossed the large room to stand near the bed. "I just came to tell you that someday I'll forgive you, but right now it's hard. I know it's not very Christian of me to carry a grudge." She paused to let her sister respond. Megan said nothing, and her eyes rested somewhere below the middle of Reena's robe. Reena went on, "This is going to be very hard on me for the next couple of days, and I'd appreciate it if we could avoid each other as much as possible. I especially don't want to see you with Louis."

"I didn't plan this, Reena. It just . . . happened. Louis and I were talking, and—"

ALAN MORRIS / BY HONOR BOUND

Reena held up a hand. "I really don't want to hear about it."

Megan nodded and looked glum. "Yes, I'll keep away from you."

"Thank you," Reena said stiffly, then went to the door.

"Reena?"

Her hand already on the knob, Reena hesitated but didn't turn around.

"I think you'll make a great missionary."

Reena couldn't help but wonder if this was another ploy and felt a surge of sorrow for the loss of trust in her sister. She ran Megan's words over in her mind but couldn't detect a hint of victory in her tone— only sincerity. Nodding, but still without turning around, she left.

The urge to cry again came to her, but she avoided it by keeping her mind on practicalities. In her room, she sat down at her dressing table and reached for her jewelry box. The precious stones would be useless where she was going, and she decided she would give them to her mother before she left. She was fingering a pair of ruby earrings when she heard a knock at her door.

"If that's you, Megan, I don't have anything else to say," she called.

"Ahem . . . er . . . it's me," Jack O'Donnell replied, his voice muffled by the door.

"Oh, Da, come in!"

The first thing she noticed when he came in was his clothes. Her father was a very formal man, always dressed nicely with his tie straight and coat buttoned. But tonight his tie was still in the collar, but hanging loosely. His coat was gone, and his shirt was not tucked in tightly as usual. *Is he drunk?* she thought suddenly, but she knew that he never touched liquor. He rarely came to her room, especially since she'd grown up, but Reena knew why he was here.

"I've come to ask you to reconsider, Reena," he said without preamble. "I know it would be hard on you, but since I run a bank, and therefore have the responsibilities of avoiding scandal wherever possible, it would mean a lot to me."

"Sit down, Da." Reena went to the small settee on the wall across from her bed and sat down.

Jack hesitated, then seated himself and crossed his legs. "You know, ever since I took over that bank sixteen years ago, people were whispering that I was 'new money,' and that we would never make it. Well, we *were* 'new money,' so to speak, and with me being an immigrant there were some bad feelings. Now it's become one of the strongest banks in Chicago, but I feel that they are still saying things behind my back—waiting for me to fail."

"You're very well respected, Da!"

He put two fingers to his forehead and rubbed it. "I could be wrong, of course. Maybe it's just my ol' Irish suspicion," he drawled, sounding very much like his brother. He'd worked very hard to lose his accent, and now when he met someone for the first time, they had no idea he was first-generation Irish.

"I know what you're saying, Da," Reena agreed softly. "But I thought of something this evening that I haven't told anyone."

He sat up straight, and a glint came to his eye. "Well, ye know how we Sons of Erin love hearing secrets, lass."

Reena smiled, but it was tinged with sadness. She could tell he was hoping that he'd already said enough to change her mind, but he was going to be disappointed. "All that has happened to bring me to my decision has happened in a very short period of time. You know that." She took a deep breath and continued, "I believe the Lord is trying to tell me that I'm needed there as soon as possible—that something's about to happen with those people."

Jack's eyes lost their merriment immediately, and he abruptly stood up. "Confound it, girl, aren't I more important to you than a tribe of savages?"

"You'll always be important to me, Da! I'm just tired of hearing about everyone's social status!"

"This is business!" Jack fairly shouted, then he put a hand over his mouth and visibly tried to take control of his temper. "Business, Reena."

"Those poor Indians need God! They're being ruined and corrupted by white man's whiskey! You've heard Uncle Faron talk about it; don't you think the Assiniboine need the Lord more than you need a few customers?"

Sighing and shaking his head, Jack said, "So I can't change your mind?"

Reena shook her head, distraught at the hurt on his face.

"All right, Reena. I don't like it, but I respect your decision. I haven't told you, but I respect you for *all* of this, though I must admit I don't understand it. To go out into the wilds of Canada with no experience or training—" He closed his mouth with a snap and gave her a contemplative look. "You'll need money."

Reena shook her head. "Not really. I'll be with the Indians, and—"

"Reena, do you hear what you're saying? Do you really hear yourself? You've never even *seen* an Indian. How can you just . . . just . . . show up and live with them?"

Reena rose and stood close to him. Sounding more confident than she felt, she stated, "God wouldn't ask me to do anything I wasn't capable of."

Jack ran his fingers through his hair and shook his head yet again. Then his shoulders lost their tenseness and he pointed a finger at her. "You're still taking money. A lot of it. I don't care if you don't spend it, but my little girl's not going to be caught without money if she needs it."

"Da, I love you," Reena declared in a choked voice and slipped into his arms. She felt him nod curtly.

"I love you, too, Reena."

On his way out of the room, Reena heard him murmur something about "Irish stubborn" before the door closed.

# CHAPTER FIVE

# Journey

Overall, there was only so much packing for Reena to do. She tried to imagine the rugged conditions in which she would be living, and with Uncle Faron's help came up with a list of practical clothing. Her mother went with her to buy them—two warm coats, denim pants, sweaters, a Stetson hat, sturdy boots—and did everything but hold her nose at purchasing such unladylike attire. Reena laughed at her, but the next three days she felt an uncomfortable sadness settle over her that wouldn't leave. It seemed every time she turned around she was telling a lifelong friend goodbye. Sally Ames had cried helplessly, sure she would never see Reena again.

"I'll come back, Sally," Reena consoled her. "It's not like I'm walking off the edge of the earth!"

"But . . . but what if you're *scalped*!" Sally wailed. "What if a polar bear gets you?"

"There aren't any polar bears in Canada, Sally. They're near the North Pole—that's why they call them polar bears, remember?"

"Well, there are other kinds of bears, aren't there?"

"I'll watch out for bears." Her friend's innocence cut to Reena's heart, and she ended up crying right along with her.

Through it all, Reena prayed and prayed for strength. She definitely felt an all-encompassing approval from God, but her troubled emotions made many attempts to balk at her decision to leave. Her feelings of total unpreparedness for her uncertain future grew so strong sometimes that her breathing quickened with fear. Reena had never been out of the city and had no idea how she would react to seeing a snake or, yes, even a bear.

Megan was true to her word about staying out of the way, and Reena rarely saw her. Megan skipped dinnertime with the family, choosing to eat in her room or go out. One time Reena caught a glimpse of Louis' carriage bringing Megan home late one night, but Reena quickly left the window and immediately found something to occupy her thoughts.

Reena didn't see Louis once.

Finally her day of departure arrived. Uncle Faron woke Reena up early, before the sun rose. As she was getting dressed in her new western clothes, her mother came in. Her eyes were puffy, and Reena knew she probably hadn't slept much and had cried some, too.

Virginia examined Reena's gray denim breeches and simple white blouse, and Reena nearly burst into tears at the look on her mother's face. "You seem like a different person," Virginia observed.

"Wait until you see me in my hat." Reena finished tucking in her shirt and placed the wide-brim Stetson on her head.

Tears brimming her eyes, Virginia walked over and took Reena in her arms. "Oh, I've been dreading this day!"

Feeling hot tears course down her cheeks, Reena took off the cumbersome hat and squeezed her mother tightly. "Me, too, Mother. More than you know."

They held each other for a few minutes, quietly weeping, not talking, until Virginia pulled back and gripped Reena's arms. "I know this is what the Lord has planned for you. I just wish . . . I wish—"

"That it *wasn't* what He'd planned for me?"

"Yes," she agreed, smiling through her tears. "Is that wrong, do you think?"

"If it is, then we're *both* wrong," Reena whispered, then hugged her again. "Oh, Mama, I'm so scared!"

"I know . . . I know. But God will take care of you."

Reena could have stayed in her mother's arms all day, but Faron's booming knock rattled her door.

"Are ye ready, darlin'?"

"In a minute!" Reena reluctantly let go and wiped her face quickly. She took one last look around her bedroom, but she knew she'd packed everything.

"Reena," Virginia said softly, "*do* try to forgive Megan and Louis. It's better that you found out what sort of man he was before it had been too late."

"I'd already thought of that," Reena said, picking up a knapsack that contained personal items she hadn't wanted packed in her trunk.

"And your sister—well, she's just your sister. Always looking out for her own best interests and no one else's."

"I know, Mother."

"Reena!" Faron called from the hall.

"You can come in now, Uncle Faron."

He was dressed in his favorite outfit: fringed buckskin from neck to toe. His eyes were bright and alert, and his teeth gleamed through his beard. "It'll be a glorious day, lass! I can feel it in me bones. Let's see how fourteen hours in a buckboard suits ye!" He strode over to Reena's bed, took two feather pillows off, removed the light blue covers, and threw the pillows to Reena one at a time.

"Faron, those are good pillows!" Virginia exclaimed.

"Aye. For yer daughter's sake, I hope they're real *soft* pillows. Let's go!"

Even before they made it downstairs, Reena heard the wailing of Elmira Cotter.

"My baby goin' on an' leavin' me! I's can't *bear* it!" Hiram stood beside her, his hat in hand, looking small and extremely uncomfortable about Ellie's open display of emotion. Liam took Reena's pillows and knapsack and went with Faron to load the wagon.

"Ellie!" Reena cried, going to the big woman and giving her a long hug. The embrace she received almost crushed her. Ellie's usual scent of dough and hickory smoke surrounded her, and Reena knew she would miss it. "Ellie, I'll be fine, don't worry."

"I's just feels like I's gonna *die*!" she howled, backing away and blowing hugely into a kitchen towel.

"You take care of my family, Ellie, you hear?"

"Oh, I's take good care of 'em," she cried. "But who gonna take care o' my baby! Lawsy, I's can't stands it!" This new round of sobbing caused Ellie's knees to threaten to give way, and Hiram grabbed her and did the best he could to hold her up.

"Ellie, you stop that crying now," Virginia ordered. "Reena feels bad enough as it is!"

The wailing stopped at once, but Ellie's face remained buried in the towel as her body shook.

"Goodbye, Hiram," Reena said, and would have shaken his hand, but it was filled with Ellie.

"Be careful, Miz Reena."

Dawn was coming, and the early morning sky was filled with eerie blue light. Reena's father was standing beside the wagon, his hands clasped behind him. She went to him and gave him a kiss, and he em-

63

braced her, shortly but with feeling. "Take care of yourself, daughter," he said simply, and Reena nodded.

"Reena?" She turned to find Liam looking slightly embarrassed and holding something out to her. "I made it myself." It was a carved wooden cross as big as her hand, with a leather necklace. The wood was very light colored and smooth as her skin. Delicately engraved on the horizontal part of the cross were the words, "*Deo Gratias.*" She ran her thumb over it and looked up at him questioningly.

"It's Latin," Liam said. "It means, 'Thanks be to God.' The wood is ash."

Reena removed her hat and slipped on the necklace. "It's beautiful, Liam. Thank you." She hugged him tightly and kissed him on the cheek, which only embarrassed him to the point of blushing.

Virginia hugged Reena once more, whispering, "I'll pray for you."

Reena climbed into the covered-wagon seat, then stared down at her family. A sudden feeling of unreality washed over her. Through her sad smile she was thinking, *I can't believe I'm doing this . . . I can't believe I'm really doing this . . .* , but she knew she couldn't say the words out loud.

As the two horses pulled the wagon down the street, Reena twisted around and waved to her family. She happened to look up and saw Megan standing at her bedroom window. Reena's heart skipped a beat, and then Megan slowly raised a hand. Instantly Reena whirled around and faced forward.

Faron, the reins held loosely in his meaty hands, glanced at her strangely. "Are ye all right, girl?"

Reena stared forward for a moment, confused, then slowly turned back to the house and raised a tentative hand to her sister.

In the dim light, Reena couldn't see Megan's face. It was only a small moon against the dark bedroom, but she imagined a small smile curling Megan's lips—a smile filled with memories of playing with dolls and swimming in the river and telling secrets to her little sister.

———

As Faron headed due west, they watched the city of Chicago stir to wakefulness around them. Newspaper boys were already out, bundles in hand, hawking the *Tribune*. Shops began raising shutters and opening canopies, getting ready for the business day. Reena couldn't remember the last time she'd been out and about so early, but she knew it had been a long time.

When they reached the outskirts of town and moved among

sprawling farms, Faron muttered, "Almost forgot—stand up, Reena."

Reena looked at him questioningly but did as he said. Reaching behind him in the wagon, he produced the feather pillows and plopped them down on Reena's seat. Patting the pillows, he told her, "Plant 'er there."

"But I'm comfortable enough," she protested as she sat down. "You should've left the pillows with Mother."

"Reena, darlin', by tonight yer haunches would've been squealin' with pain loud enough for *me* to hear 'em. As it is, even wi' those fancy cushions your lower back will be thinkin' about mutiny from the rest o' ye."

"What about you? You're not sitting on anything."

"Bah!" he snorted contemptuously. "My body's so used to punishment, it don't even bother complainin' anymore!" He leaned over and looked behind them. "Say goodbye to your city, lass. After we top this hill there'll be no lookin' back."

Reena turned and saw that Chicago had shrunk to a hazy brown mass of buildings. She said nothing and faced front again, noticing out of the corner of her eye that Uncle Faron was watching her.

"Are ye scared, lass?"

"Yes."

"If ye don' stop fingerin' that cross, there'll be nothin' left o' it in a month."

Reena wasn't even aware that she'd been grasping Liam's gift and peered at it with her first taste of homesickness. *I won't cry. I'm through with crying!*

"Don' ye worry," Uncle Faron winked, "ye'll be seein' your brudder again someday."

They rode in silence for a while, until Faron began humming a tune Reena didn't know. She suddenly thought of something she'd been meaning to ask him for a week. "Why did you come to Chicago, Uncle? It's so far. You surely didn't just come for a visit, did you?"

The humming stopped, and Reena saw a serious look come over his strong features. It made her realize how rarely he *was* serious. Uncle Faron always looked at the world sideways with a skeptical grin and twinkle-eyed amusement. But now he stared into the bean field they were passing and seemed to be counting the tiny sprouts.

"If it's none of my business—" Reena began.

"No, it's not that . . . not that at all." His dancing blue eyes took on a faraway stare as he said, "I admire ye, Reena. I really do. Ye're about to see some sights up north in Canada that ye'll think are too beautiful to be real. I wish *I* were gonna see 'em again for the first time." He gave the reins a slap, and the horses picked up their step. "Hah, ya see—just thinkin' about 'em made me want to get there faster!"

"It sounds wonderful, but what does that have to do with your coming to Chicago?"

"Do ye know about the romantic notion of the grizzled ol' mountain man that goes into the hills and never comes out? Well, that's not just a notion—that's real." He paused and shook his head. "I could feel the Rockies pullin' me, Reena, as sure as ye feel gravity yank ye to the ground after a stumble. I got to the point where my feet were itchin' to head thataway and never bring me back out o' them hills. Before that happened, I wanted to see my family once more."

Reena watched him closely, looking for the telltale crinkles at the corners of his eyes that said he was being playful; but there were none. "You mean you're going to . . . disappear after we get there?"

"You're goin' where God intended *you* to be," Faron smiled, "and I'm goin' where He intended me—where I've always belonged. I'm goin' home."

———

By the time Faron began scouting for a site to camp that night, his words of warning concerning Reena's being sore now seemed sadly underestimated. Not only did her backside and spine scream their protest, her neck felt too weak to hold her head up. This had caused a splitting headache, unlike any she'd never known. Tremors in the backs of her thighs and calves foretold a night filled with cramps. *And this is just the first day!* she thought miserably.

"There!" Faron exclaimed as he pointed. "That's the spot."

Had Reena not been in so much agony, she would have appreciated the natural beauty of the area more. A shallow stream bubbled between a small hill and a limestone cliff. Darkness was closing in fast, but she could see cardinal flowers on the hill blooming in a glorious spread of red velvet, with yellow water lilies floating lazily in a small inlet.

Faron nudged her and pointed. She followed his finger to the birch and maple trees on top of the limestone cliff and saw two flying creatures making their way through the branches. Their flight was unlike the determined flight of any bird; they seemed to *float* to their destinations, then scramble to the end of the branch and launch themselves into space again.

"Flying squirrels," Faron said, his tone tinged with awe. "You're lucky to see 'em; they move around mostly in dead dark."

Reena was so tired she could only nod.

"Ye just get down and stretch your parts, girl. I'll set up the camp and cook us a meal."

Groaning as her feet hit the ground, Reena put her hands to the small of her back and bent backward, hearing and feeling the perfect popping of her spine realigning itself. She started making her way downstream to exercise her legs, picking her way through fist-sized gray rocks. Over the gurgle of the stream she heard an incredibly high-pitched scream from above and looked up to see a dark bird streaking on high.

Faron, who was keeping an eye on Reena while she explored, shouted, "That's an eagle!"

Reena watched until the bird was out of sight, marveling at the powerful push of its wings. When she turned back downstream, she uttered a surprised "Oh!" as she found herself staring eye to eye with a deer that was watching her carefully. His head was halfway to the stream, as if interrupted before drinking, and his rack of antlers was huge. The large black eyes bore into hers, and Reena kept perfectly still, scared to breathe. *Will he charge me and gore me?* She wanted to turn and call to Uncle Faron for help, but as soon as she'd decided to make a run for it, the deer dipped his head down and thrust his muzzle into the stream. Realizing he wasn't going to hurt her, Reena stared at the muscular shoulders and sleek flanks. The biscuit-colored fur held a few marks and scars, as if from battles fought with other deer. The buck drank his fill, then with another cautious look at Reena made his way back over the crest of the hill.

Despite her exhaustion, Reena smiled and breathed deeply, smelling freshwater, moss, wood, and, most of all, crisp *cleanliness*. She leaned down, picked up a rock, and tossed it into the water. To her surprise, several shapes darted from the intrusion. Fish had been resting in the shallows only inches from her, and she hadn't even known it. She suddenly felt overwhelmed by her lack of knowledge about the wild. Her admiration deepened for her uncle's way of life, and when she turned to tell him, he was setting up a tent he had purchased for her in Chicago.

"I don't want a tent!" she shouted. He looked up but hadn't heard her. Going back toward him, she repeated herself and saw his surprise.

"Ye wanna sleep in the open?"

"Yes—it's lovely!"

"But, Reena—ye'll get cold and wake up with icy dew on ye."

"I don't care!" she stated, grinning with the freedom of the woods flowing through her. Even her soreness seemed to have dimmed a little. "It's incredible, Uncle."

"Aye, 'tis that," he agreed, smiling at her knowingly.

Reena pitched in and helped him gather wood for the fire, and he cooked ham and beans.

It was the best meal she'd ever eaten.

The night sounds kept her awake for a while after they'd bedded down; therefore, Faron was kept from sleep also.

"What was that?"

"An owl, lass."

"What an incredible sound!"

A few moments later. "I feel like something's crawling on me!"

"Prob'ly is."

"What!"

A chuckle. "Settle down, Reena. Ye've a long day tomorrow, and the day after that, and the day after that."

"Do snakes make a noise?"

"Not so's ye'd hear 'em with your mouth runnin' all the time."

"What was that howling?"

"Bobcat or wolf."

"Will they eat us?"

A heavy sigh. "No, they prefer less talkative prey."

"Do deer sleep at night?"

"If they do, I admire 'em."

Finally Reena grew silent, and Faron believed she'd gone to sleep when he heard her voice thick with drowsiness.

"It's really beautiful, Uncle."

A moment later, Faron heard the deep, even breathing of the exhausted.

———

After two weeks, Faron began to believe that his niece's curiosity would *never* be quenched. She questioned him about everything from ticks to tigers, from leaves to mountains.

Following the first few days of nearly unbearable stiffness, her body had slowly adjusted to the brutality of twelve hours a day in a swaying wagon and to sleeping on the hard ground. Her face and arms were toned to a deep bronze from the sun. Faron showed her how to shape and mold her hat to slough off the driving rains that hit with sudden ferocity. During the first few thunderstorms, Reena climbed into the bed of the wagon under cover, but soon she insisted on staying with him through the showers and learned the beauty of a Dakota downpour. He taught her how to shoot his Navy Colt and powder musket. And though he pretended to gripe and complain about her insatiable thirst for knowledge of the frontier, he was more than pleased—and Reena knew it.

"We'll be stoppin' up here in Fargo for supplies to last us on to the Cypress Hills," he announced one day, examining her appearance. "Stuff yer hair up under yer hat and cover them skinny arms." He placed the Colt in her lap. "Stay in the wagon, an' don' let go o' that. Do ya *hear* me, Reena? Stay—in—the wagon! An' don't talk to no one."

"What's the matter?"

"We're on the edge o' civilization as ye know it. Don't let yer eyes pop out o' yer head if ye see an Indian, neither."

Fargo was a hastily built affair with a general goods store, saloon, blacksmith shop, and livery. Reena heard tinny piano music and bawdy laughter coming from the saloon, even though it was only midmorning.

Faron had one more word of advice before going in the supply store. "Try to look mean."

Putting on as formidable a face as possible, Reena watched the swinging doors of the saloon, expecting several dusty, hard-eyed men to gather at the window and point at the impostor in the wagon across the street. She pulled the Stetson down low to her eyebrows and tried to blend in with the scenery.

"Them horses for sale?"

She jerked away from the voice at her elbow. Looking down, she saw a large, very fat man with a head like a pumpkin and eyes set so deep they were all but invisible. He hadn't shaved, and his beard was as thick and ominous as a blackberry bramble. The smell of him was overwhelming, and Reena unconsciously slid away even farther.

"What's a matter, boy? Your lips locked?" he asked with a grin that revealed sharp yellow canines. When he saw Reena full-face, the grin disappeared and he leaned closer. "You shore is a *pretty* boy!"

Shouting came from the saloon—voices raised in anger. Reena chanced a quick look around but could see no one inside. She turned back and searched the windows of the dry goods store, looking for Uncle Faron, but saw only large sacks of feed stacked high. A meaty paw reached out and hit her thigh.

"Them horses for sale or not?" the man shouted, and at that instant men came boiling out of the saloon like bees from a hive on fire. Two men separated themselves from the others, facing each other with deadly glares.

"I told you, that claim's mine!" a tall, thin man shouted, obviously drunk. He pulled his knee-length tan coat back to reveal a holstered gun.

The other man was calmer but weaving also. He was blinking furiously, as if he had something in his eye.

"Them two been at each other all mornin'," the fat man at Reena's side commented. He watched from behind the buckboard, as if afraid to show too much of his considerable body. "Somebody's gonna get killed."

"Let's settle this once and for all," the blinking man said as his hand inched to the butt of his pistol.

*They're going to draw!* Reena thought with horror. She risked another look back to the store window, but Uncle Faron still hadn't appeared. *I don't believe this!* Just as she turned back, the men pulled their guns and began blazing away at each other. Many shots were fired—to Reena it seemed like twenty, but that was impossible—until the blinking man suddenly fell backward with a shout and lay still.

The silence after the explosions was eerie, and puffs of blue smoke hung thick in the air. All the spectators stared at the unmoving body for a moment, then, as if in agreement, all eyes shifted to the thin man. To Reena's surprise, his face was filled with pain, and he began to cry. "Guess the claim's mine now!" he shouted to the corpse in a cracked voice. He turned toward the crowd of men outside the saloon doors, who looked on with neutral expressions. "I've knowed Bob all my life," the thin man said, tears rolling down his cheeks. "And now I killed him." The men stared at him for a moment, then began making their way back inside the saloon without a word. Just another death on the prairie.

The horror of the scene ran through Reena, and she watched as the man went to his friend's body, fell to his knees, and stared down with his face a blank mask.

"I ain't gonna ask you again, boy," the fat man said beside her, the shoot-out apparently witnessed and forgotten. "How's about them horses?" He saw Reena's eyes dart behind him but was too late.

"Unless ye'll be wantin' a buffalo gun to blow a hole through yer fat middle big enough to toss a mule through," Faron uttered dangerously behind the man, "ye'll be backin' off." He punctuated the threat by cocking the musket aimed at the man's back.

"I'm leavin'!" the fat man croaked, his huge body frozen. "I jest wanted to make an honest buy for them horses."

"And I'm the queen of England," Faron answered. "Walk away easy and don't turn around."

The fat man kept his back to Faron as he walked around the horses and headed for the saloon, passing the prone figure in the street and the immobile man beside it without a glance downward.

Faron handed Reena the musket. "Keep that darlin' trained at those doors, girl." He turned and picked up their supplies and loaded them in the back of the wagon. Despite his warning to watch the doors of the saloon, Reena couldn't help but stare at the man beside his dead friend. He hadn't moved, and his pale face now held the look of disbelief and sorrow.

Faron climbed into the seat beside her and slapped the reins without a glance at the gunfighters.

"Shouldn't we do something, Uncle Faron?"

"Nope . . . none o' our affair."

"But . . . he just *killed* that man! He was his best friend! He's sorry for what he did. Look at him!"

Instead of turning to look, Faron studied Reena with knowing eyes. "Everybody's sorry when they kill somebody, Reena. If they're human anyway."

The image of the man's drawn, shattered face stayed with Reena for days afterward.

———

The spring weather was a relief for Reena as they traveled. Her skin had begun to itch beneath the heavy clothing she'd been wearing, and along the latter part of the journey she treated herself to a few sponge baths at various creeks and streams. The evenings would still become cool with the sweeping prairie winds, but despite this her excitement rose with the temperature change.

As they neared the Cypress Hills, Faron began teaching her as much as he knew of the Assiniboine language, which was basically Sioux. He knew enough verbal and sign language to make trades with them, but Reena realized that teaching the Word of God would be out of the question until she learned more of their language. However, she surprised them both with her quick grasp of the strange tongue.

The day finally arrived to meet the Indians. The Cypress Hills in which they lived were low and unusual, Faron told her. They ran from east to west for eighty miles, with a width of anywhere from fifteen to twenty-five miles. Numerous valleys made the upland appear hilly, but the Hills were actually a flat-topped plateau dissected into three segments by two north-south valleys. The Assiniboine village was on a creek flowing through the south side of the westernmost segment.

Reena uselessly adjusted her hat, already nervous about meeting the Indians. "How much farther?"

"Just around that hill there—but they already know we're here."

"They do?"

Faron smiled, but didn't answer.

When they'd skirted the hill, Reena's breathing quickened. Smoke curled lazily to the sky from various small fires, and a flat area beside a flowing creek was dotted with many tepees. The whole village was nestled in a valley surrounded by hills, except for the entrance they were passing through.

Several Indians were spread out in a line in front of them, each carrying a weapon of some sort. The man in the middle was taller than the rest, and when he saw Faron, his black eyes lit up and he called out a greeting, which Faron returned. The man's attention immediately came back to Reena, and she found all of them staring at her curiously.

"That's Standing Bear in the middle," Faron said. "Ah, here comes Gray Dawn."

A dignified older woman made her way toward them, with what seemed like the whole village behind her. Reena was surprised at the size of the tribe and was slightly overcome for a moment. *All these people! How can I lead this many to the Lord?*

Gray Dawn greeted Faron warmly, but worry lines returned quickly as she tried to explain something to him. Faron nodded and clarified some things, then turned to Reena as he started to get down from the wagon. "This is Lone Elk's wife. You remember, he's the chief that ye dreamed about. I think she's tellin' me there's somethin' wrong with him. Let's go."

Reena felt what seemed to be thousand eyes watch her every move as she dismounted and followed Gray Dawn and Faron. Children, their curiosity getting the better of them, tentatively reached out and touched her clothing as they swarmed around her. Reena laughed, but a sharp word from Gray Dawn sent them all scattering.

They went directly to a tepee near the center of the village. Support poles poked through the top like wooden fingers, and red-and-black broken stripes were painted all around the outside of the dwelling. Gray Dawn pulled aside the flap, and the first thing Reena noticed was the smell of smoke and dirt. A small fire surrounded by stones was situated in the middle, its smoke curling upward through the hole created by the support poles. Various paintings of battle scenes covered the walls. The dirt floor was beaten down as smooth as glass, giving the impression of cleanliness. One side, probably the sleeping area, was covered with the skins of animals; on a raised bench in the middle lay a very sick-looking man.

Faron said something to the Indian woman, who locked eyes with Reena. Gray Dawn's gaze was so intent, Reena felt as if the woman knew her every thought. Then the chief's wife took her hand and led her to the prone figure of Lone Elk. Even though the chief seemed near death, there was no doubt he was the man she'd dreamed of. His features had been strong at one time, but his cheeks were now sunken deeply, giving the disturbing impression of a breathing corpse.

"What . . . what's wrong with him?" Reena asked no one in particular, her attention focused on Lone Elk.

"It'll be that blasted whiskey," Faron said vehemently. "Looks like the chief's had himself about two hundred too many drinks."

"But . . . he can't die!" Reena protested. "I dreamed of him! He's the reason I'm here!" She turned to Gray Dawn. "Don't you understand?" The woman watched her closely but couldn't comprehend. "Tell her, Uncle!"

Using sign language and the few simple words he knew, Faron clumsily attempted to communicate with Gray Dawn, but the woman only stared at him.

"I will help him!" Reena said forcefully, locking eyes with Gray Dawn. She held up the wooden cross around her neck. "God will help him—I promise! Do you understand?"

Not fully understanding, Gray Dawn nodded, as if hypnotized by Reena. She had seen a few white women before, but none with eyes like this one—and right now, Gray Dawn felt as if those incredible sky-blue eyes had her pinned to a lodge pole with their intensity. Whatever this white woman was saying, Gray Dawn sensed she meant it, and it would happen. The certainty of it was immensely comforting, and Gray Dawn felt relieved that someone had come to help share her burden.

———

Two days later, Reena and her uncle stood by the wagon, which was once again hitched up and ready to go—only this time, Reena wouldn't be going. He'd stayed long enough to get her settled in her own tepee, and to make introductions to so many people Reena had already forgotten half their names.

"Uncle Faron, I don't know where to start thanking you."

"Nonsense, darlin'! Ye don' have to thank me."

"I couldn't have done this without you. I believe God brought you to Chicago at that time to bring me here."

Faron looked at her closely. "Will ye be all right, Reena darlin'?"

His concern touched her, and she threw her arms around his neck, ignoring his scratchy, full beard against her smooth cheek. "Oh, I'm sick of goodbyes!" she cried. "I never want to say goodbye to anyone again!"

Faron chuckled, squeezed her tight, and said, "Ye can avoid that word, ye know. Back in Ireland we would say, 'til we meet again.' Doesn't seem so *final*, now, does it?"

Reena pulled back without letting go of him. "Will we? Meet again, I mean?" She remembered his words about disappearing into the Rockies—"going home" he'd called it. That day seemed like years ago, but it had only been a month.

Faron held up a thick, gnarled index finger to her face. "That'll be *another* saying we had, lass." He lightly tapped her nose with each word: "Never say never!"

# PART TWO
April–June 1873

# FIERCE EXTREMES

*Feel by turns the bitter change
Of fierce extremes, extremes by
change more fierce.*

John Milton
*Paradise Lost*

# CHAPTER SIX

# Rain and Fire

For the third time, Hunter Stone felt eyes on his back and turned quickly to scan the low, barren hills he'd just passed. Unlike the times before, he fully turned the horse as his gray eyes carefully searched the broken horizon. After scrutinizing the knobby hills, he watched the flat prairie for a moment, trying to detect any movement among the shallow ravines that crisscrossed the landscape. The cold, biting wind made his eyes water.

Seeing no motion, he shook his head with irritation and patted his horse s neck. "Come on, Buck. We're just jumpy, I guess." Stone nudged the animal with his knee to turn him, but Buck stayed in place, nostrils flaring. "What *is* it, boy?" Stone asked in frustration.

Buck's uneasiness would probably have gone unnoticed to an unfamiliar rider. Stone had raised the buckskin from a wobbly legged colt to the supreme range mount that he was, and the end result was that he knew Buck's little quirks better than he knew his own. On their normal journey home from the trading post where Stone worked, Buck would canter along at an easy trot. But during the last mile his ears were active—pricking up suddenly and twisting to the rear, as if trying to detect and sort noises not heard by Stone. The last time he'd behaved in the same manner, Stone had turned to find a curious bear studying their progress from behind a tree.

"Enough of this," he said, pulling the reins forcefully, "we've got supper waiting." He nevertheless cast yet another glance over his shoulder as he spurred Buck into a gallop. Stone feared no man, but on the yawning expanse of the wide open prairie that surrounded him, the best policy was caution rather than negligence.

Stone's tall and well-proportioned frame rolled easily to Buck's canter, an indication of his lifelong seasoning in the saddle. He was twenty-four years old, and the hands that held the reins were long and broad against heavy wrists, with a sprinkling of the same light, sandy-blond hair that covered his head. His face was more square than oval, with a strong cleft chin and determined jaw.

Stone's disposition brightened considerably a few minutes later when his home came into view. He cherished the silence of his treks to and from the trading post, for those times were solely his, whether to sort out jumbled thoughts or to simply enjoy the cloudless blue dome of heaven overhead. But his nights belonged to Betsy, his wife of two years.

Buck whinnied as he always did, bringing Betsy to the door. Sometimes Stone believed Buck missed her as much as he did. Even from one hundred feet away he could see her white teeth flash in a welcome smile, not aware that she could see him as well.

"Got any grub, ma'am?" Stone drawled as he dismounted and tied Buck close to the trough.

"Come on in, stranger, and pull up a stump." Betsy talked as if a huge wad of tobacco were tucked away in her cheek. Her liquid brown eyes danced with mischief, for she loved their playful banter. Then she looked at him closely and worry lines etched into her forehead. "Hunter Stone, your lips are blue! Get in this house—I told you to wear your heavier coat this morning."

Stone had been so preoccupied with Buck's skittishness that he hadn't noticed the biting prairie wind. "Why don't you warm them up for me?" he teased as he put his arms around her and she lifted her warm lips to his. He loved the sensation of her melting in his arms, and the natural scent of her skin never failed to thrill him. Neither of them had ever wanted another since they'd met at the awkward age of thirteen in a small schoolhouse on the outskirts of Dufferin on the American border. Remembering the day eleven years before, he pulled her back and let his eyes take in the fullness of her beauty. "I swear, Betsy," he breathed, "you grow more lovely every day."

A good-natured rebuttal came to her mind, but when she saw the earnestness in his eyes her only reply was a heartfelt, "Thank you, Hunter." Deep affection surged through her, and she was once again astounded by the suitability of their marriage. Just that morning, studying her face in the mirror, she'd detected the beginnings of crow's-feet around her eyes. And now her husband was telling her exactly what she needed to hear. This didn't surprise her. What *did* surprise her was his incredible ability of saying the right things at the right times over and over again.

Stone kissed her lightly. "I'll unsaddle Buck while you get dinner ready."

"Did you change your mind about riding over to the Osbournes' to ask them to dinner tomorrow night?"

He winced and confessed, "I forgot about that. I'll go right after we eat." Betsy really liked Olivia Osbourne, and Stone silently berated himself for his mental lapse, because it had been his idea to have them over in the first place. Unlike himself, Betsy had come from a large family of four girls and one boy. Though she'd never admit it to him, she seemed to miss having someone to talk to besides him. Olivia and Betsy had spent many evenings studying the Bible together, for it had been Olivia who had led her to God.

"Come on, then," Betsy said, taking his hand and leading him inside, "I want you back before dark."

Stone washed up at the sink and stood close to the fire as she set the table. Watching her compact movements and admiring the spotlessly clean house, his eyes came to rest on the baby crib in a corner of the room. Smiling, he asked, "Did you do anything special today?"

"Not really, I just—" Betsy stopped as she set a bowl of sweet potatoes on the table. Seeing his smile, she knew what he was really asking about. The corners of her wide mouth turned up in a secret smile, and she crossed to the crib, murmuring, "Just a little something. . . ." She reached inside and produced a tiny pair of white socks, her brown doe-eyes shining. "Do you think I'm crazy?"

He went to her and took the socks in his large hands. "Of course I don't, love. There's nothing wrong with dreaming. I do it too sometimes."

"I'm sure the Lord has a reason for making me wait this long to get pregnant." She looked down at the booties and the smile left her. "I suppose this is just my way of telling Him we're ready."

He placed the socks in her small hands and enveloped them in his. "It'll happen, darling. It'll happen." Kissing her forehead, he realized how awkward he sounded whenever she brought up the subject of God. His feet had never crossed the threshold of a church except for his father's funeral. Betsy never pressured him to go with her and Olivia, and both Stone and Gaston usually found some "urgent" chore to perform on their farms when Sunday rolled around.

Betsy kept her face hidden when she said, "Supper's on the table." As she started toward the dining room table, Stone could detect the tears that were just below the surface. Feeling helpless, he took his place at the table.

They ate in silence for a while, until Stone could stand it no longer. Around a mouthful of chicken he commented, "It's almost May, so I'll be leaving the trading post in a couple of weeks to find a buyer for the cattle. Twenty head won't bring much, but it'll be enough to tide us over until a crop comes in."

"It's so nice of Sam to let you run the trading post for him during the winter."

Stone chuckled. "I don't know if it's niceness. My father had a lot of pull with the Hudson's Bay Company because of his store's success. I think he may have had a hand in my hiring."

"It's about time for another letter from your mother." Betsy seemed to be carrying on the conversation while her mind wandered elsewhere. He noticed that she was just moving her food around her plate without really eating. Stomach troubles frequently overtook her, and he suddenly wondered if that malady had somehow affected their ability to have children.

Realizing she was waiting for a response, he filed the thought away for later consideration. "She's been good about writing, hasn't she? Better than me, anyway." He wiped his mouth and pushed his plate away, resting his elbows on the table. "I sure didn't think she would be capable of taking over the store when Dad died, but she's turned out to be just as shrewd as—"

Stone's hearing shifted to the outside of the house. Buck was snorting and whinnying, and Stone was so accustomed to the silence of the prairie that every sound which was out of place seized his attention. On his feet instantly, he started toward the wall where he kept his Henry rifle but realized it was still in the saddle sleeve.

"Hunter, what is it?" Betsy asked, but he was already out the door by the time she'd finished.

"Stay inside, Betsy!" he called over his shoulder before closing the door. The biting wind reminded him that he was in shirt-sleeves, but he quickly forgot it as he saw Buck nervously prancing at the hitching post, his eyes wild. "What is it, Bucky?" Stone called as he took a quick look around the perimeter of the house.

Going to Buck and laying a calming hand on his rump, Stone slid the rifle from its sheath, never taking his eyes from the horizon. A board creaked behind him, and he wheeled, cocking the hammer of the rifle and bringing it up to his shoulder.

Betsy was standing wide-eyed just outside the door and gasped when she saw Stone bring the rifle around to her.

Stone raised the barrel into the air at once, shocked at how close he'd been to firing. "Betsy, I told you—"

"Why are you so nervous, Hunter?" she asked. Then her round-eyed gaze slid to the south and she said, "Oh, my, look at those storm clouds!"

Stone turned and looked at the sky. He'd been concentrating on the prairie and had all but ignored the dark clouds hovering over the horizon. The flat land allowed visibility for as far as the eye could see, and often they'd sat on the porch and watched as a thunderstorm worked its majestic fierceness miles away. This particular storm was still in its beginning stage, and the dark gray, almost violet clouds were swirling just above the horizon.

"Hunter—is that a funnel cloud?"

Stone had seen the light gray phenomenon at the same time; puffy and billowy at the top edge of the clouds, it trailed down to the distant ground in a thinning twist. But something about the denseness caught his eye—a mild sort of transparency that didn't fit. . . .

"Fire," he whispered to himself, still absorbing the thought. His numbed mind assimilated two facts at once, one on the heels of the other: a prairie fire could destroy his and Gaston's ranches, and the fire was coming from the *direction* of Gaston's ranch.

"It's the Osbournes, Betsy!" he shouted, spinning to shove the rifle into the sleeve and untie Buck. "That's smoke from a fire!"

"Oh no!" Betsy wailed and disappeared inside.

Stone mounted Buck and was ready to take off when she dashed outside and threw him his buffalo coat and hat. "Be careful, Hunter!"

He caught them, pulled them on, and with a strained look spurred Buck into a dead run. The Osbourne place was about six miles away, and Stone pushed the buckskin all the way. Confused thoughts charged through his head as he rode low in the saddle. He found himself hoping it was Gaston's barn that was on fire, because a prairie fire was totally uncontrollable. After chastising himself for selfishness, he thought, *Maybe Gaston's just burning some brush. We could have some good laughs about my rushing over as if a pack of wolves were on my tail!* But he knew there wasn't enough brush around for miles to produce the pillar of smoke he'd seen. Suddenly, he began to dread what he would find.

A huge clap of thunder rolled over him as he came into sight of the Osbourne ranch. He glanced up at the ominous-looking clouds as the first coin-sized drops of rain began falling around him. One of them stung his cheek, making him flinch as the spatter went into his eyes.

81

When he'd cleared his vision, a fierce dread overcame him as he saw the Osbourne house *and* barn on fire. The barn was beyond help, but he instantly decided he would try entering the house if needed because the inferno wasn't as great.

He looked around for the cattle and horses but saw none. They'd either run off by themselves to escape, or been stolen. *Indians!* Stone thought suddenly. *And they could still be around.* He stopped Buck immediately and dismounted. The horse was well trained and would come to him when he whistled, but Stone didn't trust Buck's training in the face of a raging fire. Tying him to a large bush, he withdrew his rifle and moved cautiously toward the house, eyes constantly searching for any signs of movement.

As if a giant spigot had been unplugged, the storm suddenly dumped raindrops on him in torrents. He shivered involuntarily as the wind picked up, and the strong gale tore his hat from his head before he had a chance to put a hand on it. Blinking furiously, he charged across the yard and jumped up onto the porch of the house. The door was open and he could see fire licking at the rafters of the ceiling. He stopped in the doorway and through the thick smoke saw Olivia on the floor by the sofa. The heat from the fire forced him back onto the porch, and he felt as if his eyes were seared. But nothing would burn out the memory of the quick glimpse he'd had of Olivia. He felt his gorge rise as he recalled seeing that her head had almost been severed from her neck.

Stone stumbled back down the porch steps, shocked at the mutilation. He'd seen no sign of Gaston in his abbreviated look around inside and was willing himself to go back in when he saw a form lying on the ground on the north side of the house. A small moan escaped his lips as he woodenly tramped through the mud to Gaston's body.

He was lying on his side, his back to Stone, with two arrowheads protruding from the upper middle part of his back. Stone had no choice but to turn him over and make sure there was no life left in him, though he knew it would only be a perfunctory action. Stooping down and gently rolling the body over, he stared at Gaston's face for a moment, then promptly turned to the side and lost his supper. He dropped to his knees in the mud, his limp fingers releasing his rifle, and thought crazily but calmly, *Here's another memory I'll live with until I die.* Gaston had been cleanly and efficiently scalped.

Trembling, Stone sat back on his heels and stared at the ground. For a few moments he didn't move a muscle. Time lost all meaning, and his mind self-defensively shut down against the sudden horror that had been forced upon it. He had witnessed the faces of death before, one of them caused by his own hand. However, he wasn't prepared for the sight of people he knew—*friends*—dying a grisly death.

A loud creaking noise shook him from his vacuous state, and he raised his gray, almost colorless eyes to watch the skeleton of the barn lean slowly sideways and collapse hissing into the mud. The rain was still coming down hard, though not in sheets as before, and darkness was gathering outside the flickering light of the fires. That was when he saw the Indian.

Astride an ebony horse with a white mask, his red, black, and white face paint smeared from the rain, he watched Stone with calm interest. The firelight flickered on his wet face, and combined with the running paint, the Indian appeared to Stone to be a horrible merchant of death itself. Though he wore a buffalo hide coat, the overall impression was one of grace, strength, and power. So still was he, Stone began to wonder if he was looking at a photograph of a macabre apparition. Then he saw the dark horse paw impatiently at the ground, causing the rider to sway and confirm himself as a member of Stone's world.

The movement activated Stone, and he reached quickly for his rifle, dropping it once from the slick mud on the stock. Even as he raised it to his shoulder, he knew the powder would be too wet to fire. His finger tightened on the trigger, but he let the pressure off at the last second as he realized that the barrel could be blocked by the mud and might explode in his face. Lowering the gun, he saw a twisted grin spread across the Indian's features, as if he could read Stone's mind and thought him amusing and contemptible.

With a sudden, vicious kick to the pony's flanks, the Indian started straight for Stone, unleashing a coup club—a thick stick with a large rock tied to the end. Stone rapidly looked around for shelter, but only the open plain lay behind him, and the thought of Buck tied to a bush flashed through his brain. He switched his hold on the rifle, taking the barrel in both of his hands, and with a cry he rushed toward the charging pony. His momentary fear and hesitancy had vanished, replaced with horrific images of his butchered friends and an all-consuming rage.

The pony covered the fifty yards that separated them in seconds, and Stone aimed his swing of the rifle butt at the swift rider. The Indian brought his club straight out at shoulder level, and just as Stone started his wild swing, he slid to the other side of his pony's back. Gauging the arc of the rifle butt, he instantly ducked underneath and brought the club around in a backward swing to the side of Stone's head with a crunch.

Stone slumped to his hands and knees, losing his grip on his rifle, and saw sparks of light in his vision. He groaned in pain, and he shook his head to clear it, but the action only made him dizzier than he already was. He tried to rise but succeeded in only falling to his side in the mud. Totally helpless, he waited groggily for a killing blow or the swift burn of his throat being cut open, but over the roaring in his ears he heard the thump of hoofbeats . . . and they were receding. An earsplitting shriek of joy and victory reverberated through his aching skull, and he was left with only the sound of the flames greedily lapping up wood.

When the world stopped spinning, Stone managed to gain his feet while tenderly exploring the scalp behind his ear. His fingers came away crimson. Chaotic thoughts zipped through his mind: *I've got to get a shovel and bury Gaston and Olivia—I've got to notify some kind of authority—I've got to start tracking that murderer—I've got to get to Betsy, and—Betsy!*

With a startled cry, he snatched up his rifle and took off at a dead run, ignoring the torturous throbbing in his head. *Please, God, don't let him have stolen Buck! Please, God, don't let him have stolen Buck!* Over and over the litany coursed through his mind, until he saw the nervous horse prancing around the bush.

Frantically untying the reins, he ignored the stirrups and leaped into the saddle. Buck, sensing his master's frenzy, didn't need spurring to entice him into a blistering pace. The buckskin had already covered about twelve miles that day, some of it hard running, but there was nothing Stone could do about that, and he urged the tired horse on. He thought the Indian had taken a westerly direction, but he couldn't be sure, since his mind had been in disarray at the time. Even if he had, that didn't mean that he couldn't turn north to Stone's ranch—and to Betsy.

Stone silently cursed himself for not backtracking on his journey home and making sure he wasn't being followed by Indians. But there had been no rumor of marauding bands in the area. The only Indians Stone ever came in contact with were the peaceful Blackfoot or Cree that came to the trading post to swap furs for food, or sometimes guns and ammunition. He was sure he'd never seen the fierce warrior in the post. He would have remembered that face, even devoid of paint. If Betsy were hurt—or even worse—because of his negligence earlier in the day, he would never be able to forgive himself.

Buck began to falter in his gait, his pace noticeably slower by the minute. Stone, who was shivering violently now from the freezing air, prayed to a God he'd never known—a Being he could only think of as "Betsy's God." He prayed that he wasn't killing his horse, even as he drove him on. He prayed for Betsy's safety and well-being. Whether his awkward and jumbled supplications fell on any ears besides Buck's and a few prairie dogs', he didn't know.

A cry of relief tore its way out of him as he saw a light in the distance. Not the light of a fire, but the warm glow of an oil lamp shining through the window of his home. *She's safe! Thank you . . . thank you!*

If his powder hadn't been wet he would have discharged his gun to bring her to the door. He wanted to be *certain* that she was inside and unharmed. Instead, he bellowed hoarsely, "BETSY!" as loud as he could when he was still some distance away. When there was no response, he tried again, and this time the front door opened and he saw her cautiously peep outside. As she stepped onto the porch, he saw in the dim light the familiar worry lines etched across her forehead.

And he thanked "Betsy's God" for that wonderful, lined forehead.

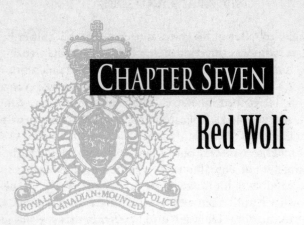

# Chapter Seven

# Red Wolf

Following the white man was ridiculously easy for Red Wolf.

The deep prints in the wet grass of the prairie were plain, and Red Wolf had no trouble seeing them by the light of the moon that shone after the storm had passed. For a while, he could hear the white man talking, almost shouting as he rode.

Red Wolf smiled, but the upward curve of his lips didn't match the cruel eyes, the icy countenance. Red Wolf's flowing black mane of hair framed a handsome face, with a fine Roman nose and strong jaw. Intelligence glinted from the sinister eyes, combined with an unsettling contempt and arrogance for all things living.

His smile was one of self-satisfaction at his own cleverness. *Nothing cries in the night but owls and wolves—and this strange white man. I will name him Owl Dog. I would name him Owl Wolf, but he is not worthy to carry my name—I have counted coup against him.*

Among Red Wolf's Crow people, and many other tribes, counting coup against an enemy was a greater accomplishment than killing him. To simply strike an armed enemy with a coup club demonstrated courage, skill, and ultimate disrespect. However, Red Wolf had seen many braves count coup, only to be blown off their horses by the white eyes as they celebrated. He had seen the great numbers of the white eyes, and it made no sense to him to sacrifice a fine warrior's life for honor. Glory could just as easily be obtained in battle and at the same time reduce the number of the enemy. Red Wolf would much rather kill than count coup.

He hadn't taken the life of Owl Dog because his bloodlust had been satisfied. Also, some things about Owl Dog had fascinated him.

For a white eye, he was a fine specimen—extremely handsome, tall, strongly built, and, Red Wolf found out, quick as a snake's strike. Owl Dog's rifle swing had nearly taken his head off. Instead of running or begging for his life as most of Red Wolf's victims did, Owl Dog had defiantly stood his ground—his strangely colored eyes glowing a fiery red from the fire's reflection. Red Wolf had been taken aback for a slight moment at the eerie sight. Finally, the blow Red Wolf had dealt with the club had been substantial. Red Wolf thought he might have killed him and was shocked to see Owl Dog come running out of the inferno at full speed, as if unhurt.

Crow warriors were respected for the caliber of their enemies. Red Wolf's people were held in high esteem for their continued wars with the mighty Sioux despite being heavily outnumbered. As long as Owl Dog walked the earth, Red Wolf knew his own legend would only grow more mythical with the telling of this story.

He stopped his pony as Owl Dog reached a house. Dismounting, he silently walked forward another hundred feet and studied the man and woman with his keen eyesight. Owl Dog was obviously very affectionate and protective of her as he embraced her, then ushered her inside quickly. She was also the most beautiful white woman Red Wolf had ever seen.

After a few minutes, Owl Dog came back outside, and Red Wolf thought for a moment he'd been spotted as the white man stared intently in his direction. Finally, he took his horse to the barn. Red Wolf continued staring at the window, hoping for another glimpse of the woman, but none came. Knowing he had to return to his small band of warriors, he reluctantly went back to his pony and rode off to catch up with them. On the way he thought about Owl Dog's cattle, horses, and woman—but not necessarily in that order.

———

Betsy had finally fallen asleep on the sofa after tending to her husband's bruised scalp. The club had left a large, ugly gash, and the area around it was swollen and red. Only after making sure he was all right was she able to mourn her friends. She'd cried and cried, and Stone had extinguished the lamp and placed her head in his lap, stroking her hair. When her weeping was finished, she rose and changed the wrapping on his wound, then began crying again until she eventually drifted into a fitful and dream-filled sleep.

"Hunter, did you stay up all night?" Betsy asked accusingly as she rubbed the sleep from her eyes.

Stone smiled weakly at her from the chair he'd moved to the window. The morning sun shone through the bedroom window in the room behind her, framing him in its glow. His eyes were red-rimmed, and the sparkle of his whiskers added to the effect of exhaustion.

A reprimand came to Betsy's mind, but she realized he'd stayed up all night going from window to window, guarding them against an attack. *And his head must ache terribly!* Eyes softening, she went to his chair and knelt down in front of him, placing her hands on his stubbled face. "I'm sorry I fell asleep." He started to shake his head, but her hands held him. "I should have kept watch all night, after what you went through. Now please go in there and go to bed. I'll keep an eye on things, and when you get up we'll go tell the authorities."

Stone snorted. "What authorities? There aren't any this side of Fort Garry."

"But there was talk of a mounted police force. Weren't they ever organized?"

"No. That's all it was—just talk." He took her hands in his own and squeezed them gently. "We're all alone out here. At least until I can find a way to send you to your family for a while."

"Those murderers will just go free?" Betsy hadn't considered the possibility, and the idea made her slightly sick. Then his last statement sank in and her eyes narrowed. "Don't even think about sending me away, Hunter Stone! I'm your wife, and I stay with you."

Stone leaned closer to her and reasoned, "Betsy, listen to me. I've been up all night thinking about it, and I know you're lonesome for your family sometimes, and—"

"You don't know anything of the kind!"

"Yes, I do!" he argued, a bit more strongly than he'd intended. His face softened as he said, "Whether you miss them or not, I can't leave you alone for a moment until I know that savage has been captured or has left the territory completely."

"You want to go after him, don't you?" she asked quietly.

He was startled into silence, for that was exactly what he intended to do. Recovering quickly, he lied, "No, I don't." But he knew he was too late with the denial.

"Don't lie to me, darling. I can tell when you're lying to me," Betsy smiled. "You shift your eyes."

"I can lie like a politician—if I want to."

"Not to me, you can't. Hunter, this won't be tracking down bounty jumpers like you did for that justice of the peace in Dufferin."

"I know that."

"I don't think you do. I could see how spooked you were when you described that Indian. If you hadn't been so impressed with him, you wouldn't have described him in such detail. And you want to chase *him* down and kill him?"

"Yes—I—do," Stone said, pronouncing each word forcefully. "You weren't there, Betsy. You didn't see Olivia and Gaston—you didn't see them."

"What if there's fifty of them, Hunter? What if he was the last one out—just a regular brave, and the other forty-nine are more fierce-looking than him?"

"Believe me, he wasn't just a regular brave, and there *are* none scarier than him."

His normally full lips were set in a grim line, and as she watched him his cheek twitched slightly. She wouldn't have noticed if she hadn't been so close to him, but the tic combined with the hollow-eyed look told her all she needed to know. She'd never seen a haunted expression on his face, but she was seeing one now. "Nobody's going anywhere, Hunter. We're both staying here until your head heals, then you can go back to work until it's time to plant."

Stone sighed long and deep. He knew from her tone that she wouldn't budge from her declaration, and he was too tired to argue with her for now. "All right, Betsy. But when I get up later, we're going over there to bury them. I'm sorry, but you'll have to come with me. You don't have to see anything. You can stay away from their house, but I won't leave you alone here."

"I'll go," Betsy whispered. "They need a decent burial."

Stone slept for seven hours. The last thing he wanted to do upon waking was to move his head, but with Betsy's help he rose, ate a little stew, and saddled the horses. Mounting Buck proved to be an adventure, for when he swung himself painfully up into the saddle, a wave of dizziness rolled over him, and he was forced to hug the horse's neck to keep from falling off.

Betsy had already mounted and spurred to his side to make sure he wouldn't fall. "Why don't we wait until tomorrow?"

"No," Stone muttered through gritted teeth, "today." He was already dreading the ride, and when his vision cleared, he urged Buck into an easy canter that took them all the way to the Osbourne place.

If Betsy hadn't been with him, he would have missed the tracks. As they neared the burned-out ranch, the ground turned soft from the soaking rain of the night before. "Whose prints are those, Hunter?" She pointed to deep indentions that ran parallel to Stone's tracks of the night before but turned west close to the spot where the barn had stood.

Savagely, Stone jerked Buck to a stop and uttered a vile curse.

Betsy was stunned. First of all, because he never treated Buck roughly—he spoiled the horse as he would a child. Secondly, she hadn't heard him curse since her conversion to Christ almost two years before. He'd either stopped the habit outright, or was simply careful when she was around. She'd never asked the reason. His face was still a bit pale from the pain in his head, but now his haggard expression had been replaced with a mask of rage.

"He followed me," Stone said tightly as he glared at the hoof-prints. "That dirty, murdering . . ." He glanced quickly at Betsy, who suddenly felt the need to step back from his blazing eyes, but then she remembered his anger wasn't directed at her. "He knows where we live. He knows where we sleep. He knows we have horses and cattle. He knows everything about us, and we don't know *anything* about him."

———

Red Wolf tore a chunk of beef from the ribs with his strong white teeth and smacked with pleasure. He grudgingly nodded to Deer Runner, who had cooked the side of beef. Deer Runner was lazy and a whiner, and Red Wolf planned on killing him when the time was right. For now, Red Wolf would enjoy his cooking and let him live another day.

"We're almost out of meat," Little Pony observed.

Red Wolf shrugged and continued eating.

"We could go steal the cattle we sold to the trappers," laughed Spotted Hawk, Red Wolf's brother. "And then sell them back to the fools!" The group around the campfire exploded with laughter.

Red Wolf smiled at his brother's joke. After wiping his greasy hands on his deerskin leggings, he pulled his buffalo robe around himself tighter. Though it was springtime, the cold weather at the foot of the Rocky Mountains would not break. However, it was a safe place to rest and hide from any pursuers, though he doubted there were any.

A month had passed since their bountiful raid on the white man and woman. After selling some of the cows, they'd traded the rest for new guns and ammunition. Nothing could stop them now; not even a troop of the so-called "mounted police" he'd heard about. He regarded the nine Crow braves around him. *They grow fat from their spoils. It is time to make war again.* He recalled some other business.

"Long Feather, tell me the news from our tribe."

Long Feather was yawning when Red Wolf asked the question and closed his mouth with a snap. He'd ridden long and hard to find them and unlike the others was extremely tired. A look of disdain crossed his long face as he said, "The once courageous warriors of our tribe have turned into old women and harlots for the horse soldiers. They sign treaties that are never honored and even offer themselves as guides to help the paleface track our brothers. Red Wolf was wise to leave the cowards and make war on his own."

Murmurs of consent flowed around the fire. "Tell us the tale again, Spotted Hawk," Little Pony asked.

Spotted Hawk glanced at Red Wolf, and an unspoken communication passed between them. Spotted Hawk's dark eyes gleamed as he said, "Seven years ago, when every tribe feared the Crow, a warrior joined the annual sun dance. He was fifteen winters old and made no sound when the medicine man pierced his breast once, then twice with the eagle talons. The medicine man attached the ropes to the talons, and the young brave was lifted high into the air above every onlooker. Again he made no cry of pain."

Every man around the fire was entranced with the story, though they'd all heard it before, and those that were eating ceased all movement.

"Even the strongest of warriors would only last a few hours while hanging this way. But the silent brave immediately went into the spirit world and hung for the rest of that day and most of that night.

"Finally, the medicine man was convinced the boy had died. No man could stay in the spirit world for so long without his soul being snatched away. The medicine man cut him down, but before he could see if the boy was still breathing, the boy sat up and began to speak."

Spotted Hawk paused, and all eyes turned to Red Wolf, waiting for him to fulfill his part of the play.

Red Wolf hesitated, savoring the breathless air. When he spoke, his voice was strong, and his eyes were locked on a distant point in the cottonwoods. He recited the words he'd uttered on the day of his sun dance: "The Great Spirit has sent me a vision. I have seen the death of our people—starving, freezing, and homeless from the buffalo being taken from us. Massacres at the hands of the pony soldiers, who spare no one, not even our women and children! I saw all of our people being herded into one place and a fence being built to keep us under the white eyes.

"My guide through all of these nightmares was a wolf. His eyes were yellow and wild. His fur was matted with great amounts of blood—not his own blood, but the blood of Crow enemies. After every sight he showed me, he would whisper, 'Seek the blood! Seek the blood!' ''

The campfire popped, and in the total silence of the listeners the sound was an explosion, yet no one moved.

Red Wolf continued to stare into the woods for a moment, caught up in the memory of his seven-year-old hallucination. It proved to be the most important day of his life. The Great Spirit had chosen him to force fire, pain, blood, and death upon the enemies of the Crow nation. *And I have only just begun!* he thought.

With an ecstatic shudder of power, he brought himself back to the present. Surveying every face around him one at a time, he proclaimed, "I still seek the blood. And everywhere I go, the bloody wolf is with me—grinning with long, sharp teeth that could tear a man in two!" He leaned forward, fixing his intent gaze over Deer Runner's shoulder and whispering, "He's with us now! Right behind *you*, Deer Runner!"

Deer Runner's eyes appeared ready to pop from his head. Every brave slowly turned his head to look behind him, and just when Deer Runner felt he had to turn around or die from curiosity and fright, Red Wolf exploded in laughter that caused the frightened braves to jump as one body. After the initial shock, the rest joined in—chiefly from relief that the horrendous wolf *hadn't* been in their midst. Running Deer made a determined attempt at laughter, knowing that if he didn't, Red Wolf would hurt him or kill him. But in his chest, his heart was pounding so hard he felt as if he would collapse at any moment.

After the laughter had died down, Little Pony asked, "When is our next journey, Great One?"

"Tomorrow," Red Wolf stated firmly. "We have many miles to go." For the past two nights, Red Wolf's dreams were of a beautiful plains girl with long brown hair and the soft brown eyes of a doe. When she appeared in the dreams, she was always followed by the grinning, cruel, crimson-splashed wolf.

———

"Hunter, it's been over a month. You can't stay with me every minute for the rest of my life!" Betsy reasoned as she kneaded dough in the kitchen.

"Why not?" Stone grinned. "I like it."

"Be serious!" Betsy cried, stamping her small foot.

"You're getting flour all over yourself."

Betsy made a disgusted sound, tore off a part of the dough, and hurled it in his direction. He ducked, and the small piece bounced off the door behind him and fell in the bowl of cleaning oil he was using for his guns. Fishing it out of the mess, he held it up and said, "Now, that ought to fry up nicely!"

Betsy gave him a beseeching look. "Hunter, please!"

"All right, all right. I've been thinking about it, too." He finished wiping excess oil from the pistol he'd been cleaning and began to assemble it. "I'll go to the post tomorrow and get everything I need to start planting. You stay here and do your little wifey things all by yourself. Okay?"

"Just like that?"

"Just like that."

"You won't just get out of sight and circle back to watch the place like you did last week?"

"Cross my heart." And he did.

"That was really silly, Hunter. Didn't you think I would wonder where the things were that I sent you after?"

He shrugged. "You're just too smart for me."

"Well, thank you, but it's no great effort."

Stone leaped from his chair and she only had time to squeal before he was tickling her. She managed to smear dough paste on his face, and when she saw him, she began to laugh even harder.

"Oh, stop it, Hunter!" she cried breathlessly. "I can't breathe!"

"Say you're sorry."

"I'm sorry!"

"Say I'm the wisest and smartest man to ever walk the earth."

"Do I have to?" Betsy asked and erupted in a new round of giggles as he doubled his efforts.

———

That night after supper, Stone came in from bedding down the animals for the night and found Betsy staring off into the distance with her Bible in her lap. It wasn't the first time he'd found her this way. Sometimes she would tell him what she was pondering, while other times she would eventually sigh and continue her reading. Stone had picked up her Bible and flipped through it before, but the words were so alien he'd always given up quickly. He was curious about his wife's obsession with it but had never taken the time to find out about it. As for Betsy, she was content to witness to him whenever the moment presented itself, but she never forced God's Word on him.

Stone found himself with nothing to do and sat down on the sofa beside his wife. "Heavy thinking?" he asked, then was startled to see a tear weaving its glistening path down the side of her face.

Betsy didn't answer right away, and Stone was content to wait until she found the words.

"It's hard not to hate him," she said softly.

Stone didn't need to ask to whom she was referring, but her statement confused him, and for some reason angered him. "Why shouldn't you hate him? I do, and if I ever see him again, I'll kill him, scalp him, and burn him—just like he did to our friends!"

"No, Hunter," she said, appalled at his vehemence.

"No?" He pointed to her Bible. "Doesn't that say 'an eye for an eye'?"

"Yes, but that's the law of Moses in the Old Testament. Jesus Christ came and changed all that."

"How?"

"Listen to this," she said. Opening up her Bible, she read: " 'And when they were come to the place, which is called Calvary, there they crucified him, and the criminals, one on the right hand, and the other on the left. Then said Jesus, Father, forgive them; for they know not what they do.' " Betsy locked her eyes with his. "Jesus teaches us to forgive the ones that hurt us, just as He forgave the Romans for nailing Him to a cross and leaving Him to die."

Stone couldn't believe it. *Forgive that monster? That's impossible! A man capable of that kind of butchery deserves to die as no other.*

Betsy saw his confusion. "Jesus taught that over and over again." She flipped through her Bible and pointed at another passage. " 'Love your enemies, do good to them which hate you; bless them that curse you, and pray for them which despitefully use you. And unto him that smiteth thee on the one cheek offer also the other.' "

"But that's . . . that's . . . incredible! *Nobody* can do that."

"Jesus did."

"He was the Son of God—He was perfect, wasn't He?"

"He was a *man*, Hunter. Just like you. And He doesn't ask anything of a normal man that He wasn't capable of. He set the example for all men to follow."

"I can't be that way, Betsy," Stone said solemnly. "There's no way."

"There's a way," she said confidently and smoothed the blond hair on top of his head. "With God, anything is possible."

Stone kissed her. "I don't understand you, darling, but I sure do love you."

"I love you, too, Hunter."

———

Betsy felt him get up before dawn in a lazy, distracted way. She knew he wanted to get an early start so he would make it back before dark. He'd told her before they'd drifted off to sleep that he shouldn't be long, but not to worry if he was.

She sighed contentedly and rolled over to his side of the bed where his warmth still held. Hearing a far-off rumble, she opened one eye and looked out the window to determine if he was in for a wet ride, but the rain seemed to be far enough away. Snuggling close to his pillow, she sank into a deep sleep.

Two hours later, Betsy came out of a dream in which she was standing on one side of a raging river, while watching Hunter swimming desperately to reach her. Behind her was open prairie, and she couldn't understand why Hunter was struggling against an obviously powerful undercurrent. *Why doesn't he go downstream and try to find a calmer point to cross? Where's Buck? Buck is a good swimmer and would have no problem carrying Hunter over. And why is he so frantically trying to reach me? I don't understand any of this!*

Finding herself face down in her pillow, she perched on her elbows and rubbed her eyes before opening them.

Yawning hugely, she turned over and looked up into the cold and merciless eyes of Red Wolf.

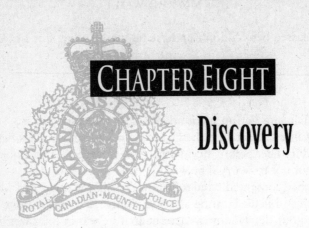

# Chapter Eight

# Discovery

"What do I owe you, Sam?" Stone asked, waving a hand over the supplies he'd gathered and placed on the counter. He then began to tie the bean and corn seed, sugar, oats, and flour bags together.

Sam Pairvent smiled crookedly. Whenever he did so, a red horse-shoe-shaped scar on his right jawline stretched white. "You know better than that, Hunter."

"Now, Sam, I've got to pay you something. This is a lot of merchandise."

"Your money's no good here. Even if you don't run this trading post right now, you will come fall, just like last year."

"I don't think the Hudson's Bay Company would agree with your generosity." Stone finished tying the bags and looked Pairvent in the eye. He felt he'd been away from Betsy long enough and wanted to be on his way. "Give me a price, Sam."

"You're the stubbornest and proudest man I've ever met, Hunter. Five dollars Yankee." Though they were in Canada, almost everyone in the remote territories used American dollars.

Stone quickly calculated his purchase. "Done." He knew he was getting a bargain, but the amount would cover the Company's cost, anyway. Reaching for his money, he asked, "Heard anything about those renegade Indians?" Pairvent had told him when he'd walked in the door that a band of Indians had raided a trading post close to the Rockies a few days after the Osbourne incident. They'd killed the proprietor and made off with some supplies and four horses. Stone knew it had to be the fierce-looking Indian's gang; there weren't any other uprisings reported before or since.

Pairvent shook his head as he took Stone's money. "They must've gone into the mountains—or headed back down to the U.S. Oh, by the way—" He reached behind him and pulled a newspaper from a shelf, slapping it down on the counter with a WHACK! "This here article makes me feel safer already," he said with heavy sarcasm.

Stone picked up the paper and read:

May 3, 1873
JUSTICE BILL PROPOSED
    OTTAWA. . . . Sir John A. Macdonald, prime minister of the Dominion of Canada, and his deputy minister in the Department of Justice, Hewitt Bernard, introduced a bill into the House of Commons that would begin paving the way for a mounted police force in the North-West Territories. Voting on the bill will take place on May 4, with little or no opposition expected.

    The bill would provide for the establishment of courts, the appointment of magistrates, and the erection of jails in the Territories. If passed, the Act would be an enabling measure, giving the Government authority to implement provisions for a police force by Order-in-Council.

    Establishment of a force has been slow. Eastern Canadian politicians are in no hurry to spend much-needed Government funds on the sparsely populated Territories. Macdonald, who makes no secret of his iron intent to establish a mounted police force, argues that the Territories are being populated with more and more settlers every day. "They [the settlers] are in constant danger of an Indian war, and once that commences who knows where it may end."

    Macdonald maintains that the force would pay for itself, pointing out that the members would be customs officers and would therefore contribute to the public purse. . . .

"Bunch of mealy mouthed politicians!" Pairvent complained. "They'll never get us no police. If it's not happening in their backyard, they don't want to hear about it." He planted his elbows on the counter as he leaned closer to Stone, expelling bad breath toward him. "Your friends might be alive today if we had them lawmen. You're respected around these parts, Hunter. Why don't you write a letter to some of those fat boys in the Commons? Tell 'em how alone we are out here?"

Stone backed up a step, looked down, and pretended to inspect his boot to escape the man's sour breath. "They know, Sam. These things just take time and money. Look at the Americans. The same thing's going on in their West."

"Yeah, but their land's ten times bigger than ours. Seems to me if one of them scalawags in Ottawa was to have a *family* member butchered like the Osbournes, we'd have the whole British Army swarmin' in on us!"

Stone's stomach tightened anxiously as he recalled the carnage at the Osbourne ranch. He had worked in a slaughterhouse when he was a boy and thought himself immune to the sight of blood after that. But that was animal blood, not human, and he'd found out there was definitely a difference. Sleep had been elusive for a few nights after the massacre, and he'd never before had trouble sleeping.

". . . all right?"

Stone's eyes came into focus on Pairvent's worried face. "What?"

"I said, are you all right? You turned white there for a minute."

Stone blinked and cleared his throat, which had gone bone dry. "Yes, I'm fine."

Pairvent looked sideways at him as if he didn't believe a word of it. Hunter was not one to daydream.

Stone straightened himself and gathered a handful of the rope that bound his supplies together. Then he snapped his fingers. "Do you have any chocolates?" Betsy loved the sweets, and he always tried to remember to pick some up when he came to the post.

Pairvent chuckled. "I knew you were forgetting something. Don't worry, *I* didn't forget—I was just waiting for you to ask." He bagged the candy and handed it over.

"Thanks. And I'll think about writing that letter."

"You do that. Take care of yourself, Hunter."

On the ride home, Stone admired the spring day. It had started out cool, but the noon sunshine forced him to remove his coat. He took off his hat and put it on the saddle horn while he raised his face to the warmth of the rays, trusting Buck to know the way without his guidance. A flight of geese soared overhead, returning after their annual exodus to the warmer south. Hearing a chattering noise, he looked to his right and saw two gophers playing, chasing each other with incredible swiftness.

He smiled to himself and inhaled deeply, breathing in the prairie perfume of heather, lilies, and sage. He loved the wide open plain and actually resented time spent inside a house. The nights were especially mesmerizing with the countless stars and the moon draped across the ebony sky. Sometimes, the full moon rising on the horizon appeared so huge and close, he pictured himself throwing a rock and watching the small puff of moon dust where it landed. Then he would sit on the corral fence and watch it shrink so many miles away, and his mind would ache with the awareness of his own insignificance in the face of such majesty.

Sometimes Betsy would join him, sitting beside him without a word, and the only sound that escaped them would be the gasp over a shooting star, or the soft murmur of their love for each other. He would put his arms around her and hold her while they gazed, or occasionally Betsy would climb down to stand in front of him, her head firm against his chest, and he would stroke her hair. At times like those, Stone could only shake his head in wonder at love and togetherness and heaven's canopy.

Stone reached the low hills that broke the flat horizon and remembered the day of the Osbourne massacre when Buck had been so spooked. *Had one of the Indians been hiding in these hills, watching me? Or was it just a mountain lion or coyote? If I was being watched that day, why did they choose the Osbournes instead of me? What factor ruled me out, or made them seem more vulnerable?* He would never know.

Emerging from the short pass, he looked in the direction of his home—and his whole body stiffened when he saw the smoke. His heart leaped as dread washed over him. A choked, strangled sound emitted from his throat as he tried to swallow the insipid taste of fear that had sprung into his mouth.

Buck's nose was assaulted by the sudden smell of distress emanating from his master, and he took a faltering half step to the side before feeling a vicious kick to his flanks. Instantly he was on the run, long black mane flying in the wind.

Stone bent low over Buck's neck, attempting to soften the stiff wind resistance caused by the buckskin's speed and a natural westerly breeze. Feeling an awkwardness in Buck's gait, he turned and with a powerful heave lifted the supplies and threw them to the ground. The flour bag split open when it landed, showering a small snowstorm over the other sacks.

His lips were drawn in a taut line, deepening the cleft chin, and the ocean of apprehension that held him created a square-jawed look of consternation. The nightmare of Olivia Osbourne's corpse again assaulted his brain, and before he knew it her face was replaced by Betsy's. "NO!" he shouted to the wind and began whipping Buck's flanks mercilessly with the reins.

He could see the ruins of the house and barn. The fire had already done its damage; both structures were flat and smoking, with little evidence of flame. The chimney stood blackened but intact, a lone monument to happy times spent sitting at its hearth. One section of the corral fence had been torn down, with both horses and the ten head of cattle gone. Stone's eyes frantically searched for a sign of Betsy and found none. The thought struck him that he didn't know whether to hope for her bleeding body to come into view or not. If it did, she was dead. If not, she could still be alive.

Buck hadn't fully come to a stop before Stone was off and racing toward the house. The heat from the embers burned his face and stung his eyes. He scanned the smoldering mess and thankfully saw no evidence of a body. Instead of feeling relief, for a moment he was stunned. *He took her—why would he take her?*

His breathing was harsh and labored. A lump formed in the back of his throat as he realized he was staring with watering eyes at what had once been his life. No matter what happened—if he rescued Betsy, if she was killed, whatever—his life would never be the same again. Despite living on the endless prairie, he'd felt an invulnerability—a security that Betsy's God was in His heaven and this spring's crop would sprout in health for the harvest and soon he would be bouncing a baby on his knee. They'd lived in their own little world, far away from war, poverty, politics, corruption, and heartache. Betsy had depended on him for their security, and he had failed miserably, possibly leaving her to pay an unthinkable price.

Anger charged through him, and he was brought back to the present by a violent tremor that shook his body. *This is my fault. All of it. And it's time to make it right.* His lips drew into a taut line, and his mind began to assess the situation. He glanced down at himself and realized his sole possessions were: the clothes he wore, Buck, a revolver, a Henry .44 rifle, a knife, a canteen, field glasses, a saddle, and a bedroll. Instead of feeling dejected about his scant possessions, he felt well-equipped for what he had to do. Those items were the only things he'd carried when hunting down men before, and they were all he needed now.

Sorrow and despair were gone, replaced by a stinging, chafing wrath. Rather than blind him, his powerful emotions seemed to help focus a clear tunnel vision that took over his movements and chased away defeating thoughts.

He strode to Buck and tightened the saddle cinch. The horse turned his head to look at him and Stone said, "We've got some hard riding to do, my friend. Hard riding." Removing his canteen, he poured out the tepid water and refilled it with fresh water from the pump.

His movements were purposeful and automatic, yet unhurried. He knew the Indians had a good head start on him, but their path would be simple to follow. Mounting Buck, he surveyed the destruction for the last time. For a moment he reflected on the plans he'd made before deciding to marry Betsy; he'd been a free man, able to roam where he wanted and take nature in his grip and *celebrate* independence. But loving Betsy had changed all that. He'd given in to his fears of becoming bored and settled down with her—and liked it. Now it was all washed away, like a child's sandcastle yielding to the inevitable tide.

All because of a vicious Indian and his twisted desires.

His sandy eyebrows were split by two fierce frown lines. Every nerve in his body was alive and tingling. He heard the far-off, shrill cry of a hawk. He saw a drop of water hanging from the mouth of the water pump and watched as the weight of it created a teardrop shape before falling to the mud below. His ears registered the *plop* even from twenty feet away, over the crackling and simmering of what had once been his home.

*I'm coming for you, Betsy. And God help anyone that gets in my way. . . .*

———

"Why do you not fear me, little rabbit?" Red Wolf asked as he held a strip of beef in front of Betsy's face.

The fact that he spoke English shocked her. She hesitated before allowing him to feed her, despite her ravenous hunger. Her hands were tied behind her back, as they had been all day. Traveling well into the night, Red Wolf had called a halt to rest the horses and cattle. He showed no concern for her growing tired. Betsy remembered Hunter telling her that Indians sometimes placed a higher value on their horses than on their wives and families.

"I don't fear you because I draw my strength from God Almighty." She accepted the offered meat and chewed quickly.

Red Wolf studied her for a moment before cutting off another piece of beef from the steak he held in his hand.

They'd butchered a steer right before Betsy had gone to sleep, exhausted from the long, tense day. Red Wolf woke her up when the meat was done, and she had no idea what time of night it was. The beef was still cooking over an open fire, and she heard the fire sizzle as the fat fell in a steady flow. The rest of the braves, minus one probably on guard, were asleep. She wondered if Red Wolf ever slept.

"I have had many captives before," he stated conversationally, "and all have been afraid."

Betsy didn't respond, because there was nothing to say. She took another piece of meat, examining his face closely. His head was large for his body, and his resolute jawline was pockmarked with acne scars. The black and white paint had been scrubbed from his face, but she noticed a small patch that he'd missed by his right ear, gleaming a pale white in the weak light from the fire. But the disturbing feature was his eyes, so black and bottomless that both pupils disappeared in an inky abyss. What was *not* seen in them was the most disturbing. No compassion. No mercy. No conscience. *He's lost his soul*, she thought suddenly, and it chilled her. *Is that possible, Lord?* She knew the answer immediately: everyone created in His image had a soul. Red Wolf's was just . . . buried somewhere.

Betsy had seen nothing like those eyes before, and to stop the fear that was welling inside her, she said the first thing that came to her mind. "My husband will come for me." She felt an odd satisfaction when those very formidable eyes widened slightly.

Red Wolf recovered his arrogant control immediately—so quickly that Betsy wondered if she'd really seen the falter. "Why should I fear your husband?"

"Because he is a great warrior."

"Hah!" he snorted. "The last time I saw this man he was crying in the night after I hit him with my club. He was too pitiful to kill."

Betsy cocked her head and looked at him knowingly. "I don't think you're telling me the truth. You *have* no pity." With effort, she held his smoldering gaze without blinking. "Did you fear him?"

"I do not fear dogs that howl in the night."

"Dogs can bite—and even kill."

Suddenly, he was directly in her face. She could smell sweat and horses and smoke. "Listen to me, little rabbit. If your man comes for me, he is a fool! I let him live before, but if I see him again I will carve out his liver!" His black eyes bored into hers, and when she attempted to shift her gaze, he moved directly into her line of sight and forced her to look at him.

"What do you want from me?" she asked.

A smile touched his lips as he moved back into the squatting position he'd been in before. "It is not what I want *from* you. It is what I want *for* you." He held up two fingers. "Two ponies. The Sioux will pay that much for a white woman slave."

Betsy nodded slowly and looked at the ground.

"This God of yours—He comforts you?" All trace of anger had left him, and he was now curious, as if nothing had happened.

"Yes, He does. And He would comfort you, too, if you asked Him."

"Do you think I need comfort?" he asked, bemused.

"Everyone does—even you."

He fed her another piece of beef while looking at her skeptically. "I have all I need. And what I do not have, I steal from someone who does." He shrugged his shoulders as if it were the simplest solution in the world.

"Stealing is wrong," Betsy said around the mouthful.

"Only if I am caught. I have never been caught."

"You will be, someday. And they will hang you."

He regarded her with something like admiration. "The little rabbit has sharp teeth."

"When you die, you go before God to be judged. If you don't know God's son Jesus, you will burn in hell for all eternity." Betsy much preferred to talk of God's love and compassion, but she didn't think he would grasp the concept. Violence and threats he would understand.

"When I die"—he stopped and pointed at her—"and when *you* die, we go to the earth and become one with it. Just as we were before being born."

Betsy shook her head. "Not our spirits. Only our bodies. Our spirits live forever, either with God in everlasting joy, or in hell with eternal misery. God wants to love you, and He wants you to love Him. That's all He asks."

Red Wolf popped the last strip of beef in his own mouth. She watched his jaw muscles work as he chewed. Standing, he said with amusement, "You talk too much, little rabbit. You were silent all day, and now that you start talking, you cannot stop. Get some sleep." He walked over and brutally kicked one of his sleeping men and gave him an order. With a dark look at Red Wolf's receding back, the brave went to relieve the guard.

———

Runs-in-the-Night blearily drew his moccasin closer to his face, trying to see better by the firelight. As he did so, he jabbed himself in the finger with the sewing needle he was using to stitch his worn footwear back together. Cursing, he put his finger in his mouth and ran his tongue over the small dot of blood.

Laughing, Bear Claw thrust the half-empty whiskey bottle toward him, its contents sloshing faintly. "Here," he said in their Cree language, "maybe this will help."

"Nothing will help Runs-in-the-Night," Gopher John pronounced distractedly as he peered at his face closely with a broken mirror. He'd had a hard time putting the glass down since he'd traded for it at the Bow River post. Quite honestly, he'd never seen a more attractive Cree brave. "If Runs-in-the-Night were a woman, he would be thrown to the wolves, he's so clumsy."

Runs-in-the-Night turned a dark glare on Gopher John, who didn't notice.

Bear Claw drank deeply from the bottle Runs-in-the-Night had refused. He liked whiskey and drank it whenever possible. Gopher John never drank, which suited Bear Claw and Runs-in-the-Night just fine because it left more for them. Bear Claw absently rubbed his left knee. He'd gotten so drunk the night before, he'd fallen and awkwardly bent his leg under himself. The pain had *really* hit in the morning and had hindered him all day.

Gopher John put down his mirror and listened to the horses and cattle as they moved in the night. "Your father will be proud of our trading skills, Bear Claw."

"I know. I don't think even *he* could have done better. We should have enough beef to last through the summer." The idea of his father showing pleasure for something he did, instead of anger, made Bear Claw happy. Of course, Gopher John would exaggerate his own part in the bartering, but Bear Claw wouldn't be outdone this time. He planned on keeping Gopher John in his sight while the story of their journey was told. It meant keeping away from the whiskey and preserving a clear head for a day or two, but he could handle that, he hoped.

"It's about time for Snow to come back," Gopher John said. "It's your watch, Runs-in-the-Night, if you ever get that moccasin fixed."

"Almost finished." Runs-in-the-Night was sitting as close to the fire as the heat would allow. Besides the low light hindering his work, his eyes kept crossing from the amount of whiskey he'd consumed. "Wait—it's not my turn!"

"Yes, it is."

"No, it's not!"

Gopher John leaned toward him and stated carefully and slowly, "Yes . . . it . . . is." He had penetrating eyes, and thanks to his mirror, he knew it. He'd practiced many looks when no one was watching and was surprised to see how stern he could appear.

Bear Claw said, "You're not the leader here." He was having trouble following the simple conversation, and it made him mad.

Gopher John turned his gaze on Bear Claw and sneered, "Do you think you are?"

"Yes—my father is chief," he announced and sat up a little straighter.

"Your whiskey is chief! And your father knows it!" Gopher John was aware of Bear Claw's drunkenness and loved baiting him.

Just as Bear Claw was getting ready to climb to his feet, the world exploded around them.

Gopher John had been aware of a crashing through the woods at his left, but he'd figured the disturbance was Snow returning for some sleep. Snow was fat and couldn't keep quiet. Just when he realized that Snow wouldn't be *coming* from the direction of the woods, the gunshot sounded. All three men around the fire jerked with surprise and fear, barely having time to rise when a rider on a huge horse leaped into their midst. His hat hung low on his brow, and from under the brim Gopher John could see red eyes. Superstitious fear clutched him, for he'd heard legends from Indians that had traveled this trail of a crazy white man that had red eyes and sharp, pointed teeth. When the man turned his head slightly to cover Bear Claw, Gopher John saw with relief that it had just been the reflection of the fire—the white man's eyes were gray, but an unsettling gray that shone with barely subdued fury. He held a carbine on Gopher John, and a pistol on Bear Claw and Runs-in-the-Night, the barrel of which was still smoking from the round fired from it.

The intrusion had been so swift, and the shock of seeing the fierce rider so disturbing, Gopher John hadn't noticed the plump shape of Snow flung across the big buckskin's neck until the rider put a knee under Snow's limp shoulder, heaving the body to the ground at Bear Claw's feet. Snow landed face down with the limpness of a dead dog. Gopher John couldn't tell if Snow was dead or merely unconscious—and didn't really care at the moment. From the menacing glare of the white man, they were all in mortal danger.

"Where's the woman?" the big man asked, his voice hoarse.

The three Crees looked at each other out of the corners of their eyes, careful not to move their heads.

"You!" the man cried, thrusting his rifle toward Gopher John, who twitched noticeably. "Where is she?"

Gopher John found himself wishing they *had* a woman with them. He didn't want to disappoint this man. Swallowing, he said uncertainly, "Woman?" He knew little English and hoped the man didn't ask him something he couldn't understand.

"That's right. Woman. Where?"

Gopher John shook his head vigorously and looked to his friends for confirmation, saying, "No woman. No woman." Bear Claw and Runs-in-the-Night shook their heads, too.

The rider swayed in the saddle as his horse stamped impatiently, but his aim never wavered. He studied each of them intently, as if searching their faces for a sign of recognition. Disappointment crossed his features, and he seemed to relax slightly—but only slightly. "How many more in your party?"

Gopher John understood "how many," but that was all.

The man swung his rifle around at each of them, then pointed toward the prairie. "How many braves?"

Bear Claw was the first to grasp the meaning of the question. He slapped his own chest and began to gesture to the others, but the sudden movement brought the hammer of the pistol back with an audible click. He froze, considered the rider's eyes, and very slowly and deliberately pointed to each brave, including the unconscious or dead Snow. Spreading his hands he said, "All. All braves." Then in Cree, in case there was a chance the man would understand: "We are the only ones. No woman."

The horseman obviously didn't understand the language, but he seemed to accept their word about being alone. He glanced quickly behind himself, over both shoulders. *A capable and cautious white warrior*, Gopher John thought. *White death. I am glad I don't have his woman.*

The man lowered his guns and rested his forearms on his thighs, but he kept the barrels trained in their direction. He looked at them thoughtfully for a moment. "I seek a fierce warrior. Black and white face. Black and white pony. He has my woman. I want her back."

"Red Wolf," Gopher John said immediately and with awe.

"Eh? What's that?"

"Red Wolf," he repeated and waved a hand in front of his face. "Black and white." He pointed at the buckskin. "Black and white. Crow warrior. Bad medicine. Kill Cree"—he slapped his chest at the word—"kill Blood, kill Blackfoot, kill Assiniboine. Kill white man, white wom—" Gopher John closed his mouth instantly.

The man's eyes narrowed, and his face flushed. "Yes, I know. He kills white women, too. I have seen his work." His eyes focused over Gopher John's shoulder for a moment, and the Cree wondered what he was seeing with such haunted eyes. The gray eyes eventually came back to him. "You say he's Crow?"

Gopher John nodded certainly. "Crow. Bad Crow."

On the ground at the buckskin's feet, Snow stirred painfully. His pudgy hand went to the back of his head, exploring tenderly, until he felt that something wasn't right in his surroundings. He brought his head around slowly, saw the horse and rider, and started to scramble away on his hands and knees. Bear Claw helped him up and made a sign for him to be calm. Snow looked from Bear Claw to the rider to Gopher John in confusion.

"Tell your friend I'm sorry I hurt him," the horseman said to Gopher John.

He understood and relayed the message in Cree.

"I leave now." The man uncocked his rifle and pushed it into its scabbard. His pistol he held on to but aimed away from them.

Gopher John held up a hand, pointed to the fire, and said, "Eat." He suddenly didn't want this man to go. Even if they were limited by language, he was sober. Gopher John was tired of talking to drunk Crees, and he had a feeling the man would have a very interesting story to tell if they could communicate well enough.

The big white man appeared tempted for a moment, but with a shake of his head repeated, "I leave now."

Runs-in-the-Night leaned over and picked up a chunk of dried beef. Slowly he went to the big horse and gestured to the saddlebags with a questioning look. The rider nodded, and Runs-in-the-Night placed the beef inside and stepped away, never taking his eyes from the white man.

An unmistakable look of gratitude came over the man's face as he nodded to them. Then he turned the horse and rode into the night.

The braves listened to the receding hoofbeats in silence. When they'd faded completely, Gopher John turned to Snow. "What happened out there? Were you asleep?"

Snow shook his head carefully to avoid pain. "I was wide awake, getting ready to come in. I never saw or heard a thing."

They all looked at each other with unspoken meaning. Snow was indeed fat, but his eyes and ears were better than any brave in the tribe.

"He could have killed me if he had wanted to," Snow added.

"He could have killed all of us," Gopher John stated with certainty.

"I am glad he was not after us," Runs-in-the-Night said with round eyes.

For once, Gopher John agreed with him.

# CHAPTER NINE

# Death

Though thoroughly exhausted, Stone slept fitfully. He resented the fact that he couldn't track at night. Trying to go to sleep, he tossed and turned in his blanket, *certain* that the Indians he pursued were making time against him. He knew they had camped the night before because he'd come across the site earlier in the day. Therefore, they would probably stop again this night, but that did not comfort him.

Finally falling asleep, the smallest of sounds awakened him: Buck's soft movements, a coyote's far-off howl, even the wind caressing the prairie grass. His first thought upon waking was that maybe the sun would be just beyond the horizon. Maybe the ebony sky in the east would be tinged with gray and blue, and he could rise and fix himself coffee. Every time he woke and found the horizon dotted with stars, he made himself go back to sleep again, fighting the demons of doubt. He knew he needed the rest, but he was also aware that realistically his body could go for days without sleep; Betsy might not last that long with the cutthroats that had kidnapped her. Sleep seemed to be a waste of time.

His attempt at night tracking had almost gotten four innocent Crees massacred. Somehow, he'd accidentally picked up their trail in the dark. He'd had all day to contemplate his actions of the previous night. The fury that had overcome him at the moment of discovering the camp was frightening. He'd been *sure* he'd found Betsy's kidnappers from the signs—a small band, a few head of cattle and horses—and with trembling fingers he'd loaded his Henry rifle. He was just thankful he'd knocked the guard unconscious instead of following his initial instinct to cut his throat silently.

Stone had experienced the baffling state of unleashed fury once before when working as a bounty hunter. A man named Cyrus Gurtz had gone berserk one night in Winnipeg and burned his own house down after a serious row with his wife. Mrs. Gurtz and their twin boys had been in the house at the time, and Cyrus was caught and arrested immediately.

After tricking the jailor one night, he'd escaped and Stone had been sent after him. When Stone caught up with him near Lake Manitoba, a curious, all-encompassing wrath had taken over. Stone had felt the trembling in his hands, and the distant pain of grinding his teeth together, but otherwise his every move seemed as if it were already planned out. He'd entered a state of fearlessness; a coming together of mind and body that required no conscious effort or direction. Cyrus Gurtz never heard Stone coming until he was right on him. Gurtz tried to pull a gun, just as Stone knew he would, but Stone had been ready.

Afterward, while returning the body to Winnipeg for burial, Stone found himself with feelings of regret. However, he'd always followed a code of predestiny. Deep inside, he knew it was a lazy man's answer for everything that happened, but his knowledge of God was limited, almost nonexistent, and he was content with his ideas. According to destiny, Cyrus Gurtz was meant to die violently for a disgusting crime; Stone was merely the delegate to deliver the justice. However, he'd thought of Gurtz many times in the four years since the incident— usually with an uneasy feeling of self-reproach for *not* feeling more guilty about his death.

Why his actions against the Crees hadn't resulted in instant death for them was beyond him. In a way, Stone was thankful for the detached state. Despite feeling out of control, he felt very much *in* control. It was as simple and as complicated as that.

When dawn finally painted the east a deep red, Stone rose, fixed coffee, and fed Buck some oats. His water supply was almost gone, but he would be crossing the South Saskatchewan River today if Red Wolf followed the same southeasterly course.

The trail was ridiculously easy to follow, and Stone spurred Buck into an energy-saving, easy gallop. He would much prefer an all-out run, but the Crows had at least a half-day's head start on him, probably more.

At midmorning, a covered wagon appeared to his left. He veered toward it, hoping for news of a sighting. A thin hope, he knew, since Red Wolf apparently didn't like leaving witnesses.

The wagon was tattered but rolled steadily on the flat plain. A deeply tanned man of about forty drove, with a chubby little girl sitting beside him. The man stopped the wagon warily and reached behind the seat, resting his hand on what Stone knew would be a gun. The man's eyes were light gray, almost identical to Stone's own. His face was strangely cadaverous, with high, prominent cheekbones and no chin to speak of. The little girl had a yellow ribbon lost in her naturally curly blond hair and considered Stone with an interested eye. He was probably a welcome distraction from the tedium of the drive across the barren prairie.

"Morning," Stone called.

"Good morning," the girl returned in a friendly tone, and her smile revealed two dimples. The man continued to stare with his hand behind the seat but said nothing.

"You folks settlers?" Stone addressed this to the man, but the girl answered again.

"Yes, sir. Are you lost?"

Stone smiled. "No, honey, I'm not lost." He turned to the man and asked him directly, "I was wondering if you'd run across any Indians?"

Still the man said nothing. On closer inspection, Stone noticed a diagonal scar that ran across his upper and lower lips. The man turned and glanced quickly in the back of the wagon and banged his hidden hand on the seat three times.

"My daddy doesn't talk."

"Well, what's your name, then?"

"Sally Gravette."

From the opening in the wagon behind the two, a woman's head emerged, then another older girl, then a boy. All at once, five people were staring at Stone with round eyes.

Stone touched his hat brim. "Ma'am. My name's Stone."

She smiled and said, "I'm Delia Gravette, and this is my husband Tenny." Her hair was short with streaks of gray already showing. She appeared younger than her husband by about ten years and had broad shoulders for a woman. "I heard your question, and no, we ain't seen any Indians. There some around?" She shifted her eyes around the area nervously, as if a screaming savage would rise from the ground at any moment.

"I don't mean to alarm you, Mrs. Gravette, but I'm on the trail of some pretty bad renegades. I think they're south of us and heading for the Cypress Hills, but I'd keep an eye out just in case."

"The Cypress Hills?"

"Yes, ma'am."

The family traded meaningful glances.

"Is something wrong?" Stone asked, noting the frowning faces.

Delia looked at Tenny, who nodded his head slightly. Delia said, "Some Indians were massacred there just the other day."

"Massacred?"

"Yep," she answered with a firm nod of her head. "We don't know much about it. We heard it when we stopped at a trading post near the Sand Hills. Fifty men, women, and children killed, they said."

Stone gazed at them, stunned. "How—what tribe, do you know?"

"The man didn't know. Just Indians."

"What happened?"

Delia shrugged her thick shoulders. "Word is, the ones that done the shootin' were Americans, up from Fort Benton, Montana. The Indians stole some horses, and the Americans caught up with 'em and started shootin'. That's all we know."

He wondered if Red Wolf was heading in that direction for revenge, or if he even knew about the killings. Whether he did or not, the Crow was definitely heading straight for the area. With an unpredictable man like Red Wolf in a volatile place like that, war could erupt. And as far as Stone knew, there was no police of any kind to stop a bloody warpath by the Crows.

Stone saw Tenny Gravette watching him intently, as if reading his thoughts. "Mr. Gravette, I have to go. Thank you for your information." Gravette nodded, his eyes betraying no thoughts. "Watch over your family," Stone added, and with the look that passed between the two men's identical gray eyes, Stone had the eerie feeling that Tenny Gravette knew exactly what he was talking about, and why he'd said it.

Stone turned Buck, but Delia called out, "Mr. Stone, do you know of a good place to settle in the Territory?"

Stone stopped the horse abruptly and waited a moment before turning his head. He did not look directly at her when he answered, "Up on the Red Deer River. Just keep heading in the direction you're going." And, as an afterthought, "Good soil and water."

Delia Gravette watched the handsome, but obviously tired, rider leave quickly without another word. She was sorry she'd asked. Delia had never seen such a haunted look on a man's face.

———

"Take two others and kill that man," Red Wolf ordered.

Spotted Hawk searched the empty prairie they'd just crossed. "What man, my brother?"

Red Wolf slowly turned his heavy gaze to him. "The woman's husband—Owl Dog." He inclined his head to the north, the very area Spotted Hawk had scanned. "Out there."

Spotted Hawk was bewildered. He glanced uncomfortably to the rest of the braves at the bottom of the natural hill, waiting to cross the Saskatchewan River. The cattle and horses were milling about impatiently, anxious to enter the water to drink and cool off. The white woman was sitting on her horse, staring at the other side of the river, expressionless.

Spotted Hawk again scrutinized the plains, squinting harder.

"Trust me," Red Wolf said, "he's out there."

Spotted Hawk saw *nothing*. Not a movement anywhere for miles. He knew his brother's eyesight was extraordinary, but he didn't know it was *this* good.

Red Wolf saw his hesitation and grew angry. He wasn't accustomed to his orders being questioned, much less ignored, even from his brother. "Maybe I should ask another to lead the party."

"No!" Spotted Hawk answered instantly. "I will lead."

"Today, sometime?" Red Wolf asked sarcastically.

Spotted Hawk nodded and started down the hill.

"Spotted Hawk?"

He turned, and Red Wolf looked into his eyes.

"This man is strong and quick. Do not underestimate him. Let the other two kill him, and stay back."

Spotted Hawk grinned. "Of course, brother."

Red Wolf knew the white man was as good as dead. Spotted Hawk was a good fighter, and he saw him select Long Feather and Bison to go with him, both capable warriors. Owl Dog would perish in the face of such fierce enemies. Still, Red Wolf had to admire the man. Most white men upon finding their dead would weep and mourn for days, long after the trail was cold. Then they would waste more time by contacting the authorities and waiting for a posse. But Owl Dog had almost caught up with them—*would* have caught up with them had he ridden through the night. The woman's warning had stayed in Red Wolf's mind, and when they'd come to the first hill, he'd searched and seen the tiny dot at the edge of his vision. He could just make out the buckskin horse Owl Dog rode.

*Maybe* I've *underestimated this man,* he thought suddenly. *I did not think he would live when I hit him with my club. He did, and then rode ten miles to protect his woman. I did not think he would give chase to us—nine seasoned warriors—and he has, nearly catching us.*

Red Wolf shifted on his feet, uncomfortable that he had perhaps made a miscalculation. He watched the braves cover the open fields swiftly, becoming smaller and smaller.

He turned to the woman, who was sitting quietly on the horse. Her lack of fear disturbed him; even now she observed the excitement with a detached attitude—almost as if she were merely biding her time, waiting for . . .

Red Wolf ran down the hill, seeing the shocked, upturned faces of his band staring at him. They began to glance around, looking for an enemy. Instead, Red Wolf ran directly to the woman and savagely pulled her off the horse.

Betsy still had her hands tied, with no way to break her fall. Fortunately she landed solidly on her side, her whole body absorbing the shock. She was winded, but nothing was broken. She looked up at Red Wolf in fear and surprise.

"Your husband—was he ever a horse soldier?"

"N—No!"

Red Wolf crouched down suddenly, his face only inches from hers. "Don't lie to me!" he hissed.

"No—never!" Betsy was confused at the sudden violence and strange questions. She struggled to catch her breath.

"Your friends—the ones that I killed one moon ago. Did soldiers come after that?"

Betsy's face darkened at the memory of her friends' murders. "No one came. No one." All at once she understood why he and Spotted Hawk had gone to the hill and talked about something they were seeing, and the subsequent excitement of Spotted Hawk and the other two leaving. Now she was being asked questions about her husband.

Hunter was out there. They'd seen him and gone to kill him. She closed her eyes tightly. *Dear God, please keep him safe! Dress him with your armor!*

Red Wolf, satisfied that she was telling the truth, walked slowly toward the north. He could still see his brother riding in the distance, just barely, but unaided by the height of the hill he couldn't see the white man. But he was out there.

And he was alone.

Red Wolf smiled.

Hunter Stone knew he was getting close to the Saskatchewan River. He stopped at a small offshoot and let Buck drink his fill.

He'd already begun to plan his move for when he caught up with the Crows. Charging in with guns blazing on eight or nine warriors would probably get him killed. The Crees he'd surprised were farmers, untrained in war, and were easily overcome. Experienced Crow braves on the warpath would be much more alert and deadly.

He could try to get ahead of them and pick them off one by one with his Henry. But in order to get close enough to fire effectively, he would have at least four or five Indians on top of him before he knew it.

A night attack would be best; or better yet, take as many of them as he could in one night, then bide his time and attack again two or three nights later, if he wasn't killed. And if they didn't kill Betsy in the raid.

Betsy was the wild card. Were she not involved, he wouldn't have to worry about repercussions. But her welfare had to be considered first, and he hadn't figured out how to get her in the clear before the trouble started.

*Maybe she's already dead* . . . .

The thought intruded brutally and he quickly put it away, refusing to consider the possibility. He had to *believe* she was still alive, and that Red Wolf had a plan to sell her.

Stone squatted upstream from Buck and filled his canteen. His knees popped with loud cracks in the still air. He stayed by the stream for a moment with his head down, painfully aware that he had gotten soft since his bounty hunter days. He couldn't remember the last time he'd ridden fourteen hours straight as he had the day before, but his muscles and spine reminded him of how long it had been.

Before mounting Buck he happened to glance over the saddle and see three riders, only blurs in the distance. He removed a pair of field glasses from its case on the saddle and focused on the Indians, riding hard directly toward him. There was no mistaking their intentions. Two of them brandished rifles, and all of them sported warpaint.

Stone glanced around him and decided that the best defensible area was exactly where he was standing. The small stream cut a four-foot-deep ditch through the flat plain, creating a natural barrier to hide behind. He unsheathed his Henry and led Buck across the water. The horse would stay behind the shelter with him; Stone didn't want to be left afoot if Buck were wounded or killed.

The Henry .44 held fifteen copper-jacketed rounds under the

twenty-four-inch barrel, and he cocked the lever, loading one into the breach. He raised the front sight and adjusted the range to a half mile, hoping to get lucky with a long-range shot. Even if he could manage to bring one of the horses down, it would give him some much-needed time.

He sighted along the iron barrel and picked one of the galloping riders coming ever closer. The Henry discharged with a great roar and a blast of smoke that the wind thankfully carried to his right. The rider kept coming. Stone didn't even know how close he'd gotten, or if the braves had heard the 216 grain ball whizzing past. For all he knew, it may have fallen short.

Jacking another round in the chamber, he drew a bead on the same rider and fired. He saw the Indian duck suddenly, so he knew his shot had been close. They were only two hundred yards away, and Stone lowered his sights. The next shot brought horse and rider down, but which one was hit he didn't know.

A cloud of dirt rose a few feet to his left, causing Buck to jerk away, but he didn't bolt. Stone ducked down behind the riverbank as a bullet whined over his head. Hoping they didn't have repeating rifles as he did, he raised up and fired off a wild shot that hit nothing. When he worked the lever too quickly, the cartridge jammed at the entrance to the breech. Cursing, he dropped down and fumbled with the bullet until it slid neatly in, then looked over the embankment for another shot. An arrow whirred by his head, missing him by inches, and his mind registered the fact that another flew toward Buck and buried itself in the saddle with a thud. Buck skittered away nervously while Stone aimed at a powerful-looking Indian with a line of red paint from his forehead to his chin. The Henry exploded, and Stone watched as the Crow was blown backward over the horse's back to lie unmoving on the prairie.

Stone had run out of time. If the gun hadn't jammed, he might have been able to take the other Indian, but with a loud drumming of hooves, the pony jumped into the cut, and Stone felt a body land on top of him. He managed to shrug the brave to the ground at the edge of the water with a heave of his shoulders. Taking the Henry's barrel into his hands, he rushed at the Indian and swung down at him, but the Crow rolled away with lightning speed. Stone took in the strong smell of the man, who was shorter than he, sporting the figure of a buffalo painted in black in the middle of his chest.

With his back now to the Indian, Stone ducked instinctively and heard the air above him cut with the *whoosh!* of a tomahawk swung forcefully at his head. He brought the Henry around in a sweeping half-circle and felt a satisfying thud when it connected with flesh and bone. The brave grunted painfully but still danced away from Stone's returning swing at him. He was bent sideways, favoring his right side, and Stone saw a flicker of alarm in his black eyes as Stone spun the stock of the gun back into his hands after the swing's momentum. When he'd half cocked the gun's lever, the Crow threw the tomahawk with an agonized look on his face from the strain to his broken ribs. The throw had no force and poor aim behind it, but the flat top of the tomahawk struck Stone on his left collarbone. The weight of the striking weapon was enough to send a searing bolt of pain through his shoulder, but not enough to prevent him from fully cocking the Henry. Incredibly, the Indian charged him unarmed, and when he was only two feet away, Stone fired. The big bullet hit the man dead center in the chest, throwing him backward, and through the powder smoke Stone saw the painted buffalo on the Indian's chest grow red with blood.

Stone turned away from the dead man, only then remembering the first brave he'd brought down in the distance. Stone saw him mounting his horse awkwardly, obviously wounded in either his left arm or shoulder. The bloody arm hung limp and useless. From the pony's back he stared at Stone for a few moments, then with a whoop he turned and headed back the way they had come. The second Indian he'd shot out of the saddle hadn't moved. The three eagle feathers he'd worn on his head blew softly in the breeze.

Stone was breathing heavily from the battle and trauma, and he noticed his hands were trembling. Unable to summon the will to give chase to the wounded Indian, he slumped down on the embankment with a groan. His shoulder was on fire now, and he knew without exploring the area that his collarbone was cracked or broken. He still held the Henry in his right hand and was glad that Sam Pairvent had talked him into buying it. He hated to think of what would have happened if he'd tried to take on three Crow braves with a single-shot musket.

The wounded brave was taking bad news back to Red Wolf, and Stone knew he had to get going. The sheer unpredictability of the man was frustrating, to say the least. Where was he heading? Why had he kidnapped Betsy, instead of killing her as he had Olivia Osbourne? What was he going to do with her? Stone shook his head. He'd asked himself the questions so many times, he was sick of them. There was only one way to find the answers, and that was to ask the man himself— *if I don't kill him first.*

Whistling to Buck, he rose and flexed his left arm and fingers. He found he could raise his arm above the level of his shoulder—a good sign that the bone was only cracked—but the act itself was excruciating.

He sheathed the Henry and pulled the arrow from the saddle. Without knowing why, he tucked the tomahawk under his bedroll before mounting painfully. He knew he didn't have time to bury the dead, and after passing the body of the Indian with the three feathers, he didn't look back.

————

Traditionally, when a Crow raiding party returned to their home after suffering a defeat, a lone messenger was sent to a prominent point near the villiage and signaled the news by firing a gun or waving a robe. The elders of the tribe would go out to meet the messenger, hear the full story, then return to lead the tribe in mourning. The warriors would remain in seclusion for ten days before setting out again to avenge the earlier losses.

Long Feather had no such messenger to send to Red Wolf and break the bad news. The thought terrified him. Red Wolf was so full of hate, Long Feather doubted that he felt affection toward anyone. Anyone, that is, except for his family, which consisted solely of Spotted Hawk. Long Feather had seriously considered not even *returning* to face Red Wolf's wrath—to ride as far away as possible, letting Red Wolf think all three of them had been killed. But facing the consequences of today would be ten times easier than a chance meeting between the two sometime in the future, especially if Red Wolf thought he had died gloriously for him. Long Feather didn't even want to *think* about that possibility, and the prospect of looking over his shoulder for the rest of his life didn't thrill him, either.

All this depended upon if he lived, and from the way his wound was bleeding, he wasn't sure that he would survive. The bullet had caught him at the joint where his arm met his shoulder, shattered it, and exited. After making sure the white man wasn't following him, Long Feather had stopped at a creek and applied mud to the wound. The mud eventually dried and flaked away, and he started bleeding again. He felt himself growing weaker by the minute, so that by the time he caught up with the band, he was bent over the pony's neck, holding on desperately.

He collapsed into helping arms, and then Red Wolf was standing over him. "What happened? Where is my brother?" Long Feather, despite feeling as if he would pass out or die any moment, noticed a strange look on Red Wolf's face. After his fevered brain sorted it out, he realized that for the first time since he had known Red Wolf, he was witnessing worry lines on the man's forehead.

"The white man—" Long Feather paused, grimacing, as a particularly nasty bolt of pain hit him. "The white man killed Spotted Hawk and Bison. I saw them fall with my own eyes, Great One."

Red Wolf blinked in genuine surprise, and Long Feather mentally noted another first. Red Wolf's eyes narrowed, and his lips drew into a tight line. His gaze shifted to the direction from which Long Feather had come, but when he brought his attention back to him, Red Wolf's nostrils were flared with barely controlled fury. Long Feather knew what was coming.

"If my brother is dead, why are you still living?"

Long Feather chose his words as carefully as he could, considering he was now seeing two of Red Wolf. "The white eyes had a long gun that holds many bullets. I could not get close to him, just as Spotted Hawk could not."

"And Bison?"

"Bison reached the man but was defeated." Long Feather saw Red Wolf draw his huge knife and knew he was dead. But Red Wolf merely stood over him, his large hand gripping the handle of the knife with white knuckles. Red Wolf studied the knife carefully, as if for the first time, even gently running a finger over the sharp blade. Long Feather could see that Red Wolf badly wanted to kill him, but something held him back. The rest of the braves stood by quietly. If Red Wolf chose to cut his throat, no one would dare interfere.

Red Wolf reached a decision. "I will not kill you today, Long Feather. Maybe tomorrow, if you do not die from your cowardly wound." He scanned the faces around him, his face a mask of inner pain and anger. "I will take my revenge on the white dog. But first he will suffer pain as I have this day."

He turned his penetrating glare on Betsy Stone.

# CHAPTER TEN

# Casualties

While Stone rode along, favoring his painful shoulder by keeping his left arm close to his body, a memory came to him that suddenly helped explain the steady jolts he was suffering.

When he was nine, his father, William, had taken him to a horse race. Matt Stone, his father's brother, announced to everyone that he had a stallion that sported a different stride from any other, and was the fastest horse alive. A neighbor disputed the fact, and a contest became inevitable.

Most of the county turned out for the event, since everyone had heard Matt's boasting, and Matt himself was strutting with pride and anticipation while people crowded around to see the stallion. Matt was surprised to find Hunter and his father present, since William and Matt Stone were never close and rarely talked. Hunter had asked his father about the distant relationship once, to which William had mumbled something about he and his brother "not seeing eye to eye on things." Hunter never found out what the rift was about, but that day the brothers greeted each other politely enough.

"What's so special about this horse, Matt?" William asked after they'd exchanged hellos.

Matt removed a fat cigar from his mouth to speak. "At one point when he runs, all four hooves are off the ground at the same time." This announcement was made with much pride.

"Why, Matt, *all* horses do that!" William exclaimed in shock.

"They do not! Prove it!"

"I don't have to prove it—everybody already *knows* it but you!"

"You watch and see, William!" Matt warned and marched off with his big cigar.

Hunter's father hadn't backed either horse that day. Matt's stallion had been edged out by a nose at the finish line, and his uncle had even argued about *that*. Hunter heard his father grunt with satisfaction immediately after the race and mutter something about "the old fool."

Hunter hadn't questioned his father's theory about horses that day because of William's dark mood. In fact, he'd never given it another thought until now as he rode along while nursing a cracked collarbone.

With painful regularity his shoulder was jolted rudely—a rhythmic pounding that could only be caused by all four of Buck's hooves thumping the ground at the same time. *So, my father was right all the time*, he thought with conviction. He'd held his arm in every position he could think of but there was no relief since his whole body was bouncing up and down. He could only grit his teeth and ride on.

Small hills rose ahead of him, and he knew they were the banks of the Saskatchewan. The Cypress Hills were now visible to him on the skyline—a welcome sight after the monotony of the flat prairie. His eyes followed the tracks of the raiding party and saw that they disappeared into a narrow pass ahead. He entered cautiously, his rifle held in one hand, searching for any sign of ambush. By now Red Wolf would be aware of Stone following, and there was no telling what the Indian would have in store.

Trees and bushes suddenly became plentiful, soaking up the river's nourishment. He passed around the last hill before the river, glad of escaping attack, but his relief was short-lived as his heart skipped a beat and then sank to his belly for the second time in two days. Amidst the greenery of the grass and shrubs, against the backdrop of the slow-moving Saskatchewan, a light blue color caught his eye at the river's edge.

Stone had seen the color countless times before, always before bedtime. It was Betsy's nightdress. As his stunned eyes took in more detail, to his horror he saw that it wasn't merely the garment beside the river—Betsy still wore it, face down and motionless.

This was the moment he'd dreaded; the sight he'd forced from his mind for two days and refused to think about. And in one awful lightning bolt of consciousness, he knew she was dead. Not sleeping. Not senseless. Drowned.

For a moment he could only stare in a numbed state of shock. Then the corners of his mouth turned down, his lower lip began to quiver, and his eyes filled up with hot tears. He slowly dismounted, never taking his eyes from the still form, and with dread like a rock in the middle of his stomach made his way to her side.

Stone took his wife in his arms and hugged her to his breast. He pushed the wet hair from her face and kissed her forehead. Even in death, she was beautiful. He saw a drop of moisture fall on her cheek and crazily wondered how it could rain out of a clear blue sky until he realized it was one of his tears.

Ignoring the searing pain in his shoulder, he picked her up and carried her to the shade of a spruce tree. He was weeping openly now as he sat down and rocked her to him. The front of his shirt and pants became wet from her drenched nightdress. He told her he was sorry over and over. At one point, he found himself trembling with anger, cursing the vicious Indian with oaths he'd never used before. When he heard himself raving against God and the heavens, he stopped abruptly, remembering that one of the last things Betsy had said to him was about forgiveness and love in the face of wrongdoings. He didn't stop because he forgave—but because of Betsy's love and respect for God, and even though she was beyond hearing him, it seemed blasphemous. He cursed his own gods of destiny, asking "Why?" again and again and again. Eventually his voice gave out from overuse and thirst, and for hours he merely held her.

Stone emerged from his trance sometime into the night. He wanted to stay there with her in his arms, crying his sorrow to her, but his tears would no longer come. He walked to Buck, who had been standing patiently for the whole day, and removed the bit so he could graze. Stone drained his canteen without pausing and replenished it at the river.

Hunter Stone buried his wife beneath the spruce tree that night. He had only a strong, crude tree limb for digging, but the ground was soft and he finished at dawn. He made a cross from tree limbs, too. When the task was finally over, he didn't know what to do, since he'd never prayed in his life. What came from his mouth was this: "God, you and I don't see eye to eye on a lot of things, but if what Betsy said was true, then we both love her. The only difference is, you have her now and I don't. That's one of the things we don't see eye to eye on— why was she taken from me? Why couldn't I have had her a while longer? Why couldn't You at least let me tell her goodbye?"

Stone shook his head and stared at the crude cross. After a few minutes of silence he went on, bitterness coating his voice, "I didn't think You'd answer. I never understood why Betsy would talk to You every day, because as far as I could see, *she* never got an answer either."

He lifted his head to stare at the morning sky. "Anyway—I'm going to find this . . . this . . . *animal* that killed her, and *I'll* see that justice is served. What did Betsy call it—the law of Moses? *That's* a man that I could understand. 'An eye for an eye.' It doesn't get much plainer than that. So You take care of my Betsy—" He paused and pointed to the heavens. "And don't You *dare* take that murdering scum before I get to him! *Do You hear me?*" he screamed and glared at the sky with wide-open, burning eyes.

With a last look at the grave, he whistled to Buck, replaced the bit and harness, and crossed the Saskatchewan River.

————

Red Wolf made camp alone in the Cypress Hills. His band had come across some Blackfeet who had told them of the massacre in the Assiniboine village. He wanted to find the men responsible, but his warriors were tired and homesick and only wished to see their families across the border. They had been raiding for months, and that was the only reason Red Wolf let them go. After determining a meeting place for one month in the future, the braves headed south with the cattle and horses.

Red Wolf despised the Assiniboine tribe, just as he did every Indian that wasn't Crow—the True People. But he fancied himself a warrior for *all* Indians, whether they wanted him or not, in the face of the white threat. He would try to find the white murderers and exact his revenge for the peaceful Assiniboine.

A heavy thunderstorm moved in, and Red Wolf sat beside his sputtering fire beneath a tree. He wore no shirt, despite the cold rain, and idly sharpened his knife while waiting for sleep. He required almost no sleep, but he had been traveling hard and fast for days and he felt a tiredness in his bones.

He thought of Owl Dog and knew that his pain was great. Red Wolf suffered no remorse over the murder of the man's woman. The law of the plains was clear—hurt your enemy in any way possible. Surely Owl Dog had understood that when he'd killed Bison and Spotted Hawk, the woman would die. Didn't he?

Red Wolf shook his head, the water falling from his drenched hair. It didn't matter if he understood or not; what's done was done. He wondered if the white man had turned to go home—to bury his dead and mourn his loss. Red Wolf thought so.

A flash of lightning cracked across the sky, and seeing something out of the corner of his eye, Red Wolf turned to his left. Chill bumps rose on his shoulders, and not from the cold rain.

The white man himself, Owl Dog, was staring at him from twenty feet away. His clothes were soaked, and Red Wolf noticed that the cold apparently didn't bother him, either, because he wore only a shirt with no coat. His hat was pulled down low, and his strange gray eyes pierced into Red Wolf's. Hatred and fury burned in them to a degree Red Wolf had never seen before, tempered with a strange calmness that seemed to say, "Here we are. Let's end this." Despite himself, Red Wolf felt a small chill of apprehension course through his body. In Owl Dog's hand was not the rifle he'd used to kill Red Wolf's brother, but a knife with a long, thick blade.

Red Wolf was shocked. *No one* had ever surprised him in his own camp, even with rain and thunder for cover. However, he recovered quickly and said, "We meet again."

Stone said nothing.

"I thought you would be home by now, nursing your heart wounds."

Stone only stared in an unnerving way, his fingers flexing over and over again on the knife's handle. Red Wolf saw that he had large, strong hands.

"It seems I have underestimated you again." Red Wolf hated admitting this, but he couldn't help feeling a certain respect for this white man. *He has the heart of a warrior. As I do.*

"You killed my wife," Stone uttered softly, his voice hoarse. Red Wolf could barely hear him over the pounding rain. "So now you will pay."

Red Wolf slowly stood, alarmed that his right foot was almost asleep. He felt like shaking it but didn't want Owl Dog to understand the problem and charge while he was handicapped. Thunder roared, and he waited until the echo died before saying, "You killed my brother. You shot him off his horse—like a coward."

Stone's eyes flickered with comprehension. "An eye for an eye," he said grimly, almost to himself.

Red Wolf had heard the saying before. "You understand. Maybe we are more alike than we thought."

Stone started shaking his head before the statement was out, as if he knew what Red Wolf was going to say. "We are nothing alike! You're a butcher of women, and today you will die."

The rain suddenly started to come down with such force that the two men could barely see each other. Red Wolf watched his opponent carefully, and the instant Stone moved, a blinding flash of lightning lit the clearing. Red Wolf had a glimpse of white teeth flashing, the knife blade glinting, and then the man was nearly upon him. Red Wolf charged the final few feet to meet him, his own knife clutched in his hand.

The battle was short, but horribly brutal. Animal-like growls punctuated each parry with the knives. Both men were slick with rain, making it almost impossible to obtain a firm grip. To make it worse, they were soon on the ground and rolling in mud. Each received slashes from the razor-sharp blades, and blood added to the slipperiness. At one point, Red Wolf's head crashed into Stone's cracked collarbone, making him gasp with pain. Red Wolf noticed, and with every chance he delivered a blow to the general area.

They rolled into the dying fire, and Red Wolf cried out as the coals seared his bare back. Stone attempted to keep him right in the middle of the embers but was thrown off. They jumped to their feet and stared at each other for a moment, both at the ready with their weapons. Their chests heaved with labored breathing, and Stone took advantage of the respite to move his knife to his left hand, wipe his right hand dry, and switch back. His shoulder felt completely broken now, and his left arm was useless. Red Wolf understood and attacked with even more ferocity.

Stone parried the blows as best he could, but Red Wolf finally overpowered him. As he fell to the ground again, Stone saw an opening and plunged his knife into Red Wolf's belly. At the same moment, he felt a deep burning in his own side—once, twice. His eyes were closed in agony, and he felt Red Wolf collapse to the ground beside him. Stone heard the Indian's groans of pain, strangely mixed with his own. The edges of his vision were darkening, and he struggled desperately to sit up, but his strength was drained completely. *Help me, God!* he found himself praying, and had the bitter thought that just hours before, he had been cursing Him. The pain was all but intolerable, and the weakness would not leave him. He lay on his back, waiting for a killing blow—if Red Wolf had the strength to deliver it.

Red Wolf, despite his own terrible wound, managed to crawl to Stone's side. He put the knife to Stone's throat, and a red line appeared beneath the blade where it slightly indented the skin. The rain had stopped, and the only sounds were moisture falling from the trees softly, and their own harsh, strained breathing. They stared at each other for a long moment with pain-filled eyes.

Stone was very close to passing out or dying, he didn't know which. "What are you waiting for?" he croaked.

To Stone's surprise, Red Wolf slowly gained his feet and limped to his blanket. With his knife, he cut the soaked cloth in two and wrapped one of the strips around his bleeding middle. Then he went to Stone and did the same. "What—why are you doing this?" Stone gasped. Whatever his intentions, Red Wolf was none too gentle with his movements and Stone couldn't help crying out.

Red Wolf let him fall to his back again and gazed deeply into his eyes. "You may die from your wounds tonight. And you may not. That is left to the Great Spirit." He paused and wiped the sweat from his eyes. "Crow warriors are judged by the courage of their enemies. If you live, it will only add to my power. If you die, I will find another to take your place."

He turned to leave, but after a few steps he faced Stone again. "What is your name?"

As if from a dream, Stone whispered, "Hunter Stone."

Red Wolf considered this and nodded slowly. "A strong name." A spasm of pain doubled him over momentarily. When he raised himself up, his mouth was twisted. "If I see you again, Hunter Stone, I will kill you and be done with it."

The Indian vanished from Stone's line of sight.

After staring at the cloudy night sky for a moment, Stone succumbed to a warm and beckoning place where there was no pain.

# AFTER-SILENCE ON THE SHORE

*It is not in the storm*
*nor in the strife*
*We feel benumbed,*
*and wish to be no more,*
*But in the after-silence*
*on the shore,*
*When all is lost,*
*except a little life.*

Lord Byron

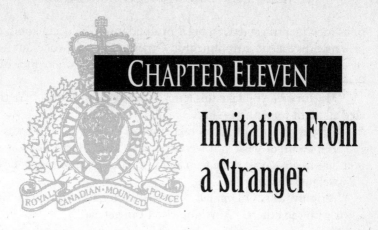

# CHAPTER ELEVEN

# Invitation From a Stranger

Reena O'Donnell was furious.

Her light blue eyes flashed against the background of raven black hair that framed her delicate features. "Those murderers are still *there*, Mr. Farwell! The nerve of that!"

Abel Farwell nodded and tried to look calm, though he was flustered by the show of temper from so beautiful a woman. *And a missionary, too!* he thought wonderingly. The first time he'd seen her stroll into his trading post, he'd nearly dropped the bag of flour he'd been carrying. Then he'd glanced around quickly to see if his wife had seen his jaw drop. Luckily, she'd been in the back washing clothes, as she was today.

"Miss O'Donnell, what can we do? Yes, they killed all those Indians, but ain't no law here to arrest 'em. None!" He glanced at the missionary's ever-present companion, Chief Lone Elk. Farwell had never heard the man say a word, and he didn't look as if he would speak now.

"I know, I know," Reena said with exasperation. "What I detest is the way they just *sit* there after what they've done! They don't even feel as if they have to escape because they know they won't be arrested. Meanwhile, the people they've *destroyed* are living in the hills like animals, afraid of their own shadows!" With only a slight pause, she shifted the subject. "Have our letters been mailed yet?"

"Ma'am, I told you they only pick up mail twice a month here. They're due here any day now—*if* they keep the schedule."

Reena drew an envelope from her bag. "Well, here's another one. I had every surviving Indian in the tribe make his mark on it."

Farwell's face softened. "Miss O'Donnell, it's a good idea for all of us to write protest letters, but I'm afraid it won't do any good. It'll take months for the government in Ottawa to get someone out here. By then those varmints will be over the border, back where they came from, I hope!"

"Mr. Farwell, you take this letter," Reena commanded. "We traveled all night to get here—in the rain."

"Oh yes, ma'am, I'll surely take it. What I was tryin' to say was—"

"I'm aware of what you were trying to say!" Reena knew it was pointless to get angry at the man and with effort calmed herself down. "Please, just mail it."

"Alrighty, Miss O'Donnell." Farwell took the letter and put it in a box with the others. "Anything else I can getcha?"

"Some cornmeal, please. And salt." Reena sighed deeply, as frustrated as she'd ever been in her twenty-one years. The fifteen wolf hunters from Fort Benton, Montana, had come to the area tracking horse thieves. Not all of the hunters were Americans—French and English Canadians were included also. The band of horse thieves they were after were Crees, but like most white men they didn't really know or care about different tribes. As she'd heard a grizzled trapper say once outside the trading post, "A dirty, stealing Injun was a dirty, stealing Injun."

The hunters had broken out the whiskey, even giving some to the Assiniboines. Before long drunkenness ruled, and the hunters reasoned that the Indians right in front of them were extremely shootable and easier to track than the swift Crees. So they'd opened fire on a village of two hundred innocent Assiniboine Indians.

Reena closed her eyes tightly. The memory would never leave her—men, women, and children running and screaming, some of them falling to the ground to never move again. . . .

"Here you go," Farwell chirped, setting the supplies on the counter. Without a word, Lone Elk lifted the heavy bags easily and went to stow them in the wagon.

Farwell studied Reena's face intently for a moment, knowing this would probably be the last time he would see her for a while. He kept looking for a flaw in her features—something that would confirm the fact that she was human, and not an angel from heaven. He discovered that if he had to pick something out, just *had* to, he would say that her nose was a bit too narrow and sharp. But at the same time it complimented her high cheekbones and oval face.

Farwell sighed deeply. *Nope, I'm done lookin' for flaws. I'm just gonna enjoy the sight from now on. And one of these days I'm gonna ask her what she's doin' out here in the middle of nowhere with a bunch of Injuns. She oughta be on stage somewhere.*

" . . . doing?" Reena was saying.

"Hmmm? What was that?"

"I asked how Mrs. Farwell was doing."

Farwell knew he looked guilty even as he spoke, but Reena showed no sign of reading his thoughts about her. "She's fine, Miss O'Don-nell—doin' just fine. Thank you for askin'." He shot a quick glance over his shoulder to see if the lady in question just happened to be standing behind him.

"I'm glad," Reena smiled, trying to make up for the hard time she'd given him. He seemed to be a good man, even though he liked to stare a lot. "It's got to be hard out here for her, don't you think?"

"Oh, I'm sure it is," Farwell agreed. *And just like that, here's my chance!* "Um—if you don't mind my askin', ma'am . . . uh . . . how did you come to be out here all by yourself?" He held up a hand quickly. "If it's none of my affair, why you just sing out! I ain't a nosy man. It's just that we've never really *talked*, if you know what I mean, and—" Reena smiled, and Abel Farwell felt as if he would melt.

"It's all right, Mr. Farwell, it's really simple. I was born and raised in Chicago. My father's a banker, and the Lord just chose me to come to these people."

"Just like that, huh?" Farwell asked expansively, leaning his elbows on the counter to get closer to her. *Skin as smooth as glass*, he thought.

"Hello, Reena!" Mary Farwell crowed as she appeared from the back washroom. She was a tall, thin woman with iron gray hair and a determined mouth.

"Mrs. Farwell."

"Oh, hello, dear," Farwell exclaimed, jerking upright and nerv-ously tapping his fingers on the counter.

"What are *you* looking so guilty about, Abel?" Mrs. Farwell asked icily. She stood six inches taller than her husband and invariably stared down her nose at him.

Reena glanced out the door to see Lone Elk sitting patiently in the wagon. She knew they needed to get back, but once in a great while— she felt with a pang of guilt—she wanted to have some conversation with white people. Lone Elk could speak English, but to talk to someone with the same culture as hers was something she'd been longing for. Besides, since the massacre, small talk was lacking in the Assiniboine tribe.

To busy himself and avoid his wife's accusing eyes, Farwell began rummaging through a small wooden box containing the receipts for the month. "Miss Reena was just telling me how she came to be here," and he finished explaining her story.

"You seem so *young* to be out there all by yourself," Mrs. Farwell commented. "How did your parents feel about your decision?"

"My mother was very supportive, and my father—wasn't." Reena stole a glance outside again and saw that it was almost fully light now. "Listen, I've really got to get back. Maybe we can talk again sometime when things aren't so—confused."

"I'd like that," Abel said instantly, then endured another heated glance from his wife.

"Goodbye," Reena smiled.

As soon as the door was closed, Mrs. Farwell commented, "A *very* pretty young woman, wouldn't you say, Abel?"

Farwell suddenly had an urge to adjust his apron. "Mmmm? Oh yeah, I guess so. Hadn't really noticed myself."

Mary Farwell reached out and tweaked his ear, then marched back to the washroom.

"Owww! What was that for, Mary?"

———

Reena listened to the old buckboard creak and groan as they rode back to the camp, mentally checking off her various duties for the near future. Strong Woman was only a week or two away from having her baby. Though the women of the tribe were able to deliver, Reena always liked to be there to assist during childbirths.

Star Light, a boy of eight, had been showing more and more interest in the teachings of Jesus Christ—before he'd seen his parents gunned down by bullets. He hadn't uttered a word since.

A year had passed since Reena had first come to the Indians. After a very awkward and uncomfortable beginning, she'd finally settled in to the everyday life of the Assiniboine and been accepted by the people. The language problem had been rectified rather easily; the sign language the Indians used was as practical as it was simple and easy to remember. Gray Dawn, Lone Elk's wife, gave Reena lessons every day until she was comfortable to communicate with the others without an interpreter. From there, the problem arose for Reena of reading the Bible in English, converting it to Sioux in her mind, and telling the Indians what it meant both verbally and in sign.

Reena found that she was *not* a preacher, preferring to talk one on one with them, or with very small groups. The tribe's medicine man had died shortly before she'd arrived, and this had paved the way for the people to be more open minded when they heard her message about God. After Lone Elk and Gray Dawn had accepted Jesus, nearly the whole tribe had followed, until there were very few left clinging to the old ways.

"Please have mercy on Star Light, Lord," Reena murmured. She realized she'd spoken out loud and glanced at Lone Elk. He acted as if he hadn't heard, but Reena knew he was growing accustomed to her impulsive, heartfelt prayers. She was grateful for the man's company. He rarely spoke, but when he did have something to say, it was usually important.

"Lone Elk, what can we do to help Star Light?" Reena asked, watching him closely. She thought he was about forty, but many times she'd been wrong when guessing the Indians' ages. He had a small head and wore the headdress she'd seen in her vision so long ago: golden eagle tail feathers dyed red, tipped with yellow-tinted horsehair. She'd learned since that red symbolized spiritual energy and power to the Indians.

He blinked and thought on the question. Lone Elk rarely gave hasty answers. "We pray for him—like you just did."

Reena waited for him to continue, but he said nothing more. Lone Elk epitomized the view most white men had of Indians: stoic, deadly serious, and solemn. Reena had found out that he was in the minority rather than the majority. The pranks and playfulness of the Assiniboines were very real, and Reena had found herself the butt of a few jokes.

One other Indian in the tribe had Lone Elk's strong characteristics. "What about Standing Bear? Are you going to let him go get himself killed by trying to revenge that day?"

Lone Elk paused even longer. "Standing Bear is no longer a boy and will do what his heart tells him to."

"And you'll stand by and let him go to a sure death—and even while he's dying, he may be bringing more killing to your people." Reena formed this as a statement instead of a question.

Reena waited for an answer, then heard the longest reply he'd ever given her. "My people are trying to follow the Christian way. But they are Assiniboine, as were their fathers, and their fathers' fathers. They try to fit the old ways in the Christian ways, but it is hard for them. Standing Bear has had a vision of revenge, and his heart is heavy for the dead. Visions are very important to the Assiniboine. Very important. If I tell him to ignore his vision, the people might turn against me, and God."

He was right, and Reena knew it. One fact she hadn't considered when making her decision to witness to the Indian nation was the frustration of dealing with a completely different culture. Old habits die hard, especially with a race of people that depended on tradition as no other. They were accustomed to relying heavily on the messages they received in visions and dreams. They practically worshiped nature, and Reena had been hard put to explain that the physical things of the world were not to be worshiped, but rather the Creator of them. Their belief in the "Great Spirit" had paved the way for her to explain the omniscience of the one Almighty God.

Their wagon was passing through the valley that split the western-most hills from the center. The rise was steep on their right, all the way to conglomerate cliffs that stood over the valley. Reena scanned the deep woods casually, her eye catching an out-of-place color through the white spruce and aspens halfway up the rise. "Stop, Lone Elk! Look, it's a deer!"

Lone Elk stopped the wagon and peered after Reena's pointing finger.

"Quick, get your musket!" Reena said excitedly, but without waiting turned herself and began fumbling for the heavy gun in the bed of the wagon. For an instant, it flashed through her mind that only one year before, she would have been appalled to suggest killing something so beautiful. But she'd quickly learned that the Assiniboine lived and survived off the land and its animals. Fresh meat was always welcome and rarely presented itself by chance.

Lone Elk was still examining the sight, and without looking he put his hand behind him and stayed Reena's groping fingers. "That is not a deer," he stated softly. "It is a horse."

"A horse. . . ?" Reena narrowed her eyes and studied the splash of brown color more closely. The animal was fidgeting about nervously, and when it pranced into a natural alley through the trees, she saw a saddled buckskin. "What's the matter with him? He acts as if he's been there a long time and he's trying to break loose. Do you think he's a hunter's horse, and something happened to the man?"

Lone Elk reached back and withdrew his rifle and canteen. "Or something is stalking him. Bear, maybe." He jumped down from the wagon. "Stay here."

Without hesitation Reena clambered down from her side of the wagon. "With a bear around? I think I'll go where the gun goes."

He didn't respond, and Reena found herself struggling to keep up with the Indian's forceful stride. The steep slope was a problem for her leather-soled boots, and the trees had shed many leaves that carpeted the ground and caused her to slip more than once.

Lone Elk, steady and sure, was inspecting the area around the nervous horse by the time Reena caught up with him. Placing her hand on the buckskin's neck, she spoke soothing words to calm the animal. The whites of his eyes shone as he pranced and tried to adjust to strangers being so close. He was well-groomed and obviously cared for, which made Reena wonder why the owner had abandoned him. A sense of foreboding came over her.

"He has been here all night," Lone Elk stated, straightening from his kneeling position. He took the cap off of his canteen and poured water in his hand, offering it to the horse. The buckskin drank greedily, and Lone Elk repeated the gesture over and over while his eyes searched for the owner's tracks.

"He's a splendid horse," Reena murmured, still stroking the animal. "What do you think—?"

But the chief was walking to the east before she could finish her question.

"Wait a minute, Lone Elk! Where are you going? What about the horse?"

"Leave him," he called over his shoulder, never breaking stride.

With an uncertain glance at the horse, Reena again set off to follow the Indian, this time holding on to trees as she made her way. After a short time, they came upon a small clearing, and both stood stunned for a moment. The remains of a fire was visible in one corner, with the body of a man close by.

Reena put a hand to her mouth. "Oh no. . . !" she breathed.

Lone Elk rushed to the man, with Reena at his heels. He was a white man, and at first Reena thought that he had to be dead. His face was chalky white, but when she put a hand on his face, she discovered that he was burning with fever.

*Still alive*, she thought. *Thank God!* His clothes were damp from the previous night's rain, but his tattered shirt was patchy with darkened stains too numerous to count. An old worn Indian blanket was wrapped around his middle. "This must have been quite a battle," she observed grimly.

Lone Elk had lifted the dirty blanket and was inspecting a large stain in the rib area. He carefully moved the stiffened shirt fabric aside, and Reena saw two puckered, gory wounds.

"Stabbed with knife," Lone Elk said casually. He glanced around the woods suddenly, as if expecting to find an assailant bearing down on them, waving a bloody knife.

Reena leaned close to the man, smelling sweat and smoke. Stroking and patting his face, she whispered, "Can you hear me? Hello?" His breathing was very shallow, almost imperceptible. A fine glaze of sweat covered his face, and she gently pushed his hair back from his forehead.

Without opening his eyes, the man whispered very clearly, "Betsy?"

"Yes?" Reena said immediately, leaning even closer. "I mean, no, I'm not Betsy. My name is Reena. I'm here to help you. Can you hear me?"

He mumbled something unintelligible and moaned softly.

"What can we do?" she asked Lone Elk desperately, but he was already at work. He'd rolled some grass and mud together and was applying the coarse mixture to the wounds.

"Take him with us," he shrugged, as if the answer was obvious.

"But . . . what if he dies when we move him?"

Lone Elk looked at her. "He will die if we do not."

Reena watched him finish with the mud application and was abruptly aware of how *big* the man was—well over six feet, and probably two hundred pounds.

"How do we—?" she started to ask, but Lone Elk had already slipped his hands under the man and lifted him with a grunt. The stranger made no sound. "He's too heavy to carry that far! What—"

"Get the horse," Lone Elk grunted through tight lips as he started walking heavily.

Reena watched in amazement as the slight-looking Indian chief carried the big man. With no support, the stranger's head lolled back awkwardly. Lone Elk stumbled but kept his feet with a grunt, and the misstep snapped Reena into action.

She ran by the struggling Indian, untied the horse, and rushed back to meet Lone Elk. With groans of effort they managed to lift the stranger over the saddle onto his belly. The man cried out with pain, and while Lone Elk led the horse, Reena walked beside the man's head, helplessly trying to reassure him, not even knowing if he heard her.

He moaned again as they moved him to the wagon bed, and Reena saw that despite the quickly applied mud, the wounds were oozing blood. After trying to cover the wounds again, she found a knife, ripped wide strips from the hem of her dress, then pressed the rags against the mass of blood and mud.

For a moment she thought she would throw up. She had seen many horrible bullet wounds after the massacre, but there was something about the ragged wounds of a knife that were different—more *open* somehow. The nauseous feeling passed, leaving her gasping.

The man mumbled something else, his face twisted in pain.

Reena soaked a cloth with water and tenderly wiped his face. When she finished, she took one of his rough, dirty hands in both of hers.

Feeling completely helpless, she closed her eyes and began to pray. "Father, please help me comfort this man. I don't know who he is, or why you've put him in my life, but he's in terrible pain. You are the Great Comforter—please work through me to help him."

She continued to pray for a while, and gradually the anxiety left her. To her surprise, she felt a slight tightening of the stranger's hand. When she opened her eyes, she found him staring at her with direct gray eyes. The whites were bloodshot, but there was no mistaking that he could see her face.

"Betsy," he whispered again, and a smile touched his full lips. "You're alive."

Reena opened her mouth for another denial, but at the last moment decided against it. She gripped his hand harder and leaned forward smiling.

"Don't you ever stop praying for me?"

Reena continued to smile at him, wishing desperately for an inspiration. *It must be his wife. What would she say at this moment?*

"Thought you were dead," he continued, the words beginning to slur and run together. "Thought I was too late."

"You need to rest now," Reena said softly. *What kind of horrors has this poor man been through?*

"Wanna go gaze at the moon?" He closed his eyes, still smiling.

Reena hesitated, not sure whether he was waiting for an answer or had passed out. She glanced at Lone Elk, who had turned to listen when the white man had started talking. His face was impassive, as usual.

" 'member that, Betsy?" the man asked, a bit more insistently. He opened his eyes and stared straight into Reena's. "Do you remember?"

"Yes," Reena whispered and nodded.

"Do ya wanna go again? Now?" He lifted his head a bit, and the gray eyes were pleading.

Reena leaned over and gently laid his head back down, stroking his face. "I'd love to go gaze at the moon with you."

He smiled again, and the gray eyes closed.

*Whoever you are*, Reena thought.

# Chapter Twelve

# Prayers for the Heart

For two days Reena's patient lingered near death. He had lost a lot of blood, and his body had been near exhaustion when he was wounded, which worsened his condition. When he woke, which was seldom, his words were unintelligible and his manner wild.

Reena stayed by his side, changing the dressing and nursing his many cuts. She had no medical training and would have never known that his collarbone was broken if it had not been for Lone Elk. As he and another man were undressing and bathing Stone, Lone Elk saw the odd protrusion and discoloration. He set the bone and wrapped the right shoulder and arm in bandages.

"I'm afraid he's dying," Reena said to Gray Dawn.

"His spirit is weak," she agreed. She was a short, stout woman, very strong, with long hair flowing to her waist. Strands of gray had just started to appear, but her whole being gave off the impression of youthfulness and vitality. Her squarish face remained unlined despite her thirty-eight years.

"We don't even know his *name*!" Reena expressed in frustration, dark eyebrows knitted. She spoke to Gray Dawn without taking her eyes off the tall, sleeping man.

"His fever will break, or it will not," Gray Dawn said calmly. She shrugged her thick shoulders. "His breathing will get better, or it will not."

"The wound must have punctured a lung. That's why his breathing is so labored," Reena said.

Gray Dawn shrugged again as if to say: *You can call it whatever your white medicine calls it. I say the man cannot breathe.*

Suddenly the man's eyes popped open and he tried to raise himself to a sitting position. "Red Wolf! Red Wolf!" His voice was harsh and gutteral with fury, and his eyes were locked on a spot across the tent as if Red Wolf were only a few feet away. The two women barely caught him as he fell back on the blankets, and the air exploded from his mouth in a coughing fit.

Reena lifted a soaking cloth from the bowl of water beside him and wiped his face, soothing him back into unconsciousness. His breath rattled alarmingly, the worst Reena had heard yet.

Gray Dawn was looking not at the man, but at Reena. She felt the need to comfort Reena, for the girl had barely left the man's bedside since she and Lone Elk had brought him back to the villiage. The tribe—especially Standing Bear—had been adamantly against letting them bring a white man into the villiage. Standing Bear and Lone Elk had argued for a few minutes before Standing Bear had acceded to the chief's wishes. Nevertheless, he had cast a dark glance at the figure of Hunter Stone as they'd carried him into Reena's tepee.

Gray Dawn somehow knew that as Reena nursed the man, her friend had taken upon herself the responsibility for his healing. If the man died, Reena would take it personally. Gray Dawn didn't fully understand this; she had never nursed a wounded brave from outside her tribe. *Maybe the white woman is lonely for her people.* The thought struck Gray Dawn with surprising clarity.

Putting her hand on Reena's, she said quietly, "His spirit cries to live. But his body does not."

"I'm not so sure," Reena said thoughtfully.

"What?"

Reena sighed and watched the man's laboring chest rise and fall erratically. "He's talked a lot, Gray Dawn. Most of it makes no sense, but some of it does. He keeps mentioning Betsy, who I believe was his wife. He rants about someone named Red Wolf, as you just saw, but sometimes he says the name in something like awe or fear. I haven't figured out who Buck is, or Osbourne."

Gray Dawn waited, for even though Reena had stopped speaking, she sensed that the girl wasn't finished.

Reena studied her hands, then looked at Gray Dawn with haunted blue eyes. "I think Red Wolf killed Betsy, and I think this man believes it was somehow his fault."

Gray Dawn glanced at the man for a moment, lost in thought.

"I think he wants to die—to atone for his failure to save his wife—and there's nothing I can do to stop him."

The older woman forced a smile. "Part of what you say is true, little one."

Reena nodded solemnly, then looked up at Gray Dawn quickly when she realized what she'd said. "Part?"

"There is nothing you can do to stop a man when he wants to die. I learned that before you came to us."

Reena nodded again but was puzzled by the strange gleam in Gray Dawn's eyes.

"If you remember, Lone Elk was just as this man at one time. Not hurt like this," she said, smiling and placing one of her rough, work-hardened hands on Stone's wounded side. Her hand then moved to his bare chest. "Wounded here—in his heart."

Gray Dawn had been sitting on her heels, but now she sat down on the blanket very close to Reena. "We never talked about how it was before you came. Lone Elk loved the white man's whiskey. He traded the most beautiful furs you have ever *seen* for the whiskey. He would drink it and become someone else—not the man you see now. A man who was not wise, who would fight with his braves over silly things— most of all the whiskey. A man who would beat his wife and then go to other women."

Reena, embarrassed for her, studied a drawing of a buffalo hunt on the tepee wall.

"No, it is all right now, Reena," Gray Dawn smiled. "One night, Lone Elk went to the post to buy whiskey, alone. Some white men were there and beat him badly and stole his furs. He made it back here and could not move for two suns. On the third day, he told me that he had failed his people and me, and only wanted to die. I begged with him not to die, but he became even weaker. That is when you came. After you told me what you had planned for our people, to lead us to the God that heals hearts, I told him of you when he woke. He said, 'I will see this white woman, for my heart is dead.'"

"I remember that day. . . ." Reena whispered.

"And when I brought you to him, you looked as if you knew each other," Gray Dawn continued. "You prayed for him and he accepted God into his dead heart." She looked down at the stranger sadly. "This man has a dead heart, too."

"But . . . I can't *talk* to him! He can't *hear* about God's love."

"How do you know what this man hears and does not hear? He might be listening to us right now."

Reena considered the slack face of the stranger. His eyelids were partly open, and the whites of his eyes appeared as two half moons. If she hadn't heard the raspy breathing coming from his mouth, she would have sworn he was dead. *How could he possibly hear us? If he can, then . . .*

"Would you pray for him with me, Gray Dawn?"

"Yes."

Reena instinctively laid a hand on Stone's arm and prayed as fervently as she had ever done. She prayed for God to show the man His love and give him the will to live; to heal his broken body, but especially to heal his heart and mind of his burdens.

"Finally, Father, let him forgive himself as you forgive—with all-encompassing mercy and compassion. Instill in him a forgiveness for this Red Wolf, whoever he is, and show him your way of grace. Thank you for what you are going to do. Amen."

When Reena looked up, the stranger was staring at her. She couldn't tell if he was seeing her or not—his gray eyes seemed unfocused, but when she leaned forward they appeared centered.

"Hello," she said softly. "Are you awake?"

He blinked but said nothing.

Reena wiped his face with the cloth. "Can you talk? Tell us your name? I feel silly calling you 'that man' over and over again."

No response.

Reena smiled and leaned even closer. "It's all right. You don't have to talk. Just let God wrap you in His arms and rock you back to sleep. You need it."

He mumbled something that she couldn't understand, and then his eyes closed.

---

Reena woke to the sound of activity in the village. She was momentarily disoriented, but the sliver of light through her tepee flap provided enough illumination to notice she'd fallen asleep a few feet from the stranger.

Rubbing her gritty, tired eyes, she started when a small Indian girl with dimples and lively brown eyes stuck her head inside and called excitedly, "Come, Miss Reena! Come outside!" Then the moon face vanished as quickly as it had appeared.

Reena checked her patient, found he was in a deep sleep, and smoothed her worn brown blouse as best she could. She hadn't intended to sleep in her clothes; she couldn't even remember *falling* asleep.

Running her fingers through her thick black hair, she stepped outside into a new day. The sun was still behind the hills, and she shivered in the cool air. She hurried back inside and retrieved the buffalo shawl that Strong Woman had made for her before the last winter. It had kept Reena warm on many chilly mornings.

The camp was coming to life quickly, with men, women, and children all emerging from their tepees in various stages of dress, eyes round with fear at the alarm. The people on the other side of Reena began to point to a path down the mountain that she couldn't see from where she stood. Falling in step with the throng moving in that direction, she saw two riders and four horses entering the camp. They were white men, and Reena saw more than a few guns gripped in the brown hands of the Assiniboines.

Reena went to stand beside Lone Elk and Standing Bear, who were both holding weapons. Other braves gathered behind them, with the women and children staying close to the tepees in case they had to start running if any shooting started.

The two men were as different as night and day. The one riding in front was dressed in a spotless white shirt with a heavy black coat, tight riding trousers with suspenders, and shiny black calf-length boots. He wore a black beaver hat, and below it his face was narrow and open, with thin lips and a long, straight nose. Brown eyes surveyed the gathered party in front of him with a casual air.

"Good morning!" he called. "And a beautiful one it is, hey?—very nearly, but not quite as beautiful as you, m'lady." He swept off his hat and bowed in the saddle. The proper, crisp English accent was unmistakable. "My name is Jaye Eliot Vickersham, and this"—he waved a hand toward the other man, who had stopped his horse slightly behind—"this is Del Dekko, my assistant."

Dekko leaned over and spat a brown stream of tobacco juice. "Ain't no *assistant*!" he hissed. "Wish you'd stop callin' me that. Mornin', ma'am." He touched his hat with an instant smile that revealed tobacco-stained teeth. Del Dekko was everything Vickersham wasn't. He looked to Reena as if he hadn't had a bath in weeks, whereas Vickersham would be able to attend the queen's ball. Dekko sported a worn, sweat-stained outfit of heavy denim. Reena thought it once might have been dark blue, but she couldn't be sure. A scraggly, graying beard covered most of his face, nearly all the way up to his bulging eyes. She peered more closely and saw that one of those eyes was trained on her, while the other wandered off to her left. She glanced away quickly, hoping she hadn't offended him by staring.

"My name is Lone Elk, and these are my people."

"Very glad to make your acquaintance, Chief Lone Elk," Vickersham replied. "And, m'lady, you are—?"

"Reena O'Donnell."

"Miss—Mrs.?"—Reena shook her head at the latter—"*Miss* O'Donnell, you are a welcome sight in a savage land."

"These people are more civilized than many Anglos I've known, Mr. Vickersham."

"No, no, please, you misunderstand me! I'm from England, as I'd wager you've guessed, and this country fascinates and intrigues me as nothing I've ever had the pleasure to see! I was merely trying to compliment your beauty, not cause offense to you or these people. Can you forgive me? And you, too, Lone Elk?"

Reena and Lone Elk exchanged glances. "Yes, we forgive you, Mr. Vickersham," Reena said with a slight smile.

"Thank you ever so much." He put a finger to a pencil-thin mustache and stroked it thoughtfully. "O'Donnell, O'Donnell . . . that name sounds familiar. I once met an O'Donnell, didn't I, Del?"

Dekko rolled his eyes and grabbed at the pockets of his grubby shirt in exaggerated fashion. "Well, let me just find my list I keep handy of all the people you've met—"

Vickersham snapped his fingers and said, "Faron! Faron O'Donnell—do you happen to know him?"

"Know him!" Reena exclaimed. "He's my uncle!"

"You don't say! Jolly old chap he was—met him in the Wood Mountains. Had an interesting view of English history—claimed we were a bunch of land-grabbing wogs that had no business walking around on two feet. 'Lower than a snake's belly,' I believe were his exact words. Nearly shot the man over that."

"Shot him!" Reena blinked.

"Oh, but I didn't, you see, and I'm glad. We spent a delightful evening with him, and he cooked the best venison I'd ever tasted. Anyway, that night—"

"This is very interesting, Mr. Vickersham," Reena interrupted, after noticing Lone Elk shifting his feet impatiently. "What exactly is your business?"

Vickersham studied her for a moment, then said, "I apologize again, Miss O'Donnell. I'm rambling, aren't I?"

From Dekko came an exaggerated sigh and sharp glance at Vickersham. "Gettin' to the point, ma'am, which seems to elude us—listen to that, Vic, you done got me usin' them fancy words!" He scowled at Vickersham and continued, "We're goin' after them bushwhackers that killed all them Injuns, and we was wonderin' if you might know where they went."

Reena was stunned. "Are you . . . the law?"

"Not exactly, ma'am."

"What does 'not exactly' mean?"

Dekko and Vickersham exchanged glances. Dekko nodded and said, "You can have that one, Mr. Talky."

"Thank you, Del," Vickersham said dryly. "Lone Elk, was it your people who were . . . um . . . attacked?"

Lone Elk nodded.

"Then I extend my condolences to you and your tribe."

"Me, too," Dekko added, then scratched his armpit.

Lone Elk nodded again. "Thank you."

"Miss O'Donnell," Vickersham said, "that is why I call this land savage. The scourge of humanity are left to roam and do as they please, with no fear of lawful consequences. Del and I are tired of innocent people suffering for that. We have no authority, but *someone* has to do *something*."

Standing Bear spoke for the first time. "The murderers went south—where they came from. I was going to make war on them, but they left in the middle of the night."

"South you say? Thank you, my good man." Vickersham turned to Dekko. "If they went back to the United States, this may be more difficult than we thought."

Dekko spat on a passing bug, scoring a direct hit. "Law down there's 'bout as spread out as up here. Ain't no big deal."

Reena regarded the two characters in a much different light after hearing of their mission. Thinking they were just adventure seekers had made her anxious to send them on their way. Now she was intrigued and wanted to hear their stories, especially about Uncle Faron. "How did you two meet?" she blurted out.

"Now there's a story!" Vickersham crowed.

Dekko rolled his eyes. "Excuse me, ma'am, but did you have to ask that question? I was hopin' to make some miles today, but I see now we might as well climb down and get comfy—this'll take a while."

Vickersham, his face turned away from Dekko, grinned at Reena and winked. He obviously enjoyed baiting his partner. "But maybe the story would be best told around a campfire on a cool evening with a pot of hot tea."

"I bet she's *real* sorry she asked that question now," Dekko mumbled.

"What was that, Del?"

"Nuthin'."

"How else can we help you, gentlemen?" Reena asked, covering her smile.

"We have all we need, but thank you for asking," Vickersham said pleasantly.

"I'll say we got all we need," Dekko drawled, indicating the two horses behind him loaded down with supplies. "This here's all *his* stuff—most of it clothes. If we run across a ballroom dance out here in the middle of nowheres, he'll be ready."

Vickersham ignored the remark and tipped his hat with a brilliant smile. "Until next time, Miss O'Donnell—and I do hope it's soon."

"God go with you both."

"Lone Elk, it has been a pleasure, sir."

"I wish I could go with you, but my people need me," Lone Elk said with genuine regret.

"I understand. Somehow I feel they are fortunate to have you." Vickersham saluted, and Dekko waved, and they began to make their way back down the mountainside.

"A ballroom dance, Del?" Reena heard as they rode off. "You are sometimes really too much."

"Well, I ain't ever *seen* a man with so many clothes! Is there a law somewheres over there where you come from that says you gotta carry that much junk?"

"It's called a gentleman's wardrobe, Del, and no one commiserates with you."

"I ain't asked nobody for no commissery! I just don't see why . . ."

––––––––––

When Reena returned to her tepee, her patient turned his head and looked at her.

"Well, good morning!" she greeted, hoping he was lucid this time.

"Good morning," he croaked through dry lips.

"How about some water—" she started, then stopped when she saw his eyes. They were no longer feverish and bloodshot, but a translucent gray. For the first time Reena felt he really could *see* her. "Oh, thank the Lord!"

He watched her curiously. "What is it? Where am I?"

Reena poured some water into a cup and gave him slow sips. "First things first, please. I've been wanting to know your name for four days. I'm Reena O'Donnell."

He savored the water on his parched tongue for a moment before answering. "Hunter Stone."

Reena smiled and gave him another sip. "To answer your questions, Hunter Stone, I was thanking God for your improvement. And you are in an Assiniboine Indian camp in the Cypress Hills."

Complete bewilderment swept over his face. Stone didn't even know where to *start* asking questions.

Reena saw his confusion and told him how she and Lone Elk had found him. ". . . so you've been here trying to die on me ever since."

"What's . . . what's wrong with me? I hurt all over."

"You don't need to be moving, anyway. Your shoulder is broken, and you have two knife wounds and various cuts and abrasions. I think you were exhausted, too. Other than that, you're fine."

Stone considered her words for a long time. He could remember the fight with Red Wolf, but everything after that was blank.

"Are you hungry? Do you want some broth?"

"Where's Buck?"

"Who's Buck?"

"My horse—a big buckskin."

"He's in our corral, happy and well-fed. I've had to fight off half the braves in camp from stealing him—"

"No! Don't let them take him!" Stone said, raising his head, then grimacing with pain.

Reena laid a hand on his forehead and with great relief found his skin warm, instead of the heat of a blazing fever as in the past few days. "Easy, Mr. Stone," she said seriously, "I was only joking. These men wouldn't steal your horse. Not all Indians are thieves."

"The ones I know are," he said bitterly. He was still gasping after his small outburst. He felt horrible, and it didn't help that his first waking thought had been that he would have to live his life without Betsy. After he'd found her by the river, his only feelings had been overwhelming grief for her, and then a raging anger had taken over when he'd caught up with Red Wolf. Now remorse hit him, along with a profound sense of anguish. Even as he recognized his feelings, he despised them. He hated self-pity in other people—how could he tolerate it in himself?

Reena watched the range of emotions pass over his face. "Mr. Stone, you—said some things while you were delirious. Would you like to talk about them?"

"No."

She nodded. "Too tired?"

"No, I just don't want to talk about them."

Reena was anxious to ask about Betsy and Red Wolf, but Stone was clearly distraught. He was pale and had a hollow-eyed look, with dark half moons under his eyes. As she held his gaze she saw that he was already tired and needed more rest. "We need to get some food in you before you go back to sleep."

"I'm not hungry," he answered softly, turning his head away from her.

Reena stood and started for the flap of the tepee. "I didn't ask if you were hungry. I said we *need* to get some food in you." She stopped, put her hands on her hips, and pronounced, "You've already tried to die on me once—you won't do it again."

Stone turned his head to face her, surprised at the firm tone. For a moment he thought she was scolding playfully, but after considering her body language and the stubborn glint in her bright blue eyes, he knew it was something more. "Who *are* you, anyway?" he whispered, his throat dry again. "Why are you here?"

"I'm a missionary."

"You don't look like a missionary."

"Thank you," she replied. Hiding a smile, she went to get him some broth.

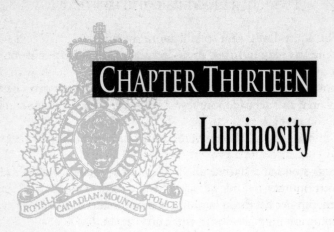

# CHAPTER THIRTEEN

# Luminosity

Star Light watched intently as Reena changed Stone's dressing, and Stone took advantage of the opportunity to examine the boy closely.

His shoulder-length, square-cut hair was circled with a beaded headband of light blue. Wearing only a deerskin vest and breeches, the boy's skinny arms were crossed while resting on his knees. The black eyes held what could only be defined as a deep sadness. A wide nose and full lips made Star Light's features strong despite his eight years.

"Why doesn't he ever talk?" Stone asked Reena. His voice was still weak and hoarse.

Reena was inspecting the bandages she'd just removed. Glancing at Star Light she said, "He hasn't said anything since he saw his parents murdered by the hunters."

"He *saw* them killed?" Stone shot a stunned look at the boy, who continued to watch Reena.

"He's not the only one who saw a family member killed, but he's not handling it well." Reena held out her hand for the fresh dressing. Star Light solemnly placed it in her hands. "He sure is fascinated with you for some reason."

"Does he speak English?"

"Not very well, but he has a good grasp of it."

Stone looked at the boy, wishing he could think of something to say. He hadn't been around children very much, and as far as he was concerned they were from a different planet. Knowing nothing about them, he'd planned on learning from his own children, and Betsy. *So I guess I'll never learn about children*, he thought with the now-too-familiar wrench of sorrow in his gut.

"Thank the Lord, there's still no sign of infection," Reena said, discarding the old dressing. "It's been a week since we found you, so I think we're out of danger now."

Stone coughed, a deep, phlegmy rattling that seemed to come from his toes. His face screwed up in pain from the jolting to his shoulder and side.

Reena watched him, worry lines creasing her forehead. His breathing had gradually improved, but the cough had not.

Gasping, Stone asked irritably, "Can I *please* sit up? I'm so *sick* of being flat on my back, staring at the top of this tepee. I don't think I'm going to get any better unless I move around, either."

"But everything I've heard is that bedrest is the best thing—"

"I don't care what you've heard!" Stone argued, louder than he'd intended. He saw her recoil and immediately felt sorry for the outburst. "I'm sorry, Miss O'Donnell," he said, looking away.

Reena's lips compressed. She spoke to Star Light in his native tongue and the boy left.

"Do they have their own language?" he asked.

"It's Sioux. The Assiniboine are from the Sioux family. They defected to join the Cree when they obtained firearms."

Stone met her blue eyes. There was no denying the fact that she was the most beautiful woman he'd ever seen—and there was no avoiding the lady herself. She was his nurse, and she was there every time he awakened. He admired her, as if admiring a sunset, or the paintings he'd seen of the Sistine Chapel. He was struck by the contrast of her glow with the relative squalor of their surroundings. His mind fuzzily recalled that she was a missionary, and he made a note to question her further on that unusual decision.

"What is it?" Reena asked.

"What?"

"What are you staring at?" Her hands instinctively went to her face. "Is there something on my face?"

"No, there's . . ." He paused, unsure of what to say. He wanted to tell her what he was thinking, but he didn't want to embarrass her or make her uncomfortable. "Could I have a drink of water?"

"Certainly," she said, moving to get him a drink.

Lone Elk and Star Light entered the open tepee flap, with Lone Elk carrying Stone's saddle.

"Mr. Stone," Lone Elk greeted.

"Good morning. What's this?"

Giving Stone a sip of water, Reena said, "I need your help, Lone

Elk." She put down the cup and motioned for him to set the saddle behind Stone's head while she gathered some blankets. After arranging them on the saddle, she said, "Would you lift Mr. Stone, please?"

Lone Elk and Stone looked at her for a long moment, then Lone Elk placed his hands under Stone's armpits. "Are you ready, Mr. Stone?"

"As ready as I'll ever be." Grasping his left arm to stabilize his shoulder, he was already gritting his teeth in preparation for the pain. A grunt escaped him when Lone Elk lifted him, and Reena quickly pushed the saddle under Stone's back. The thick blankets cushioned the saddle's harsh curve, and after settling back with a groan, Stone was breathing heavily, but was not uncomfortable. He looked around the tepee for the first time and noticed a chair and small table across from him, which seemed out of place on the earthen floor. An oak chest was by the tepee flap, probably holding the missionary's clothes. Tendrils of smoke curled upward from a cook fire directly in the center of the tepee, its thin trail disappearing through the lodgepole opening in the top of the tent. Line drawings decorated the buffalo hide interior, but the details were too dim to make out from where he lay.

"How's that?" Reena asked.

"Better, thanks."

Reena studied his pale and sweating face closely. "Are you sure?" She pressed down gently on his bandage to see if either wound had opened, and with relief saw that no blood soaked through.

"Yes, I haven't seen my feet in days." He wiggled his toes and considered them for a moment. "They're the only part of me that's not cut, bruised, or broken." He'd intended it to be a lighthearted statement, but it came out cloaked with bitterness, and Reena didn't smile.

Lone Elk held his hand out to Star Light, and the boy handed him a tomahawk. "Mr. Stone, this was in your belongings. I was not going through your things. It fell out of a bag."

Stone considered the weapon with no expression or comment.

Lone Elk went on evenly, "It is Crow." Still Stone said nothing. "They are the enemies of the Assiniboine."

"They are my enemies, too." Stone shifted his gaze to Lone Elk, whose face betrayed nothing. They stared at each other until the chief nodded slowly. Stone knew he was fishing for an explanation, but he didn't feel comfortable enough to give one. Despite his acceptance into the Assiniboine village, he couldn't help but feel a distrust of all Indians. He was aware that his hatred for Red Wolf had caused this prejudice, but he couldn't shake the feeling.

"Was it Crows that nearly killed you?" Reena asked pointedly.

Stone looked at her, his face a mask.

"Why don't you answer?"

Stone's eyes involuntarily flickered to Lone Elk, who noticed the look.

"I must go," the chief said immediately.

Reena watched him leave, with Star Light following, unsure of what had transpired between them. She turned back to Stone. "What was that all about?"

"What do you mean?"

"Why didn't you talk to him? If there's anybody on this earth you can trust, it's Lone Elk."

Stone shifted, trying to avoid a part of the saddle that had become uncomfortable. "It's not that I don't trust him, it's just . . . ah . . . well, maybe I don't know what to say around him."

"You can say anything you want around him." Reena sat down and put a hand on Stone's arm. "Mr. Stone, I don't know much of what you've gone through. I hardly know anything about you—today is the first day you've had anything to say. But I want you to know that whatever has happened, whatever brought you to our home, you're welcome here for as long you want. That's not only me talking, that's Lone Elk, too. He's a good man. But if there are Crow warriors looking for you, I think he should be aware of it so he can look out for his people. They've got enough trouble with the white man already without worrying about Crows."

Stone watched her as she spoke. Her hand felt cool on his arm, and her rich blue eyes expressed a pleading that touched him. The voices of children playing some sort of game outside filled the tepee for a moment as they ran by. He suddenly found himself very tired, though he'd only been awake for an hour or so.

Reena, thinking his silence was an unwillingness to answer, started to get up. "I'll leave you to your thoughts, Mr. Stone."

"Would you bring Lone Elk here, please?"

She looked at him, surprised, but he was staring outside the tepee at the children. With a small nod, Reena left.

*She's right*, Stone thought, sighing deeply. *As chief, Lone Elk deserved more respect than I gave him. What's the matter with me?*

When they returned, Star Light still following silently, Stone motioned for them to sit near him. "Lone Elk, I'm sorry for my disrespect. I don't know if you'll understand, but my trust has been destroyed. Everything that was dear to me has been taken by a Crow named Red

151

Wolf. I don't know why this has happened, and all I feel is hatred and bitterness."

Lone Elk paused before answering simply, "I understand."

Stone realized how small his problems must sound to this man who had seen his own people butchered, and he scoffed at himself. "Of course you understand. How could I be so blind?"

The chief shrugged. "Your pain is very real and fresh to you. I know your pain, and it is great."

Stone hesitated before continuing. He'd never had a conversation with an Indian before, yet he couldn't shake the feeling that somehow this man really *could* see right inside his heart. "I don't think this Crow Red Wolf will be coming for me, but I was wrong about him before and paid for it. He burned my house, stole my stock, and kidnapped my wife. I tracked him, killing his brother along the way. I didn't know it was his brother. There were three of them, and I only defended my-self." His eyes narrowed and strayed to a spot behind Lone Elk's shoul-der. "He killed my wife in revenge. Maybe he was going to kill her all along, but that's the reason he gave me when I caught up with him."

Reena put a hand to her mouth and looked down. Even though this was what she'd thought had happened, the loss, despair, and anger on Stone's face unsettled her.

"You defeated three Crows in battle?" Lone Elk asked, slightly wide-eyed.

"Well, one of them got away."

The older man nodded slowly. "That is a great feat, my friend. The Crow are fierce warriors."

Star Light did something that surprised everyone present, espe-cially Stone. He scooted to Stone's side and pressed something into his hand, then closed it with his small, grubby fingers.

Stone held up the figure of a buffalo, made with blue and white colorful beads surrounded by leather. He looked questioningly at Lone Elk, but the chief was staring at the boy dumbfounded.

"Star Light, what are you doing?" Reena asked, as surprised as Lone Elk.

The boy didn't acknowledge her question. He kept his eyes on Stone.

"What is it?" Stone asked.

Reena turned to Lone Elk, who had regained his composure and said wonderingly, "It is a talisman, given to him by his mother."

"A talisman?" Stone peered closely at the finely detailed work.

"To ward off evil spirits. Once a talisman is presented to someone, it is never given away. Especially to . . ." Lone Elk trailed off, still wearing a puzzled look.

"Especially to white men?" Stone asked.

"To . . . to . . . someone outside the tribe."

"Thank you, Lone Elk, that's a nice way to put 'paleface.' " Stone gently ran his thumb over the buffalo, searching Star Light's round face. The boy matched Stone's scrutiny with an inspection of his own. His eyes roamed over Stone's face, from his dimpled chin to his sandy hair. There was no childlike curiosity in the inspection; he seemed to be filing away Stone's features one by one, as if for future judgment.

"Star Light, your mother gave that to you," Reena said. "You haven't let go of it since she . . . since she went to heaven. Why are you giving it to Mr. Stone?"

The boy said nothing and acted as if he hadn't heard her.

Stone held out the talisman to him. "I can't accept this, Star Light—"

"Don't do that!" Reena whispered. "It's very bad manners to refuse such a gift."

Ignoring her, Stone continued, "My feelings won't be hurt if you want this back." Star Light slowly reached up and pushed Stone's hand away. "What does it mean for you to give me this? Can you tell me?" Still the boy didn't answer.

"Lone Elk?" Stone asked.

"I do not know. I have never seen this before. Only the boy can tell you what it means."

Stone stared at Star Light, *willing* him to talk. He'd been aware of the boy's presence for the past few days whenever he'd gain consciousness. Apparently, Star Light had developed some sort of kinship or infatuation with him, for reasons beyond Stone's understanding. He fingered the buffalo again and mumbled, "Thank you," embarrassed for some reason.

"You need some rest, Mr. Stone," Reena observed.

Lone Elk rose and adjusted his headdress. "Thank you for your information, Mr. Stone. I have one more question. This Red Wolf—is he still alive?"

"Yes, I think so. I wounded him, but—" He paused and searched his memory. Red Wolf had said something to him before vanishing, but he couldn't remember exactly what it had been. All he could recall was deep pain and the Crow's fierce knife at his throat. "He left me alive," he whispered. His thinking had been muddled for days, and when he *could* think, he'd only dwelled on Betsy's death and his loneliness. *Why didn't he kill me?* Uneasily searching his feelings, he found that he wished Red Wolf *had* killed him. *If Betsy's dead, I should be too.*

As if reading his mind, Reena said, "Yes, he let you live, for whatever reason. And that's *good*—you have so much to live for."

"I have nothing!" Stone spat out vehemently.

Reena was taken aback by the anger and despair in his voice.

Willing himself to be calm, Stone muttered, "I'd like to sleep now." Without waiting for an answer, he clutched the talisman to his chest and closed his eyes.

---

The first items Reena had purchased from Abel Farwell's trading post were the small table and straight-back chair. Sitting on the ground didn't suit her, and she allowed herself those two luxuries to avoid backaches. She enjoyed her time of reading the Bible in the evenings much more now, since she wasn't constantly shifting to find a more comfortable position.

After an hour's reading that night, she rubbed her eyes and glanced at Stone. Noticing the gathering shadows beyond him, she reached for the second article she'd purchased from Farwell, an oil lamp. The light spread a warm amber glow over Star Light's round face as he watched her from Stone's side. The boy had gone outside only twice all day and had returned quickly both times.

Reena stoked the fire to heat the water in a pot hanging above, sure that Stone would wake up before long. He'd stirred about mid-afternoon and had refused food and water. His only request had been to lie back down, so Reena had hailed a passing brave and together they'd eased him to the blankets below. All of Reena's attempts at conversation had been ignored; Stone had only stared at the spot in the roof where the support poles joined. After a while, he'd fallen back to sleep.

She was reading Paul's letter to the Thessalonians when she heard a moan. "Mr. Stone—? Are you all right?"

He stirred with a heavy sigh but gave no answer.

Going to the fire, Reena said, smiling, "You're not going to get out of eating this time, I'm afraid."

Stone was looking at Star Light and said hoarsely, "Why are you here, boy? Why don't you go play?"

Star Light, as usual, said nothing.

Reena declared lightly, "We've got a chore to do before you eat."

"Chore?"

She held up a straight razor and hot towel. "You need it—badly."

Instinctively, Stone's hand went to his whiskers; he was surprised to feel the thick stubble. Reena pressed the steaming hot towel over the lower portion of his face.

"Ouch!"

"Do you think it's hot enough?" she asked innocently as she stropped the razor. "I hope you don't mind if I went through your saddlebags to find this."

"Of course not," he said moodily, his voice muffled by the towel. "What's mine is yours."

Reena whipped up the shaving soap in a tiny bowl, removed the towel, and began dabbing great blobs of the frothy mixture to Stone's jaw.

"Have you ever done this before?"

"No, but I'll be careful." She saw his Adam's apple move as he swallowed hard. "Are you going to tell me that you're afraid of little ol' me?"

"After the past couple of weeks, I'm a little nervous around sharp objects. I've fallen into a bad habit of bleeding heavily when one of them is around."

Reena couldn't help but smile, and inside she rejoiced that he was at least *attempting* to joke, even though it was morbid. "There," she said, satisfied that the thick lather completely swathed his lower face. "Are you ready?"

"Start on my left side."

"Why?"

"Before . . . all this, I always started on my right side."

"Any particular reason?"

"Not really."

"So why start on the left side all of a sudden?"

"Maybe it'll change my luck. I think my luck could use a healthy change, don't you?"

Reena pulled a face. "Wallowing in self-pity, are we?"

"No, I—"

"Hush. Here we go."

Very slowly and carefully, Reena slid the blade down his left cheek to his jawline. A soft, scratchy noise was the only sound in the tepee. Beside them, Star Light watched, fascinated. Wiping the razor on the towel, she positioned it where she'd left off and began down his neck.

"Careful," he warned, barely moving his lips. "If I cut myself, it's usually there."

"Would you like Star Light to do this—or maybe one of Lone Elk's braves that has more experience with sharp blades?"

A hint of a smile played at his eyes but didn't make it to his mouth. "No, you're doing fine."

"Thank you—may I continue?"

"Of course."

Reena finished both sides of his face and neck and moved very close to him to shave around his mouth. She could feel him studying her face while she worked, and she became nervous. "Could you stop staring at me?" she asked without meeting his eyes.

"You're right in front of me. What am I supposed to look at?"

"Then close your eyes."

"I don't *want* to close my eyes. They've been closed for almost a week—ooowww!"

"Oh, I'm so sorry! Now, see what you made me do?" She grabbed the towel, found a clean spot, and dabbed at the small cut.

"What *I* made you—"

"Are you all right?"

"It's okay. What's a little more blood loss?"

"Mr. Stone!"

"It's all right—really. I've done it a thousand times. It's that blasted dimple on my chin. Hard to navigate around it."

"You have a very handsome chin, Mr. Stone." The statement simply popped out, and Reena felt her face flush. He looked at her closely, his face drawn and sad and tired, but he said nothing. Hugely uncomfortable, Reena wished she could magically retract the statement, but it hung in the air like smoke.

"I think, after this, that we should switch to a first name basis, don't you?" he asked with elaborate casualness.

"That would be fine."

"It's Reena, isn't it?"

"Yes, with two *e*'s." She dabbed the cut again and finished shaving him.

"That's a very pretty name. Where did it come from?"

"My given name is Serena, but I've been called Reena ever since I can remember." She gently wiped the shaving cream from his face. "Here, hold this on that cut while I clean up and get your supper."

Stone watched her as she went to dip her hands in a clay bowl of water. He'd never seen a woman in denim pants before, and he tried to imagine her in a nice dress. After a moment, he decided that she would probably be lovely no matter what she wore. "Miss . . . er . . . Reena—why are you doing this?"

"Doing what?" She stirred the venison that was boiling in the pot over the fire.

"Taking care of me. Surely you've got more important things to do, and an Indian woman could do all this."

"Star Light, here's yours," Reena said, handing the boy a plate with huge chunks of venison and potatoes. Pouring some broth and meat in a bowl, she began cutting the meat into smaller pieces for Stone. "What do I have to do that's more important than saving the life of one of God's children, Hunter?" The name sounded strange on her lips after calling him "Mr. Stone" for so long. She began feeding him.

"Well, when you put it like that . . ." The deer meat was so tender he barely needed to chew. "I hate to ask, but this would be easier if you could raise me up again."

Instead of going to find a man to help her, Reena got behind him and managed to lift him up far enough for Star Light to slide the saddle behind him.

When everyone was settled, Reena continued, "I couldn't ask any of these women to take care of you. Not after what's been done to them by white men. Star Light, chew your food. You're wolfing it down too fast."

The boy regarded her with his big dark eyes, then carefully and methodically started to chew more slowly.

"Where does he stay?" Stone asked, nodding at Star Light.

"He's been sleeping in Lone Elk's tent, but during the day he wanders anywhere. That is, until you came along." Reena fed Stone another bite. "I just don't know what to do for him."

"Maybe there's nothing to be done for him right now."

Reena stirred the soup in the bowl, reflecting on what he'd said. *And what about you, Hunter Stone? Is there anything that can be done for you?* She studied him while he wasn't looking and noticed that his appearance had changed dramatically. His clean-shaven cheeks gleamed in the light from the fire and oil lamp. The dimple on his chin seemed even deeper in the soft glow. She watched his jaw muscles work as he chewed, then something occurred to her, and she blurted, "You thought I was her, you know."

He stopped chewing and locked eyes with her. The lights behind her threw her figure into shadow, and in a jolt of memory he saw her praying over him, praying with such feeling that he was left wordless.

Her hand had rested on his arm, very lightly, but still it was a comforting touch of warmth and compassion.

Just as abruptly, another recollection hit him: she'd been sitting near him reading her Bible. The fire had died, and the lamp had cast a light that reminded him of warm summer twilights. How many times had he seen his wife in the same light—twenty, thirty, a hundred times? And then—in his blurred feverish state—Reena *became* Betsy. "Betsy, my darling, pray for me," he'd said, or maybe he'd only thought it, because the dream-Betsy hadn't heard him. Her delicate, illuminated eyelashes came together when she'd blinked and turned a page. She was so beautiful.

"I'm sorry," Reena breathed, witnessing the increasingly haunted gray eyes. "I'm so sorry . . . I don't know what I was thinking. . . ."

"I *did* think you were her," he murmured softly. "You *were* her. She wanted me to . . ." He paused and licked his dry lips, the knowledge wrenching at his heart. "She wanted me to know that she was praying for me," he finished, his voice barely audible. "Oh, Betsy. . . ."

Reena and Star Light watched as he put a shaking hand over his mouth, and tears began to course down his smooth cheeks, their trails winking in the gentle light.

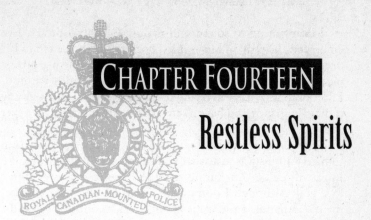

# CHAPTER FOURTEEN

# Restless Spirits

**S**trong Woman and Gray Dawn were stretching buffalo skins over a frame, while Reena sat under a spruce tree nearby preparing to write the most difficult letter of her life. The July day was crisp and clear. Everyone in the village was out in the sunshine, either playing or working.

A typical day for Reena, between caring for Stone, was to sit with the women of the tribe and help weave baskets and make blankets, the Assiniboine's main source of income and trade. Then she would translate stories from the Bible until time for lessons in the early afternoon. This day, however, found her unable to go to her translations until she took care of a matter that had been pressing on her for days.

Dear Megan,

I know this letter may come as a shock after all this time. Through the letters Mother has written, I know you and Louis are married and are doing well. This pleases me.

The circumstances surrounding my departure were upsetting and hard to deal with at the time. However, over the year I've had to think about it, I've realized our God truly does know what's best for us, even if we don't. The work I'm doing is more fulfilling than you, or even I, could imagine. These people are like no one you've ever met or seen. In my old Chicago world, a broken fingernail or torn dress was devastating; here, the pressure is to find food to last through the days, or to keep a watch out for marauding bands of white men or enemy tribes. Here, the urgency is merely the survival for our lives.

I don't mean to sound self-pitying. On the contrary, I've embraced this way of life as if I'd been raised in the tribe. It's been eerie the way I've fit in—like some sort of living puzzle piece. Or maybe *they're* the puzzle piece fitting into *my* life— I don't know. What I'm trying to say in a very roundabout way is that I'm happy and have a sense of fulfillment that I've never known.

Anyway, I've said all this to say this: I hope your decision to marry Louis was just what you needed, and I trust that the Lord will guide your future together. You're my sister, and I love you. Although I don't approve of the way your engagement was handled and came about, I can't continue to hold a grudge against you. This is not out of the goodness of my heart, it's out of learning the wonder and joy of forgiving that I've found through God. I do hope and pray for the best for you and Louis.

Gray Dawn heard Reena sigh and looked up from her work to see her friend leaning her head back against the tree with a profound expression of relief on her face. After tying an edge of the beaver skin to the round frame, she asked, "Is everything all right, Reena?"

Reena had almost forgotten about the two women, so absorbed had she been in writing her letter. "Yes—why do you ask?"

Pushing another stitch through the tough skin, the older woman didn't answer directly. "Do you miss your family?"

"Sometimes," Reena nodded as she folded the letter.

Gray Dawn smiled but said nothing. Reena watched her hands deftly tying the skin to the frame. The two women were making a warm cover for Strong Woman's baby, which was due at any time.

"How is Mr. Stone?" Strong Woman asked Reena.

"Very depressed. He's stopped talking again."

"What do you want him to say?" Gray Dawn inquired with a hint of a smile.

Reena shrugged and ran her fingers through her wind-blown hair. "I don't know—anything's better than silence. He has so much hurt inside."

"Everyone deals with loss and pain differently," Gray Dawn said. "Some of our people have shut themselves away to mourn, and others are staying very close to loved ones. He has no loved ones left. All he has from his life is the man that took away everything he had—the man he hates the most." She finished the stitch on the last knot and gave

Reena an appraising look. "And he will go find him, unless God softens his heart."

Running footsteps sounded behind Reena, and suddenly Star Light was standing over her, his eyes huge.

"What's the matter?" Reena asked anxiously, but even before the boy pointed to her tepee, she knew. Grabbing her letter, pen, and ink-well, she took off at a run.

Curious glances from the villagers followed them, and as they neared the tepee, Lone Elk appeared, a look of alarm on his leathery face. "What is it?"

"I don't know," Reena replied breathlessly. "Mr. Stone . . . ." She didn't stop to explain, and he fell in behind them.

Star Light leaped through the flap of her home, and when she'd stepped inside and saw Stone, she demanded, "Hunter, what are you doing?"

Blankets thrown aside, he was resting on his good arm, trying to get his legs under him as he struggled to stand. His face was pale and sweaty, his lips drawn back to expose white teeth. As Reena watched, his arm began trembling violently, and before she could reach him, he fell back with an explosive cry of pain and a black curse.

"Are you insane?" Reena asked, her voice rising. She saw with horror that his bandages were spotted with blood. Irritated, she realized she was still holding her writing tools and paper, so she set them on the table. "You've opened up your wounds! Where did you think you were going? Lone Elk, get me some more bandages."

Stone was gasping for breath and his face was twisted with pain. "Out . . . outside. Out of *here*!"

"What were you going to do—crawl? You're too weak to stand!" Removing the bandage and inspecting the stitches, she found that it wasn't as bad as she'd thought it would be. Only a few had pulled loose, and Reena again admired Gray Dawn's neat, tight stitches. She doubled the bandage and pressed it tightly on the oozing gash. "Lone Elk, forget about the bandage for right now, we have some restitching to do." She glared at Stone as she spoke, and Lone Elk left to find his wife.

"I'm sorry . . . I just . . . I thought I could make it—"

"Well, you didn't," she said harshly. "And now it's going to take even longer for you to get on your feet! Star Light, hold this," she ordered, indicating the bandage. She went to the flap and found a small crowd had gathered outside. Gray Dawn appeared with her husband, and Reena explained what had happened and asked her to repair the damage. When Reena went back inside, she stood over Stone with her hands on her hips.

"I'm sorry, Reena, I didn't—"

"You already said that."

"What's the matter? Why are you so angry?"

"You've got to give yourself time to heal, Hunter! I know you can't wait to ride off and let Red Wolf finish what he started, but it's going to take time." Instantly she regretted the words as she saw his face harden. Putting a shaking hand to her forehead, she turned away. *I'm taking my frustrations out on him, and that's not fair. Help me, Lord, I think I'm going crazy.*

Stone was thoughtfully staring at her when she turned and faced him again. His face was different somehow, but she couldn't decide what the change could be. Putting his hand over the bandage, he whispered to Star Light and the boy left. Stone didn't want him to see the restitching.

His gaze came back to her and wandered over her clothes. "You've really taken to the Indian way of life, haven't you?"

She looked down at her deerskin dress. Fringes adorned the hem, and a simple, white beaded belt circled her slim waist. Her feet were bare.

"It looks very good on you."

Color flooded to her cheeks, and she tried to cover it by drawing his attention to the dress. Running her hands over the soft leather, she said, "Thank you. It's so comfortable, I find myself wearing it more and more." She moved to sit beside him, not meeting his eyes. "Listen, Hunter . . ."

"It's all right. I'm just not much of a patient, and it was a stupid thing to do. I've never stayed inside much, and I miss the outdoors."

"I shouldn't have lost my temper like that, and I need to ask you to forgive me."

For some reason, the deep mask of sadness came back into his features, and all at once Reena knew why his expression had been different a few moments before. She'd been looking at the normal Hunter Stone—the one who had forgotten his grief for a little while as he considered someone else's problems. *He was worried about me for some reason*, she thought.

"With all I've put you through, it's *me* that should be asking forgiveness," he said.

"Then let's forgive each other."

They stared at each other in silence, then he said, "You remind me so much of—"

Gray Dawn came in, muttering darkly in Sioux, and Reena heard something about "stubborn men." The Indian woman knelt beside Stone and began—none too gently—by cutting the loose stitches. Stone turned his head away and gritted his teeth. When she ran the first new stitch through with the large needle, he managed not to cry out—how, Reena didn't know. Five times Gray Dawn pierced his skin, then expertly tied off the final stitch.

"This is the last time, Mr. Stone," she warned as she wound the deergut thread around a piece of wood. "Next time you do something foolish like that, you bleed to death."

"Yes, ma'am," he said seriously, feeling like a schoolboy who had been caught putting a frog down a girl's dress.

Reena raised her eyebrows in an "I told you so" fashion when Gray Dawn left, then began putting on the fresh bandage.

"Is she always so grim?"

"She wasn't completely serious—I don't think. Gray Dawn has a good heart, and she's been like a mother to me."

"You probably need someone like that, being out here all alone," he commented, watching her reaction closely.

"She's been good to me."

"Tell me about yourself, Reena. You know all about me, but I hardly know anything about you at all. Are you happy doing this?"

Reena couldn't hide her surprise. "You're very direct, aren't you?"

Stone shrugged his good shoulder. "And curious."

Finished with the bandaging, she washed her hands in a bowl of water and shook them dry. "Yes, I'm happy. The conditions here—"

"Are you really?"

She looked at him. He didn't seem skeptical or disbelieving—but his interest in her answer was clear. She decided to be as honest as possible. "Sometimes it gets lonely. It was especially scary when I first came here. I didn't even know the language, much less the customs."

"Where are you from?"

"Chicago."

"Chicago?" he echoed, raising his eyebrows. "You came all this way by yourself?"

"No, my uncle brought me here." Restlessly she rose, picked up the soiled bandage, and placed it on the ever-burning fire. After smoking heavily for a moment, the flames burst through and hungrily consumed the material. "Are you sure you want to hear all this?"

"Of course. It's not like I'm busy, or anything," he said wryly.

Reena told him her story, pausing every once in a while to wipe his sweating face. He didn't interrupt and seemed genuinely interested in her every word.

When she finished, he stared at her for a moment with a troubled look, then said quietly, "You gave up a life of ease—money, status, anything you wanted . . ." He glanced at their surroundings. "For this?"

"No, for those people out there," Reena pointed.

"And this Louis fellow," he said slowly, "he hurt you pretty bad, didn't he?" Reena glanced away, but not before he saw the hurt on her face. "I'm sorry, I didn't mean to pry."

"He and my sister took away my trust in people."

"Even me?"

"I don't know you well enough to trust you."

Stone considered that and nodded slowly. "Your story is incredible. The courage it took to do that . . ."

"God gave me the courage—it's not me." This time *he* glanced away quickly to the buffalo talisman he'd picked up while she was talking. He said nothing, but Reena could tell he was disturbed about something. "What is it, Hunter?"

"My wife was like that," he murmured, not looking up. "Strong convictions, courage . . ." His lips tightened, and Reena could see the veil dropping over his face—the withdrawal into his own private grief and pain. He suddenly jerked the sling from his arm, raised it from around his neck, and flung it away from him. Flexing the fingers of his hand, they both watched the numerous muscles work in his forearm, and then his face distorted as he stretched out his arm to its full length. Trembling began, first in his outstretched arm, then it worked its way to his whole body.

Finally, feeling her fingernails biting into her palms as she watched his face strain with effort, she could stand it no more. "You really shouldn't be doing that, you know."

"It's time," he grunted as he attempted to raise his arm over his head, but it only traveled a few inches higher. His trembling became more intense, and cords of muscle stood out on his neck. Swollen veins began to form on his forehead from his hairline down to the creases between his eyebrows.

Reena gently placed her hand on top of his quivering arm and applied a small amount of pressure. "Enough," she whispered softly. "You have to give the bone time to mend."

His arm came down to his side, and an explosion of pent-up breath escaped him. Snatching up a wooden bowl and spoon close by with his right hand, he threw them across the tepee as hard as he could, where they fell to the dirt floor with a clatter. "It seems like I've been here forever!"

"You were wounded horribly. You have to give the wounds time to—"

"Don't you see, he's getting *away*!" Stone exploded, his eyes boring into hers.

Reena stood abruptly and dusted the dirt from her skirt. "What is the *matter* with you men? Why is revenge so important? If you happen to find him and kill him, will it bring your wife back? No! Will it bring your farm back? No! Will it bring *you* back?"

Stone watched her in mute surprise.

"I want an answer to that one, Hunter Stone! Will it bring *you* back?"

His face grew cold and detached, and he turned away from her.

Reena spun on her bare heel and marched out.

————

Stone woke later that day to find Lone Elk and a warrior Stone didn't recognize entering the tepee with a litter. Tied between the two long poles were colorful animal skins, and when the chief laid the litter down beside Stone and gave him a questioning look, Stone nodded eagerly.

They lifted and placed him on the stretcher as gently as possible. Stone ignored the painful jolts in his excitement to go outside. Star Light was waiting in the sunshine, and as Stone was carried to the creek, the boy placed his small hand on the litter and walked beside him. Many of the tribe had never seen the white man that their chief had brought to the village almost two weeks before, and Stone bore many curious stares, which he returned with inquisitive looks of his own. The Assiniboine were a handsome race, with strong, straight noses, determined jawlines, and intelligent eyes.

He breathed deeply of the fresh air and faced the bright sun with closed eyes, drinking in the warmth. The Indians placed him on the bank beside the creek at an angle that allowed him to survey the pastoral scene. Downstream, women washed clothes and children played beside them in the cool water. He saw a hawk streaking through the woods, skillfully maneuvering through the branches at lightning speed. A smile played on Stone's lips, and he sighed deeply, glad to escape the confines of the tepee.

"We will come for you later," Lone Elk said as they turned away.

"I'd like it if you would sit with me for a while, Chief."

Lone Elk considered him for a moment, then sat down on the grass at the edge of the embankment. He reached in a small bag slung from his shoulder and produced a potato. Unsheathing a knife at his belt, he slowly began to peel it.

"I thank you, Lone Elk, for this pleasure."

"Do not thank me," the chief shrugged, "thank Reena."

Stone smiled. "I should have known." He glanced at the silent Star Light, who was staring into the water. "How about some water, boy? I'm dry." Star Light obediently rose and trotted off to get a cup. Lone Elk held out a chunk of potato, which Stone accepted with a nod. They munched contentedly for a moment, then Stone asked, "Why does that boy follow me around, Chief?"

Lone Elk, as usual, paused before speaking, thinking about his answer. He popped another piece of potato into his mouth and spoke around it, "He senses your loss and feels close to you."

"Many of your people have had loss—why me? A white man?"

"That I cannot tell you."

"Can't—or won't?"

Lone Elk was expressionless as he handed Stone another piece of potato. "I like potatoes. Always have." His dark eyes watched the women washing downstream. "Star Light's father died charging the white hunters as they shot my people down. His mother was killed by a stray bullet while holding on to the boy in their tepee. When we found them, she was lying on top of him. He could have gotten out from under her, but he chose to stay there—not from fear of more bullets, but as a way of staying close to her for what little time he could. He has never cried, that I know of."

Stone shook his head in disbelief over the horrible story and kept his eyes locked on the older man's impassive face as he continued.

"He has turned into an angry boy. He fights with the other boys and is disrespectful to adults. He kicks our dogs whenever he passes by them. The only time the restless spirit leaves him is when he is with you. Then he is calm and waits."

"Waits for what?"

Again Lone Elk didn't answer. Instead, he sheathed his knife and wiped his hands on his breeches.

"Come on, Chief—waits for what?" Stone repeated.

He heard a shuffled step and Star Light ran by them to the stream, filled a cup with water, and brought it to Stone. "Thanks," Stone said, bringing the cup to his lips, but keeping his eyes on the boy. Star Light sat down beside him and his eyes went to the bone handle of Lone Elk's knife. He pointed to it questioningly, and Lone Elk unsheathed it and handed it to the boy, who began scratching in the dirt and grass with it.

"Once, when I was a young man," Lone Elk related, "my father brought three prisoners to our village. They had stolen some of our horses, and it was a great feat for him to go out and capture them. It was customary for the women and children of the tribe to beat and abuse the prisoners before the braves did what they had to do. The mothers and children would form two lines, holding sticks and rocks and clubs, and the prisoners would be forced to walk between them all the way through. For the first time in my life, my father gave me permission to join the lines, but before I rushed off, he said, 'Do not choose to do this because everyone else does it. You must choose your own path—the Red Road of War, or the White Road of Peace.' "

Lone Elk paused and watched Star Light carving crude figures in the dirt. The drawings were beginning to take shape as men, with large western hats and long rifles.

"I joined the lines that day, and every time after that when prisoners were brought back to camp," Lone Elk continued, his eyes far away. "Soon I was a warrior, capturing prisoners of my own and torturing them after the women and children were through." He looked at Stone meaningfully. "I chose the Red Road of War, and now that I have the Son of God living in my heart, I regret the men that I have killed. Not a day goes by that I do not think about them, even though I know I have been forgiven."

Star Light's dirt scratches had turned into a passable drawing of six men standing on a hill. Stone heard chattering and looked across the creek to see two red squirrels running madly through the branches of a white spruce. The tree was spotted with white blooms throughout the blue-green needles, and after the squirrels landed particularly hard on one branch, the powdery blooms exploded and swirled around in the sunshine like a florid snowstorm.

"Why do you tell me this story?" Stone asked the chief.

At that moment, Star Light lifted the bone-handled knife far over his head and brought it down with all his strength into one of the figures he'd drawn. The blade sank into the soft, dusky earth to the hilt, and the boy pulled it out and brought it down to pierce the next crude figure. Over and over he performed the act, grunting with effort and purpose, until the ground at his knees was churned to a deep, rich brown and all evidence of the men had been obliterated. His breathing was labored when he stopped, and his small lips were curled back to expose gritted white teeth. He stared at the routed soil with the knife gripped tightly in his small, white-knuckled hand. Stone noticed absently that he was left-handed.

Neither man spoke to the boy. The rage he'd shown had been startling, sudden, and mesmerizing—an outpouring of passion that left both men wordless. Stone had seen none of Star Light's fights with the other boys, or the reckless abuse of man and animal that Lone Elk had spoken of earlier; the boy had always been still and quiet in Stone's presence, but the animal fury that had surfaced left Stone slightly in awe of the powerful emotions raging inside the small body.

Lone Elk reached out and gently took his knife from Star Light's small, stiff fingers, wiped the blade on the tail of his buckskin shirt, and sheathed it. "We will return for you later, Hunter," he nodded, and with one more glance at Star Light, made his way back to the village.

Star Light stretched out beside Stone on the creek bank, laced his hands behind his head, and together they gazed at the velvet blue sky in mute admiration.

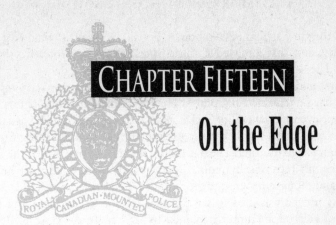

# CHAPTER FIFTEEN

# On the Edge

Two months passed, and Hunter Stone slowly healed. The puckered, angry scars on his left side were the only physical evidence of his battle with Red Wolf. At night, lying in the tepee that had been provided for him by Lone Elk, he would lightly run his fingers over the raised skin. The area was numb from shattered nerves, but every night he found himself caressing the lesions absently, while his thoughts dwelled on revenge and blood and broken dreams.

The nights were the worst; during the day, he let the simple life of the Assiniboine envelop him like a cocoon, keeping his mind occupied as a defense against the crimson thoughts of the night. By sunlight, his world was visual. He observed the women make and mend clothes from the hides and furs of animals, he learned their cuisine, and he watched as Reena taught the children English so that they could read the Bibles she'd gotten for them. But at night, when the only sound was the dying fire popping faintly inside his tepee, his vision turned inward. The memories of the day were quickly pushed aside for the deeper, darker ones that haunted him before and during sleep.

The tribe was unfailingly courteous, but at the same time he was a stranger among them that could disappear and be out of their lives at any given moment. The silent, watching white man with eyes the color of mountain slate was treated with respect, but it was the respect reserved for the mountain lions or grizzlies that roamed the Hills: he was one of God's creatures, but unpredictability hovered just below the surface.

Reena continued to nurse him until he was able to care for himself. Both had apologized for their altercation concerning revenge when he'd first arrived, but since then Reena found herself with a guarded attitude much the same as all the Assiniboines. For all she knew he could be gone any day, and that knowledge caused her to build a protective shield around herself that made their relationship more formal than before. She couldn't understand why he hadn't already left, but she thanked God for every day he remained and prayed He was working in Stone's heart.

One evening, Jaye Eliot Vickersham and Del Dekko rode back into the village. Reena had heard the excitement but thought it was Stone returning from hunting. The day before, he'd gone out and for the first time hadn't returned by nightfall, and everyone nodded their heads sadly and thought he was gone for good. When Vickersham and Dekko arrived, Reena was glad to see the two self-made crusaders, but the knot of worry for Hunter remained inside her. It was close to dusk, and she was concerned that he might be out in the wilderness hurt or incapacitated. *What if he really hasn't left for good? What if he's lying out there in the same condition I found him?* With an effort, she shook off her morbid thoughts.

"Ah, Miss O'Donnell," Vickersham smiled as he and Dekko dismounted near Lone Elk's tepee. "You're as beautiful as the day I first saw you."

Reena shook her head. "You're a charmer, Mr. Vickersham. I'll have to keep my eye on you. Hello, Mr. Dekko."

"Ma'am," Dekko smiled, removing his battered hat. "And call me Del, please. Ain't nobody *ever* called me Mr. Dekko, and I nearly looked around to see if my long-dead daddy was behind me."

Lone Elk came out of the tepee and greeted them, motioning to the cook fire nearby. "Sit down."

"Thank you, Chief," Vickersham nodded. Two braves took their four horses away to feed and water them.

"It's been a long time," Reena commented. "What brings you two back this way?"

Vickersham, dressed as immaculately as before in a black suit and gleaming boots, crossed his legs and rested his arms on his knees. Reena noticed the sparkle of a huge ring on his right hand. His clipped English accent rang clear in the gathering shadows. "Well, as you're already aware, we went down to Montana Territory to see if we could find those murderers that attacked your people, Lone Elk. But we jolly well might have been sight-seeing, for all the good it did."

"What do you mean?" Reena asked.

"By the time we arrived they'd disbanded and ridden off in fifteen different directions. We received absolutely no help from the local authorities in raising a posse since we aren't officers of the law, and there was nothing we could do." His tone conveyed anger and frustration. "I'm sorry, Chief."

Lone Elk nodded as if he'd expected nothing less.

"Wouldn't anyone listen to you?" Reena wondered. "What did the law say when you told them what the men had done?"

Vickersham exchanged a glance with Del. Reena was unnerved for a moment by Del's eyes, as she had been when they'd met for the first time; one of them seemed to be looking at her while the other was on Vickersham beside him. Then he brought the one looking at his partner around to her, and the other wandered off somewhere to Reena's right. "They weren't very cooperative, ma'am," Del explained bitterly. He looked quickly at Lone Elk before continuing and shifted his weight. "Seems they were celebrating a great victory in Fort Benton over the—excuse me, Chief—'murderous and treacherous redskins.' Their words, not mine." He and Vickersham stared into the fire, not wanting to meet their eyes.

Lone Elk had no reaction, but Reena's eyes widened with shock. "That's the most *outrageous*—! How could anybody think like that?"

No one answered her. Del retrieved a thick chunk of jerky from his coat pocket, sliced off a piece, and put it in his mouth. "So they just ride off into the sunset," Reena murmured, "free as the wind." The injustice of it made her want to apologize to Lone Elk on behalf of all white people.

"Rider comin'," Del said around his mouthful of jerky, and his hand went to a huge pistol in his belt.

"It is Hunter," Lone Elk said.

Reena heard the relief evident in his voice. She turned and saw Stone entering the village from the western mountainside, his hat low over his eyes. He wore the clothes they'd found him in; Gray Dawn had mended the tan shirt where the Crow's knife had torn it. Reena couldn't hide her own relief and went to meet him.

He stopped Buck and looked down at her with the hint of a smile. Tied across Buck's hindquarters was a freshly killed antelope.

"I thought you were gone," Reena said softly as she patted Buck's neck.

"Not this time."

"I'm glad."

"Who are our visitors?"

"Come on. I'll introduce you."

Star Light appeared out of nowhere, and Stone dismounted, retrieved his saddlebags, and handed him the reins without a word. The boy led Buck away to give the antelope to a brave for skinning and dressing.

"Nice kill," Del drawled as they neared the fire.

Reena made the introductions, and Vickersham got to his feet to shake Stone's hand. Reena had thought that Vickersham was the same height as Stone, but seeing them together she saw that Stone was a few inches taller.

After they'd sat down, Stone handed Reena the saddlebags. "Pin cherries and saskatoons."

"Thank you, Hunter."

"Pin cherries?" Lone Elk echoed. "You were on the north side?"

"Yes."

"That is far."

Stone shrugged. "It's just where I ended up—didn't plan on it."

Reena saw Vickersham and Del watching Stone with questions in their eyes. "Hunter came to us a few months ago and stayed on." She would let Hunter explain his story however he chose.

"By the looks of that fat antelope, you were well named," Del commented. "'Bout as big as an elk."

Hunter stared into the fire and said nothing. Darkness was closing fast, and the reflection of the fire made his clear eyes appear red.

"Are you from around here, Mr. Stone?" Vickersham asked.

"Up north a little bit—near the Red Deer."

More questions came to Vickersham's mind, but the man held a guarded look that told him they could wait. Del, however, was not as observant. "What brought you down thisaway?" he asked innocently, but when Stone looked at him, he saw the red reflection and involuntarily swallowed.

"Hunting," Stone stated in a low voice that left no room for more questions.

Reena felt the electricity in the air and changed the subject. "Mr. Vickersham and Del just returned from—"

"Please, Miss O'Donnell, call me Vic. I'd always wanted a nickname in England, but they're too formal for that. Del started calling me Vic, and I'm fairly proud of it, as a matter of fact."

"I weren't about to call you 'Your Majesty,' or whatever it was," Del grumbled.

"It wasn't 'Your Majesty,' Del, it was 'Lord Vickersham.' And that's just a courtesy title."

"Whatever *that* is," Del mumbled.

"You're an English lord?" Reena asked.

"Well . . . sort of," Vic stammered. "You see, my father is the Marquess of Bennington—"

"Here we go again," Del said, rolling his wayward eyes.

"—and I'm his youngest son. Therefore, my oldest brother will inherit everything of my father's—everything—which makes him an earl, and I have a courtesy title of 'lord.' I was supposed to—sort of lounge around looking royal, I suppose, but I tired of that fairly soon and decided to set out for adventure."

"And ain't we lucky we got ya," Del said, inspecting his worn boot. "Anyways, what it comes down to after that long-winded explanation, I weren't about to call 'im 'lord.' "

"I didn't *expect* you to, Del. That's just the way I was introduced to you by the jailer."

"You two met in a jail?" Reena asked with raised eyebrows. "Who was visiting whom?"

"Uh . . . ahem . . ." Del coughed. "I was wrongly accused."

"Wrongly accused!" Vic exclaimed. "There were so many cards up your sleeves, they could have created a new deck!"

"They was only four, and I'd've cleaned them boys out if'n I hadn't got confused on the last one I skimmed from the deck!"

"You weren't only a cheat, you were a very poor one."

Del whipped around and pointed a finger at Vic. "I told you not to call me that!"

"Which one? A cheat, or a very poor cheat?"

"All right, gentlemen," Reena interrupted, laughing. "Can I get back to my story?"

"Of course, Miss O'Donnell, I'm so sorry," Vic smiled. Del continued staring at Vic with a burning intensity, but Vic ignored him. Del mumbled something about "snotty lords," pulled his boot off, and began scratching his foot through the holes in his socks.

"Anyway, Hunter," Reena continued, "they went down to Montana trying to find those butchers that killed all these people."

Stone looked at the pair with newfound respect. "Any luck?"

Vic told him about their lack of help from the authorities. "So, there was nothing else we could do, and we came back here."

"You will stay the night," Lone Elk spoke up, "or as long as you want." It wasn't a question, and Vic nodded his thanks gratefully. Gray Dawn brought strong coffee, and they drank silently for a while, listening to the loons calling out in the night.

Stone broke the silence. "Did you hear of any renegade Indians down that way? Crow, maybe?"

"No, we didn't, Mr. Stone," Vic answered slowly, noticing the keen look Reena gave Stone. "Why do you ask?"

"Just wondering."

"What will you do now?" Reena asked the pair, wanting to change the subject as quickly as possible.

"Ah, that's the interesting part," Vic said, holding up a finger. "We're going to Winnipeg to join the North-West Mounted Police."

"The what?"

Vic grinned. "It's official now. They're recruiting in Winnipeg and the Maritime Provinces for a march to this area to restore order."

"Why, that's wonderful!" Reena exclaimed. "Lone Elk, did you hear that? We're finally getting law and order here!"

Lone Elk nodded and smiled, but it vanished quickly and a troubled look clouded his face. *He's thinking that they're a few months late*, Reena thought. *And he's right.*

"I know it doesn't help much now, Chief Lone Elk," Vic said, "but the incident here was the deciding factor for the government. Lieutenant-Governor Morris of Manitoba had been warning Ottawa that something like this would happen, and now that it has, the government had to do something." Vic wasn't lying, but he wasn't telling the whole truth, either. The government's main purpose to act now had been fear of Indian retaliation for the massacre, not *because* of the incident. But Vic wasn't about to tell the proud chief this.

Stone spoke for the first time in a while. "How many men?"

"Three divisions of fifty men each."

Shaking his head, Stone remarked, "Won't be enough."

"The Act called for not more than three hundred, so I think it's just a matter of time before they call for the other hundred and fifty." Vic stared at Stone appraisingly for a moment. "Why don't you come with us?"

Reena and Lone Elk looked at Stone sharply. Reena thought excitedly, *That would be perfect! Just what he needs to bring him back to life!*

Vic and Del noticed the anxious glances, and both of them wondered again about this man's story. Del had once met a man with the same sort of quick, aggressive flash in the eyes that Stone had. He'd been a veteran of Robert E. Lee's battered Confederate army and had been through every campaign of "Marse Lee's" career. Del had met him in Dakota Territory in '69 and spent a restless, sleepless night on the cold prairie wondering if he'd wake up with his throat cut. The man had been nice enough, but quiet, with haunted eyes that seemed to look right through him as if he weren't there. Del would have left and camped a few miles away by himself, but he'd known that a few miles wasn't far enough from that man to guarantee sleep. When Del had awakened the next morning, sore and gritty-eyed, the man had vanished as if he hadn't even been there. Del, a superstitious man, shivered at the memory of the ghost-man.

Instead of facing Vic to answer his question, Stone looked at Lone Elk and said, "I think I'll pass."

"Why, Hunter?" Reena debated. "It sounds like something that would fit you perfectly."

"If you don't mind, Reena," he declared, getting to his feet, "I'll decide what's best for me right now."

He walked off, and Reena felt her face color. *Fine*, she thought bitterly, *that's the last time I look out for* his *welfare! He can be so kind one moment, then cruel the next!*

"May I ask what that fellow's problem is?" Vic asked, watching Stone's receding back.

"He makes me nervous," Del muttered.

"He is a troubled man," Lone Elk answered.

"No excuse to be rude to a lady," Vic sniffed.

———

Autumn arrived, and Stone's expeditions into the Cypress Hills lengthened from overnight stays to a few days, then to weeks at a time. Sometimes he took Star Light with him, but more often he traveled alone. When he was in the village he rarely talked anymore and never smiled. Reena always knew when he was preparing for another trek by his butchering of meat and preparation to make jerky. While the meat was smoking, he would sit outside his tepee, or sometimes by the creek, and clean his Henry rifle, slowly running an oiled cloth up and down the long barrel over and over. His face held a strange concentration as he did this, as if the task required all of his attention.

One gray, overcast day, Reena drove by his tepee in a wagon on her way to Farwell's trading post. Cold, biting wind had driven most of the people into their tepees to huddle by their fires, but Stone was sitting outside, cross-legged and staring at nothing. Seeing him there, stoic and unreadable, shivering slightly, the thought leaped into Reena's mind that she'd been pushing away for some time: *He's losing his mind. Oh, Lord, please help him!* She hadn't allowed the idea to form before, and the truth of it, cold and shiny as a bone stripped of flesh, pierced her heart.

Throughout the time of his withdrawal from the world, Reena had unfailingly tried to bring out the gentle side of him that she knew was there. She spoke to him whenever she saw him but only received one-word answers for her efforts. As she looked at him, some instinctive part of her knew he was on the verge of crossing over into unreality, and she couldn't resist trying one more time to bring him back.

Stopping the wagon, she got down and went to kneel beside him. He studied her with his faraway gaze that seemed to see beyond her somehow and greeted, "Good morning."

"Hello, Hunter. A little cold to be outside today, isn't it?"

"I don't mind." He wore a light buckskin coat, but his cheeks were blushed from the cold wind, and his hands trembled slightly. His face was covered with a few days of beard stubble, and Reena remembered the time she'd shaved him months before. *Back when he was helpless and sensitive*, she thought. *Not the husk of a man here.* The tragedy of his life and what he'd become overwhelmed her, and she instinctively reached out and ran the back of her fingers gently against his rough whiskers.

"Time for another shave?" she asked softly and felt tears welling in her eyes.

Stone kept his eyes on her, and as she watched, something shifted behind them—maybe a remembrance of that night when she'd clumsily cut him because of her anxiety at his closeness—but as soon as she recognized it, his face again turned stony, contemplative. "I'll be leaving soon, Reena."

Even before he said it, she'd known what was coming, and she nodded as her grief for him spilled over her cheeks.

"You saved my life—I owe you for that."

"You don't owe me a thing, Hunter Stone," she whispered, bringing her hand back down to her lap. "But you do owe yourself."

"What would that be?"

"A long life. Rebuilding. A family someday."

He shook his head wryly. "You never give up, do you?"

Reena wiped her cheeks and said, "No. It's called faith, and I'll keep praying for you even after you're gone." She stood and pulled her coat around herself tighter. "Would you do me a favor, Hunter?"

"Yes."

"Don't leave without telling me goodbye?"

He nodded slowly. "I can do that."

"Thank you," Reena said and managed to hold back the rest of her tears until she was out of the village.

———

Stone watched her leave.

Something inside of him burned to chase after the wagon—to climb into the seat beside her, place her soft hand back on his cheek, and tell her everything. Tell her how his mind was betraying him. Tell her how he missed contact with her, contact with a caring human being that only wanted what was best for him. Tell her that she was smart and considerate and brave—give something back to her that she'd attempted to shower over him for the past months: dignity, honor, and a sense of worthiness. Tell her about Betsy, and what a joy the world had been when she was in his life, and how the future held only a gray dimness now that closed over his eyes like a curtain and held no objective, but one.

*Red Wolf.*

For a while, Stone had forgotten his hunger for revenge. The loss of Betsy had hit him, really *hit* him, until all he could think about was what could have been. He'd watched the Indians getting on with their lives after losing loved ones, clinging to the very faith that had sustained his wife. He'd heard Reena teaching love and forgiveness, and to trust in Jesus to take away the pain. But the words had been just that—words—and hadn't penetrated the fog in his head.

*Red Wolf.*

Then the anger came, blotting all else out but basic, day-to-day functioning. His thoughts would bleed crimson hate, and time became meaningless. He would lose whole *days* sometimes while roaming in the hills, finally becoming aware of his surroundings at dusk, sitting beside a dead fire and holding a cup of coffee he'd prepared that morning. On those occasions, he'd shaken himself and slowly stretched his aching muscles, knowing that he should be disturbed over losing consciousness for hours, but somehow unable to grow concerned enough to feel threatened.

He wanted to go after Reena and tell her everything.

But he didn't.

That night he camped on the south side of the Hills, where a grizzly's spoor had led him. The heavy clouds of the day had blown over and left a full moon that illuminated his sparsely treed position and the valley below. He chose not to build a fire and ate the dried jerky he'd prepared previously. Resting with his head on his saddle, he surveyed the stars and listened to Buck's gentle movements behind him before sleep overtook him surprisingly fast.

In his dream, he was riding Buck at a smooth gallop, in no hurry, and with no destination in mind. It was extremely dark, with no moon, and a flash of lightning revealed a rider beside him that he hadn't been aware of before. There was no mistaking the ebony horse with the white mask, and Stone's eyes went to the rider. Red Wolf's fierce, strong face was painted as white as his horse's, and his dark eyes watched Stone unwaveringly. Instead of feeling alarmed, Stone merely stared back at the Crow calmly. There was nothing else in the dream but the two riders and the occasional lightning—no ground, landscape, or sky—but somehow they could see each other as if they cast lights of their own.

"I have waited long for a man such as you to ride by my side," Red Wolf voiced clearly. "Together, no one can stop us. We can go where we want, take what we want, and all of the Territory will be at our feet."

Stone nodded at the truth of it but said nothing.

Buck snickered nervously and threw his head back, biting at the reins.

Suddenly, Stone was looking at himself astride Buck and realized he was in Red Wolf's body. The searing pain of dozens of Red Wolf's victims crashed through his head, and when he opened his eyes, he saw and heard his other self say, "You know the reality of it all now, don't you? I am you, and you are me. One and the same, just as it has always been." The voice was Red Wolf's, coming from Stone's own lips. The horror was overwhelming. Then he was back in his own body, and Red Wolf began laughing from deep in his throat until the blackness around them rang with his pleasure.

Buck snickered again, urgently this time, and Stone's dread and aversion increased until he broke through the surface of sleep and found himself sweating in the cold night air, hugging himself tightly. He sat up immediately and looked around for the phantom of his dream, but there was only Buck in the small corral Stone had made for him with rope around four trees. The horse seemed to be staring right at him in the dim light, and he snorted quietly.

"What is it, boy?" Stone asked, rising and stroking his muzzle. Stone turned and viewed the valley, and his eyes widened as he became absolutely still. He saw five shadowy riders, and in the front, a white dot bobbing up and down. As his eyes became adjusted to the distance and moonlight, he knew he was looking at the stark white mask of a dark horse.

Like the one he'd been dreaming about.

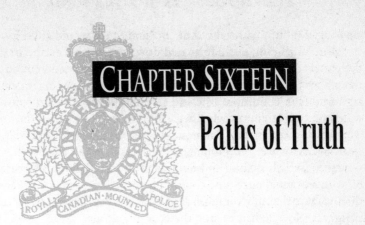

# CHAPTER SIXTEEN

## Paths of Truth

All the air rushed out of Stone's lungs as a black rage surged inside of him. He couldn't make out the riders, but he could tell the horses bore no saddles, and that fact made them Indians. For a moment he was frozen with shock that his enemy had appeared right in front of him. *I was just dreaming about him! And I was just about to leave to find him!* The coincidences were overwhelming, but his mind shifted quickly when he saw the group turn into the pass that led to the Assiniboine camp. *No!* he thought numbly, *God, no! Reena!*

Stone saddled Buck faster than he ever had in his life, pausing only as he fumbled with the cinch, his trembling hands betraying him momentarily. After savagely cutting the corral rope with a lightning flick of his knife, he mounted Buck and dug his heels hard into the horse's tan flanks. Expecting to hear gunshots any second, he ignored the valley and drove Buck directly toward the passage, slicing across the downward slope of the low hills. A misstep was more likely that way, but Stone needed *speed*, and that was the shortest distance between two points. As he rode, leaning awkwardly to the left to help Buck balance himself, he drew the Henry rifle from its scabbard and jacked a round in the chamber.

A muffled rifle exploded ahead in the direction of the village. Then another, followed by another. *I hope that's you firing, Lone Elk!* Stone thought desperately. A horrible image leaped to his mind of women and children running, and Red Wolf drawing a careful bead with his rifle on innocent victims, a savage glint in his eye, shooting them down like clay targets. In the back of Stone's mind, he wondered fleetingly why the Crow was here—*why would he take on odds of over twenty to one?* But it didn't matter; he was here, and Stone would kill him.

More shots rang out. He angled down the last hill to the head of the pass, intending to cut off any retreat the Indians had in mind and to ambush them from the rear. As he burst into the opening, he pulled up abruptly in confusion. The Indian riders were headed directly toward him, and Stone saw why they had come: in the midst of the group were a half-dozen horses belonging to the Assiniboine. *They're here to steal the horses, not kill!* he understood in a flash. Horses were as essential to Indians as food and water, and to steal them was a crushing blow to any tribe, but Stone couldn't help feeling a sense of relief that thievery was the only thing on Red Wolf's mind, instead of senseless slaughter. Now he had to stop the charging group.

He fired two shots in the air, one after another, as fast as he could, leaving three shots for himself. The group hesitated and milled about, shocked to find their escape cut off. Stone could hear shots from behind them; someone from the Assiniboine camp was giving chase on foot. The thieves were in shadow under the towering spruce trees, but Stone could just make out Red Wolf and his masked horse behind another rider. He could sense their confusion and uncertainty, and that was all he needed. Taking careful aim at the dim figure of his enemy, his finger tightened on the trigger until he felt the recoil jam back into his shoulder and heard the huge explosion.

At the last second, the rider in front of Red Wolf moved into the line of fire and with a shout flipped backward off of his mount. Stone cursed and worked the lever of the rifle. The horses were on the edge of breaking away in the direction of the village, when Red Wolf raised his fist in the air with a scream and charged Stone. The Indians to the rear were suddenly putting their hands in the air, Stone noticed absently, and he realized that whoever had been chasing from the village had caught up with them and forced surrender.

Red Wolf rode low over his horse's neck, and something about the solitary figure made Stone hesitate momentarily. But rage took over, and he gritted his teeth and spurred Buck savagely, charging through the murderous red mist that had descended over his vision. When they were twenty feet from each other, Stone became aware that the other horse was being guided to avoid instead of confront. At the last second, Stone manuevered Buck directly into the other horse and leaped toward the Crow at the same time. Stone held the Henry in front of himself with both hands as he flew through the air and felt it connect solidly as his momentum carried him over the masked horse and to the ground beside Red Wolf.

As he rolled to cushion his impact, Stone screamed triumphantly—a primal howl of victory that reverberated between the walls of the passage. When he gained his feet, he wheeled instantly and went to his foe, who was still on his back. Stone could hear his own ragged breathing and feel hot blood pumping through his face as he raised his rifle. They'd landed in a pocket of bright moonlight, and the long, polished iron barrel flashed with a cold luster. The face at which he aimed was the visage of both his worst nightmares and his most satisfying fantasies. In the torn half of an instant, as his finger tightened on the trigger, he thought with supreme, maniacal pleasure, *This is what I've waited for—this is justice* . . . .

"Hunter, no!"

*Betsy—? Is that you?*

"Hunter, *please*!"

The voice was off to his left, out of his field of vision. He glanced quickly, saw Reena with her hands clasped in front of herself in a begging gesture, and looked back to his target. Stunned, he found that the grim, mocking countenance of Red Wolf had been replaced with a boy—a terrified, cowering boy that held thin, wasted arms in front of his face. He suddenly noticed how quiet the night had become, and that he was holding his breath while his lungs cried for air. Blinking rapidly, his mind reeling in chaos, he let out his breath and took a shuffling step backward.

"They're just boys, Hunter," Reena said softly beside him. "Just little boys." She grasped the barrel of the rifle, gently pushing it away.

The Indian boy looked no more than thirteen, and he gazed at Stone with wide, terrified eyes. His arms were still held protectively in front of his face, and Stone noticed the bones of his elbows jutting out grotesquely from his lean arms. "What—how did—?" he began, but his thoughts were a maze.

Reena took the Henry from his limp fingers while examining his face. "Hunter, what's the matter? You're pale as death!" Lone Elk walked up with a group of braves guarding the other boys, and she absently handed him the heavy rifle.

Lone Elk said, "The boy that was shot is only wounded—he will live."

*I shot a boy*, Stone thought dully with dread and shame. The fact barely broke through his dazed mind as he looked around blankly at Reena, Lone Elk, the boy, and the horses. *The horse!* he thought abruptly. "Chief, ask him where he got that horse."

Lone Elk's black eyebrows raised questioningly. "What horse?"

"That one right there!" Stone said impatiently, gesturing to the nervous, winded colt that stood with the others nearby. As he pointed, he noticed for the first time that the horse's rear feet were white also, and his heart fell. Red Wolf's mount had been pure black behind the white mask. He was sure of it—he would never forget the fierce stallion bearing down on him at the Osbourne farm that rainy night. Distantly he heard Lone Elk say something in Sioux, followed by the boy's high-pitched reply.

"He says he has had the horse since its birth."

Stone understood now—understood everything. His dream of the horse and the hatred that burned within him for Red Wolf had blinded him. Now he knew why the rider had appeared strange as he'd charged: the figure bent over the horse's neck had been too small to compare with Red Wolf's large frame. Stone shook his head as he gazed at the stockings on the colt's hind feet.

The boy on the ground carefully rose to his feet, favoring his right leg, and spoke again. Lone Elk translated, "He is Cree. He says the men are off fighting the Blackfoot, and his people are starving. They were stealing our horses for food."

Stone looked at the boy, who visibly shrank back from his gaze as he spoke again. Lone Elk said calmly, "He asks me to stop the savage white man from killing him."

The irony was almost too much for Stone to bear. *This skinny Indian boy is describing me with the word I've used so many times for Red Wolf—savage. And he's looking at me with the same fear and dread that Red Wolf's victims probably show him before they die. The dream was true—he and I are the same. I'm no better than what I despise.*

"Hunter?" Reena asked, touching his sleeve. "Are you all right? You're not going to kill him, are you?"

Stone looked at her sharply, then noticed that *everyone* was watching him and waiting for his answer. *They really believe I could shoot that kid in cold blood!* he thought in amazement. *Do they honestly think I'm capable of that? Even Reena? What have I become?* He covered his face with shaking hands for a moment, then dropped them to his side limply and whispered, "No, Reena. I'm not going to take that boy's life." Not able to meet their eyes, he turned and walked slowly to Buck, took the reins, and led him back to the village through the tree-scattered moonlight.

————

Stone remained in his tepee all the next day. Reena found herself glancing in that direction many times as she went about her duties, hoping to see him. The day grew colder instead of warmer, and at midday fat snowflakes began to fall, the first snow of the autumn. The children Reena was teaching became excited, and she finally gave up trying to keep their attention on learning English. They ran outside the tepee, jumping and playing and trying to catch the flakes on their tongues. Reena wondered if the children of the Assiniboine had been doing that for all time.

Tired from the long, exciting night before, Reena went home and considered taking a nap. The Cree boys had told of massive herds of buffalo disappearing from their land, slaughtered by white men with repeating rifles. Tears came to their eyes as they told of the land around the Bear Hills, strewn with stinking carcasses of the huge beasts, stripped of their hides and left to rot. Lone Elk had let the boys go after giving them some elk meat and corn. The generosity had shamed them, and they'd thanked the chief many times. The boys had left at daybreak and headed north to their tribe.

Reena stretched out on the thick furs of her bed and fell asleep instantly. She didn't move for two hours. When she turned over, fuzzily aware that she should get up, she heard a voice outside.

"Reena?"

She rose and rubbed her face groggily, tried to straighten her black hair, and went to the flap. "Hunter, hello! Come in."

"I'm sorry, did I wake you?"

"Is it that obvious?" she asked, putting a hand to her face. The snow was still coming down lightly but hadn't started carpeting the ground yet. She shivered and stepped back. "Come in, it's freezing!"

"I've got company, too," Stone said, and Star Light appeared from around the side of the tepee, tentatively smiling.

"Well, you can come in, too, Star, you know that," Reena smiled. "I'll make some coffee." Putting a pot of water over the fire, she watched them enter the tepee and stand awkwardly. Stone had his hands clasped in front of his thick, bearskin coat. He'd shot the bear himself, and Gray Dawn had insisted on showing him how to dry the skin and make the cuts for the pattern. Stone had been reluctant at first, but after a while he'd listened carefully and studied her skillful movements, and felt confident he could make another one in the future. "Go ahead, sit down," Reena gestured.

Removing their coats, they sat cross-legged by the fire and put their hands close to the flames to warm them. "It's been so long since I've been here," Stone said softly as he looked around. He remembered every line and stitch of the tepee, since he'd spent a month staring at the walls. "I was actually afraid it would bring back bad memories, but it doesn't."

"I'm glad. You were very near death here." Reena wondered why he was here as she considered his face closely, noticing with pleasure that he was freshly shaved. His overall appearance seemed well-groomed, very different from the shambling, sickly looking man of the previous months. His eyes rested on her, and they were clear and lucid. As she noted that his normally tight-lipped mouth was relaxed, he smiled, almost shyly.

"I guess I've seemed kind of crazy lately," he confessed.

"Yes, but for all I knew you were acting normally, since I didn't know you before all this happened to you. That's why I've kept my distance."

"Good point," he nodded. "But it's not how I used to be."

"I didn't really think so," she smiled.

"Last night—I saw something in myself that I despised. I let hatred completely take me over, and a little boy almost died because of it." He glanced at Star Light, who was watching him intently. "Do you understand what happened to me last night?" The boy didn't answer. "Do you understand what hateful feelings can do to you? It snatches your soul, Star. Right here"—he patted the boy's chest—"poof! Gone."

Star Light looked away, troubled.

"Reena," Stone continued, "one of the last conversations I ever had with my wife was about forgiveness. She was the most caring person I ever knew, but even *she* was having a hard time forgiving that Crow. You see, he killed our friends about a month before he took Betsy. I was the one that found them, and he saw me. When he came to my farm and did what he did, that made it personal."

Reena saw the water boiling and began pouring the dark liquid into pottery cups. "Go on," she encouraged.

"All my life I've followed the law and never wavered from it. But this was *personal*. I've kicked myself every day because I didn't shoot that dog when I had the chance that night. Instead, I had this crazy notion that we should fight hand to hand, man to man. I wanted him to *know* who was going to defeat him—but it didn't turn out that way. Now there's no telling how many more lives he's taken because I acted so stupidly."

Reena handed him a cup of hot coffee. "I'm glad you didn't kill him, Hunter. A revenge killing is never going to be right."

"Even if he's killed more families?" Stone asked testily.

"You're not God, Hunter. It's not your place to decide whether someone should live or die."

"You're not married, but what if he killed your mother or your father? Do you think you'd still feel that way?"

"I'd hope so," Reena said fervently. "I would hope nothing would make me abandon what I believe in."

Stone nodded slowly and took a sip of the steaming coffee. He watched her over the rim of the cup as he blew on the drink to cool it. "Hang on to that hope, Reena. Pray that you keep that hope, because to lose your principles leads to internal chaos, believe me." The haunted look clouded his face again for an instant, then was gone as quickly as it had appeared.

"You're a good man, Hunter Stone. I knew it all along, even if you didn't."

"Thank you," he smiled. "It helps when there's someone who believes in you. Whether you're aware of it or not, you've helped me a great deal. I think if it hadn't been for you, I'd have been gone from here as soon as I could walk." He reached over with his free hand and took hers, leaning over slightly and gazing deep into her eyes. She held her breath, thinking he was actually going to kiss her, and she was mired in confusion until he said softly, "I wouldn't have made it without you, physically *or* mentally. You're a special lady, and I thank you."

His lips were parted slightly, and she had the sudden urge to kiss them but fought it down at once. Blushing, she squeezed his hand and withdrew hers. "You're a strong man, Hunter," she pronounced, trying to cover her embarrassment. *Could he see what I was thinking?* "You would've been all right."

Stone nodded but looked doubtful. "I came by to tell you—tell you both—that I've made a decision." He glanced at Star Light, who perked up noticeably. Taking a deep breath, Stone declared, "I'm going to join the Mounted Police."

"Hunter, that's wonderful!" Reena said, joy and relief filling her.

"I can't waste my life trying to find that man and kill him. If I ever do see him again I don't know how I'll react, but I'm not going looking for him."

"You don't know how happy this makes me."

Star Light suddenly reached in Stone's coat pocket where he knew the buffalo talisman was kept, snatched it out, and waved it in front of Stone. Small growling noises emanated from deep in his throat, gain-ing intensity and volume, and his eyebrows came together in a deep scowl. "N-n-no!" he stammered.

Stone and Reena watched his reaction in shock, unable to move. Stone didn't know which was more surprising, his response or hearing the sound of his voice for the first time.

"N-no! Find them! We find them!" he shrieked, pushing the talisman closer to Stone's face.

"What's he talking about?" Reena asked Stone, even though she had a good idea what it might be.

"So that's what Lone Elk was talking about," he said thoughtfully. "He told me that Star was waiting for something, waiting for *me* to do something, and I didn't understand. But now I do: he wants me to hunt down the men that killed his parents."

The boy nodded, and his face lit up with hope.

"Oh, Star," Reena moaned, "is that why you've followed Hunter everywhere? Because you thought he would take revenge for himself, then help you take yours?"

Nodding again, Star Light motioned to Stone and himself. "We go," he stated and gave Stone an expectant look.

"No, Star," Stone disagreed gently. "We *don't* go. That's not the way." The boy's face transformed with sudden intensity, and he rose to his feet quickly. Stone grasped his small arm, urging, "Wait a minute, sit down."

Star Light attempted to pull his arm away, but Stone tightened his grip.

"You lie!" Star hissed.

"No, I didn't lie to you. I never said anything about going after the white hunters—you just took it for granted that I would. Do you understand?"

His lower lip began to tremble as he stared into the steaming pot of water by the fire. The buffalo talisman was bent double in his fist as he clenched it tightly.

"Star Light, you're so full of anger, and it'll eat you up. Believe me, I know. You've got to let it go and get on with your life."

"He's right, Star," Reena agreed, leaning toward the boy. "You're so smart, and everyone loves you and wants what's best for you." A tear rolled down the boy's cheek, winking in the fire light. "God loves you more than any of us *ever* could, Star Light. I know you've heard me say that when I've been teaching the Bible. I've seen you watching me, and I know you understand—why don't you let the Lord take care of you?"

"Bad men," Star Light whispered.

"Yes, they were bad men," Stone agreed, "and bad men have a way of running into the law very soon and going to jail. Those men made a mistake when they went down to the United States, because there are soldiers and marshals down there. If they'd stayed here, there would have been no one to put them in jail, until the Mounted Police get here." He patted the boy's back. "And when they *do* get here, I'll be with them and maybe I'll run across those fellas and put them in jail *for* you."

"We have to depend on the law," Reena told Star Light, "and let God bring those men to justice."

Star Light raised his eyes. "Just-just—?"

"Justice—it means fair punishment," Reena smiled. "To pay for the bad thing they did."

Nodding, Star Light looked down at the talisman clasped tightly in his hands. He slowly released his grip and ran his fingers over the beads gently and whispered, "Mama."

Reena felt a lump in her throat and moved around Stone to wrap her arms around the hurting little boy from behind. He began to cry and shake, releasing his pain for the first time in five months, and she held him tightly and stroked his silky black hair.

Watching them, Stone felt his own eyes moisten. He knew exactly how the boy felt, and without a word he moved beside them and encircled them both with his arms. They clung to one another for a long time.

———

The snow had continued to fall gently all through the night, and in the morning a four-inch carpet of white covered the ground. Word of Stone's departure spread quickly, and a few of the women hastily prepared food for his long journey east.

But the biggest news was Star Light's breakthrough. All of the women in the tribe had felt unmistakable maternal emotions for the sad little boy that had chosen to have no home or family. It just wasn't *right*, and Star Light had remained an unspoken reminder of the horrible day of the massacre—a silent, mourning ghost that moved among them every day. So when a woman named Stands Tall emerged from her tepee for firewood that snowy morning and saw the boy walking by with Stone to feed the horses, she smiled at him as she always did. "Good morning," Star Light said to her shyly, and the poor woman nearly fainted. Then, after recovering from her shock and seeing Stone smile knowingly at her, she ran after the little boy, took him in her arms, and laughed and cried as she showered him with kisses. Soon every woman in the tribe was seeking the boy, and Star Light endured hugs and kisses until his ribs were sore from all the squeezing. "Maybe better not to talk," he confided to Stone later, massaging his middle, and Stone had broken a long dry spell of his own—he'd laughed.

Reena and Gray Dawn were standing outside admiring the snowfall when they saw the man and little boy talking and laughing. "I never thought I'd see the day," Reena said softly.

"It is good," Gray Dawn agreed, and her face glowed with pleasure. "Hunter will be all right. Will you?"

"Me? Of course I will—why?"

"You are fond of him."

"Yes, I am. Just as you are."

Gray Dawn smiled but said nothing else.

By noon, Buck was saddled and ready to go. Stone had had to refuse most of the gifts of food and clothes from the Indians, because Buck would have been much too weighted down to bear the load. Their generosity had touched him deeply, and he'd taken the time to thank each thoughtful giver.

"We have been blessed by your presence," Lone Elk stated as he shook Stone's hand. "Go with God."

"Thank you, Chief Lone Elk," Stone returned formally, then he impulsively embraced the shorter man. "I'll never forget you—or you, Gray Dawn," he said as he put his arms around her, too.

"You will come back someday?" Gray Dawn asked, her dark eyes shining as she looked up at him.

"You can count on it." Stone felt a tugging at the hem of his bear coat and found Star Light holding out his talisman. Squatting down, Stone locked eyes with the boy and said gently, "That buffalo got me through some hard times, Star, but I want you to keep it to help you through your own troubles. Do you understand?"

Star Light considered his words for a moment. "You no want?"

"I'd love to have one, but your mother wanted you to have that one. Tell you what—why don't you make one for me, just like that, for when I come back?"

Smiling, Star Light nodded and threw his arms around Stone's neck. Stone held him tight, and for a moment he had the wild idea to take this wonderful, fatherless boy with him and fulfill a desire for both of them. He closed his eyes tightly, knowing he was dreaming, but not caring. "You help Lone Elk take care of your people, you hear?" He felt the small head nod on his shoulder, and he hoped the boy wasn't crying; but when Star Light pulled away he was smiling and confident. Stone ruffled his hair and turned to Reena, who was stroking Buck's nose.

"You look like a totally different man," she commented, smiling up at him.

"I *am* a different man." A shadow of sadness passed over his face before he took her hand and grinned mischievously. "Especially since we first met—I'm upright, and I'm not bleeding all over the place." Reena laughed, and after a moment he said seriously, "I'll miss that."

"What?"

"Your laugh—your smile."

Reena squeezed his hand and felt her eyes moisten. She'd promised herself that she wouldn't cry, and it took every bit of her strength to avoid it. *This is a happy time, Lord; help me remember that. He's got his life together again.* "I'll miss you, too. You *will* come back, won't you?" His answer was suddenly very important to her, more than she wanted to admit.

"I'll be back. I promise." He smiled and took her in his arms.

"Be careful, Hunter," she whispered close to his ear. "I'll pray for you."

"I'll be careful. Thank you for everything, Reena."

She shook her head but didn't trust her voice enough to speak. He stepped back from her, mounted Buck, and waved to the Indians gathered around. "Thank you *all*."

At the first bend of the passage, before Buck took him out of sight, he turned in the saddle and waved to her once more, already looking forward to his next visit with the Assiniboine—and a missionary named Reena.

———

Stu Durant was mumbling as he stocked the shelves of his trading post, located on the east side of the Sweet Grass Hills in Montana Territory. He and his wife, Missy, had lived for a while in Fort Benton, about one hundred miles south of the Hills, until Stu had had a grand idea. The dry goods and mercantile stores in Fort Benton were making a killing off of Indians, hunters, and settlers coming down from Canada to purchase supplies. Stu had talked Missy into moving up to the Sweet Grass Hills to open their own trading post and intercept all that money going south.

For the last three months, it had worked. Most of the time, Stu was in a great mood as he mentally patted himself on the back for his un-canny sense of business. Missy, however, viewed the move quite dif-ferently. Stuck out in the middle of nowhere, with nothing to do and no one to visit, she complained every day. "What good does it do if we make money?" she would ask countless times. "We don't have any-where to spend it!" Stu would patiently point out the brand-new bath-tub he'd ordered for her, or the Boston rocker, or the Chippendale furniture—but it never was enough. Missy wanted to flaunt their new-found wealth, pouting in her deep-South twang, "But who am I going to flaunt it at, the gophers?"

So Stu was set to grumbling as well. His bad humor didn't improve when he opened an unmarked box he'd just received in a shipment from Fort Benton. Six red velvet cords lay coiled like snakes in the box, and attached to one end of each was a brass knob. "What in the—?" Stu removed one of the soft coils and turned it over and over, totally baffled. Out of the corner of his eye, he saw a white piece of paper in the bottom of the box, and he snatched it up.

For a moment, he stared in disbelief at what had been purchased with his hard-earned money. His eyes went to the bottom of the doc-ument to see who'd ordered the items, as if he didn't know already. "M. D." the initials read. *"Missy!"* Stu hollered at the top of his voice.

"Yes, Stu?" Missy called from the living area in the back of the store.

"What are we doing with bellpulls for door chimes?"

"Oh, are they here?"

"Yes, they're here!" Stu shot back with irritation. "But *why* are they here?"

"You never know, Stu," Missy said lightly, her careless tone causing Stu to become even more annoyed. "Someone might come in today and want one."

Stu hung his head in exasperation. "Well, I'll offer one to the next beaver trapper that comes in—maybe he'll want one for his cave!" He took the box in his arms and stood. "Or maybe the next dirty Injun that—" Stu's mouth closed with a snap.

Just inside the door stood the most frightening Indian he'd ever seen. Cold, black eyes watched him with the tiniest hint of amusement. Every Indian he'd seen had been of average stature or shorter, but this one was *big*. Cradled carelessly in his arms was a long rifle. Stu had heard no noise at all—*nothing*.

For the first time since he'd come to the Sweet Grass Hills, Stu was acutely aware of the complete meaning of remoteness. There was no sheriff to call, no cavalry to come to their rescue, and his loaded pistol was in the back with Missy. Completely surprised and concentrating on slowing down his speeding heart, Stu held out the box to the Indian and spoke the first words that came to his mind. "Bellpull, sir?"

The ebony eyes flickered to the box, then locked on Stu's face again. One corner of his full mouth raised into a half-grin, and Stu's blood chilled as he struggled with the sudden impulse to shiver.

"I . . . uh . . . about that 'dirty Injun' comment, sir," Stu began, hearing the pleading in his own voice, "it's just a figger of speech, you understand—"

"Fifty caliber cartridges," the Indian interrupted as the half-grin vanished.

"Yes, sir, right away, sir," Stu nodded, starting to pass in front of the Indian to get around the counter. The long barrel of the rifle came down in front of him, stopping him instantly.

"And keep your hands in sight," the man said softly.

Stu couldn't meet his eyes and felt a drop of sweat fall from his forehead. "Yessir, you got it." The Indian let him pass, and Stu instantly set the box of bellpulls on the counter and held his hands high as he rounded the counter. Then he realized he faced another dilemma. "Um . . . I . . . uh . . . I have to reach under the counter to get your shells, sir . . . uh . . . may I?" he finished weakly. He suddenly thought of Missy and prayed she stayed in the back.

The Indian nodded, once, and laid the barrel of the rifle across the counter, aimed directly at Stu's chest. Stu kept one hand in the air and his eyes on the rifle as he leaned down and retrieved the box of shells. He'd never been so scared in his life and hoped his trembling knees didn't buckle under him.

The Indian seemed bored in an arrogant sort of way as his eyes wandered to a newspaper on the counter. He seemed to focus on an item on the front page. "What does this say?" he pointed.

Stu slid the box of cartridges toward him and glanced quickly at the paper he'd already read. "It's about a mounted police force they're forming in Canada. They're gonna march across the country to the North-West Territories to 'stablish law and order and settle the—" Stu shut his mouth, for he'd almost said, "settle the Injuns." His dry throat clicked as he swallowed and finished: "Um . . . settle the settlers."

The Indian looked at Stu with the horrible half-smile again. "Law and order? Maybe I should go turn myself in right now."

He seemed to wait for a reaction, but Stu didn't know what to say, so he continued concentrating on not falling down. The shaking in his knees had spread to his whole body, and he felt like a marionette being jerked around by a mad puppeteer. His eyes could not stop going to the huge black hole at the end of the rifle barrel, and he expected an explosion at any second.

"Those *police*"—the Indian spat the word—"have a long way to travel from Winnipeg. Anything could happen between there and the Territories. Do you agree?"

"Yep," Stu nodded instantly, feeling sweat leaking from every pore. "Long way . . . anything—"

"How much for the cartridges?"

"Nothing, not a thing . . . uh . . . special today—"

"Thanks." Obviously enjoying Stu's discomfort, seeming to *feed* off of it in an eerie way, the big Indian pocketed the shells and started to back away from the counter. Then he stopped, reached into the box, and withdrew one of the bellpulls. At the door, he grinned and gave a farewell wave with the coiled red velvet cord.

Stu's legs completely gave out as he collapsed into a chair, shaking uncontrollably. For some reason, the Indian's face had reminded Stu of a hungry wolf.

# TAMING THE RUDE SAVAGE

*We'll tame the rude savage,*
*we'll order, ordain,*
*And we'll chase the wild buffalo*
*over the plain;*
*All riots and rows*
*at our advent shall cease,*
*And we'll show them who's who*
*with the Mounted Police.*

Stanza from an anonymously written
poem appearing in the Ottawa
*Daily Citizen*, before the Mounted Police
embarked on the Great March West.

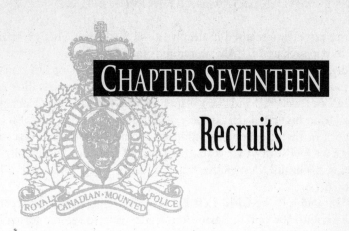

# CHAPTER SEVENTEEN

# Recruits

Del Dekko stood by one of the windows of East Barracks in Lower Fort Garry warming his hands by the woodburning stove and cackling until tears came to his eyes. Outside in the deep snow, under the overcast clouds of January 1874, Sub-Inspector Jaye Eliot Vickersham of C Division, North-West Mounted Police, stood shivering as he observed his sub-constables march on parade. *Poor ol' Lord Vic's 'bout froze to an icicle*, Del thought with glee, *and here I am, toasty and warm by the stove! Don't that beat all!* When Del's eyes had cleared from the tears, he began watching Vic again, waiting for his next body-shaking shiver that would send Del into more raucous peals of laughter.

The police marching in the snow looked anything but professional; the uniforms that had been promised had not yet arrived, and the men were dressed in the clothes they'd brought with them. However, they'd been drilled enough times so that their lines were straight, and the turns they executed were crisp. Great clouds of steam rose from forty-seven mouths as they went through their paces in the sub-zero temperature.

"Hooo-eee, them boys is gonna be cold!" Del crowed as he pulled his suspenders over his shoulders. He'd just risen from a midafternoon nap—a routine he'd established for himself since he had nothing else to do—and was planning on making some coffee for the men. *Sure am sleeping a lot lately*, he reflected uneasily, *but if anybody calls me old, I'll pinch his head! 'Sides, it ain't the age, it's the miles*, he justified to himself.

Pouring a small mountain of crushed coffee beans into a large pot on the stove, he breathed in deeply of the thick aroma before setting the burlap sack aside. "Always reminds me of me pappy," he recalled fondly, though his father had been a horrible abuser of Del and his mother. Jonathan Dekko would make fun of Del's eyes, calling him "bug" or "weevil," and then blame his wife for having a "cockeyed son." After his verbal attacks, he would usually get drunk and beat one or both of them, depending upon his temper at the time. Over the course of Del's fifty-two years, he'd buried his pain by mentally replacing his pitiful, destructive father with the image of a loving, but strict, parent.

Humming "The Girl I Left Behind Me," Del poured a bucketful of water into the pot and glanced outside again to see the formation breaking up and rushing toward the warmth of the barracks. He noticed Vic following the men, instead of heading to the officers' quarters.

The peace and quiet Del had been enjoying was rudely shattered when the door flew open and the men burst through, stomping the snow from their boots, complaining loudly, and making a beeline toward the six stoves scattered throughout the long, low building.

"Hey, Dekko!" Constable Ivan Maisel roared from the nearest stove. "This fire's almost burned down! Can't you even handle *that* woman's job?" He turned his massive head to the nearest sub-constable. "Booger, stoke this fire." The unfortunately named Gustav Boogaard did as he was told after casting a dark look at Maisel's back. His nickname was unavoidable, but coming from Maisel's mouth it seemed even more distasteful.

"Here he comes, Del," whispered Andy Doe beside him. Doe was twenty, with large brown eyes set in a baby face that barely grew whiskers. He and another sub-constable, Ken Garner, could have been twins and were often mistaken for each other.

"I'm gonna let 'im have it, Garner," Del growled.

"I'm Doe, Del."

"Whatever."

Maisel strode up to them in his cocky walk. "Couldn't you find the time in your busy day to keep the fires going, Dekko? Doesn't seem too hard a job, if you ask me."

"Well, nobody asked you, Maisel," Del countered, defiantly meeting his eyes, though Maisel stood at least eight inches taller than Del's five foot seven. He had a huge head, very square, with small brown eyes that receded under the thick bone structure of his brows. A thick mustache covered his upper lip.

"Watch your mouth—you're talking to a superior officer here. I've warned you about that."

"You *ain't* superior, and you *ain't* no officer, Maisel."

"I'm a full constable, and that's a whole lot more superior than a lowly scout."

"We'll see about that when we're out in the middle of nowheres, and you're squallin' about which way to go to find water and shelter!"

"Is there a problem here, gentlemen?" Vickersham asked as he appeared beside Doe and started warming his hands over the stove. His deep blue woolen caped coat was glistening with melted snow, and despite his easy tone, his brown eyes were narrowed.

Maisel and Doe came to attention—neither was aware that Vic had followed them inside. Maisel jerked his head in Del's direction. "Uh . . . the scout here seems to be neglecting his duties, sir. At least one of the stoves was burnt out, and I haven't had time to check the others."

"What are your duties, Constable?" Vic asked curtly.

"Sir?"

"Tell me your duties, as explained to you by Inspector Macleod."

"To obey orders at all times, and to convey and supervise those orders to the sub-constables, sir."

Vic nodded slowly and pursed his lips. "Constable, was there anything in there about supervising scouts?"

"No, sir."

"And under whose jurisdiction is Mr. Dekko?"

"In our troop, sir—Troop C—he is under Sub-Inspector Vickersham and Inspector Macleod."

"That's funny—I didn't hear you say 'Constable Maisel' in there. Did I miss it?"

"No, sir."

"Very well. Carry on, Constable."

"Thank you, sir." With a dark look at Del, Maisel spun on a booted heel and walked stiffly to the other side of the barracks, fully one hundred feet away.

Vickersham noticed Doe between himself and Del and said, "At ease, Garner."

Doe didn't move a muscle.

"I said 'at ease,' " Vic repeated.

"I'm Doe, sir."

"Then at ease, Doe."

"Thank you, sir," Doe responded, immediately placing his still-cold hands over the stove.

"Doe," Vic said thoughtfully, "I looked straight at you when I gave you the order. What difference does it make if I had you confused with Garner?"

"Because Sub-constable Garner could have been standing behind me, sir. I didn't want to take the chance that you were speaking to him and not me, sir."

"Sub-constable Doe?" Vic asked with a glint in his eye.

"Yes, sir?"

"If I had two hundred of you, I could invade Montana Territory and plant the Dominion of Canada flag."

"Anytime you're ready, sir."

Vic smiled and patted the boy on the back. "Could you give Mr. Dekko and me a moment, Doe?"

"Of course, sir."

After he'd gone, Del gave Vickersham a disgusted look. "I swear, I never thought I'd see the day when you had people sirrin' you right and left. What's the world come to?"

"Del, about the fires—"

"I know, I know. I just missed that one today—never happened before."

"Take care in the future, will you? The men are cold when they get in."

"Yes, *sir*!" Del said sarcastically. When he saw that his friend didn't appreciate it, he mumbled, "Sorry, Vic."

"I know it's different having to show respect for me, Del, but if I let you get into the habit of insubordination when we're alone—"

"Yeah, yeah—I might do it in front of Macleod—excuse me—*Inspector* Macleod, and then my hide wouldn't be worth a turtle's tail."

"That's right."

"By the way, what are you doin' here, anyway? The officers' quarters are better heated than this cave."

"And farther away." Vic glanced around quickly. "Don't tell the men, but officers get cold, too."

"Naaawww! You're joshin' me!"

"Yes, and it's a jolly good thing that I *did* come in here. Maisel looked as if he were going to have at you."

"Bah!"

"He seems to have taken a particular disliking to you, Del. I'd watch him."

"Maisel prob'ly took a dislike to his own mother. Everbody hates him. All he can talk about is how he cain't wait to get into a scrap and show them Indians and whiskey traders who's who. Man's got more hot air in 'im than Mount Bersubius."

"Vesuvius."

"Whatever. When *are* we gonna be movin' out, Vic?"

"Got cabin fever, Del?"

"I'm as depressed as a chipmunk in a cat's mouth."

Vickersham removed his coat and shook it over the stove. The drops of moisture fizzled faintly and disappeared. "The detachment in Toronto is just getting started in their training," he informed Del, taking off his woolen hat and shaking the water from it, too. He nodded in the direction of the men around them. "And these men aren't ready yet, either. Besides, Del, we can't go anywhere in the middle of the winter freeze-up."

"Excuse me, sir," Constable Preston Stride interrupted at Vickersham's elbow. He was a tall, tough Englishman with close-cropped red hair and much more professional at supervising the men than his counterpart, Ivan Maisel. Vickersham liked and trusted him. "We seem to have a problem with Sub-Constable Smith."

"A problem?"

"Yes, sir. Would you come with me, sir?"

Vickersham followed Stride to a spot near the door where a knot of men was gathered. Smith, a man with the largest ears Vickersham had ever seen on a human, was standing by the door with his hand on the knob and his rucksack thrown over his shoulder. "Is there something wrong, Smith?" Vickersham asked.

"Blame right, there's something wrong, Vickersham—"

"That's Sub-Inspector to you, Smith," Stride growled.

"I'll call him anything I want. I quit! I'm sick of marching in the snow, day after day, with nothing but bad food and you ugly brutes to look at!"

"Think about what you're doing, Smith," Vic advised. "There were fifteen hundred men that applied for the Police, and you happen to be one of them that was chosen—show some pride in that."

"You can have your pride! You're all going to be massacred by two thousand Blackfeet anyway! I think I'll miss that party, if you don't mind." Smith glanced around at the faces in defiance, then opened the door and left.

Feeling the blast of cold air from the briefly opened door, Vickersham suppressed a shiver. Smith wasn't the first man to bolt, but whenever one *did*, he always seemed to have a parting comment about the Police being doomed, either by Indians or whiskey traders. It was difficult to keep up men's morale with words like that.

"Shall I go and get him, sir?" Stride asked, obviously wanting to.

"No, Sergeant, let him go." Stride had served in a British regiment in England and preferred to be addressed by his military rank rather than "Constable." All former soldiers held the same view—even Vickersham, who'd served in the British Army for a short time and preferred to be called "Captain." But appearances had to be upheld, and Vickersham only addressed Stride as "Sergeant" when there was no superior officer around.

"Excuse me, sir." A man tentatively stepped forward from the group still gathered around. His boyish face was reluctant as he asked, "Do you think there's anything to that talk? About Indians and all?"

Vickersham clasped his hands behind his back and attempted to exude more self-confidence than he felt. "I'm not going to lie to you, lad. We all know there are Indians out there, but they're not *all* looking for scalps. In fact, I spent a few very pleasant evenings with a tribe of Assiniboine once. Couldn't ask for a more peaceful or honorable people." He paused and looked around at the anxious faces and saw a few visibly relax. "So, why don't we concentrate on our duties and worry about trouble when and if it comes, what?"

"Yes, sir," the man replied.

The door opened again, and Inspector Macleod's adjutant, Wilkes, stuck his head in. "Sub-Inspector Vickersham? Inspector Macleod wishes to see you in his office, sir."

*Now what?* Vickersham almost said aloud, but instead he nodded and turned to Stride. "Carry on, Sergeant."

"Very well, sir. You men stop standing around and get cleaned up for supper. I don't want to see one particle of dirt under any fingernails." Stride had a barking, gruff voice that left no room for hesitation, and the men scurried to do his bidding.

"Dirt? The snow's ten feet deep—how would we *get* to any dirt?" one of the men mumbled.

Stride heard the comment and considered dressing the man down. Instead, his stony features actually came close to smiling. But not quite.

———

The officers' quarters for Troop C was much smaller than the barracks Vickersham had just left; it was barely large enough for the six cots, but the two stoves provided a toasty environment that was always a pleasure to enter after even ten minutes outside in the bitter cold. Stamping his feet and removing his gloves, coat, and hat, Vickersham then threw them carelessly on his cot before knocking on the door to the small office at one end of the quarters.

"Come!"

Vic opened the door and received a shock. "Mr. Stone!"

"Hello, Vickersham—or should I say Sub-Inspector?" Stone rose from a mahogany Windsor chair and held out his hand.

Vichersham saw that his face was snow-burned a deep brown, and he appeared unmistakably weary. But he could sense a difference between the man standing before him and the angry, defiant man of a few months before. *It's in the eyes somehow*, Vic thought with conviction. *He's . . . solved something.* "Well, this *is* a surprise!" Vickersham exclaimed, privately recognizing the double meaning in his words. "How . . . what—"

"Close your mouth and have a seat, Vickersham," Inspector Macleod ordered good-naturedly.

"Thank you, sir—and hello, by the way, didn't mean to ignore you, sir."

James Farquharson Macleod waved off the apology and finished signing the papers on his desk. Scottish-born with an English father, he was six feet tall and handsome, with a full dark beard and high forehead. A soldier as well as a lawyer, Macleod had served as a brigade major in the Red River expedition of 1870. His credentials were impeccable, and he was well respected among the men for his intelligence and fairness. He gestured to Stone. "This man said he knew you, and I can see he wasn't lying."

"Yes, sir. We're . . . acquainted," Vickersham finished lamely.

Stone smiled. "Don't worry, Vickersham. I've explained my story to the inspector, so you don't have to pretend that we're the best of friends."

"So what are you doing here? To tell you the truth, I never thought I'd see you again. You had that classic 'mountain man' air about you, and I pictured you riding off and never being heard from again."

"Mr. Stone wishes to join our Force," Macleod interjected and watched Vickersham's reaction in amusement.

Vickersham felt his mouth open, and he looked back and forth at each man in surprise for a moment. "Join the Mounted? Why that's very . . . um . . . well, what I mean to say is—join the Mounted? Police?"

Stone and Macleod laughed in unison. Macleod said, "Mr. Stone, you must have been a sight to behold when you knew Vickersham before. I've never seen him uncertain about a man's capabilities since I've known him."

"Capabilities!" Vic exclaimed. "No, no, you misunderstand me, sir. I'm sure that Stone is *more* than capable of handling the duties. It's just that . . ." Vic trailed off, not knowing how to explain his reservations.

Stone held up a hand and leaned forward in his chair. "If I can explain to our stunned colleague, Inspector. When you knew me before, Vickersham, I was a lost man. I'd just lost my wife, and almost got myself killed. I was having a hard time adjusting to life, and sort of . . . *left* it for a while."

He paused, and his strange gray eyes bored into Vickersham's. Vickersham could detect no sign of the madness that had been there before—*that's* what was different about them.

Stone continued, "Anyway, I found out some things about myself that I didn't like, and I'm trying to set things right. I remembered what you'd said that night about the Mounted Police, and I'm determined to sign on, no matter how long it takes, or how many times I have to apply."

Vickersham nodded slowly, unable to look away from him. He could see Macleod gauging his reaction, and he realized why he'd been summoned to Macleod's office: to vouch for Stone's character. Making a decision—quick, but certain—Vickersham turned to the Scot. "Inspector, I would be proud to serve with this man. I believe he would do nothing but add to the strength and character of the Force."

Stone gave him a grateful look and leaned back in his chair.

"I agree," Macleod said, "but there's still the question of where to put him. Our ranks are filled, and we can't go over quota."

Vickersham grinned. "I think I can solve that one, Inspector. I had a man pack up and leave just today."

"Another one?" Macleod shook his head and absently stroked his beard. "I can't understand any man not *wanting* to be part of the history we're making here."

"Neither can I, sir, but some of these men have never seen an Indian, and they're afraid for their scalps."

Macleod harrumphed loudly. "Then it's well we're weeding them out now, instead of on the prairies. We only need men of courage, honor, and integrity out there." He looked at Stone brightly. "Welcome aboard, Sub-Constable Stone. I'm sure you'll fit in well with C Troop."

"Thank you, sir. And thank *you*, Vickersham."

"That's Sub-Inspector Vickersham to you, Sub-Constable," he corrected good-naturedly.

"Yes, *sir*!" Stone grinned.

"Oh, I almost forgot," Macleod said, reaching for the papers he'd been signing and holding them up for Vic to see, even though the print was too fine. "Packing lists for the new uniforms, Vickersham."

"Excellent! They came in?"

"Just today—and I've taken the liberty to filch a box of them for us." He considered Stone's build briefly. "You look a little bigger than Vickersham, but we'll try it." He stood and reached into one of three boxes stacked behind the desk and turned around. "How's this color to strike fear in the hearts of any savage, gentlemen?"

For a moment, Vic and Stone held their breaths. The jacket Macleod was holding for their inspection was redder than red—a color that was the very essence of the words "deep and bright" at the same time. A single line of brass buttons ran down the front, with belt loops and flap pockets on the sides, and deep gray epaulets on the shoulders. The collar was small, with matching gray trim around the top. Stone breathed, "It's the most handsome coat I've ever seen!"

"Quite right, Stone. The color is officially scarlet, but I don't think even *that* does it quite enough justice."

"It seems even a deeper red than the British Army," Vickersham commented.

"The trousers are deep gray with twin white stripes down the side for the enlisted men. Ours, Vickersham, are blue."

"Who would notice, the way that jacket captures one's eyes?" Vickersham remarked.

"All together a dashing statement, wouldn't you say, gentlemen?"

Vickersham and Stone nodded in unison.

"Well, what are you waiting for?" Macleod smiled. "Let's try them on, what?"

"Really?" Stone asked. "Now?"

"Of course, Stone! I'm the commander; it's not like I'll turn around and order us lashed to a post and thrashed, now is it? And by the way, you'll be the first man sworn in while wearing the colors, how about that? Aren't you the lucky one!"

"Yes, I am," Stone agreed solemnly.

"Here, Vickersham," Macleod offered. "This seems about your

size." He turned and sorted through the box for a moment, held up another jacket, and offered it to Stone. "Sub-Constable?"

Stone took the offered coat from him and ran his fingers over the soft, thick wool. He glanced at Vic, who already had his on and was running his hands up and down the front of the jacket with a solemn look on his face. Quickly Stone slipped his tunic on. It was a near-perfect fit down to his waist where the coat flared out slightly. The three men watched one another in mute admiration as they buttoned the jackets, and secretly none of them could wait to get to a mirror.

Macleod sighed, and his eyes glazed over as they fixed on a spot somewhere between Stone and Vickersham. "I can't wait, men. Somehow I feel that we were all born to do what's ahead of us. I feel as if I've waited my whole life to wear this uniform."

Vickersham had never heard the inspector speak his private thoughts, but in his opinion, Macleod couldn't have picked a better moment to start.

"This is almost too much to take," Stone said softly as he looked at Vickersham. "To think of where I was a few months ago . . ."

"And now you are part of the finest Police Force the world has ever seen," Vickersham finished for him.

"Not quite yet, he isn't," Macleod announced in a loud voice, breaking the spell. "He still has to be sworn in. Are you ready, Sub-Constable?"

"You don't know how ready, sir."

"Raise your right hand and repeat after me."

Stone braced his backbone, raised his hand, and echoed the inspector. As he listened to the words coming from his mouth, he felt the same sense of predestination Macleod had spoken of so poignantly a few moments before; he felt that he was *meant* to say the words and take them to heart: "I, Hunter Edward Stone, solemnly swear that I will faithfully, diligently, and impartially execute and perform the duties required of me as a member of the North-West Mounted Police, and will well and truly obey and perform all lawful orders and instructions that I receive as such, without fear, favor or affection of or toward any person. So help me God."

Vickersham beamed at him when he'd finished and held out his hand. "Congratulations, Hunter. Welcome to the Force." Only after Stone gripped his hand tightly did Vic see the tears brimming in his unusual gray eyes.

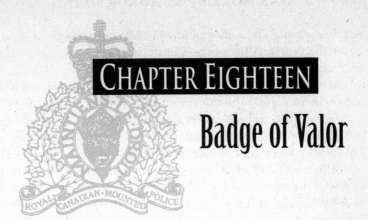

# CHAPTER EIGHTEEN

## Badge of Valor

"Here, now, Stone, what do you think you're doing there?" Ivan Maisel asked tersely. "You're supposed to be cleaning your Enfield, not that buffalo gun."

Stone looked up at the big man with irritation. Sitting on his bunk, he was running a lightly oiled rag through the barrel of his Henry rifle. "I've already cleaned the Enfield, Constable. Just thought I'd use the rest of my time working on this."

"Oh, you did, huh? Let's have a look at this Enfield you've already finished with. Everyone else is still working on theirs." Stone handed Maisel the gleaming rifle, noticing that he took it by the barrel, deliberately smudging the polish. Cracking the breech, he glared suspiciously through the short barrel and inspected the firing mechanism. "Mmmm," he grunted noncommittally, then snapped the breech shut and thrust it back into Stone's face, getting more fingerprints on the barrel. "Shine up that barrel—it's smudged," he ordered with a malicious glint in his eye. He started to walk to the next man but came back instead. "I don't like it that you're still allowed to carry that cannon," he pronounced, jabbing an impatient finger at the Henry. "The Enfield has been officially declared the weapon of the Force."

Stone said nothing. Maisel had been riding him hard for the three weeks he'd been training. The burly constable had taken a special interest in Stone for some reason, and everyone was aware of it.

"He's just jealous 'cause the men like you," Del had related one day. "You're a natural leader, and he knows it." Stone wasn't sure if that was the reason, but he didn't like Maisel or the way he bullied the men.

205

"I'm waiting for an answer, Stone," Maisel persisted.

"I didn't hear a question—Constable," Stone said, just slightly emphasizing the last word.

Maisel's beefy face reddened. "Watch yourself, big man, or I'll have you on latrine detail," he threatened, glaring as he stalked off.

Stone shook his head and began polishing the rifle barrel Maisel had blotted with his fingers, thinking about his time with the Mounted Police. He'd fallen into the routine easily, stilling the one fear he'd had of not being able to adjust to a structured, supervised schedule. But he found the ordered system of life strangely soothing and satisfying after the months of turmoil he'd endured. No more cooking his own meals, or wondering how to spend his days; he was able to throw himself into the work and training with enthusiasm and a sense of belonging. He'd faced the horrible task of writing his mother and Betsy's parents, a duty he had strictly avoided, but the letters had been another way of banishing the demons that had haunted him. They had become a confession, a cleansing, and a renewal of hope all rolled into one.

Del appeared on the bunk opposite Stone, muttering in his beard. "I swear, Hunter, you and that lunkhead are headed on a surefire collision course!" he proclaimed, nodding in Maisel's direction.

"I'm afraid you're wrong, Del. He's my superior, no matter how incompetent he is, and I won't be starting any trouble."

"*You* don't have to start nothin'." He leaned close, and Stone could smell bittersweet tobacco on his breath. "If'n anything *does* happen—like a meetin' behind the shed, if'n you know whut I mean—the boys are all behind you."

Stone finished wiping down the Enfield and picked up his Henry again. "I don't want to hear that kind of talk, Del. We're all here for one purpose, and that's to settle the North-West Territories. Not to fight each other."

Pushing his sweat-stained hat back on his wide forehead, Del stared disbelievingly at Stone. "Shooeee! Ain't you the cat's meow! Don't you see, the peckin' order's been established around here, and *you're* the rooster, not that side o' beef with brickbats between his ears!"

"Wrong again, Del." Stone smiled. "Stride's the one to follow, not me."

"Well, *there's* an argument," Del conceded, "but if ya ask anybody else, *you* belong in Maisel's job."

Stone laid the long rifle across his knees and locked eyes with Del. "That's enough, Del. No more talk of who belongs in whose job, and who's the better man. Maisel was appointed by Macleod, and that's the way it is—live with it."

"All right, all right, no need to get huffy! I's just sayin'—"

"I know what you were saying, and I appreciate it. But that's the last time I want to hear you giving that opinion—to me, or anybody else. Okay?"

"Yeah," Del agreed glumly. Then his face lit up as he said, "Hey, guess what? I hear there's a mission comin' up—the first one of the Mounted Police!"

"What did you hear?"

Del glanced around conspiratorially. "Word is, there's some whiskey traders operatin' among the Cree up on Lake Winnipeg. Macleod wants 'em arrested."

"Who told you this?"

"Heard Mr. Wilkes—Macleod's adjutant—talkin' to *my* boss, Leveille, the chief of scouts. Wilkes was askin' him about the terrain in the area, like Macleod's gettin' ready to go up there and set things aright."

"Have you ever been up there, Del?"

"Aw, hundreds of times!" Del caught Stone's sideways look and amended, "Well, a few times." Stone continued to stare at him silently. "All right, all right, once! But I 'member it like it was yesterday."

Stone nodded absently. "Keep your ears open and let me know if he's mounting a troop for it, would you, Del?"

"You betcha, I will! My eyes may leave somethin' to be desired, but when it comes to ears, I got the biggest pair around."

————

Three days passed, and Del had no more news of the raid. But Stone kept hoping, and before going to sleep at night, it was all he could think about. Del swore he told no one else about it, but soon rumors and speculations were buzzing all around the barracks.

"Do you think we'll be in it, Hunter?" Gustav Boogaard asked at mess one night.

Stone was inspecting the forkful of food he'd scooped up from the metal plate. It looked like mashed potatoes, but there were dark bits of something in it; he hoped it was meat. The food was usually edible, but sometimes the cooks served up a mystery. "I don't know, Gus." Stone refused to call Boogaard by his nickname. "The whole thing may be a false rumor."

"They wouldn't take you anyway, Booger," Charles Hallman retorted in his nasal twang. "You can't even stay on that horse yet." Hallman had been a fisherman and small-town constable from the Maritime Provinces. He had a thin, cadaver-like face and rough hands that looked strong enough to snap a bedpost in two.

"That horse *hates* me," Boogaard glowered. "He tries to buck me off every day. One of these nights I'm going to sneak in the stables and shoot him."

"If you do, you'll be staying here when we start west," Hallman remarked. "There aren't any extra horses right now."

"He always looks like he's up to something, you know? Always staring at me."

Ken Garner laughed. "If I were you, I'd be more scared of that horse than the Indians. It's more personal with him." Garner was Andy Doe's look-alike, and the only reason Stone knew it was Garner was that he was eating left handed, while Doe was right handed. At least, Stone *thought* that's how it was.

Boogaard's question proved that Stone wasn't the only one with Garner-Doe identification problems. "Which one are you?" he asked Garner, eyes narrowed. "I don't like one of you, but I never know who to glare at."

Garner smiled. "I'll never tell."

"He's Garner," Doe called from the next table. He'd been listening to them and was sick and tired of being mixed up with Garner. He wished one of them would be transferred to another company. "Stop confusing them, Ken, it's hard enough without that."

"Then you're the one I don't like," Boogaard said, pointing his fork at Garner. He looked back down at his plate and mumbled low enough so that only Stone heard, "I think."

"You sure you guys aren't twins and just playing with us?" Hallman asked suspiciously.

"What's the matter with you, Charlie?" Doe asked, his voice rising. "What's the matter with *all* of you? I don't think we look *anything* alike!"

For a silent moment, heads at both tables turned in unison to look at Doe, over to Garner, and back to Doe. Then, with most of them shaking their heads, they returned to their meals.

"Look like twins to me," Hallman insisted.

"Two peas in a pod," said one man.

"I can't tell the difference," said another.

"Freaks of nature," mumbled Boogaard.

"Cut from the same cloth—"

"That's enough, ladies!" growled Sergeant Stride from two tables away, and the jesting stopped instantly. "Wrap your mouths around those forks, or I'll have every one of you on guard duty tonight." Night guard duty was the most dreaded of tasks, since the temperature was unbelievably cold.

Stone's eyes went to Stride. Next to Red Wolf, Stride had the fiercest eyes Stone had ever seen. Those eyes locked on Stone, and just before he continued eating, Stone saw the barest hint—just a whisper—of a smile tug at the corners of his razor-thin mouth. It marked the first time Stone had seen Stride with any expression but severe, uncompromising sternness. Stone grinned sardonically as he shoveled more of the mystery meal into his mouth and thought, *So, the sergeant likes to pal around more than he lets on. Have to file that away for later.*

Macleod and Vickersham came in, stamping their feet. Stride jumped up and hollered, "Attennn-*tion!*" instantly. The sound of many chairs being hurriedly scooted backward filled the hall for a moment as men desperately tried to chew and swallow before the inspector was close.

"At ease, men," Macleod said, "and be seated."

Stone saw Vickersham give him an almost imperceptible nod. Stone had talked little with him since the night he'd been sworn in. Vickersham had thrown himself full force into learning his job as an officer, and Macleod had been more than happy to teach him. Whenever Stone saw one of them, the other was usually not far away.

Macleod nodded to Vickersham and made his way to a small room off the main dining area that was reserved for the officers. Vickersham cleared his throat and said, "So sorry to interrupt, gentlemen. Constable Maisel, Sub-Constables Garner, D'Artigue, and Stone follow me." For a brief second, Stone and Garner exchanged puzzled glances before trailing Vickersham to the officers' dining room with the others.

Macleod had removed his heavy coat and gloves and seated himself at the head of the lone table in the room. "Sit down, men," he motioned when all of them were inside. "I've some splendid news."

Stone sat beside Garner, across from Maisel and D'Artigue. He'd rarely talked to the Frenchman, the only reason being that the man's accent was so thick that Stone couldn't understand him. D'Artigue seemed to understand English perfectly, however.

"This company is coming together very well, in my opinion," Macleod began, placing his hands palm-down on the table in front of him. He looked each man straight in the eye as he talked. "And when that happens, there is a natural . . . er . . . grapevine formed that can start wild rumors and false stories. In my experience, I've learned this grapevine can also be very intuitive and informed." He paused and clasped his hands together slowly. "Would someone mind telling me the latest rumor about this bunch of whiskey traders on Lake Winnipeg?"

The four enlisted men exchanged glances, unsure of the tone of the inspector. Was he looking for a scapegoat, or merely curious about how accurate the grapevine's information happened to be? Stone thought it should be Maisel who answered, but the beefy man found a spot on the table to stare at. *Gutless lout!* Stone thought briefly, then answered Macleod. "Well, sir—we've heard that a troop was probably going to be sent to arrest the traders in question. That is, if there *are* any."

Macleod's expression didn't change as he stared at Stone with his intense brown eyes. "And what do you think, Sub-Constable Stone?"

Stone felt the need to look away from those eyes, but he fought it down. "I have no idea if the information is correct, sir. But if it is, I would sure like to be in that troop."

The only sound in the room was the faint murmur of the men in the main dining hall and an occasional clang of utensils. Macleod continued staring at him, and then nodded almost imperceptibly. "It is, and you shall, Sub-Constable." He faced the rest of the men. "All of you are to accompany me to the lake on the Force's first mission." The four men looked at one another, beaming. "We'll have a Cree guide, and leave in the morning by dogsled. Constable, I'll expect the men to be ready at daybreak, with rations for three days and plenty of warm clothes."

"You'll have it, sir," Maisel nodded.

"Very well. Off you go, then."

On the way out, Stone grinned at Vickersham but received only a curt nod in return. Stone thought it strange until it hit him. *He's disappointed because he's staying here. Why didn't Macleod choose him instead of Maisel?* More questions suddenly flooded his mind. *Why did Macleod choose the four of us? Because we're competent, or is he wondering about our abilities?* As they came out of the dining room and received curious stares from the other men, he pushed the doubts away and let his enthusiasm return. He'd been chosen for the first mission, and that was all that mattered.

———

Dog sledding was included in the training of the Mounted Police. Stone had mastered the skill easily and had even enjoyed the cold outings as much as the dogs. However, the training runs lasted only about an hour, and nothing had prepared him for the twenty miles they traveled the next day.

The wind slashed at his skin like a razor. Despite wearing a scarf around his nose and mouth, his throat and lungs burned from breathing in the cold air that hit him full force in the face. His eyes watered continually, and coupled with the blinding reflection of the sun on snow, he had to rely on the dogs to have the sense to follow the sled in front and not crash into a tree. But he was exhilarated from the change of routine barracks life.

The land stretched out in a solid sheet of white to the horizon. On occasion they would steer through a thick copse of trees with snow-laden branches. They crossed countless frozen streams and stopped only once for a quick lunch.

"The whiskey traders are camped in a cabin on this side of a small bay on the eastern edge of the lake," Macleod informed them. "We should arrive at dark. Deer Dance says there are a few rolling hills that will shield our advance. His tribe was paid a visit by the traders themselves."

Stone glanced at the short, stout Deer Dance, who spoke for the first time that day. "The whiskey men came during our *o-giwi-manse-win*, a ceremony that celebrates the gift of water to us. They handed out their poison, and soon many braves were drunk—including our elder, who was to share the wisdom he has learned in life. The elder lost his voice and became as a dead man. The tradition of *o-giwi-manse-win* was broken. For this, the whiskey men must pay." Deer Dance spoke matter-of-factly, but his dark eyes revealed a palpable hurt and rage.

"Oh, they'll pay all right," Maisel grunted, with a wink at Stone. Since the talk with Macleod, he'd done nothing but talk about the terrible vengeance he was going to inflict on the criminals.

"Nobody fires unless fired upon," Macleod told Maisel directly. "And even then, only as a last resort. We aren't vigilantes, Constable, we're officers of the law."

At dusk they entered the boreal forest. Some said the thick woods stretched all the way to the edge of the continent, while others claimed that, while immeasurably huge, it gave way to tundra somewhere along the Hudson Bay. The forest provided almost impenetrable cover of birch, spruce, and aspen trees, intermingled with pine, balsam fir, and hemlock. Bears, wolves, wolverines, foxes, otters, minks, and beavers prowled in the shifting indigo shadows.

As a boy, Stone had had to memorize a bit of Longfellow's *The Song*

*of Hiawatha*, the setting of which centered around "Gitche Gumee"—
Lake Superior. The words he used to describe the boreal forest came
back to him:

This is the forest primeval.
The murmuring pines and the hemlocks,
Bearded with moss, and in garments green,
Indistinct in the twilight. . . .

*"Forest primeval" is right*, Stone thought as the dogs whisked between trees, while he kept a sharp eye out for low-hanging branches.
Stone was glad Deer Dance led the way, and not him.

Just when Stone was seriously beginning to believe that he would
never be warm again, the party stopped. Through the gloom of dusk
he saw Macleod's white gloves motioning them forward. Gathering at
the edge of a small rise, the six men crouched in the soft snow and
peered over the top. Below, beside an endless body of water that Stone
took to be Lake Winnipeg, was a cabin that was startlingly close. A
wavering spire of gray woodsmoke curled from the small chimney.
Windows glowed with lamplight on every side, but they were frosted
over with moisture so that it was impossible to see inside. About one
hundred feet away from the cabin was an outhouse.

"How many?" Maisel whispered with a strange edge in his voice.

"Deer Dance said three men came to their village, but there may
be more," Macleod answered him.

Maisel was on Stone's right, at the end of their six-man line, with
Garner, Macleod, D'Artigue, and Deer Dance on Stone's left in that
order. Stone heard Maisel breathing heavily, and he glanced over at the
constable. His small, recessed eyes were as large as Stone had ever seen
them, and his hands flexed and unflexed on his rifle repeatedly. Despite
the cold, his cheeks were shiny with a thin layer of sweat, and his
tongue darted out to wet his dry lips.

"Let's try this peacefully, gentlemen," Macleod said, and rising he
cupped his mouth with his hands and shouted, "Hello the house! This
is Inspector J. F. Macleod with the North-West Mounted Police! We
would like to talk with you!"

No movement from the cabin. Somewhere a snow owl hooted, as
if asking Macleod to repeat his name.

"Maybe they're asleep," Garner suggested.

"Who sleeps with lamps lit?" Macleod reasoned. He turned to the
cabin again. "Please come out with your hands in the—"

A side window opened, and the black barrel of a rifle appeared. The
shot kicked up snow directly in front of Macleod, and the inspector

dropped so quickly that Stone thought he was hit. They all ducked, and Stone heard another window open with the scratching sound of wood on wood. Two more shots exploded, and through the din, he could hear Maisel's teeth chattering beside him. *The man's scared to death!* he realized with a start. Maisel was staring wordlessly at Stone, and a small moan escaped him.

"Maisel, pull yourself together!" Stone barked. Three more shots. Maisel tucked himself into a ball, trying to make himself as small as possible, though he was completely shielded by the rise.

"Return fire when ready, men!" Macleod shouted, and as one—except for Maisel—they rose and fired a volley at the cabin. The other men ducked down to reload the one-shot Enfields, while Stone continued firing until he'd emptied his fifteen-shot Henry. The heavy 216 grain bullets blew out windowpanes and shattered wood, while the rifle barrels that protruded from the windows jerked back inside awkwardly. While firing, he was aware of the angry buzzing of a bullet whizzing by his ear, and a small puff of snow blew up in front of him. Just before he crouched down behind the hill to reload, he spied a movement from the outhouse. The door had been closed a moment before, and now it swung open, only about six inches.

The other four men fired another volley in unison, and when they began reloading again, Stone yelled to Macleod, "Man in the outhouse, sir!"

Macleod nodded as he jammed another round in the breech of his Enfield. "I saw him. Go, and we'll cover! Go with him, Maisel!" In the confusion, Macleod hadn't noticed Maisel cowering down in the snow.

Stone ignored Maisel as he skirted around the huge, balled-up figure, positioning for a straight run down to the outhouse. "Maisel!" he heard Macleod scream as he made ready for his run, "Support Stone!"

The firing from the cabin suddenly paused for a moment, and Stone took off down the incline, dodging recklessly from tree to tree, praying that he could keep his footing in the snow. He knew he was charging alone, and the only plan in his mind was to get to the small house, knock the man unconscious, and hold there until Macleod made his move. He heard more shots, but they were aimed at the hill; he didn't think he could be seen, since he'd kept the outhouse between himself and the back window of the cabin.

Just before he reached the small building, the door banged open and a short, stout man emerged at a run. He never saw Stone. Stone heard another volley from the rise as he fell in right behind the fleeing man as he headed straight for the cabin.

"Good gracious, would you look at that!" Macleod breathed from the top of the rise. "He's attacking by himself! Come on, D'Artigue!" He'd already sent Garner to follow Stone after seeing Maisel's helplessness, so Macleod, D'Artigue, and Deer Dance fired another volley through the windows of the cabin, and then they began to run.

Ten feet in front of Stone, the short man began yelling in French to identify himself right before he reached the door. Stone stayed right behind him, aware that he was directly even with a gunman's line of fire from the back window, expecting an explosion and searing pain any moment. The short man burst through the door with Stone on his heels.

"Police! Drop your weapons!" Stone roared as he jerked to a stop in the doorway. The room was a mess, with blankets, food, and clothing strewn everywhere, and boxes lined along the walls. Rotating the Henry from side to side, his heart thumped when he found he was covering four healthy, armed men. The short man turned in horror—he had never realized Stone was behind him—and shot his hands up when he saw the huge Henry leveled at him.

On the floor by the west window another man lay moaning. The four armed men stared at Stone in shock for a moment. Stone could almost see them calculating the odds in their heads; then the odds changed, and four guns began to turn toward him. He pulled off a shot from his rifle that deafened everyone in the close cabin and shattered the back of a rocking chair to bits. "Drop those weapons and don't move!"

Stone heard steps crunching in the snow behind him, and Garner came to Stone's side, breathless, and brandishing his Enfield. At Garner's appearance, the men dropped their rifles with muttered oaths and dark looks.

"Good work, Stone!" Macleod congratulated as he brushed by him to help cover the men. He grinned wolfishly at the traders and bellowed, "Well, what have we in those boxes, gentlemen? It wouldn't be whiskey, now would it?"

The short man looked over at the boxes as if they'd appeared out of thin air, then shrugged expansively. "*Que désirez-vous?*"

Macleod leaned back toward D'Artigue slightly, his eyes not leaving the man. "What was that, Sub-Constable?"

"He asks what you want, sir," D'Artigue answered with a smile in his voice.

"What do I want—?" Macleod asked, then contemptuously added, "*monsieur?* Well, that's very simple. I want to strap you and your detestable friends to sleds, carry you back to Fort Garry, and plan the next twenty years of your life for you. *That's* what I want."

The short man obviously understood English, because all of the muscles in his face seemed to give out at once, and his whole body sagged.

"Garner, D'Artigue—tie these men up at once!" Macleod ordered.

Stone wheeled nervously when he heard more steps in the snow behind them and found Maisel looking pale and sheepish in the doorway. "Excuse me, sir," he addressed Macleod, and swallowed noticeably, "about my behavior—"

"Which was despicable and unacceptable as a noncommissioned officer of the Mounted, Constable," Macleod thundered as he stepped toward the bigger man. His voice rose in volume and took on a slight Scottish lilt as he continued, "I would also go on record as saying that your cowardice is unacceptable as an *enlisted* man in the Force, and I'll see you brought up on court-martial charges as soon as we return! Is that clear, Maisel?"

Looking as if he were about to be sick, Maisel nodded.

"Now, remove your overcoat."

"Sir?" Maisel asked in confusion.

"I said, remove your overcoat and hand over the scarlet! You'll not be wearing it in my presence!" Blinking, Maisel did as he was told. Macleod took the red jacket and removed the constable's badge from the breast. "Here, Constable Stone," he said formally, handing the badge to the surprised Stone. "I'm giving you a field promotion. I'll make it official when we return to Fort Garry."

"Th-thank you, sir," Stone stammered, staring at the gold shield engraved with a crown in the center.

Macleod noticed D'Artigue and Garner observing the scene, their eyes wide, their mouths open. Even the traders were regarding Macleod's temper with interest. "Well, stop gawking and tie those men up! See to your men, Constable Stone," he ordered impatiently, gesturing with his gloved hand.

"Yes, sir!" Stone answered, the new title echoing in his mind like a morsel to be tasted later. But instead of dressing the men down, he could only return the big grins plastered on their faces with one of his own.

# CHAPTER NINETEEN

# March West

June 25, 1874

Dear Reena,

I hope this letter finds you well, if it finds you at all. I've sent it care of Farwell's Trading Post, since that's the closest mail delivery that I know of.

Please don't think it forward of me to write to you—I just wanted to tell you about what has happened since I left. I am sitting here in Troop C barracks, on my cot, in the room I share with my fellow constable, Preston Woodbine Stride. Yes, he is every bit as British as his name sounds, and I can't imagine a better man for the job. I've learned a great deal from him, and he seems to hold me in high regard, too, though I don't know what I've done to deserve his merit. I know you're not aware of the ranking order of the Force, but he and I are basically sergeants, with the responsibility of forty-seven subconstables under us. I received the promotion soon after I joined and enjoy my job immensely.

Jaye Vickersham was commissioned an officer at the outset, and Del Dekko is with our scout contingent. They have become my best friends, although there is the tiniest barrier between Vic and me because of the fact that he's my superior officer. Thankfully, it has not caused any problem yet. Del, of course, is Del, and manages to find many things to complain about concerning barracks life. Both men recall you fondly and send their best.

I have to say that Del isn't the only one growing tired of

our situation, but good news has arrived. We are scheduled to leave our cozy winter home and march down to Dufferin to join up with Troops D, E, and F, who are traveling by train from Toronto. Together, we will begin our trek across the prairies to the Belly and Bow Rivers in the West. There is a place there called Fort Whoop-up (it's not really a fort) where whiskey is sold to the Blackfeet. It sounds as if those Indians are in worse trouble than the Assiniboine were when you arrived. We should be passing just north of the Cypress Hills on our journey.

I know my decision to come here was right, and I've been thinking more and more about God and Providence—how events so horrible could somehow lead me to the most satisfying feeling I've ever encountered (next to being Betsy's husband). Inspector James Macleod, the supreme officer of our troop, put it best I think. He, Vic, and I were trying on our uniforms for the first time, and he said he felt as if he'd waited his whole life to wear that scarlet jacket. I've thought about that a lot, and I can't agree with him more. It's as if this whole scenario has a rightness about it for me—an orderliness that I've never known. That's why I've been thinking about God and am looking forward to discussing it with you the next time I see you.

Enough about me for now. I was only going to write you a short note, and here I am on my fourth page. How is little Star Light? I hope I didn't create a monster that no one is able to shut up. I'm teasing, of course. Give him my best, and tell him I'm still expecting that talisman when I see him. Also say hello to Lone Elk and Gray Dawn—I miss them.

I miss you, too, Reena. I miss our talks, and listening to you speak about the Bible, and the walks we took. I know you may have very few fond memories of me—I was in such a state!—but it's important to me to be able to tell you how much you affected my life, and to express my deepest gratitude.

I must go for now, but I will remain

Your friend,
Hunter Stone

———

The afternoon of July 8, 1874, was sunny, humid, and very hot. Stone, mounted on Buck, waited with Stride, Vickersham, and Dekko at the edge of the town of Dufferin. The six troops of the North-West

Mounted Police were formed six abreast in a column that reminded Stone of a long, bright red ribbon. Since the troops were lined up in alphabetical order, Stone's Troop C was situated squarely in the center of the group. He looked fore and aft admiringly, seeing the sun sparkle off a sea of white, British Army-style helmets, and the impressive arrangement of troops to horse color: A rode dark bays, B dark browns, C buckskins and bright chestnuts, D grays, E blacks, and F was mounted on light bays. It was the most impressive sight Stone had ever seen.

Del must have been admiring the horses, too, when he commented, "Guess you feel lucky to have landed in C, Hunter. You didn't have to give up your horse."

"Doesn't matter. In my mind, there never would've been any question about giving up my horse. Where I go, he goes."

"How about that storm last night?" Vickersham asked the group in general. "Don't think it was a bad sign, do you?"

Del, ever superstitious, answered, "Yep, shore do."

"Don't believe in signs, sir," Stride countered, removing his helmet and wiping his high forehead.

"What *do* you believe in, Sergeant?"

Stride placed his helmet back on his head and gazed to the rear of the column for a moment. "I believe in that, sir—the Mounted Police. No storm will keep us from our destiny."

Vickersham smiled. "Spoken like a true Englishman. Your *esprit de corps* is impressive, Sergeant."

"Decor?" Del asked. "Ain't that what ladies do with the insides o' their houses?"

"No, Del. *Esprit de corps* means enthusiasm for the troop, or devotion to a cause."

"Whatever." Del wiped his face with a dirty red bandana. "If'n ya ask me, it's too hot fer any o' that 'decor.' Too hot fer anything."

"I heard B and F didn't get their horses rounded up until midmorning," Stone commented. The violent thunderstorms had sent hail the size of walnuts crashing down, causing a stampede.

"That's true," Vickersham confirmed. "Those poor chaps didn't get any sleep after chasing their mounts all night."

"Fools should learn how to tether their horses," Stride growled. "There were quite a few tents blown down last night, too."

"What are we standin' around in the sun waitin' fer?" Del complained. "I thought they said we was ready to go!"

Vickersham said patiently, "Del, do you have any idea what they're having to organize to the rear?"

"No, but I got a funny feelin' *you* know, and are about to tell me."

"Besides getting the men and horses ready, we have over a hundred head of oxen and cattle, almost two hundred carts and wagons, two nine-pound field guns, two mortars, portable kitchens and forges, and mowing machines. This column will be over a mile and a half long, and it takes time to get all that in line."

Del leaned over and spit a stream of tobacco juice. "And jest how much time did it take you to memorize all that?"

"Here comes Inspector Macleod and Commissioner French," Stone observed. Macleod cut a sharp figure as he rode ramrod straight in the saddle, in contrast to the other rider, who appeared uncomfortable on the back of a horse. Commissioner George Arthur French, despite his name, was an Irishman—a short, stout man with penetrating blue eyes and a full handlebar mustache. He and Macleod, like Vickersham and all the other officers, sported red plumes in their helmets that danced in the wind. He'd served in the Canadian Militia as commandant of A Battery and Inspector of Artillery and Warlike Stores. Although a strict disciplinarian, he was efficient and energetic, with a genuine concern for his men's physical well-being and morale.

"Almost ready, men," French informed them in a surprisingly high voice. "We'll only try for a small lake about five miles down the trail, since it's so late." He looked at Del. "Button up that shirt, Scout."

"Yes, sir," Del said instantly. He wore the outfit Stone had always seen him wear—canvas trousers, suspenders, plain, dark blue shirt, and brown leather vest.

"We've already had the first casualties of the Force," Macleod related darkly. "Two men died—one from malaria, and one from typhoid. We're having to leave eight more behind with the same symptoms."

"Any from our troop, sir?" Vickersham asked.

"No, thank God." After a moment, his face brightened. "It's a glorious day, isn't it, gentlemen? Mark this day, for it's probably the only time all the troops will be together at one time, what with everyone scattered all over the Territory at their prospective outposts. Get your lines straightened, Vickersham—we're ready to march."

"Yes, sir," Vickersham saluted as the two officers rode toward the front of the line.

With a strange sadness Stone thought of Macleod's words, about them all being together for the first and only time, then he heard the order being relayed from the front down the long, scarlet line.

"Forward!"

And the North-West Mounted Police marched into history.

———

Four days later, on July 12, the column reached the Boundary Commission depot at Pembina. The Force was following a trail documented by the commission the year before. Besides surveying the exact U.S.–Canada border, the commission also denoted careful details of the best grass and water along the way.

The head of the column reached Pembina at midafternoon. However, much to Commissioner French's chagrin, the neat, mile-and-a-half formation that left Dufferin quickly turned into a train that stretched for five miles. The slow footwork of the oxen pulling carts, combined with the breakdowns of both cart and wagon along the way, stretched out the column like old chewing gum. The rest of the unit straggled into Pembina until dusk.

Stone and Stride had just finished supervising the men as they bedded down the horses, when Del and two other scouts rode up. One of them was huge—well over six feet, and weighing at least three hundred pounds. Stone knew him as Pierre Leveille, chief of scouts, but he'd never seen the other man, who was medium build with a sharp, angular face and quick, darting eyes. "I'm gonna bunk with this here unit, Pierre," Del informed the big man.

"Why you don' just *join* de unit?" Pierre asked with a wide smile and thick French accent. "You are weeth dem all de time, anyways!"

" 'Cause I'm too old, you know that!"

Pierre threw back his head and laughed. "And Monsieur French trew you to me, like old cloths nobody want no more!" He waved a hand good-naturedly. "See you in de mornin' at four—don' be late." Pierre turned his horse, and after watching Stone and Stride for a moment, the sharp-faced man followed.

Del dismounted and savagely waved at a cloud of mosquitoes that suddenly swarmed around his sweaty face. "Dern skeeters! I'm surprised they's a man left in this outfit that still has all his blood! And Pierre says it ain't gonna get no better, especially with all them locusts." At a few points along the way, they'd ridden over places so thick with locusts that the low, rolling land had seemed like a black carpet. Stone remembered Buck's hooves being black with their crushed bodies. "Anyways," Del continued, "you wouldn't believe what Pierre did today!"

"Who was that other chap?" Stride asked.

"Oh, that's Sallier." Del pronounced the name "Sally-ay." "Spooky feller, never says a word. And he's always *watchin'* ya, like he knows somethin' about yerself that *you* don't even know. He makes me nervous. And so does that Crow Injun."

"What?" Stone asked, fully alert. He'd been watching the hot, tired men file by them to set up their tents and had been only half listening to Del.

Noticing Stone's sharp look, Del hesitated before repeating, "That Crow Injun that hired on. Says he knows a way through a rough spot down the trail to a water hole nobody knows about."

"What does he look like?"

"Uh . . . young feller . . . speaks English pretty good—"

"Younger or older than me?" Stone found that he was leaning too close to Del and backed off as he noticed Stride giving him a strange look.

"Oh, he's younger'n you, Hunter. Not by much, I'd say, but younger."

Stone relaxed slightly. *It can't be him*, he thought, feeling his taut muscles relax. *Besides, he'd be a fool to join a police force as a scout.* Then three words hit him, one after the other: cunning, daring, and crazy. "Where is this Indian?"

Del was now regarding Stone with a worried stare. "He's in the scout camp, I guess. Say, Hunter . . . this Injun trouble you had a while back . . ."

"That was Blackfeet," Stone lied quickly. He didn't want Del to grow more suspicious than he already was. Del had a good heart, but his love of gossip was becoming legendary. "Go on with your story, Del," Stone suggested. He tried to put on a normal face, but all he could think about was getting a look at that Crow.

Del looked confused for a brief second, then exclaimed, "Oh yeah, I almost forgot! Me and Pierre and Sallier went back to see what was holdin' up the rear today, and we found a horse that wouldn't get out o' that stream we crossed a couple miles back. He was just *standin'* in the water, and they was whuppin' 'im, and beggin' 'im—doin' ever-thing but what Pierre done." He paused and stared at them expec-tantly.

After a moment, Stride obliged him. "And what did he do?"

"Thanky, I was just seein' if'n you was listenin'. Pierre jumped down in that water, went over to that horse's rear, and grabbed his tail. The horse kinda looked sideways at 'im, suspicious like, not sure what

Pierre had in mind, and then Pierre took ahold o' that brush tail and *lifted*! I mean *lifted* the whole horse's behind! Then he pushed that tail toward the bank, and naturally the horse *had* to go where his tail was goin', so out he come!"

Stone and Stride glanced at each other. "That's a pretty impressive story," Stone commented.

"It's the *truth*! Just ask anybody that was there!"

A roaring crack of thunder made all three men look at the sky. Dark, blue-black clouds were gathering on the western horizon, and as they watched, the thunderhead covered the orange setting sun in an ominous way. "Oh no, not another one!" Del moaned. "Why cain't them storms come in the daytime when nobody minds gettin' wet?"

"Let's hurry the men in getting those tents up," Stride suggested to Stone.

"Sergeant?" They turned to Andy Doe as he approached. "Sub-Inspector Vickersham wants to see both of you. He's over at the blacksmith's—that way."

"Thank you, Doe," Stride said, and Stone followed him in the direction Doe had pointed.

Vickersham was watching his horse being shoed by a blacksmith, and greeted them as they approached. "Stride—Stone. Looks like another sleepless night," he stated, nodding toward the gathering clouds.

"Yes, sir," they chimed.

Vickersham's face grew concerned. Stone thought he looked tired, but so was every man in the troop. "We may have a bit of a problem. I believe we're being shadowed."

"Shadowed, sir?" Stride asked.

"Yes. This land may be flat, but there are still some low hills to conceal a group of riders if they didn't want to be seen. Inspector Macleod thought he saw something today off to the north."

"What do you think they want?" asked Stone.

"Who knows? Could be anyone—Indians, whiskey traders, or just settlers. But the inspector wanted one of you to sort of drift to the north of the column tomorrow and see what's what."

"All right, sir." The first thought that came to Stone's mind was: *How does anyone "drift" in these bright red coats?* The second followed quickly on the heels of the first: *A new Crow scout, and riders following us—imagine that.* "How many riders?" he asked Vic.

"He couldn't tell. But if it's more than five or six, don't attack them, Hunter," he added with a grin. News of Stone's heroics at the trader's cabin had done wonders for the stale, winter-laden morale of the men. They'd cheered him at mess the night after the party had returned, and his back was slapped countless times. Maisel had resigned rather than undergo the humiliation of a court-martial, and the whiskey traders had been hauled off to jail. Vickersham had been happy for Stone, but he hadn't been able to conceal his disappointment at being left behind.

On their way back to camp, Stride asked nonchalantly, "Going to the scout camp tonight, Stone?"

"Was I that obvious?"

Stride shrugged. "For a while there, you seemed as if you'd been hit a good shot in the stomach."

They walked in silence for a while, observing the various troops preparing to settle in for the night. Some were building fires and raising tents, while a few gathered in small groups, tunics unbuttoned, glancing nervously at the ever-darkening sky.

Stone had confided only to Vickersham about his past. He felt that his story was not one to be told around a campfire to just anyone, and a small part of him believed the less he talked about it, the easier it would be for the horrible memories to leave him. Deep down inside he knew it was probably naive and childish, but there it was.

Stride interrupted his thoughts. "I'm not a man to pry, Stone. Every man has his secrets, and that's the way it ought to be. But if you know something that endangers the Force, I think it's your duty to report it. If not to me, then to the inspector."

Stone smiled wryly. "Say what you mean, Stride. Don't talk in riddles." He stopped and met Stride squarely. "If this Indian turns out to be the one I'm familiar with, believe me, I'll deal with it. But I don't think it's him."

Stride considered this for a moment, then asked haltingly, "Would you like me to. . . ?"

"No, but thanks anyway. I'm just going to get a look at him."

"That's not the part that has me worried."

"I didn't know you ever *got* worried."

"The look in your eyes earlier—*that* worries me."

Stone smiled and shook his head. "It's not him, Stride. Not from the way Del described him."

"This sounds like an interesting story," Stride commented.

"Maybe I'll tell you about it someday."

Stone left him at C camp and made his way to the scout's area. The layout of the camps had grown predictable; Stone compared it to his school years, when all the children would invariably return to the same seat they'd chosen on the first day. B would move up beside A to camp. C preferred spreading out behind them, with the scouts settling beside them a small distance away.

The aroma of beef cooking, mingled with the sharp scent of prairie sage, drifted to his nose, and he felt his stomach growl. He'd heard one of his men complain about the kitchen wagons arriving late, so supper would be delayed for the third night in a row. He glanced up at the sky again as another low rumble growled in the distance. The storm clouds were almost overhead, but there was still no rain.

The scouts were gathered around a fire, some of them sitting cross-legged, while others were sprawled on their backs or sides. Most of them were Metis—mixed-blood descendants of French and English fur trappers who'd taken Indian wives. They were considered backward and socially unacceptable by most, but they were a proud people who kept their own traditions and thumbed their collective noses at new ways. They'd proved their defiance was no small matter in 1869, when a spirited young Metis named Louis Riel had caused the Canadian government to back off and let them keep and govern their own lands on the Red River.

Stone drew curious looks as he stopped outside their scattered circle. He saw the Indian immediately, mainly because he was alone and apart. Dressed in dark pants and a light blue shirt, he was sharpening a knife intently, seemingly oblivious to the raucous banter of the Metis around him. He was indeed younger than Stone, and even though he was not Red Wolf, Stone felt peculiar. *This man is from the race of people that killed my Betsy. How many white people has he killed? Here he is in the middle of a police force, eating our meat and probably being paid with our money. Who does he think he is?* Stone felt his pulse accelerating and his fingernails digging into his palms. As if the Crow could feel Stone's glare, he looked up directly at Stone and his eyes widened.

"*Est-ce que je puis vous servir, monsieur?*" Pierre asked, breaking Stone's concentration. Sallier sat beside him, his face expressionless.

"What?"

"Er . . . need you *aide*?"

Stone saw that the whole group was looking at him expectantly. He suddenly realized that he hadn't thought of an excuse to be there, and his mind raced to form an answer. "No, I don't need help. I'm just walking—stretching my legs."

Pierre nodded uncertainly, but the stiff silence remained. The smell of rain came strongly, and as soon as Stone registered the fact in his senses, the heavens fell in huge drops. Men began scampering to their tents, but the Crow remained where he was for a moment, returning Stone's gaze. His eyes were round and uncertain, and when the rain started coming down in silver sheets, he rose and ran to his own tent, with a tentative look back before disappearing inside.

Stone was drenched in a short time, but he ignored the soggy feeling as he walked quickly back to C camp. His mounting rage had receded, and he was left with a strange sadness. The memory of Betsy's death was with him every day, but some days the pain would hit him anew, as if she'd died only yesterday instead of a year ago. As the heavy rain echoed inside his helmet, he wondered if he would ever be free from his suffering.

---

Long Feather's breath rasped in and out of his mouth harshly as he scooted to the back of his small tent and brandished the knife toward the flap. He could remember only one time when he'd been so scared, and that was the day he'd had to tell Red Wolf of the death of Spotted Hawk, Red Wolf's brother. The vicious Crow leader had let him live that day. Then, inexplicably, the white man whom Long Feather, Spotted Hawk, and Bison had tried to kill that day had let him live also. It had taken every ounce of his self-control to avoid bolting from the white man's glare, but he'd somehow managed to stay rooted to his spot. *Owl Dog is here!* he thought, slightly sick as the full force of his panic overwhelmed him. *Right here! And he did not recognize me!*

Long Feather stared at the tent flap, expecting a red jacket and cold gray eyes to appear at any moment. Then, unable to stand it any longer, he cautiously looked outside into the driving rain. His face was instantly wet as the westerly wind blew in his face, but he blinked the water from his eyes rapidly and saw the white man walking away. He leaned back and let out a great sigh, bewildered at his own ability of escaping sure death. Had he seen a flicker of recognition in Owl Dog's eyes, or had it only been frightened imagination?

*Owl Dog saw me that day I tried to kill him,* Long Feather thought with certainty. *I saw him clearly enough—why didn't he know me?* He mentally pictured that day—remembered Spotted Hawk being blown out of his saddle beside him by Owl Dog's long gun. Then Bison had fought with him, and he, too, had been killed. The memory was so vivid in Long Feather's mind, he felt a dull ache in his shoulder where he himself had been wounded by the white man's repeating rifle. Before riding away, Long Feather had screamed at Owl Dog, who'd only stared at him in fury and defiance. His look today had been less murderous, but Long Feather had still sensed anger rising in the strange eyes.

*What do I do? Do I go to Red Wolf right now? No, he would kill me. I am right where he told me to be—watching the white men in red, making a plan for Red Wolf to steal their fine horses.* Long Feather shook his head. *Why do I always have hard decisions? What if Red Wolf kills me for not telling him about Owl Dog as soon as I knew?* His elation at avoiding discovery vanished. Sometimes he wished he hadn't joined the dangerous Red Wolf—it seemed as if Long Feather was always worried about being killed by him. *I would be safer staying with the Police,* he thought grimly. Had he not been so worried, he would have smiled at the irony.

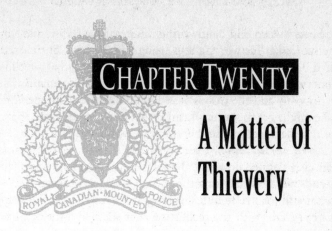

# CHAPTER TWENTY

# A Matter of Thievery

Reena picked up Stone's letter and began reading it for the third time. Almost a year had passed since he'd left them, and she was starting to think he'd forgotten about them, or, heaven forbid, something had happened to him between the Cypress Hills and Fort Garry. But when Abel Farwell had handed her the folded paper with her name across the front, she'd known who it was from before turning it over and reading the name.

Sometimes in the cold, frozen nights of the winter past, she'd found herself staring at the place he'd lain. She told herself many times that she missed him because he was a fellow white person, and someone from her own culture, which was true. But she didn't enjoy visiting with Abel and Mary Farwell for more than a few minutes, and *they* were white.

So one night she'd had an honest talk with herself. *Okay, I miss him because he's a man and handsome and intelligent and gentle and strong and handsome . . . I admit it. Did I say handsome twice? Never mind. I admit it. Just once I wish he'd hugged me when he wasn't hugging Star Light at the same time, or saying goodbye. A comforting, caring hug, just for me. I admit that, too. I felt safe around him, and I felt more needed around him. No, needed isn't the right word . . . womanly! Despite my plain, old clothes and lack of makeup and being dirty most of the time, I felt like a woman around him—pretty and dainty. Is all that so bad?* Since that little talk, Reena had thought about him every day without the small twinge of guilt that had always seemed to gnaw at her.

Bent over the letter, so close to the oil lamp she could feel the heat emanating from it, she read much more slowly than the first two times, savoring every word. His handwriting was neat, masculine, and strong, and she scoffed at his worry about being too forward. She wondered how he'd been promoted out of forty-seven men and had a feeling he was undermining some grand achievement. The information about Fort Whoop-up and the troops passing so close by had jumped off the page; she might get to see him again at that time. In addition, the sorry state of the Blackfeet had set her mind to working.

*He's even started thinking about you, Lord! Thank you for that blessing!* Her eyes skipped down to "I miss you, too, Reena," and she read it over and over before letting the paper fall to the desktop.

She sat still for five minutes, staring at nothing, until she snapped out of her reverie with the realization that she had a lot of thinking and praying to do.

————

After reaching Roche-Percée, two hundred seventy miles west of Dufferin, Commissioner French ordered the column to set up camp on the banks of the Souris River at Rivière Courte, or Short Creek. All around them were peculiar outcroppings of limestone that stared at them from the sides of hills like gray faces.

Stone was eating supper with Stride, Garner, D'Artigue, and Boogaard when Vickersham came striding up to them, his smooth face lined with concern. "How did it go, sir?" Stone asked.

Vickersham waved at the men to stay seated and helped himself to a plate of stew. Instead of answering, he asked, "Any more signs of those riders to our north?"

Stone was confused for a moment, then said, "Not since that day I went to look. Why? Did someone see them again?" He'd almost forgotten about their "shadows" to the north since they hadn't been spotted again. They must have seen Stone approaching them that day, for they'd ridden off immediately. He thought there might have been four of them, but they'd been so far away he couldn't be certain.

Shaking his head, Vickersham said, "No, no one's seen them. I just don't like all the surprises that we seem to be running into, and they've been in the back of my mind."

"What other surprises do we have, sir?" Stone asked.

"Besides no fresh horses where they're supposed to be, storms, stampedes, our ammo supply mysteriously disappearing, and our creeping pace? I'm afraid we've had a change of plans. French says the easiest part of the expedition is behind us, and—"

"Easy part!" Garner choked and quickly remembered who he was interrupting. "Sorry, sir, it's just that I didn't know we were traveling through the 'easy part.' I would have tried to enjoy it more."

Despite the interruption, Vickersham smiled with the others. "Yes, well, here it is: the horses and oxen are showing signs of exhaustion, the watering holes are going to become fewer and farther apart, and some of the men are too sick and weak to make it all the way to the Belly River."

"How much farther is it, sir?" Stride asked.

"Sergeant, we are just over a quarter of the way there. We still have over five hundred miles to go, some of it through uncharted territory."

Complete, awed silence met the answer, and Stone felt his stomach curl into a tight ball. He'd known it would be a long, difficult undertaking, but he hadn't thought the horses would be as tired as they were after only two hundred seventy miles. How were they going to make it another five hundred?

"We were supposed to have fresh horses waiting for us here at Roche-Percée, but they're *not* here, and no one knows why. So Commissioner French has ordered Inspector Jarvis of A troop to take the weakest animals and men to Fort Edmonton."

"Edmonton?" Stone echoed. "Isn't that even farther away than the Belly River?"

"Yes, but they'll have the well-marked North Saskatchewan trail to follow, and therefore be assured of food, water, and shelter." Suddenly, Vickersham looked around, irritated. "Whatever is that buzzing noise?"

Stone had heard it as soon as Vickersham, and all the men glanced at one another, then up in the air. The sound wasn't localized at their group only; Stone saw men gathered around other fires cease talking and stare at each other. His first thought was of bees, but the low hum was deeper in tone than a swarm.

"Whatever it is, I don't like it," Garner whispered.

"Grasshoppers?" Boogaard asked no one in particular.

"It seems to be coming from . . . above us," Stone said.

Vickersham stood and said, "It's getting louder." As if in unspoken agreement, every man in sight stood and scanned the sky.

A black locust landed in the middle of Stone's group. Everyone looked down at it as if it were a rattlesnake. It was three or four inches long, and as they watched, it calmly crawled toward Garner's boot.

"Speaking of surprises . . ." Stride commented dryly.

"I *really* don't *like* this," Garner repeated, taking a step backward. "I hate bugs."

Another locust landed by Stride with a small thud, then another black streak ended directly in the fire. After a moment, they all heard a *snap!* as the flames exploded the bug. The hum in the air was loud now, and Stone began to hear cries of surprise and disgust from the direction of E troop.

Then, like a dark, disgusting rain, the air was suddenly thick with locusts. The men instinctively stooped over, and Stone felt two or three bodies hit his back. Glancing upward quickly, he had the impression of being inside a hive of black bodies. The sky was saturated with them, blotting out the midnight blue heavens and leaving the impression that the air itself had taken form and was shifting crazily. Helmetless, Stone felt one land in his hair and another on his neck. He brushed them off with distaste, but they were replaced by more. A nauseous cry escaped Garner, and he dashed to the nearest tent, which happened to be D'Artigue's. The rest of them followed.

Inside, Garner was spinning in circles, desperately brushing off his uniform and head. "Eeeeyyyuuuk! You'd think fighting the mosquitoes would be bad enough, but noooo! Now we've got big bugs! Quick, check my back, Booger!"

They helped one another remove all the locusts that had attached themselves, and everyone but Garner helped pick them up and throw them outside. Stone watched as the ground and tents became black with them, while the very air, the earth, crawled and scuttled and creeped.

"Well, this is certainly interesting," Stride commented behind Stone in typical British understatement.

"Interesting!" Garner sputtered. "It's *disgusting*!" Stride gave him a withering look. "Uh . . . sir."

Vickersham began laughing, and soon all but Garner joined him. Breathlessly, Vickersham said, "I don't remember the manual's course of action when attacked by locusts!" This brought more laughter, and even Garner smiled.

"What do we do now, sir?" Boogaard asked when he'd caught his breath.

Vickersham wiped his eyes. "I have no idea. Let them eat their fill, or whatever it is they're doing, and wait for them to go away."

"What if they *don't* go away?" Garner asked, his face a mask of dawning horror.

"Then, Garner, we ride over them tomorrow, just as we did the time before when we ran across them."

"But . . . I can't just *step* on them with my boot! They"—he paused and shuddered—"*crunch*!" This brought more guffaws at Garner's expense, and Stone couldn't remember the last time he'd laughed so hard. The situation was comical, yet strangely sinister—being held hostage by bugs.

"Horrible way to have supper interrupted," D'Artigue sniffed. "Most *impoli*."

"What's that mean?" Garner asked.

"Impolite—another English word stolen from French." D'Artigue was a totally affable and gregarious man, and he was obviously trying to bait the shaken Garner by putting on a front of snobbishness. He even winked at the others while Garner shook his head.

"You French sure are a funny lot," Garner stated. "You don't like anyone trying to speak your language, then you get offended when someone borrows from it." Though Garner was distracted by D'Artigue, the bug problem was still definitely in the forefront of his mind. "Check outside again, Booger."

From the tent flap, Boogaard gave Garner a smug grin and said, "They look like they're going to stay and visit a while."

———

Stone restlessly turned on his back and listened to Stride's incessant snoring across their tent. Usually after a long day's ride he had no trouble falling asleep, but on this night his eyes wouldn't stay closed. He wondered briefly if Garner were sleeping, and smiled, knowing he probably wasn't.

Staring at the ceiling of the tent, Stone was aware that there were hundreds of locusts clinging to the canvas, but the thought didn't bother him. His mind was wandering everywhere, and he finally decided to get up. Dressing in his uniform trousers and jacket, he left his coat unbuttoned and walked outside. The locusts had thinned out a bit and scattered to find various items to chew on, leaving walking space on the ground. He decided to check on Buck and was about to head toward the corral when he saw a rifle leaning against his tent, covered with the black insects. Stone and Stride never left their rifles outside, and Stone figured it probably belonged to some man walking by when the locusts had descended, and he'd carelessly left it there. *Whoever it is, he'll be in a lot of trouble in the morning if he belongs to C troop*, he thought grimly. He brushed off a few locusts at the end of the barrel, lifted, and brought it down hard on the butt, scattering the rest of the insects. Bringing the rifle close to his face, he saw that they were actually chewing the wood of the stock. He shook his head and decided not to think about what they were doing to the tents.

He made his way to the corral, trying to avoid stepping on the locusts wherever possible. The night was quiet except for the hum of the insects, and Stone wondered if sentries had been posted. At the corral he whistled softly, and out of the twenty horses gathered, two came to him. One of them was Buck, and the other was Doe's chestnut, which walked away disinterestedly when he discovered Stone wasn't Doe. "Hello, Buck," Stone whispered, stroking the horse's muzzle. "What do you think about all these black bugs? You're not scared like Garner, are you?" Buck whinnied deep in his throat and pushed against Stone's chest with his nose.

An answering whinny came from Stone's right, behind the ammunition tents. *There's no corral back there*, he thought and quietly made his way toward the sound. The flaps of the tents were on the other side, and just as he reached the corner of one of them, he heard a "Hup!" and saw a rider break into a gallop. He was leading a horse that was loaded down with saddlebags and a few boxes.

*Those are ammunition boxes*, Stone thought suddenly and remembered Vic commenting on the disappearance of the precious commodity. He opened his mouth to call for the rider to stop, but at the same time an image came to his mind: a group of riders to the north, shadowing the Mounted Police. He closed his mouth with a snap as it all came together.

Rushing back and finding a bridle on the gate of the corral, he quickly led Buck out, fastened it on, and mounted bareback. All the while he was wondering about the sentries that were supposed to be posted every night. Just as he passed the ammo tents he realized he wasn't armed and stopped to retrieve and load an Adams .450 pistol, the official sidearm of the Force. Remounting Buck, he spurred to a run, only to immediately slow him to an easy gallop. Recalling the burdened horse the rider had been leading, Stone knew he would overtake him, and he didn't want that. He wanted to catch the whole bunch in the transfer.

He followed from a safe distance behind as the man skirted a low, limestone-burdened mesa. Dense sagebrush and white spruce trees covered the foot of the slopes, and Stone had no problem weaving in and out of the natural shield without losing sight of the dim figure ahead. After a while, he began to second-guess his own actions. *Should I have gotten help? There may be anywhere from five to ten men waiting to take the ammo—what would I do then? I only have six shots.* He almost stopped, then mentally shrugged and continued. *Too late now.*

Stone hoped that the gunrunner rendezvous would take place close to camp. But on and on he rode, until Stone calculated they must have ridden two or three miles from camp.

Suddenly, the man disappeared. One moment Stone had looked away into the woods after a rustling sound, then when he'd turned back, the rider was gone. He took a chance and rode into the open, away from the protection of the trees, to get a better look. The mesa ended abruptly; the rider must have gone around the bend.

Stifling the urge to spur Buck into a gallop, Stone headed straight for the drop-off, his pistol held at the ready. He knew he couldn't just ride around the bend in the open, so when he was twenty yards from the corner, he dismounted and continued on foot through the forest and brush. Luckily, the cover he was in stretched around the base of the mesa. As he rounded the bend, he heard voices. Stalking as quietly as possible, hoping he wouldn't step on a dry twig, he made his way to the edge of the shallow forest and saw the rider about thirty feet away, talking with three men in slouch hats. They spoke French, so Stone couldn't understand what was being said, but he saw the man hand the reins of the horse carrying the ammo to another. That was all he needed to know.

Stone's knowledge of French was rudimental, but he knew the word "stop." "*Arrêtez!*" he shouted as he stepped from behind a tree, his gun trained somewhere in the middle of the group. "Police! Throw down your weapons!"

Startled, the four men looked at Stone uncertainly as they froze.

"*Arme*—to the ground—*terre! Maintenant!*" With a shock Stone recognized Sallier, the scout, as the man who'd hijacked the ammo.

Out of the corner of his eye, Stone saw the man to his far left move quickly, and without hesitation Stone swerved the Adams around and fired. The man dropped a huge pistol as he grabbed his right shoulder. Stone brought the pistol back around to include the rest of the group, who, after a tense moment, slowly raised their hands in the air. The wounded man groaned and hunched over, but he'd kept his seat in the saddle.

"Now," Stone reasoned, "I don't know if you understand English or not, but I think you can figure out what I want. You"—he pointed at Sallier—"with your left hand, slowly take out your weapon and drop it." He managed to keep the others covered as he instructed each man to do the same. Sallier had a strange smile glued to his face the whole time.

"I wouldn't be smiling if I were you, hoss. You're probably going to hang." Sallier's face was fully visible since he was hatless, and Stone saw his eyes flicker above and behind Stone. In the flash of a second, Stone threw himself to his right, rolled, and came up firing at the shadowy figure at the edge of the woods. The man crumpled to the ground as Stone instantly gained his feet and again covered the men on the horses. Sallier was half-dismounted when Stone yelled, "Stop right there, Sallier—don't move a muscle!"

Sallier froze in an awkward position, his head turned so that Stone could see his still-smiling profile. "You just fired three shots, monsieur. That only leaves you two bullets for the three of us."

"That's all right," Stone said calmly. "One for you, and one for either of you." He gestured at the other two, who shook their heads. "But, believe me, Sallier, the first one has your name written all over it."

"Can I either get down or sit up in the saddle?"

Stone moved to the wounded man's horse and picked up the gun he'd dropped. "Go ahead and get down, Sallier. Tie these men up, and remember—you're first if anything should happen." He kept one gun trained on the three men still mounted, and the other followed Sallier as he found some rope in the wounded man's saddlebags and tied their hands behind their backs.

"What about him?" Sallier asked, nodding toward the still figure at the edge of the woods.

Stone whistled for Buck, who came galloping around the bend, his dark brown mane flying. "I don't know where his horse is, so we'll throw him across your saddle. You can walk back."

————

"Constable Stone," Commissioner French sighed in exasperation. "Why didn't you take some men with you?"

Stone cleared his throat and briefly considered the three faces staring his way: French, Macleod, and Inspector James M. Walsh of A troop. Walsh was a serious-looking man, with dark, penetrating eyes and a bushy mustache. It was said that he, along with Macleod, were the best leaders in the whole Force. They were in French's large tent, with the three senior men seated behind a table and Vickersham standing stiffly at attention by Stone's side.

Stone had led the five horses into camp just before daybreak, and he'd turned the men over to an astonished Stride. The locusts had vanished sometime in the night, leaving the area with strange splotches of bare ground where they'd eaten every blade of grass.

Vickersham had listened to Stone's story, smiled with amusement, and shaken his head. Then he'd turned the matter over to the superior officers. Stone had waited outside the tent, pacing anxiously, tired but still aware of adrenaline pumping in his blood from excitement. The officers had discussed it for half an hour before Vickersham had come outside and summoned Stone.

"What is your answer, Stone?" Macleod asked.

"Sir, there was no sentry in sight, and—"

"He'd been knocked unconscious by Sallier."

"Yes, sir, but I didn't know that at the time. He was nowhere to be seen, and I didn't want to lose Sallier. Also, it would have been very difficult to escape detection while following him with a troop instead of just one man." Stone kept his eyes locked on the far wall of the tent, standing erect, waiting for whatever was to come.

"You could have gotten yourself killed, man," Walsh commented, his stony expression never changing.

"Yes, sir, but I reacted on instinct without thinking, sir."

"Not a very good idea, do you think?" French asked disapprovingly.

"No, sir."

"What you should have done was report to your superior officer, Sub-Inspector Vickersham, and let him handle it. You might have failed, and then we would have been short even more ammunition had the thievery continued."

"Yes, sir, I apologize, sir."

French, Walsh, and Macleod looked at one another without speaking. Then, as if silently reaching a decision, French sighed again and declared, "Now we have one dead Metis and four criminals, with no stockade in which to incarcerate them. What would you suggest we do, Constable Stone?"

Stone was taken aback by the question and risked a quick glance to the stern commissioner's face. "I . . . don't know, sir. I'd think that would be *your* decision."

"Hmmm, quite, quite," French nodded. "Well, you leave us no choice, Constable."

The three officers rose, and Stone's heart leaped into his throat. *I just arrested five men! Why do they look so grim?*

French turned and reached behind his chair. When he faced Stone again, he was holding an officer's helmet, signified by its red plume, and smiling mischeviously. "Or should I say, Sub-Inspector?"

Stone could only blink, stunned.

"Congratulations, Stone," Macleod smiled. "Well done."

Vickersham reached out and slapped Stone on the back, grinning hugely, then returned to attention.

French came around the table and stood in front of Stone with the helmet held in front of his barrel chest. "Hunter Edward Stone, under the sight of God and these witnesses, I hereby promote you to Sub-Inspector. For your bravery in apprehending five criminals set on thievery and villainy against this fine unit and the Dominion of Canada, please accept the gratitude of myself, our fellow officers, and every member of the North-West Mounted Police." He then placed the helmet on Stone's head and held out his hand. "You're just the sort of officer we need to lead our men, Stone. Congratulations."

"Thank you, sir," Stone said, swallowing and feeling weak in the knees. A few moments before, he'd been expecting some sort of reprimand, and now he found himself promoted to *officer*! The word sent a chill up his spine. Macleod and Walsh shook his hand, and then Vickersham stepped up to him.

"Congratulations, Hunter," he said, pumping his hand. A smile played across his thin lips as he leaned closer. "Try to remember not to call me 'sir' in front of the men, will you? It just wouldn't look right. And how about saving some brave deeds for the rest of us?"

"I can't believe this, Vic," Stone whispered. "I just can't believe this!"

Vic grinned and slapped him on the back. "Believe it, old chap." He glanced around quickly to see if they were safely out of hearing distance of the other officers. "Good heavens, man! If you keep this up, you'll have French's job!"

# CHAPTER TWENTY-ONE

# Power and Beauty

Long Feather couldn't get Owl Dog out of his mind. When the white man's wife had been kidnapped, he'd actually followed Red Wolf and tried to defeat him, an unheard-of feat among Red Wolf's warriors. When Long Feather had joined the Police, the first story he'd heard was of the white man's courage at Lake Winnipeg. Now, as he chopped firewood with the other scouts for the bleak and barren one hundred miles of prairie they were about to enter, the talk was of Owl Dog's arrest of Sallier. Long Feather listened, and his fear grew.

"Them fellers didn't have a chance against that Mountie," Lemasters said ominously. He was a small man with a weathered, leathery face and bushy eyebrows. "They said they didn't hear nothin'. He just *appeared*, like an Injun." He shot a glance at Long Feather, who didn't look up from his chopping.

"I heard he *is* part Indian," a man named Peronnes offered.

"Now that's the stupidest thing I ever heard. The man's got blond hair and blue eyes."

"They're not blue, they're almost clear—no more color than a ghost."

"Well, that sure don't make him no Injun. Long Feather, you ever see an Injun with eyes like that?"

"I have never seen *any* man with eyes that color."

"See, Peronnes? That's stupid talk about him bein' part Injun, and I don't wanna hear it anymore. Gives me the willies."

Peronnes and Lemasters were loading split logs in a cart, and Peronnes stopped to wipe his wide forehead and look around conspiratorially. "I also heard that he killed more than one of those men and just left them on the other side of that mesa for the buzzards. Now, what kind of man would do that?"

Long Feather ceased his chopping and thought with horror: *A man like Red Wolf—that's who.* He shivered despite the early morning heat that pressed down on them.

Lemasters' eyes widened. "Now, I ain't heard *that.*"

"I don't know if it's true, but it sure *sounds* true."

"Yep. Any man that could sneak up on Sallier can do most anything. Sallier scared me—always lookin' at you with them dead eyes, like he was sizin' you up to kill you."

"Well, at least we don't have to worry about him anymore. But now, this Stone scares me more."

"Peronnes, what you got to be scared about? You ain't never done nothin' wrong in your life!"

"That's right, and I'm not *going* to do anything wrong with *him* around. I feel sorry for whoever gets on his bad side."

Long Feather swallowed and with great effort silenced the voice inside of him that told him to leave *now.* *What if Owl Dog recognizes me?* he thought with a chill. *What if, one day, I feel a tap on my shoulder, and he's staring at me with those gray eyes? Would he kill me, or, worse yet, torture me as Red Wolf does?*

"What's the matter with you, Long Feather?" Lemasters asked. "You look like you just seen a phantom!" He elbowed Peronnes in the side. "You ever seen an Injun go pale?"

"Nothing is wrong. I am only hot." Untying the blue bandana around his neck, he wiped his sweaty face as he walked over to the shade of a spruce tree. He needed an excuse to get away from the scouts and their curious eyes.

Long Feather knew he couldn't leave. First of all, the place where he was supposed to meet Red Wolf was still two hundred miles away, and secondly, Red Wolf himself would kill him for failing to carry out his orders. *I will stay as far away from the white man as I can. If I see him, I will turn the other way. I will become as a spirit and make myself invisible.* His eyes wandered to the east as he wiped his face and neck, and he froze.

In the distance, buzzards were circling over the mesa.

Superstitious fear gripped him, and he shivered again. *Surely it is the carcass of a coyote or a prairie dog they have spotted. Owl Dog would not kill men and just leave them for the black birds of death.*

*Would he?*

On August 4, one week after Stone's promotion, the column left the security of the Boundary Commission's trail and swung northwest up the parched, bare slopes of the Missouri Couteaux. The Metis called the line of hills the Dirt Hills, and Stone tended to agree with them. "Couteaux" mistakenly conjured vivid images of plush, green mounds of gentle rolling hills, whereas the Dirt Hills were just that—dirt. They were traveling barren land, home to the rattlesnake and prairie dog and burnt, brown grass. With each day's grueling march the expedition became a test of endurance and determination for both men and horses. The summer sun gave no quarter as it blistered down from capacious blue skies.

"You know we're going to have to cross those hills, don't you?" Vickersham asked Stone one day as they rode together at the head of the troop.

"I'm trying not to think about it."

"Your horse looks as if he's just begun our little journey."

Stone reached down and patted Buck's sweaty neck. "I've never had a finer one. We've been through a lot together."

Vic turned and regarded the long line of men behind them and waved Stride forward. "The eastern horses aren't going to make it," he stated grimly. "They stampede at the drop of a hat, they're slower, and they don't have much stamina."

Stone nodded. "We're going to have to start giving the horses a break and alternate riding and walking every mile or so."

"But that's not going to help the ones pulling the carts and wagons."

"We'll do what has to be done, Vic."

"You wanted to see me, sir?" Stride asked as he rode up.

"Yes, Sergeant," Vic said. "How are the men? They don't complain to Hunter and me, but I'm sure you've heard your share."

Stride licked his dry lips, and Stone noticed an angry red blister at one side of his mouth. He avoided their eyes for a moment, then said, "That fool Hallman filled his canteen at a small watering hole a few days ago, and now he's complaining of stomach cramps and bowel trouble."

"Dysentery," Stone remarked with a shake of his head. The sickness was becoming more common every day throughout the Force. It was only a matter of time before Hallman would be incapacitated and another hindrance to an already troubled expedition.

"Looks that way, sir. But overall, the men are still in good spirits, I'd say. Del says there's a good place to water on the other side of the hills."

"Jolly good," Vickersham remarked. "It'll give the men something to look forward to."

That evening before the column halted for the night, Stone and Vickersham rode forward to ask French when they'd be crossing the Dirt Hills. A constable pointed them in the direction of three figures on horseback in the distance, at the edge of a small mesa framed by the setting orange sun. "The commissioner and inspectors have been up there for a while, sir. Don't know what they're doing."

When they reached the officers, Stone and Vickersham stopped twenty feet away, and Stone shouted, "Permission to come forward?"

The three men turned in their saddles, and Macleod, who was obviously excited about something, waved for them to advance. "Come here—quick! You fellows have to see this!"

As they rode forward, a panoramic view of the flat prairie met their eyes, and Stone caught his breath.

"They're magnificent!" Macleod stated. "I've never seen such a sight."

"Power and beauty," Inspector Walsh proclaimed in awe.

As far as the eye could see, the plains appeared to be a rolling, undulating mass of chocolate brown as a massive herd of buffalo heaved restlessly below them. Their number was staggering, and even as Stone had the thought, Vickersham, his voice choked with astonishment, breathed, "How many of them *are* there?" to no one in particular.

"Legion," Macleod answered.

"Countless. Infinite," Walsh added.

"The description 'herd' simply doesn't do this justice," Commissioner French stated.

Stone began to pick out individual animals, from the imposing, ponderous bulls to the smallest calves. The flanks of the bulls teemed with thick muscle like knotted ropes. The dense mass of fur that covered the front half of their bodies only added to the suggestion of brutal and deadly power. Young, spirited males patrolled the outer reaches of the group, and when a calf or cow strayed, they would nudge the stragglers back into line with their horns.

Macleod glanced at the silent Stone. "Stone, your jaw appears to have come unhinged. Don't you have a comment?"

Stone realized his mouth *was* hanging open, and after closing it and swallowing, he croaked, "Majestic, sir. I can't think of another word right now."

Macleod smiled. "Well, gentlemen, I've heard majestic, powerful, beautiful, and magnificent. And I don't think even those eloquent words fully describe what we're seeing right now." His eyes suddenly widened as an idea occurred to him. "Commissioner, may I make a suggestion?"

"Of course, Macleod, what is it?"

"You mentioned just last night that the Force needed a symbol or image that would convey the spirit of the Force itself." Macleod paused as every man looked at him with dawning comprehension. Expansively sweeping his arm over the plain before them, he declared, "I think we have it, don't you?"

"Good heavens, Inspector, I think that's a splendid idea!"

"Excellent, Macleod," Walsh added, his dark eyes taking on a faraway stare. "In addition to the official badge, we could stamp every button of every uniform with the figure."

They stayed on the ridge until the sun had dropped over the horizon. No more words were spoken, and each man felt a strange satisfaction, as if he were the one that had been blessed with the inspiration for the motif of the North-West Mounted Police.

———

That evening, two hundred fifty miles away, Reena O'Donnell made her decision.

The story Stone had told in his letter of the oppressed Indians at Fort Whoop-up had stayed with her night and day. She'd prayed continuously for guidance from the Lord, and on that night she learned from Lone Elk the significance and horror of a breakdown in tribal rituals.

"From the stories I have heard, the tribe that has lost its way can be compared to the war that occurred in the United States a few years ago. Brothers compete with brothers to the death, and sons lose respect for their fathers. The women are confused and must choose sides. All trust is gone, and if a natural leader does not show himself, the result is terrible. When certain rules are broken, there is no limit to how far the tribe may fall. To add to the pain, there is whiskey."

Reena listened intently as she watched him carve the roasted breast of an antelope. His knife was sharp, and his movements were deliberate and smooth. "So how is it stopped?" she asked, afraid of his answer.

The old chief shook his head sadly. "It does not stop. It is like the disease that the white man brought to the Assiniboine many years ago."

"Smallpox?"

"Yes. I saw many of my tribe die day after day, until there were hundreds of us gone." He shrugged lightly. "I do not know why I did not die. Both my mother and father did."

"God had a plan for you, Lone Elk. It was to bring your people to Him." The sight of the steaming slices of meat made Reena's mouth water. Gray Dawn came inside the tepee carrying a bowl of boiled potatoes, and she smiled at Reena. *How can I leave these people?* Reena thought suddenly. *They're like my family.* She remembered with painful clarity the day she'd left Chicago, and she knew that it would be no easier to leave these people. *Is that what the rest of my life holds? Getting close to people, only to leave them?* The idea depressed and saddened her.

Lone Elk finished carving the meat and looked at her, his dark eyes glittering in the firelight of the tepee. "It is good that you came to us when you did. The whiskey was destroying us, and we were going the way of the Blackfoot at this Fort Whoop-up. They need someone like you to help them now. Will you consider this?"

Reena wasn't sure she'd heard him correctly. She glanced at Gray Dawn, who knelt beside Lone Elk and said, "There are women who are losing their husbands, just as I was."

"I know. I've thought of that. In fact, I've been thinking about it for a long time, and I believe it's time for me to go." Reena felt her heart wrench as she said this. Until recently, she'd been under the impression that she would be with the Assiniboine for a long time.

Lone Elk and Gray Dawn smiled their understanding but said nothing.

Reena looked down at her fingernails. While in Chicago, she'd had fine, strong nails that she'd been proud of; now they extended no farther than the edges of her fingertips, and they were split and rough-looking. "I came here expecting you to beg me to stay. Now that you're encouraging me to leave, I don't know how I feel."

Gray Dawn reached across and took Reena's hand. "We don't *want* you to go, Reena. We will miss you very much."

"I know. I didn't mean to sound disappointed. It's just . . . my work here *is* finished, isn't it?"

"Our children speak English well and are able to read their Bibles. The tribe has taken God into their hearts and are happier than they've ever been. All of this is because of you, Reena."

"No, I can't take the credit for all this—it's the Lord working."

"Through you," Lone Elk contended, pointing at Reena. "Through you, Little One."

His recent pet name for her brought tears to her eyes.

———

The officers' awe of the great bison turned to alarm the next day, mixed with a healthy respect for the sheer size of the herd. The buffalo were gone, but they'd left an endless wasteland in their wake. Every blade of grass within sight had disappeared, either eaten or trampled. The water hole at which the Force had intended to replenish their supply was now a large thick paste of mud.

Nearly every man in the column had to help the horses and oxen in the crossing of the Dirt Hills by pushing the carts. One horse died of heatstroke and had to be cut from the reins halfway up. While descending the other side, the men attached ropes to the wagons and stayed behind them, grimly hanging on to prevent the carts from overrunning the tired animals on the steep slope. By the time they were on the west side of the Dirt Hills, every man and animal was exhausted and thirsty.

Stone stood beside Buck and drank the last drops from his canteen. Buck brought his long nose around and nudged at the container, as if he, too, was aware of the emptiness inside. "That's right, boy. From here to Old Wives Creek is going to be a *long* way."

"You ain't gonna believe what they's doin' down at that mudhole," Del drawled as he lumbered up to Stone with Vickersham.

"Taking a mud bath?" Stone asked without humor.

"Naw, they got 'em some empty barrels, poked holes in the bottoms of 'em, and are sinkin' 'em down in the mud to soak through some water. Awfullest lookin' stuff you ever saw."

"The color of ink," Vic agreed with a grimace, "even after they pour it through a filter."

Stone turned his empty canteen upside down in front of them and smiled grimly. "In a few days, I'm sure that water will look as tasty as a mountain stream."

Every day for the next week, the column inevitably straggled out until it trailed five miles long. Three more horses died, along with one ox. Stone had thought he'd be physically prepared for the long journey, but an ache was beginning to gnaw at his back every day after only a few hours of riding. He began to alternate riding and walking even more frequently than before, since walking eased the pain somewhat.

More of the men were getting sick; Hallman was so weak he could barely ride, and others were starting to feel the effects of the bad water. Stone drank the dark fluid as little as possible, but he knew he wasn't ingesting enough to satisfy his body's needs. Before long he would be in danger of dehydration. The water they came across along the way was no better than what they had. Some of it was not drinkable at all, due to the heavy saline content.

Finally they reached Old Wives Creek and moved about two miles northwest to a small lake where there was good grass and water. Here French decided to rest the men and animals for a few days, while Macleod went south to Wood Mountain depot to buy a supply of oats. Stone, along with many others, took advantage of the respite to enjoy long, soaking baths in the lake and streams.

The first day, Stone and Vickersham stayed submerged in the lake so long that the tips of their fingers wrinkled like prunes. While they were floating on their backs, feeling the midmorning sun explore their tanned faces with warm fingers, Vickersham commented off-handedly, "We'll be reaching the Cypress Hills in a few days."

"Mmmm."

A pause. "Do you think Miss O'Donnell's still there?"

"I don't know. Probably."

"I'll bet she is. I mean, where else would she go?"

Stone didn't answer.

"A very pretty lady."

"Mmmm."

"Am I bothering you, Hunter?"

"Not much."

Vic saw him smile and laughed. "You sure aren't much on words, I'll say that."

"Are you thinking of deserting us for a few days to call on Miss O'Donnell?" Stone asked, feeling a startling and surprising twinge of jealousy.

"And risk Macleod pinching my head off? I don't think so." Vickersham let himself drop down in the shallow water until he was sitting in the soft silt. "But I do have to admit the thought had crossed my mind. What about you? You scrubbed those uniforms pretty hard this morning—planning on a detour of your own?"

Stone also sat down, cupped water in his hands, and splashed his face. He was stalling while trying to assess the disturbing jealous feelings of a few moments before. There was no doubt he'd thought of Reena quite a few times along the way and had actually daydreamed of going to see her, but he doubted he would be granted permission.

*Besides, I still love and miss Betsy. How could I be jealous over another woman?* To Vickersham he said, "I think it's too soon for that, Vic."

"Too soon for—? Oh yes . . . I'm sorry, Hunter, sometimes I just forget. You never talk about her and . . ." Vic finished weakly, immediately uncomfortable.

Stone gazed out over the gently rippling water and heard the joyful cry of someone diving in the water down the bank. Drops of water fell from their hair and plopped softly in the water behind them. "She was wonderful. Always happy and smiling. You know, since she died I've learned to appreciate her more. She never wanted anything for herself—everything she did was for me. And I can't thank her now, that's the hardest part. She knew I loved her, but I can't *thank* her, you know?"

Vickersham smiled and shrugged. "Never been married. But I think I know what you're talking about."

"We should tell whoever we love 'thanks' every day, because you never know if . . . well, you never know."

Studying his friend's stoic profile, Vickersham tried to imagine the hurt and sorrow that accompanied the loss of a loved one. He'd never even lost a friend, much less a member of his family. Words seemed so inadequate at this time, so he said nothing.

"You know something, Vic? It wouldn't be so hard if there were a *reason* for her to die. If she'd been saving the life of a child, or . . . *something*! But what happened was . . ." His face flushed under his deep tan, and his lips disappeared in a thin, tight line. "Useless," he whispered, shaking his head. "Useless."

# CHAPTER TWENTY-TWO

## Reunions

Long Feather received the shock of his life when he stirred from his sleep on the morning of September 2, 1874. He hadn't gotten to bed until the wee hours of the morning. Another scout had somehow secured a few bottles of whiskey, and they'd even invited Long Feather to help them drink it—from his own cup, of course. Even the mixed-blood Metis didn't want to drink after an Indian. He hadn't held it against them, however, and they'd toasted the night away to concepts and men that were totally alien to Long Feather, except for the many times they'd mockingly raised a cup to the Police camped a comfortable distance away from the carousing.

When Long Feather felt the inhospitable kick to his leg that woke him, he was in no mood for Metis pranks. He swept an arm behind him to slap away the kicking leg, missed, and attempted to settle back down for more sleep. Another kick, more vicious this time, landed on his rear. "Get up, Crow!" Long Feather sat up quickly and the pain in his head was unbearable. His eyes were dry and gritty, and when he opened them he looked straight into the eyes of Owl Dog.

Long Feather immediately forgot about his hangover and crawled backward a few feet. *He has come for me! He finally remembered where he had seen me before, and now he is here to kill me!* He didn't see a weapon in the white man's hands and realized he'd come to kill him with his bare hands.

"It's time," Owl Dog said, and Long Feather could smell his own stale breath as he began a strange wheezing. "It's time for you to earn your pay. Get up."

Long Feather sprang to his feet instantly, blinking into the early morning sun. Owl Dog's expression was menacing under the brim of the white helmet as he ran his gray eyes up and down Long Feather's form. His lip curled slightly at Long Feather's disheveled appearance. Long Feather tried to speak, but what came out of his dry throat was nothing but a croak.

"You hired on with the promise of finding water," Owl Dog continued, "and we need water."

A myriad of thoughts and emotions flashed through Long Feather's mind, the strongest of which was fear—absolute and perfect in its form. He had no idea where to find water and had never planned on anyone asking him to find it. His gullet clicked as he attempted to swallow. "I knew of many places around Old Wives Creek. I am not as sure about this area." He knew they were west and south of the Cypress Hills, but he couldn't lead the man directly to a water hole.

"Then why are we still paying you?"

The question caught Long Feather totally off guard, and he felt his mouth working for an answer. He watched as Owl Dog picked up Long Feather's hat and ran his finger over the beaded hatband that was made in the colorful motif of the Crow nation. After a moment, the gray eyes pierced him again.

"You ever hear of a Crow named Red Wolf?"

Long Feather just *knew* his face was giving him away even as he shook his head—which he probably did too quickly to be believable. "No, I have never heard of him."

"You're lying."

"No. I speak the truth."

"He's a famous man in these parts—a butcher of women and children, and a member of your own race. I'd go so far as to say he's a popular subject around Crow campfires. And you're going to tell me you've never heard of him?"

Wanting very much to tell him the truth, to have the blitzing, accusing eyes off of him, Long Feather somehow found the strength to stick with his story and shook his head again. "I am sorry. I do not know this man."

Stone was in a foul mood. The Mounties had traveled two hundred miles since Old Wives Creek, and every man was thirsty and exhausted, with quite a few of them sick. They'd left Old Wives Creek carrying all the water and food they could manage, but in a week they'd found themselves in the same situation as before, with supplies running out and no way to replenish them. However, they'd run across another bison herd, and this time, instead of admiring, they'd killed enough to provide over 1700 pounds of meat. The water situation was another matter, and Stone had grown tired of drinking the putrid fluids. Then he'd remembered Long Feather and had decided to pay him a visit.

As he continued to stare at the Indian, Stone knew that he was lying, but he couldn't exactly force a confession out of him. He didn't like to admit it to himself, but he was enjoying Long Feather's obvious discomfort. Stone made the Indian very nervous, though he didn't know why.

Long Feather felt he *must* break the long, uncomfortable silence and was grateful for a sudden helpful idea. "There is water in the Cypress Hills, though it is a day's ride away."

"You stay out of the Cypress Hills," Stone responded immediately. "Do you understand me?"

"Yes, sir."

"Don't go *near* them."

"Yes, sir."

"Hunter!" Vickersham hailed from behind Stone as he walked toward them. "Here you are—I've been searching all over for you."

Long Feather had heard nothing but good things about Vickersham, and he was immensely relieved to have him join them. *Owl Dog will not kill me in front of this other man . . . will he?* He shook his head in exasperation. *It seems I am always worried about someone killing me. Very disturbing, this life. In the next life, I wish to be a bear and not worry about dying all the time.*

"Why are you looking for me?" Stone asked Vickersham, keeping his eyes on Long Feather.

"Because you missed a meeting with the Commissioner. He's decided the Force will camp here for a few days, while Macleod, you, and I take a detail to Fort Benton in Montana for more supplies and—believe it or not—to collect our pay." The men still hadn't received any money, and it had become a running joke among them.

Stone made a curt, slicing gesture with his hand. "Don't talk in front of *him*, Vic."

Vickersham looked at Long Feather, then back at Stone in confusion. "It'll be common knowledge in a matter of hours, Hunter. What difference does it make?"

Stone ignored Vic's question and said to Long Feather, "Remember what I said."

"Yes, sir," Long Feather nodded. Owl Dog contemptuously flipped his hat to him, and Long Feather watched them walk away.

Long Feather knew what he had to do.

———

"When do we leave, Vic?" Stone asked as they made their way back to C camp.

"Day after tomorrow. We have to let the horses rest before we start out. I say, Hunter, what's the lowdown on you and that Indian?"

"What do you mean?"

"I think you know what I mean. If looks could kill, he'd be a dead man."

"I don't trust him, and I think he just lied to me."

"Concerning what?"

Stone stopped and faced his friend. "What's he doing here, Vic? As far as I know, he hasn't done anything but tag along for the ride. Why?"

Vickersham shrugged, and his face softened. "Listen, Hunter. Not every Indian is a frothing killer. You should know that after spending time with the Assiniboine. We have no knowledge of Long Feather's accomplishments on this trek since the scouts keep to themselves. Maybe he's avoided a particularly bad area for us, or led us to a water hole that had dried up, and we just haven't heard about it." He patted Stone on the arm. "Relax, will you? There's a good chap."

"I'm going to see Reena," Stone said abruptly.

"What? When did you decide this?"

"Just now."

"Hunter, you can't just ride off like that!"

"I can if you cover for me."

Vic chuckled uneasily, removed his helmet, and wiped his brow. "How in the world did your stubborn head come to this—? Oh, never mind. Just go! Maybe it'll put you in a better frame of mind."

"Thanks, Vic."

"But I'm warning you. I can only lie about your whereabouts for so long. Macleod's not daft, you know."

Stone put his arm around Vickersham's shoulders and led him to the camp. He'd been blessed with few close friends in his life, but Vic had become the best one he'd ever had. "You're a good friend."

"I'm a *brainless* friend is what I am for letting you do this. And you be back here tomorrow night, safe and sound."

"Yes, Mother Vickersham."

"I'm serious, Hunter!"

"I know—I'll be here."

They walked a way in silence until Vickersham blurted, "Whatever made you decide to go see her? One moment we were talking about Indians, and the next you're off on a mysterious quest."

"Well, I've been thinking. What if I'm posted in the far northwest, in the middle of nowhere? This may be my last chance to see *any* of them."

Vic considered this and nodded. Then a thought occurred to him. "Wait a moment, what about me? I could say the same thing."

"Sorry, Vic, my idea."

"You're a sly one, Hunter," Vickersham sighed. "Sometimes I wish I still outranked you."

———

Red Wolf rolled the dice on the flat ground in front of him. The dice were made from fruit pits, with slashes carved in the sides for numbers. Until recently he'd despised any man who would play the game, thinking it silly and a waste of time. But one time he'd picked up the dice when no one was around and had invented his own game to compete against himself and the odds. Now he found that he could lose hours of the day playing the dice. After thinking on it, he decided that the reason he loved them so much was because the roll of the dice was much the same as life itself, in his opinion: pure chance. He could appreciate the irony.

Becoming aware of a gnawing hunger, Red Wolf shoved the dice into a beaded leather pouch, stood, and stretched with a groan. Once again, time had slipped away from him while he'd played, and he was surprised to see a rider coming straight toward him from the west. He was camped on the western side of the Cypress Hills at the appointed meeting place for Long Feather, in a copse of spruce trees that left him invisible from the prairie. After shadowing the Mounties for a few days, he'd known Long Feather would try to find him sometime soon, and he grunted with satisfaction as he saw the bright headband on Long Feather's hat shining in the late afternoon sun.

Red Wolf gave a low whistle when Long Feather was within hearing distance. Always suspicious, he scanned the plains behind Long Feather for anyone following; he wouldn't put it past the man to betray him. Red Wolf firmly believed that being overcautious had kept him alive so far.

Long Feather's eyes searched the thick trees as he rode in, surprised to find his leader alone. "Where are the others, My Chief?"

"I sent them to find buffalo."

Dismounting, Long Feather attempted to calm his nerves. Besides being nervous about seeing Red Wolf after so long, he was never certain about the reaction he would receive when he brought surprising news. Upon hearing of Owl Dog's presence in the Police, Red Wolf was capable of either flying into a rage—which could be dangerous to innocent bystanders—or laughing with delight.

Red Wolf grasped Long Feather's shoulders and locked eyes with him. "I have been waiting for you, Long Feather. I thought you would have come to me by now."

"I waited as long as I could, Great One."

"Sit, and tell me news of this Police." Red Wolf sat with his back against a thick spruce tree and picked up an elkhorn quirt that Long Feather had never seen before. As they talked, Red Wolf absently turned the quirt over and over in his massive hands.

Long Feather told of the Mounties' weapons, materials, and manpower, then said, "Their horses are useless to you, Chief—most of them are half dead from exhaustion and starvation."

"Yes, I saw them from the north side of the Hills. I will not waste my time with stealing them. But you have other news, yes?"

Long Feather wasn't surprised; Red Wolf could read minds, as far as he could tell. "Yes. A small troop goes to Fort Benton tomorrow or the next day to get oats, food, and money."

"Money?"

"Yes, much money. The men have not been paid since they began the march."

Red Wolf snorted derisively. "Fools."

Long Feather could see Red Wolf's mind swelling with thoughts of greed and formulating plans to steal the Mounties' pay. Taking a deep breath and cautiously attempting to slither out of quirt-swinging distance, he said, "I have other news."

"What is it?"

"Owl Dog is with them." Long Feather inwardly cringed when he said this and was aware of sweat breaking out in his palms.

Red Wolf stared at him for a moment, completely still, then barked "Ha!" triumphantly and cracked the quirt in the air with a startling *whack*! "My old friend," he grinned savagely. "We meet again."

"He is an officer, too. He arrested five men for stealing ammunition. Some say he killed more and left them for the black birds of death on the prairie."

Staring into the trees with rapturous black eyes, Red Wolf nodded. Since he'd fought with Owl Dog, he'd gone south to join with the great Sioux chief Crazy Horse in the Dakota Territory. He'd never thought he would find a warrior as great as himself, especially from the race of dogs called Sioux, but Crazy Horse had been like a blood brother. They'd gone on many raids and killed scores of white eyes, and the need for more chaos always burned in their blood. One night, Red Wolf had told the story of Owl Dog's bravery and persistence to Crazy Horse and his braves, and he'd basked in the applause of the listeners for both the white man and Red Wolf's decision to let him live and serve as a shining monument to Red Wolf's prowess. Unfortunately, Crazy Horse had felt the need to move south and fight the ever-increasing numbers of men in blue, while Red Wolf now had his own soldiers to confront in Canada. Crazy Horse had given him the elkhorn quirt as a gift, and Red Wolf cherished it like no other possession.

Out of the corner of his eye he noticed Long Feather shift uncomfortably. Red Wolf shook off his reveries and said, "I must plan a surprise meeting with my old friend."

"I have a suggestion, Great One," Long Feather hinted warily. "Owl Dog is one of the leaders for the troop to Montana. You could meet him along the way. . . ."

" . . . and take his money, or his life. Or both," Red Wolf grinned. "Maybe I will even persuade him to join me."

Long Feather was astounded. "Join you?"

"Make no mistake about him," Red Wolf warned with a dark smile, "he has more in common with me than he knows."

Long Feather thought about the fear he'd suffered the whole time he'd been with the Police, and what would happen if Owl Dog remembered him. Many times he'd found himself sharing the same dread of the white man as he held for Red Wolf. The statement from Red Wolf began to make sense.

"There is a war inside of Owl Dog," Red Wolf continued. "A war between good and evil. Now, the evil is silent as he plays at honor and goodness with the Mounties. But there are ways to bring back the evil side again and lose the good forever."

"How, Great One?"

Red Wolf grinned once again, and this time Long Feather's blood chilled.

———

Stone recalled the fateful night of the Indian boy-thieves clearly as he rode through the pass to the Assiniboine camp. He'd come so close to shooting a child that he still shuddered slightly whenever he thought of it. The memory was also a blessing, because he *hadn't* killed the boy, and the incident had practically led him into the arms of the Mounted Police.

Dusk was fully gathered around him, and he felt a sense of relief that he no longer seemed to have eyes on his back. About the time he'd drawn even with the Cypress Hills, he'd started feeling as if he were being watched, but after stopping Buck and scanning his surroundings carefully he'd seen nothing. However, he knew that didn't mean someone wasn't observing him. Another memory came to him, one of a fresh spring day when he'd experienced the same unnerving sensation; Gaston and Olivia Osbourne had died that night.

Stone pushed the morbid thoughts from his mind as he rode into the village. The first braves to see him didn't recognize him in his scarlet uniform, but after he laughed and called two of them by name, they gathered around and shook his hand with delight. Word of his arrival spread quickly through the gathering dark, and in the torchlight he spotted Lone Elk and Gray Dawn coming toward him with huge grins of welcome. He searched every face as it came into sight but didn't see Reena.

"Hunter," Lone Elk greeted, hugging him with hidden strength. "It is good to see you again, my friend."

"It's good to be here, Chief. Hello, Gray Dawn. I see you're still as beautiful as ever."

Gray Dawn giggled. "You have a smooth tongue, Hunter." Her hand stroked his sleeve gently. "And you look so . . . what is the word?"

"Handsome."

Stone turned toward the voice and saw Reena.

"Handsome and gallant," she added. She wore a deep blue dress with puffed sleeves and a white collar made of embroidered roses. Her startling blue eyes danced with mischief as she observed his surprise, and her teeth flashed in a brilliant smile.

Stone hadn't seen a woman in months, much less one so beautiful, and the sight of her caught him off guard. He'd thought he was prepared to see her, but his affection for her flowed through him in a rush. He strode to her and took her in his arms. "It's wonderful to see you, Reena," he whispered so that only she could hear, and her arms tightened around his neck. He could have held her for a long time, but with reluctance he pulled back and stepped away.

"I was hoping you'd come," she said.

"It didn't appear that I'd be able to for a while, but Vic helped me take care of it."

"You mean he's covering your tracks?"

"Yes, something like that," Stone grinned.

"And what will you do for him in return?"

"Well, we haven't talked about that yet, but I'm sure I'll pay tenfold."

"I'm sure."

"Come, Hunter," Gray Dawn interrupted, "are you hungry?"

"No, but I could sure use a drink of that fresh spring water."

They went to Lone Elk's tepee and talked for an hour. Star Light burst in at one point and gave Stone a fierce hug. True to his word, the boy had made a buffalo talisman exactly like his own, and his eyes shone as Stone admired the detailed work. He talked excitedly of his life, and Stone marveled that this was the same boy that had gone months without speaking a word. Finally, Lone Elk began yawning, and Star Light went to bed. Outside, as Reena and Stone were leaving, Gray Dawn said, "Lone Elk gets tired much sooner than he used to."

"Would you like to come with us and let him sleep?" Stone asked.

A look passed between Gray Dawn and Reena that Stone didn't understand, and Gray Dawn said, "No, you two have much to talk about."

"We do?" He glanced at Reena, who nodded. "Oh . . . well . . . I guess we do. Good night, Gray Dawn."

"Good night."

Instead of heading to her tepee, Reena steered Stone toward the horse corral. "Let's go check on Buck." When she saw the buckskin, she asked, "What have you done to him? He looks so skinny!" Stone's face fell, and she remembered the tales of hardship which he'd just told them. "That was silly of me, Hunter. I wasn't thinking."

"No, it's all right. He *is* skinny. It's been a long, difficult march, especially for the horses."

"You look tired, too."

"We all are. We haven't had much luck on our side. Or maybe I should say we've had plenty of it, but unfortunately it's been all bad."

"I don't believe in luck."

He stared at her for a long moment. "No, I don't suppose you do, do you?"

"Wait here," Reena said. He watched her walk quickly to her tepee and go inside. He had a chance to gauge his emotions and found them as confusing as ever. Only a year had passed since he'd seen her, and yet she seemed to have gained a mature beauty and bearing that was unexplainable. If she were a man, Stone would say that she'd had her first taste of battle and seen the tiger. *And maybe she has. Something in her eyes, as if she's accepted the world as a much darker place than she'd ever thought before.*

She came out of her tepee holding a pouch by its leather draw-string. Her step was lively, and he could tell she was feeling the same happiness that he was, just by being in each other's company. She hadn't lost her sweet innocence and a certain unique vulnerability, and he prayed at that moment that she never would.

"What are you smiling at, Hunter Stone?" she asked merrily.

"I'm smiling at *you*, miss."

"Well, for some reason that smile makes me nervous."

"I'm sorry, I—"

"No, don't stop. It's a *good* nervous."

"As you wish, ma'am."

She put her arm through his as they resumed their walk to the corral and said, "You know, that uniform is really stunning. If you were coming to arrest me, *I'd* sure surrender."

"I'll keep that in mind if I have to arrest you."

"Have you yet? Arrested anyone, I mean?"

He paused and took a deep breath. "Yes."

Reena waited, and when he didn't explain, she prodded, "And?"

"And what?"

She pinched his arm. "Tell me about it! I'm dying to hear about your new life!"

Reluctantly, Stone told her of the incident at Lake Winnipeg, and the arrest of Sallier and his men. He spoke only of the bare details and tried to play down his part in both of them, but she questioned him so thoroughly that she soon had the whole story. The only fact he left out was the unfortunate death of the man that had tried to shoot him in the back. He knew it was in self-defense, but he still didn't want her to know.

"Do you mean to tell me," Reena said slowly, "that you've arrested *nine* men?"

"Well, I had help in—"

"No, no. You said you charged into that cabin all by yourself, and then you followed that man Sallier all by yourself, right?"

"Yes, but Garner was right behind—"

"Hunter Stone!" Reena fairly shouted and with surprising strength spun him around to face her. "*What* do you think you're doing?"

His mouth worked, but no words came. She seemed deadly serious, a reaction he hadn't expected.

"Don't you know you could have gotten yourself killed?"

"I . . . well, I didn't—"

"You didn't *think*, did you? You just reacted."

"I did too think!" he shot back, amazed at the defensive tone that had crept into his voice.

Reena whacked him on the chest with her small fist. "I *knew* it! When I read in your letter that you'd been promoted, I just *knew* you'd gone and done something dangerous."

"Reena, it's my job! No matter how you sugarcoat it, there's always going to be danger."

Shaking her head and huffing, she rammed her arm back through his none too gently and steered him back toward the corral. "Don't you die on me, Hunter Stone. You're my best friend, and I won't allow it."

"I'll be sure to be careful. I promise." Stone wanted desperately to change the subject, so he asked, "What's in the bag?"

"Chokecherries for Buck."

When they reached the corral, Buck came to them. He nuzzled Reena and his nose went directly to the pouch. "Are you hungry, you beautiful thing?" Reena cooed and brought a handful of the sweet fruit to his mouth. Buck munched contentedly.

"You'll ruin his gourmet diet with that, you know," Stone said.

"Poor baby. He probably hasn't had a treat since you left."

"I feed him as best I can. It hasn't been easy."

Keeping her eyes on Buck, Reena said, "I'd like to come with you, Hunter." Out of the corner of her eye she saw him take a half-step back.

"You what?"

"I've done the Lord's work here, and it's time to move on. I want to go to Fort Whoop-up and try to help those Blackfeet."

"But . . . you can't just—" Stone found himself sputtering again and deliberately took control of himself. The sweet, docile Reena he'd known was proving to be quite a handful. He took her arm and turned her toward him. The dim light from the few fires still burning in the village cast a soft glow on her high cheekbones. "Reena, listen to me. We have no idea what we'll find there. For all we know, we may be facing a war with the whiskey traders *and* the Indians. It's no place for a lady right now."

"Then you admit that it may be perfectly safe."

"I didn't say that."

"Yes, you did. You said you don't know the situation, so there may be no danger at all."

Stone rolled his eyes. "Reena—"

"Fine. If you won't let me go with you and the troop, I'll go by myself."

"What? No—I forbid it."

"Hunter, you're in no position to forbid me to do anything!"

Unfortunately, she was right, and he knew it. But he wasn't going to let her travel through hostile country by herself. Besides, if she were with three hundred armed men, how much safer could she be? Sighing deeply, he said, "You're turning out to be more trouble than I thought."

Reena smiled as Buck nudged her insistently for more treats. "It's part of my charm. See, Buck loves me."

"You *are* charming, there's no doubt about that. And I don't want anything to happen to you either. Buck isn't the only one who cares about you." He couldn't stay upset with her, and he suddenly found that he didn't want to let her out of his sight. She exuded a vulnerability and innocence that he wanted to shield from the perils of the world. Looking up at him with dancing eyes, her face turned serious as she saw his. He reached out and brushed a strand of her dark hair back from her cheek, then took her small chin between his thumb and forefinger and tilted her face toward his. She came to him willingly, with a touch of eagerness and no surprise, and he found her lips warm and exciting. He wrapped his arms around her waist and drew her to him, his mind a vortex of confused emotions. It had happened so naturally that he hadn't examined the reason he'd felt the need to kiss her; he'd just let the urgent compulsion take him. *She's so soft, and smells clean and sweet and feminine. I could take care of her. I could build her a future, just like . . .*

Reena was enjoying his large, strong hands on her waist and his cool mouth, when he abruptly jerked away. He turned and gripped a corral post, his knuckles glowing a ghostly white in the dim night. He said nothing, but she knew what had happened. She tentatively placed her hands on his shoulders and, feeling no resistance, pressed her cheek against his broad back. His breathing was heavy and uneven.

"I'm sorry, Reena. I'm really sorry."

"It's all right," she whispered, stroking his back.

"I just can't . . . I thought I was ready, but—"

Reena gently turned him around and placed two fingers on his lips. "I'm not ready either, Hunter."

He nodded and took her in his arms naturally, with no expectations or promises.

They held each other until the fires in the village burned to embers.

———————

Deep in the shadows on a hill behind the corral, Red Wolf watched the man and woman embrace. His grin held more derision and contempt than amusement. He had truly believed that Owl Dog was worthy of his admiration; Crazy Horse was the only other man with whom Red Wolf had felt an instant kinship.

Red Wolf had had a dream in which he and the man called Stone had been one and the same. It had been a dark dream with no landscape, and just the two of them riding together side by side.

But Owl Dog had one major flaw that disappointed and irritated Red Wolf. It had nearly proved to be his undoing before, and he hadn't learned from his mistake as a cautious warrior should.

Red Wolf would speak to the white man about his flaw in the near future. Owl Dog would either change and take his place beside Red Wolf, or he would die.

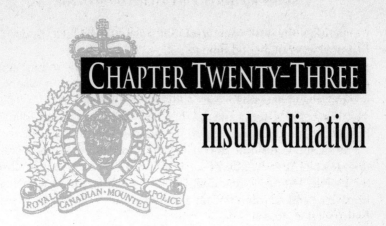

# CHAPTER TWENTY-THREE

# Insubordination

The Assiniboine tribe had known of Reena's decision to leave for quite some time; however, Stone's unforeseen arrival caught them unawares, and the feast they'd planned in her honor was now impossible. Every man, woman, and child lined up to see her off the next morning, and Reena couldn't hold back the tears that flowed down her cheeks. The most important part of her life had been spent with these people, and she didn't know if she'd ever see them again.

Parting with Lone Elk and Gray Dawn was the most difficult. The three of them wrapped their arms around one another, while Lone Elk said a prayer for her. Reena waved goodbye to them as she rode away on the horse Lone Elk had given her. After she and Stone had ridden out of sight, she continued crying until they drew clear of the Cypress Hills onto the flat plains.

Stone watched her display of emotion uneasily. To him, the sight and sound of a woman weeping made him feel totally inept and useless. Occasionally he would place his hand on her arm in an attempt to comfort, but it only seemed to make her cry harder. Eventually he contented himself with riding silently by her side.

When Reena gained control, she wiped her eyes and tried to smile. "I'm sorry. I must seem like a big baby."

"You don't have to apologize to me, Reena. I remember crying in front of you a few times."

"Yes, but that was different. You'd just lost everything you had."

"Mmmm. Just as you have right now. But you still have me." He grinned at her, proud to be able to show his masculine understanding, and was appalled when she began a fresh bout of misery. After briefly wondering if she was crying *because* he was all she had left, he decided that now was not a good time to ask.

Gradually, the uneasy sense of being watched came to him again, and he turned to look behind them frequently. Once he thought he saw movement and stopped abruptly.

"What is it?" Reena asked. When he didn't respond, she followed his gaze with red and swollen eyes. "Did you see something?"

Stone shook his head uncertainly. "I don't know. Maybe a prairie dog or wolf. Anyway, I don't see anything now." They rode in silence for a while, but Stone repeatedly found himself looking back. Finally he gave up and concentrated on what was ahead. "I hope you're ready for inspection, Reena."

"Inspection?"

"Yes. Those men have probably forgotten what a woman looks like."

"I don't mind."

He glanced at her knowingly. "You will."

Wide open eyes and gaping mouths greeted them at the camp in the late afternoon. The boisterous noise of men at leisure faded, and Stone could all but hear the whispers circling through the area with a domino effect. One man who'd been shoeing his horse spotted Reena and screamed in agony after bringing the hammer down on his thumb. Another one was dismounting from his horse when his spurs caught in his saddlebags, and he performed an acrobatic flip in the air before landing flat on his back.

Two men stood shaking their heads as Reena and Stone rode by, and when one of them found his voice he said, "That Stone. Two promotions, and now he finds a beautiful woman in the middle of nowhere. What's he going to do next, run for Governor-General?"

His partner nodded at Reena. "If he'll get me one of those, he's got my vote!"

Reena, despite being unnerved by their gawking, tried to smile and nod pleasantly to some of the men. A few had the presence of mind to remove their helmets or weakly wave back, but most of them could only stare stupidly. She gave up and kept her eyes straight ahead and was overjoyed to see Vic and Del walking toward them with huge grins.

"Miss Reena, you're as purty as ever," Del said.

"Why, thank you, Del."

Vickersham helped her dismount with a cheerful greeting and a knowing look at Stone. "I must say, I'm not a bit surprised at your appearance, Reena. Hunter can talk people into most anything. Take it from a poor soul that was left behind to make excuses for him, while he rides off to spend time with a fair maiden."

"Well, he can't take credit for this, Vic. This was my idea."

Stone was looking around at the fifty or so men that had gathered, with more on the way. "Don't you men have something to do?" None of them even looked at him. "Vic, I'm gone for one day and they've already lost respect for an officer. How did you let this happen?"

Vickersham spread his hands innocently. "You have only yourself to blame for the mutiny. We can go to our tent for some privacy."

"Go ahead. I'm going to clear this with the commissioner."

"Good luck, old boy. He's been a bit cross today."

Stone swallowed and went to find French. Vic's idea of "a bit cross" could mean that French had had two or three roaring displays of anger.

Vic and Del led Reena into a huge tent, and she was more than glad to escape the prying eyes. Hunter had been right—it had been downright disturbing to be inspected so closely. The interior of the tent was neat and tidy, and Vickersham placed a chair beside his cot for her while he and Del sat on the bed. They exchanged news, with Reena hearing more horror stories of the march. Del interrupted every once in a while to make light of their rough times to start her laughing. She told of her experiences with the Assiniboine and how she had come to make her decision to go help the Indians of Fort Whoop-up.

Vickersham gave her an admiring look. "Your faith in God is refreshing, Reena."

"Maybe you should try it," she suggested.

"Maybe I will."

Stone came back, shaking his head. "You weren't joking, were you, Vic?"

"Give you a scare, did he?"

"He gave me a dressing down that I don't ever want to go through again. But you'd better be prepared—he thinks you lied to him."

Vickersham was offended. "Not once did I lie to that man! Whenever he asked, I told him that I couldn't find you, which was the truth."

"I think I smoothed it over with him and took all the blame."

"What about me?" Reena asked.

"Oh, he doesn't have a problem with you. We'll set up a tent for you close to our company, but far enough away for some privacy."

Reena breathed a sigh of relief. She hadn't thought they'd turn her out alone, but hearing of French's acceptance put her at ease.

Stone continued, "We leave before first light, Vic, so we need to go pick some men, draw rations, and get to bed early."

"Will this trip be dangerous?" Reena asked, suddenly worried. She'd almost forgotten about their need to go to Fort Benton.

"Easier'n pluckin' a chicken," Del informed her, snapping his fingers. "Jest rip on down there, get what we need, and come straight back."

Vickersham informed Reena, "Del's been much easier to tolerate since learning he's about to be paid."

"Yup. In Yankee dollars, too. Must say it's about time."

"I don't know why they're paying *you*, since you manage to avoid most of the work."

Del appeared deeply insulted. "It's hard work avoidin' work!"

That night after supper, Stone steered Reena to a tall, stern-looking man and introduced him as Sergeant Stride. "Stride, you're a lucky man," Stone said.

"Yes, sir."

"Wait, I haven't told you why."

"Doesn't matter, sir. I've a feeling it has something to do with this exquisite lady standing between us, so therefore, I *am* a lucky man." He turned to Reena. "What'll it be, miss? Scale the tallest mountain for you? Pop out and fetch you a live bear?"

Stride's tone and facial expression never wavered from its iron bearing, and Reena had a feeling she would only have to nod and there would be no holding the man back. His clipped British accent and military stance was a bit overwhelming, but definitely reassuring. The only words that she could manage were, "Oh, my!"

Stone said, "How about just watching over her while Sub-Inspector Vickersham and I are gone?"

"Not a hair on her lovely head will come to harm, sir," was the instant answer.

"I've told you, Stride, when we're alone, you can drop the 'sirs' and just call me Hunter."

"Yes, sir, you *have* told me that."

Stone waited for more, then chuckled and told him, "Carry on, Sergeant."

"By your leave, sir." Stride whirled on a polished heel and left.

Reena watched him go and whispered, "Is he always so . . . proper?"

"Always. The best man in the whole outfit. If we're ever in a serious scrape, I'm finding him and doing whatever he says."

They walked to Reena's tent that had been set up and listened to the sounds of the night. "I love the chirp of crickets," she said dreamily.

"I have a story I could tell you that would change your mind," he said, remembering the night of the locusts.

"I'm sure you do, but I don't want to hear it." She placed her hand on his chest and looked in his eyes. "You'll be careful?"

"Yes. I promise."

"And when will you be back?"

"Shouldn't take longer than three or four days."

Reena sighed and considered her masculine surroundings. "What will I do while you're gone?"

Stone grinned. "For entertainment, why don't you ask Stride to catch that bear for you?"

Reena didn't smile. "I'll be thinking of you."

"I certainly hope so." Then turning, he said seriously, "I'll be thinking of you, too, Reena."

———

The next two days Reena slept late. She was amazed that three hundred men could be so quiet until she discovered that Sergeant Stride had threatened anyone with death if they woke her. Each morning he had coffee ready for her and a breakfast of buffalo meat, cheese, and bread. She playfully scolded him for his apologies concerning the meat's toughness, and thanked him for his thoughtfulness.

Hunter, Vic, and Del were gone, and Reena felt uncomfortable in the midst of so many strange men. Commissioner French stopped by to meet her and, as if reading her mind, to assure her that she had every right to be traveling with the Mounties. "It's our job to make the citizens feel safe, you see," he'd said with pride. She found him to be kind, but slightly stiff in his manner, and wondered if he was just uncomfortable around women. He was obviously a soldier, first and foremost, and had probably spent his entire life only in the company of men.

Reena spent the day sitting outside her tent and writing letters while enduring the stares of what seemed to be every man in the troop as they made some excuse to pass by. Their looks weren't unkind, however, and a group of them brought her dinner each night. She was amused at their extreme pleasure when she thanked them the first evening, and they milled around as if unsure of what to do next, when Stride shooed them away with, "Give the lady some privacy, lads." Reena would have been glad to talk to them, but she was secretly

263

thankful to the sergeant; she was enjoying her solitude.

The second night some of the men begged Stride to allow them to perform a skit for her, and after consulting with Reena he grudgingly gave his permission. Reena enjoyed the show immensely and found herself laughing more at the pitifully comical way the players attempted to impress her than the skit itself. They promised to have another show ready for the following night and fawned their way out of her presence with much bowing and grinning.

Reena went to bed early, read her Bible by candlelight, and left the light burning as she fell into a sleep that was filled with orderless dreams. Deep into the night she woke up thinking she was suffocating.

When she opened her eyes she was stunned to find an Indian with a large head and thin, cruel mouth smiling as he leaned over her. His hand covered her mouth before she could scream, and she could smell dirt and horse on it before she began hyperventilating.

"Do you want to die?" he whispered, still grinning as if he were asking her the time of day.

Her breathing quickened even more, and all she could do was wonder how he'd managed to sneak by Stride and three hundred men. The massive hand pressed down harder, and she felt her lips being crushed against her teeth. Her mouth filled with the salty taste of blood.

"Do you?" he asked more harshly this time. Even more frightening was the way he seemed to be enjoying her terror and pain. He was *feeding* off of it.

She shook her head as best she could under his iron weight, and he nodded slowly. A huge knife appeared in his other hand. The dim glow from the candle raced along the razor-sharp edge as he told her almost lovingly, "Then don't make a sound, or I'll split you open like a chicken!" He reached behind her and she heard a soft ripping sound as he cut a slit into the back of the tent. The next moment she was being dragged on her back, his hand still firmly clamped over her bleeding mouth, and she found herself staring at the winking stars.

The Indian yanked her up; then she felt her feet leave the ground as he lifted her easily from behind and carried her into the night.

———

Fort Benton was situated directly on the banks of the Missouri River, in the middle of the vast Montana Territory plains. An important link between the fur traders and Indians of the north with the dry goods suppliers of America, Fort Benton prospered. Supplies flowed into the small town during the summer by wagon and boat, and then moved north in the autumn by creaking cart train. The trains returned in the spring loaded down with furs and robes. Stone's troop passed one of these wagon trains heading north, and Macleod literally ground his teeth to keep from having his men search the cargo. Whiskey was undoubtedly included in the supplies, but the Mounties held no jurisdiction in Montana, and the traders weren't breaking the law until they crossed the Canadian border. These facts caused Macleod to mumble darkly into his beard as they passed by.

Besides Macleod, Stone, Vickersham, and Del, there were nine other troopers. Del shook his head before they'd even pulled out of camp. "This ain't no good. They's thirteen of us."

"So?" Stone asked him.

"That's bad luck!"

"Only to you, Del."

"Why don't you make one o' them fellers stay and leave us a nice, easy dozen? Twelve's such a *nice* number, cain't nuthin' happen—"

"Forget it, Del."

"Hmmph. You'll be sorry."

The journey south was otherwise uneventful. The tablelands they traveled were notched with creeks from which grew stands of cottonwoods. They saw nothing else but grass; mile after mile after mile of it. Stone had heard somewhere that Montana meant "mountain," but he was beginning to think that someone had been joking with him at the time. The only break in the horizon had been at the border, when they'd seen the Sweet Grass Hills to their west.

They received curious stares in Fort Benton. One drunk stumbled from a saloon near the warehouse from which they were unloading, squinted blearily, and asked Del, "Is the British invadin'?"

Del regarded him as if studying a disgusting bug. "That's the North-West Mounted Police, you fool."

The drunk thought on this, then asked, "Am I under arresht?"

"No, you're drunk. Now, skedaddle!"

When the two wagons they'd brought with them were loaded, Macleod decided to leave immediately since there were still a few hours of daylight left. Some of the men groaned; they'd been hoping to sleep in a hotel that night in a real bed. The strongbox that held the money received more than a few glances, and the men tried to think of ways to spend it as they rode. They were left with boring dreams of buying practical items like clothes or sweets from a trading post, since there were no cities within hundreds of miles of their camp in Canada.

On the third day, just before crossing the border, Stone spotted a scarlet-coated rider coming toward them. For some reason this made his blood turn cold. *This can't be good news. We've got the good news in that strongbox.* He started to say something to Macleod, but his mouth was suddenly bone-dry.

"Rider coming, sir," one of the men called from the rear. "Looks like one of us."

Macleod squinted and said, "So it is. What could that be about?" Stone noticed that his tone was edged with anxiety, too.

They spurred into a gallop. Stone kept his eyes on the horseman and eventually recognized the stiff posture of Sergeant Stride. He grew even more agitated. *What does this mean? He's supposed to be with Reena.* And then he knew. He didn't know how, but he knew. As if to confirm Stone's thoughts, Stride stopped his mount in front of them and greeted Macleod, but his eyes were locked on Stone in a silent, agonized apology.

"What is it, Sergeant?" Macleod asked.

"Sir, the missionary lady's been kidnapped by an Indian that fancies himself Red Wolf. Here's the ransom demand. Very crude writing and difficult to read, but he gets his point across." Stride handed Macleod a limp, well-worn piece of parchment and faced Stone. "I'm sorry, Hunter. I never heard a thing. It's all my fault."

Stone stared at him for a moment, while registering the fact that Stride had called him by his name for the first time. But he wasn't ready to forgive yet. "What does he want?" Stone heard himself say, and his voice cracked audibly. He felt a hand on his arm and turned to find Vic watching him uneasily.

Macleod slowly folded the paper and put it inside his jacket. "He's taken her to the Sweet Grass Hills, and wants the supplies—and the money. In exchange for the woman."

"She's probably dead already," Stone said numbly. He couldn't believe the same nightmare was happening again.

"Hunter, you don't know that!" Vickersham exclaimed.

"I don't want to hear that kind of talk, Stone," Macleod ordered.

"Bad luck," Del said, shaking his head. "I just *knew* it was bad luck."

"Shut up, Del," Vickersham said immediately.

Macleod asked, "What did the commissioner say, Sergeant?"

"He wants you to double your speed, if possible, to camp. To discuss . . . our reactions."

"There's only one reaction to discuss," Stone stated grimly. "We find him, give him nothing, and kill him."

"I'm with you, Hunter," Vic said.

"Count me in," Del agreed.

"Stop this talk at once!" Macleod bellowed, spittle flying from his lips. Their horses stamped uneasily from the palpable emotion in the air. "This is not a ladies' quilting circle where we take votes! We have our orders, so let's move!"

"Sir, you don't understand," Stone pleaded. "Even if we give him what he's demanding, he'll kill her just for the pleasure of it! I know this man. There's a chance she's still alive, so we have to act *now*!"

Macleod looked at him sharply. "You *know* this Indian?"

When Stone didn't answer, Vickersham said quietly, "He kidnapped and murdered Hunter's wife, sir."

"We're wasting *time* here, Inspector!" Stone roared.

"Don't you shout at me, Sub-Inspector!"

"I'm going!" Stone declared, starting to turn Buck.

Calmly, Macleod said to Stride, "Sergeant, place this man under arrest."

Stone drew his Adams and aimed it at Stride's chest. "Don't try it, Preston! I'll shoot you down."

"This is *mutiny*!" Macleod bellowed.

"Last chance, Inspector," Stone said, his pistol still pointed at Stride. The whole troop was frozen with horror at what they were witnessing. "Are you coming with me, or do I go alone?"

In a choked, dangerous voice, Macleod pronounced, "We have our orders from the commissioner, Stone. If you put that gun down right now and come with us, I'll forget this ever happened. Otherwise, you're facing a court-martial, lad."

Without a word, Stone wheeled and charged to the west toward the Sweet Grass Hills looming in the distance. He hadn't gone far when he heard horses following him. Thinking it was Stride, he stopped and turned, gun at the ready. He was shocked to find Vic and Del. "Go back, you two! Now!"

"We're going with you, Hunter," Vic argued.

"No, you're not! Get back there *now*, Vic! You're not going down with me!" Stone's anger and frustration were making his head ache fiercely.

"You can't tell me what to do, Hunter!"

"Me, neither," Del chimed in.

"Vic—Del, listen to me. Listen very carefully. It's *me* he wants. He knows I'm here—I don't know how—and all he wants is another chance at me!"

"That Crow scout you don't like disappeared right after you left to see Miss Reena," Del said. "Maybe they was in cahoots."

Stone nodded grimly. "That's it—that's how he knows. Anyway, he doesn't care anything about the money! So, please—if you think of me as your friend, *don't do this*! Besides, maybe I'll need you at my court-martial."

Despite Vic's anger, he could see that what his friend said made sense. He glanced back at the troop, seeing Macleod's stormy face even from a distance.

"Please, Vic."

Del looked at Vickersham, who nodded slowly. "All right. But only because you're our friend and ask it."

"Thanks," Stone said, immensely relieved.

"Hunter?" Vic asked.

"Yes?"

"Kill that savage, will you?"

Stone's face darkened as he turned Buck once again. "I plan on it."

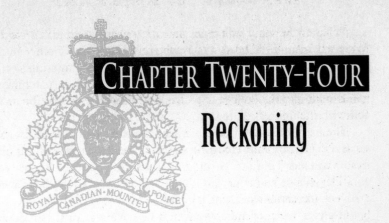

# CHAPTER TWENTY-FOUR

# Reckoning

Reena had never ridden a horse so fast in her life. The Indian quirted the huge black horse unmercifully, and after only a few miles, Reena's backside was in agony from the bareback riding. She rode in front of him, desperately clinging to the horse's flying black mane, the Indian's thickly muscled arm around her waist. He had said nothing since leaving the Mounties' encampment, and Reena hadn't bothered asking who he was or what he was doing. Her mind kept going to Hunter's wife Betsy. *Had she been as scared as I am? Could this be the same man that killed her? No, that would be too coincidental. Then who is he?*

A line of hills loomed ahead of them, and she was momentarily surprised that she could see them so clearly. As she glanced up at the brightening sky, she wondered if she'd ever see a sunrise again. Her lower lip was swollen painfully, and her head throbbed in rhythm with the pounding of the horse's hooves.

The Indian steered the horse directly toward a tall hill at the front of the range. Its circumference was studded with trees, but the top was bare and level, as if intentionally flattened with a giant hammer. The black stallion faltered as he neared the treeline, but the Indian doubled his use of the quirt and the animal bored straight in and began laboring up the slope. Reena ducked behind the horse's head as low-hanging branches swept over them. The colt began wheezing noticeably with effort. Finally they emerged from the trees and the flat ledge was in front of them.

The Indian jumped down and roughly pulled Reena off the exhausted horse. She was startled when he yelled something in his native language and another Indian came out of the trees to her left. He was smaller than Reena's kidnapper and dressed in white man's clothes. Wrapped around his head was a colorful band with a feather jutting from the back. The tall one spoke excitedly while roughly tying Reena's hands behind her back, undoubtedly telling of his skill at snatching her out from under the Police. The small one didn't laugh, and Reena was left with the impression that he was afraid of his partner.

The fierce one then tied her ankles and shoved her to the flat, bare surface of the summit. He stood watching her for a moment, his black eyes amused and curious. Struggling to a sitting position, Reena could hold her silence and anger no longer. "Don't you know that a whole troop of Mounties will come for me?"

His eyes widened mockingly, and he gave a sarcastic shudder of fear.

"I know you can speak English. Who are you, and what do you want?"

He only grinned at her.

"Talk to me!"

He reached toward her body, and she jerked away. He backhanded her viciously. The pain was excruciating, and she saw bright lights dancing in front of her eyes. When she opened them, he was holding her cross necklace in his hands, staring at the engraving. He looked at her questioningly. "What does this mean?"

Refusing to show her suffering, Reena glared up at him defiantly. " 'Thanks be to God.' "

"You are a Christian?"

"Yes." She was surprised he knew the word.

"I have met your kind before. Are all Christian white women so pretty?"

He was mocking her, and a terrible fear overcame her. "Your name is Red Wolf, isn't it?" She didn't want to be right, and hated herself for even asking the question. But she had to *know*.

"You have heard of me?" he asked, pleased.

His casual acknowledgment induced a shattering wave of nausea to Reena. She leaned over to be sick, but her empty stomach produced only gagging, teary eyes, and humiliation. When she could speak, she said, "You killed Betsy Stone."

His eyebrows lifted. "Was that her name? Yes, I sent her to her God."

Red Wolf's indifference was both frightening and infuriating. "Is that what you'll do with me?"

He paused. "You are bait."

Reena recognized that this wasn't a yes, but it wasn't a no, either. Reena knew her fate, and, strangely, she was calm for the first time since she'd been in his presence.

———

Buck was tired. Stone couldn't force him to keep up the swift pace, yet he continued to postpone slowing him down. He was aware of an awful déjà vu and felt as if he were in a bad dream that kept repeating itself over and over.

Most of all, he was overcome with anger. A black, consuming anger that tore at his senses.

He refused to torture himself the way he had while going after Betsy. He wouldn't waste time wondering whether Reena was still alive, or hurt, or if she would be killed in the struggle to come. If she was dead—killed senselessly as Betsy had been—then there was no honor left in the world. No justice. No goodness. No happiness. And no love.

Life had taught him to be gentle when gentleness was required, and brutal when brutality was brought against him. Men were exactly what they were, good or evil, and so was he. Life toughened them; it made some of them strong and wise, and others cruel. This was the way of the land and he couldn't change it. But he wouldn't tolerate those that had been warped and took pleasure in hurting others.

He concentrated on how to find the Crow savage and kill him.

If there were more braves with him, he would kill them, too.

He was Death itself, riding through the night.

———

At that moment, Red Wolf was pacing restlessly. The three of them had spent the day in near total silence. He'd been surprised that the woman had not spoken again. Sometimes he would see her with her eyes closed, praying to her God. At other times he found her watching him; not with anger or defiance, but with a peaceful curiosity and interest. For some reason, this unnerved him. He had considered her carefully that morning when she'd become aware of her inevitable death, but instead of showing fear, her face had softened and she'd nodded with calm understanding. This, too, disturbed him. Fear was his ally—his friend—and the lack of it caused him to feel at a disadvantage, though he had complete control over her.

By nightfall, Red Wolf was a tense man. He hated not knowing what the Mounties were planning, and he hadn't slept in sixty hours.

Mentally, he cursed his band of warriors that had not returned from their hunting. His trust of Long Feather's ability in a fight—and even to stay awake—was shaky, but he had to get some rest.

"You keep watch tonight," he told Long Feather, who nodded. "They will come from the east. Watch that way. If I catch you sleeping, you will never wake up again."

Long Feather nodded again. "I will stay awake, Great One."

Red Wolf walked to Reena and looked down at her. He hadn't allowed a fire to be built, and he noticed her shivering in the cool night air. She was prettier than the other woman, and he had the sudden inspiration to make her a gift to Crazy Horse. This made him smile.

"You look tired, Red Wolf," she commented.

His smile vanished instantly, and he raised his hand to strike her but hesitated at the last moment. She made no move to evade the blow or to cover up.

"You'd better get some rest," she continued, with a slight smile of her own. "Somebody's coming."

He chuckled, but it had a hollow ring to it—even to him. "Do you think it is this man—Stone?"

She nodded. "I don't think, I *know*."

"His wife, too, warned me that he was coming, and she died. He could not save her."

She didn't answer, but her smile grew.

"What does this man do to deserve such loyalty and admiration?"

The woman actually laughed. He felt his face burn, and a strange uncertainty came over him. He'd seen very few men, and *no* women, laugh in his face.

"I could try for the rest of the night to explain it to you, but you'd never understand."

Red Wolf was exhausted, and irritated with her haughtiness and disrespect, but he was intrigued. "Tell me."

Sensing that she was getting on his nerves, Reena was enjoying herself immensely. She made him wait a few seconds before answering. "There was a man that lived long ago, in another country. His name was Chaucer. He didn't know Hunter Stone, but he wrote about him even then, before Hunter was born."

"What did this man say?"

"He wrote: 'He loved chivalry, truth and honor, freedom and courtesy.' " Reena let him absorb the statement. "And *that's* why you will never understand a man like Hunter Stone."

Red Wolf nodded slowly, then placed his hands on his knees, his face inches from hers. "You are wrong, Christian woman. I understand him better than anyone." He saw her smile falter and repeated, "Anyone."

---

Stone lay flat on his belly atop one of tallest knolls in the Sweet Grass Hills. He spotted them just after daybreak.

He'd taken a chance that Red Wolf would only be concerned about riders from the east. That was why he'd come into the Hills from the south. And it had paid off.

Seeing only two men with Reena, he briefly wondered if there were more in the woods around the hill, but he doubted it. If Red Wolf had had more men, there would have been guards for every point of the compass.

Red Wolf had made a mistake for one of three reasons: carelessness, arrogance, or exhaustion. Or a combination of all three.

And Stone was going to make him pay for it with his life.

---

Reena woke the next morning stiff, tired, and hungry. The lack of a fire had forced them to eat only dried jerky and stale bread. Despite her stomach rumblings, the thought of the same diet for breakfast left her with no appetite.

Red Wolf allowed Long Feather to get some sleep. Apparently he'd managed to stay awake all night, and he curled up at the edge of the woods in a blanket. Surprisingly, Red Wolf untied her and allowed her to roam free and stretch her legs.

She was glad she'd had on thick clothing the night he'd kidnapped her; it had been cool with the coming chill of fall, and she'd been sleeping in woolen socks, warm denim pants, and a woolen sweater over a red cotton blouse. She hated to think of the shape she would be in if she'd been wearing only her nightgown.

Reena began to wonder how long Red Wolf would wait. She'd been taken the second night after Hunter and the troop had gone to Fort Benton. He'd said it would take three or four days, and this was the fourth day. Where was he? She had no doubt he would come for her, and probably bring more men with him. He didn't know that Red Wolf only had one man.

She looked up at the sky, which was overcast with huge, thick clouds. She hated to spend another day with nothing to do but wait. The thought of running came to her, but she knew how ridiculous that was. Red Wolf was sitting on the edge of the eastern ledge with his back to her, but she had no weapon, and even if she did, she doubted she could sneak up on him.

As she watched him, trying not to hate him, he suddenly cocked his head and froze, listening. A moment later she heard it: something was running through the underbrush behind them on the western side of the knoll. Running up the hill and getting closer. *Oh, God, please don't let that be Hunter charging alone into this trap! Please!* She thought of bolting toward the noise, but it could very well be more of Red Wolf's men joining him.

Red Wolf's horse was tied on the western side, and his rifle was in the saddle scabbard. He appeared beside Reena, ugly knife in hand, his bewildered eyes going from his horse to the crashing noise. He obviously wasn't expecting anyone, and he wouldn't have time to get to his rifle before the horseman came into view. He looked at Long Feather, who was still asleep, and whistled. Long Feather looked up groggily, unaware of what was going on. Reena felt a handful of her hair being grabbed, and the huge knife was at her throat. She could almost smell the hot, angry blood rushing through Red Wolf's body as he stood behind her and they faced the coming rider.

"It is time, woman," Red Wolf growled in her ear, his breath rancid. "Time to see who was right about Stone."

Reena didn't understand what he was talking about, but before she could form any words, Buck burst from the woods. She heard Red Wolf's sharp intake of breath and thought fleetingly, *He's frightened!* before they both realized that Hunter wasn't *on* Buck. No one was. The lathered buckskin stood panting heavily at the edge of the woods, looking right back at them.

Red Wolf jerked her around toward Long Feather.

Reena saw a flash of deep scarlet, and Hunter, holding a saber and pistol, emerged from the woods directly beside the startled Long Feather. Long Feather, the whites of his bulging eyes bright even from fifty feet away, fumbled at his belt for his gun and drew it. In his shock and haste, Long Feather's aim was wide when he fired, the explosion ear-splitting in the morning quiet. Hunter barely flinched and cut him down with one stroke of the saber. Reena closed her eyes quickly, but not fast enough to avoid the gory sight.

Hunter turned from Long Feather's body and strode purposefully toward them. Reena was dragged back a step by Red Wolf, and the knife bit into her skin. He was shaking violently.

"Stop right there!" Red Wolf cried.

Hunter didn't stop. Helmetless and head lowered, his face was an awful mask of hatred and fury that twisted his normally pleasing features. Reena almost didn't recognize him.

Red Wolf's breathing was harsh as he shouted, "I said *stop*!"

Hunter was only twenty feet away now.

"I'll kill her! Stop!"

Hunter raised his pistol, and Reena could feel Red Wolf try to make himself small behind her. It would have been laughable if the situation weren't so dangerous. The huge hole at the end of Hunter's gun seemed to be pointed directly at her forehead. Gasping, she felt a keen burning sensation at her throat and hot blood trickling down to her collarbone and into her blouse.

Hunter stopped at once. "Let her go." Even his voice was unrecognizable—a guttural, husky snarl.

"Why?" Red Wolf asked, already finding his arrogance again. His face was just to the right of her head. He held her hair in his left hand, the knife in his right. "It is more interesting with her here."

"If she dies, *you* die right after. There's no way out this time."

"Ah, but if she dies, even if you kill me, you will die another death, too—just as before." Red Wolf chuckled deep in his throat.

Reena's fingers dug into Red Wolf's arm that held the knife. Suddenly astounded, she realized that her hands were free.

Hunter took one more step forward, his pistol looming large. "You're too big to hide behind her, you Crow coward. I can hit you."

"Do not move! We must talk!"

"No more talk! You're sticking out all around her—your legs, your ribs—even your head!"

Reena felt the knife dig deeper into the cut and knew the end was near unless she did *something*.

"Tell her goodbye, Owl Dog!"

Sensing his grip tightening on the knife, Reena whipped her right hand back toward Red Wolf's face, fingers extended, and felt her ring finger connect with one of his soft eyeballs. Red Wolf howled in pain, and the instant he loosened his grip, she threw herself to the left. The explosion a half-second later was enormous.

Red Wolf was thrown backward five feet and landed on his back. His hands went to a growing red stain high on his chest above the heart as he groaned. In four long strides Hunter was over him, the blood-stained saber raised impossibly high. "Hunter, *no*!" Reena screamed, and in a flash she remembered the night she'd screamed the same words as he'd been ready to kill the Indian boy. That night he'd stopped instantly; this time he didn't stop at all.

The blade whistled down in a silver blur and bit into the dirt where Red Wolf's head had been a fraction of a second before. Somehow, in his excrutiating pain, he'd seen the blow coming and tilted his head just enough. Hunter raised the saber again, and this time Reena knew he wouldn't miss. She leaped to him and grabbed his arm. "Hunter, please don't! Please!" She pulled at him with all of her strength, yet it wasn't enough. His muscles were as taut as bowstrings, and she could almost hear them humming with tension. Reena heard herself crying and sobbing as she tugged on his arm desperately.

Slowly his arm lowered. His lips were pulled back from his teeth in a horrible distortion and his face was covered with sweat. While his whole body shook for a moment, she stroked his cheek and felt the savage fury slowly leave him. "Thank you," she wept. "Thank you, Hunter."

From the ground, Red Wolf watched through fuzzy vision. He smiled despite his agony and said through a mouthful of blood, "You let me live because we are the same, you and me. You cannot kill me."

Stone leaned down. "I let you live so I can watch you tried and hanged, you Crow dog. We are nothing alike. I'll not be compared with the likes of you—ever!" He sheathed his saber with a whisper of steel and holstered the Adams.

Red Wolf's grin disappeared and his eyes became heavy.

Stone leaned closer. "Honor," he whispered harshly, "is the difference between you and me. And it's something you'll never understand."

Slowly Red Wolf's eyes closed, but not before his face registered rage and frustration and failure.

After checking to make sure the Crow was still breathing, Stone turned and took Reena in his arms.

————

When Long Feather was buried, Stone spotted a contingent of troops headed directly toward them from the north. They dressed Red Wolf's wound, put him over his horse, and went to meet them.

Without preamble, Stone turned his prisoner over to the leader of the troop, Inspector James Walsh. Vickersham and Stride watched silently from behind Walsh as the inspector said with true regret, "Sub-Inspector Hunter Stone, I arrest you for lone insurrection and insubordination. You will be held in confinement until your court-martial proceedings."

Stone had taken out his pistol and sheathed saber without hesitation while Walsh spoke, and a sub-inspector from Walsh's troop reached for them. "Get away from him!" Vickersham shouted, startling the man. Vic moved his horse between the man and Stone. "*I'll* relieve him of his weapons." He shot a look at Walsh. "And I'll be the one to return them to him when he's reinstated, sir." Walsh inclined his head slightly and waved his man away.

Handing over the weapons, Stone looked Vic in the eye. "Thanks, Vic."

"Don't worry about a thing, old boy," Vic whispered. "We'll get out of this."

Reena had known what was coming, but a small part of her had dreamed that all of Hunter's sins would be forgiven. Anger rose in her as she watched Vic take Hunter's rifle. She whirled on Walsh. "This is *insane*! He saved my life! He was the only one that came to help me, and he arrested that murderer! He could have killed him, but he did the honorable thing and brought him to you! Can't you bend your stupid rules just this once?"

"Reena—" Stone began.

Walsh shifted uncomfortably in his saddle. "I have a warrant against Sub-Inspector Stone, sworn by Inspector Macleod, Miss O'Donnell. I have no choice in the matter." He turned to a man beside him. "Doctor, see to the prisoner's wound."

Reena couldn't resist. "You want him healthy when you hang him, is that it?"

Walsh didn't blink an eye. "That's correct, ma'am."

"You wouldn't have the *chance* to hang him if it weren't for Hunter! I would be dead, and Red Wolf would be off murdering someone else."

"Reena, that's enough," Stone said gently. "Let the inspector do his job."

Reena continued to glare at Walsh, who abruptly busied himself with his equipment.

———

Fort Whoop-up proved to be a disappointment to Commissioner Arthur French. Instead of finding hundreds of outlaws ready to do battle, there were only a few log houses, one of which was occupied by a starving Blackfoot family. He gave orders for the immediate construction of a gallows. The verdict from a hastily thrown together court had decreed that Red Wolf would die by hanging.

Stone, due to remarkable flexibility and trust by Macleod, had been assigned to Vickersham under house arrest until his hearing. Stone was thankful but was unable to tell Macleod since the inspector was carefully avoiding him.

On the eve of Red Wolf's hanging, Stone met with the Crow alone, a book in his hand. The wound had been superficial, for which Stone was now thankful, and had passed straight through Red Wolf with no major damage. He was obviously weak and tired, but his black eyes still managed to radiate defiance at the man who'd finally caught him. He was housed in one of the dirty log huts with his hands and feet tied, guarded by four Mounties—two inside, and two out. Stone dismissed the two men inside and sat across from Red Wolf on a well-worn, filthy cot.

"Have you come to celebrate my death?" Red Wolf asked with a smile.

"No."

"Then why are you here? To free me and allow our destinies to be one?"

"Why did you ever think I would join you, even now?"

Red Wolf watched him steadily, and Stone knew what the Crow would say even before he said it. "You, too, have dreamed of our riding together." When Stone didn't answer, he laughed. "It is written all over your face!"

"I was unstable at the time . . . on the edge of insanity. I realize that now."

"Nevertheless, it happened!" Red Wolf observed triumphantly. "I knew it! I was not certain until this very moment." He leaned forward, grimacing with pain. "It could still be. Together we could rule the Territory. Do you know what your weakness is? You play at *caring* too much. You play at *honor*. Deep inside, you are black, like me, and you will always be dark inside."

Stone felt himself getting angry, but he knew it would do no good to argue with the man.

Red Wolf smiled. "You care for no one but yourself."

Sensing he was finished spouting his hatred, Stone said quietly, "You're insane, and I pity you."

Red Wolf spit at him. "I do not need your pity!"

Stone ignored the outburst and continued, "Before you killed my wife, she taught me that there is no gain in hatred. I didn't understand at the time. Now I do, and Betsy was right. I'm only hurting myself to hate you."

"You are a fool!"

Stone stood and looked down at him. "Betsy would want me to forgive you for what you've done. *She* would have, if you'd killed me and left her to live." He shook his head slowly. "This I cannot do. Maybe someday . . . but now I'm content to watch the wheels of justice work and take satisfaction from that. Justice is the true way . . . the only way, as far as I'm concerned." Red Wolf tried to get to his feet, his face suffused with blood, but Stone easily pushed him back down and placed the book on the mattress beside him. "I promised Reena to give you this Bible. She says it will help you, if you let it."

Red Wolf snatched the Bible up and threw it as hard as he could. It bounced off of Stone's chest and fell to the floor in a flurry of thin pages. Stone calmly reached down, smoothed out the bent pages, and set it on the cot across from Red Wolf. Then he turned toward the door.

"Take this book with you!" Red Wolf shouted in helpless fury. "I do not want it, or need it! And after my death, someday, you will find that I spoke the truth to you this night! *You are just like me!*"

Red Wolf's curses and screams followed Stone into the night.

He didn't attend the hanging the next morning.

# EPILOGUE

## HONOR COURT
### NORTH-WEST MOUNTED POLICE

September 10, 1874

". . . So you see, gentlemen of the Honor Court, there were devastating circumstances leading to Sub-Inspector Stone's actions on that day. It is true that he acted in an insubordinate fashion, and he is the first to admit his mistake. But I submit to this court that he was not in his right mind when he executed these acts. You have heard the testimony of every man that was present in that troop, and without exception they all claim that Sub-Inspector Stone was caught up in an irrational state most uncommon to his normally gallant nature, as demonstrated by his honorable service to this Force so far.

"The North-West Mounted Police is under the jurisdiction and laws of the Dominion of Canada, which in turn recognizes the grand tradition and values of her mother nation, Great Britain. A sixteenth-century English poet named Stephen Hawes penned the creed of the honorable men of his time in a poem titled 'True Knighthood.' 'And no quarrel a knight ought to take, but for a truth, or for a woman's sake.'

"Hunter Edward Stone was seeking truth by bringing to justice a savage who tortured and murdered innocent men, women, and children. He risked his career, future, and life to save a Christian woman from certain death. His choice to take up this quarrel took no more thought than the swatting of a mosquito, for he *does* follow this creed. He is, you see, by honor bound.

"Does not the queen still recognize, reward, and knight those that follow this code? If that is true, why are we not decorating Sub-Inspector Stone today, instead of deciding whether or not he is worthy of wearing the scarlet?

"Once again, I thank you for the opportunity to speak on record, and for your attention."

Vickersham took his seat beside Stone at the defendant's table. Stone gave him a grateful look and smile, and Vic patted his arm.

The honor court, seated at a long table in front of them, consisted of Commissioner French, the newly appointed Assistant Commissioner Macleod, and the Inspectors of A, B, and F Troops. French stood and turned to the rest of the panel. "We have heard the evidence and rebuttals. Would you gentlemen join me, please?" They rose as one and began to follow him toward the flap in the back of the huge tent.

"May I say something?" Reena asked. She and Del had been seated behind the defense table, and when she stood, Del scrambled to his feet, too.

The men turned, surprised, and after receiving questioning looks from all of them, French nodded and said to the court reporter, "Let the record show that Miss Reena O'Donnell wishes to speak."

Reena took a deep breath. She didn't know if her speaking on record was proper or not, but she didn't care. "I feel that it's your duty to have the official record reflect my feelings in this matter, since everyone is aware that I am one of the direct reasons for Sub-Inspector Stone's actions."

She paused to gain their full attention and make sure the madly scribbling sergeant was recording her word for word. "I have no doubt that I would not be standing here were it not for the bravery of Hunter Stone. I would only be one of many silent voices crying from the grave for justice. He is one of your own, and one of the finest officers in the whole Force. You should be proud of him, instead of deciding his fate as if he were a common criminal.

"Today, in this place, much has been spoken of honor. I stand here to announce that on *my* honor, if justice is mocked here, then I will travel to Ottawa and take this matter to Parliament and the Governor-General himself. There will be no rest for you *or* them until the abortive judgment is rectified." She'd planned on being calm and analytical, but as she'd spoken her voice had slowly risen with a passion that she couldn't hide. "Thank you for letting me speak."

The honor court was slightly stunned and unsure of how to answer this fiery speech with its direct threat. "Uh . . . ahem—" French stuttered. "Thank *you*, Miss O'Donnell. Gentlemen?"

Del stared at the normally demure Reena in awe. "I'm glad you're on *our* side! Those were some powerful words, Miss Reena."

Stone went to her and took her hands in his. She was startled to find tears in his eyes when he whispered fervently, "Thank you . . . thank all of you. I couldn't ask for better friends."

"It was the *least* we could do," Vic said.

Reena nodded. "I just hope it did some good. They didn't look too happy when they left."

"They shoulda let me have *my* say," Del muttered dangerously.

Vic slapped him on the back. "Somehow, old friend, I think we're better off without that."

"What's that mean?" Del asked suspiciously.

Stone said, "It means that they probably wouldn't have been able to record most of the . . . um . . . words that you would've used."

"You got *that* right."

Vic took a deep breath. "This may take a while. Why don't we go have some lunch and—"

They all turned in surprise when the door opened and the panel filed back in, with Macleod in the lead. After a breathless moment, Stone whispered to Vic, "That was quick. Is this good or bad for me?"

"Hunter, in all my experience with courts, I can truly say that I have no idea. Let's go see."

Everyone remained standing. The honor court stared directly at them, giving nothing away by their stony expressions. Stone's nervous excitement was making him nauseous. These men were about to decide his future.

Macleod cleared his throat and said, "Commissioner French has asked me to announce the verdict since I was the officer who brought the charges." His eyes bored into Stone. "Sub-Inspector Hunter Edward Stone, your bravery and integrity are beyond question, and you are one of the finest officers I've ever had the opportunity to lead. But the charge is insubordination, of which you freely admit to be guilty. In your oath of service, which I personally read to you and heard you repeat, you swore you would, quote, 'Well and truly obey and perform all lawful orders and instructions that [you would] receive as such, without fear, favor, or affection of or toward any person,' end quote. Without question, this oath was broken and cannot go unpunished."

Stone remained standing at attention, though his legs seemed to have lost all of their strength. *I'm out,* he thought miserably. *I'm about to lose the most important thing that ever happened to me, for doing what I thought was right.*

Macleod continued in a stern voice, "It is the decision of this honor court to relieve you of a full month's pay." Incredibly, Macleod smiled.

Stone thought he hadn't heard him correctly.

Macleod barked at the court reporter, "Off the record," and said to Stone, "You're doing this wrong, Sub-Inspector. You're supposed to *draw* pay, not *forfeit* it. You haven't even received any money, and you're trying to give some of it back." His strict demeanor returned instantly. "Back on record. This sort of insubordination will not be tolerated in the future by any man without the severest penalty—namely, the subsequent discharge from service. Those are the findings of this court. Adjourned."

Stone was vaguely aware of fierce hugs from Vic and Del, and a delicious kiss on the cheek from Reena, but his eyes remained on Macleod, who came toward him with a smile. "Sir, I can't thank you enough—" Stone began.

"Nonsense, Stone. You were definitely in the wrong, but I can't ask that you be thrown to the wolves under the circumstances. Well done on arresting that scoundrel."

"Thank you, sir."

Reena impulsively kissed Macleod, who blushed furiously and stammered, "Well . . . um . . . I-I must say, *that* was worth the cost of leniency! You have remarkable friends, Stone."

"Yes, sir. I know that more than anyone." After Macleod left, Stone turned to Vic and Del. "Would you two excuse us?"

"Ah, I see how it is," Del said, nodding sagely. "Get what ye want from us, and drop us fer the girl." He turned to Vic. "Ain't that *always* how it is?"

Vic put his arm around Del's dusty shoulders and winked at Stone and Reena over his shoulder as they turned to go. "Del, in all the time I've known you, I've never heard more verisimilar words come from your lips."

Del's face was pained as he looked up at his friend. "Vic, would it just *kill* you to answer yes or no now and then? Always givin' a speech when—hey, what was that fancy word? Very-what?"

"Verisimilar. It has to do with the probability of truth."

Del regarded him suspiciously, and just as they went through the tent flap, Stone and Reena heard him say, "I think you make most o' this stuff up."

"Del!"

"Don't you 'Del' me! You make it up 'cause you're a fancy lord or somethin', and you think I'm just a lowly *commoner*. . . ."

Reena was giggling when Stone turned to her. He watched her

dancing blue eyes for a moment, then said, "That was quite a speech."

"I haven't thanked you for—"

Stone silenced her by placing two fingers gently over her lips. "It was the right thing to do," he said simply. He clasped his hands behind his back, suddenly uncomfortable. "I want to help you find those Blackfeet and start your new work."

"I'd like that." Reena looked down at her hands, then back to his face. "Hunter . . . there's something . . ."

"Yes?"

Reena didn't know how to say it, so her words came out in a rush. "I'm very attracted to you, and I think you feel the same way about me—am I being too bold?"

"Not at all."

"And those feelings confuse me because I don't want anything getting in the way of my work—the Lord's work—and even though I hide it, Louis hurt me so much that I . . . I . . . can't see how I could—"

Stone noticed she was wringing her hands unmercifully, and he took them in his own. "Reena," he said softly, "it's all right."

"No, let me finish. This has to be said before . . ." Reena smiled weakly and met his eyes. "I don't judge you, Hunter, please don't get that idea, but you're not a Christian. Besides the fact that I couldn't . . . have a relationship with someone that wasn't, I worry about *you*. Your soul. Could you please think about that? It's the most important decision you'll ever make."

Stone said nothing but took her arm and led her outside. The wind caught at them immediately, and he turned her into it so her hair wouldn't blow in her face. "I understand what you're saying, Reena. Thank you for your concern." He put his head back and drank deeply of the cool, clean air. His eyes on the brilliant sky, he said, "It's been a horrible year and a half. I haven't had much peace in that time, and that's what I'm looking forward to the most: peace—a chance to heal." He brought his gaze back to her. "I think about her every day. She's never far from me. Do you understand?"

"Of course," Reena said softly. "If it were any other way, I wouldn't care for you so much."

Stone nodded and gave her a sly smile. "Do you know what I want to do today?"

"What?"

"Take you for a picnic. Just the two of us. And I want you to tell me about David."

"David?"

"The giant killer." He began leading her to the temporary stables that the Mounties had constructed.

"He's known for much more than killing that Philistine."

"Tell me. We've got all day."

Reena began telling.

Hunter moved her closer to him as they walked, in order to hear her soft voice over the moaning and whistling prairie wind.

————

## THE END